BY LEONARD GOLDBERG

The Art of Deception

Disappearance of Alistair Ainsworth

A Study in Treason

The Daughter of Sherlock Holmes

Plague Ship

Patient One

The Cure

Fever Cell

Brainwaves

Fatal Care

Lethal Measures

Deadly Exposure

Deadly Harvest

Deadly Care

A Deadly Practice

Deadly Medicine

Transplant

A

ALSO B

The D

T

THE ABDUCTION OF PRETTY PENNY

A Daughter of Sherlock Holmes Mystery

Leonard Goldberg

MINOTAUR
BOOKS
NEW YORK

This is a work of fiction. All of the characters, organizations, and events portrayed in this novel are either products of the author's imagination or are used fictitiously.

First published in the United States by Minotaur Books, an imprint of St. Martin's Publishing Group

www.minotaurbooks.com

Designed by Omar Chapa

Library of Congress Cataloging-in-Publication Data

Names: Goldberg, Leonard S., author.
Title: The abduction of Pretty Penny : a daughter of Sherlock Holmes mystery / Leonard Goldberg.
Description: First edition. | New York : Minotaur Books, 2021. | Series: The daughter of Sherlock Holmes mysteries ; 5
Identifiers: LCCN 2020056394 | ISBN 9781250224224 (hardcover) | ISBN 9781250224231 (ebook)
Subjects: GSAFD: Mystery fiction.
Classification: LCC PS3557.O35775 A63 2021 | DDC 813/.54—dc23
LC record available at https://lccn.loc.gov/2020056394

First Edition: 2021

10 9 8 7 6 5 4 3 2 1

For Paige and Julie

All the world's a stage,
And all the men and women merely players;
They have their exits and their entrances;
And one man in his time plays many parts.

—*SHAKESPEARE,* AS YOU LIKE IT

Contents

THE ABDUCTION OF PRETTY PENNY

Chapter 1

Pretty Penny

March 1917

As chroniclers for the world's most famous detectives, it was our weekly custom, when not otherwise caught up in an investigation, to glance over the notes of previous cases which we believed merited publication. This dreary Wednesday morning found my father, John H. Watson, M.D., the friend and colleague of the long-dead Sherlock Holmes, reviewing dusty records from the mysteries the Great Detective had so admirably solved, while I studied similar pages from the twenty-odd cases unraveled by my wife, Joanna, whose analytical skills were now believed to be on the same level as those of her revered father. Outside, a clap of thunder broke our concentration, which gave us a moment to relight our pipes and enjoy the warmth of a cheery three-log fire.

"Here in 'A Case of Identity' was where Holmes uttered his often-quoted axiom," my father remarked.

"Which was?" I asked.

"That the little things are infinitely the most important," my father replied.

"And that is exemplified by the woman I have been studying for the past ten minutes," said Joanna, who was peering out the window of our rooms at 221b Baker Street.

"Pray tell what is the little thing you observe?" inquired my father.

"A woman with a walking stick," she answered.

My father and I rose and joined Joanna, so that we, too, could view the woman under consideration. I could see nothing out of the ordinary about the subject, and the expression on my father's face told me that he held the same opinion. The individual in question bore the signs of an average, commonplace woman, somewhat rotund and slow walking.

"Please describe what you gather from her outward appearance," Joanna requested.

"Most noticeably, she is wearing a broad-brimmed hat, with a curling green feather atop it," said I. "Her jacket is a light shade of brown, buttoned at the neck, and has what appears to be leather patches on its sleeves. She has on scant jewelry and is adorned only with dangling silver earrings. I cannot see her boots, nor do I have a good view of her gloveless hands. I would say she is quite ordinary, perhaps a housewife out on a shopping tour."

"And her walking stick?"

"Relatively inexpensive, for it has no metal ornaments."

Joanna clapped her hands gently at my conclusion and chuckled under her breath. "Excellent, John. You are coming along wonderfully well, and your description is spot-on, particularly your keen eye for colors. But unfortunately, you have missed everything of importance."

"Such as?"

"The details, dear John, for they are the most instructive. Do not simply observe the walking stick, but wonder why it is being used. As you have noted, this woman cares little for ornaments, and thus one might well conclude that the stick has some particular value."

I once again studied the woman who continued to stroll up and down the footpath, looking straight ahead except for occasional glances across Baker Street. For a moment, I had a clear view of her entire body as she moved between other shoppers. "She limps!"

"Yes, and that is why she employs a walking stick," Joanna remarked. "Now, Watson, you being an experienced practitioner of medicine for over thirty years, please observe her gait and inform us which of her joints is so afflicted that it requires additional support."

My father leaned in closer to the window and scrutinized the woman's every step. "It is her right hip which is damaged, for that is the side she supports with her walking stick. You will also note that she flexes and extends her knee with ease, which is more evidence that it is the hip that causes her problem."

"And the cause of her joint damage?"

"Being in her middle years, I suspect she has cartilage degeneration from wear and tear, although a traumatic cause cannot be excluded. I see no evidence of generalized arthritis."

"Most helpful, Watson," Joanna commended. "So then, let us place all of our observations together and see what conclusions can be reached. We have a middle-aged woman, with a painful right hip, strolling back and forth on a wet footpath, and she continues to do so despite the chill and drizzle which threatens to become a steady rain."

"But to what end?" I asked. "She seems to have no purpose."

"Oh, she has a purpose, for with each turn she steals a peek at our window," Joanna explained, just as the woman performed such an act. "Her purpose is us, you see, for she wishes to visit and no doubt seek our help, but is hesitant to do so. We are looking at a most worried and determined woman."

"But why then does she hesitate?" I asked.

"There are two likely reasons," Joanna replied. "She either feels her problem does not carry the gravity to interest us or she fears she does not have sufficient funds to pay for our services."

"Which do you favor?" my father queried.

"I never guess. It is a shocking habit which is destructive to logical reasoning," she stated, before pointing a finger to the street below. "Ah, she makes her move now. We shall have the answer to your question shortly."

"If either of your reasons is correct, we should at least give the poor woman a hearing," my father proposed.

Joanna shrugged indifferently. "Any port in a storm, Watson."

I had to nod at my wife's words, for there had been a definite, prolonged lull in criminal activity over the past month. Other than the occasional shop burglary, the newspapers had reported no notable felonies, and Scotland Yard had not called even once to enlist our services. It was as if the criminal element of London had gone on holiday. I easily filled the open time with my work as an assistant professor of pathology at St. Bartholomew's Hospital, while my father busied himself chronicling another, but as yet unpublished, mystery of Sherlock Holmes. Joanna, on the other hand, sat at the fireplace moodily and puffed on cigarettes or paced about aimlessly, for she abhorred the dull routine of our current existence. She required challenging work which necessitated the use of her finely tuned brain. The more difficult the problem, the more exaltation she felt at its solution. My father told me that Sherlock Holmes behaved in a similar fashion when his mind was stagnant, and that this trait as well seemed to run in the family's genes.

My thoughts were interrupted by a gentle rap on the door, followed by the entrance of our landlady, Miss Hudson, who announced, "I am afraid there is an early-morning visitor to see you. She is most insistent and refuses to return at a more convenient hour."

"The woman with the walking stick?" Joanna asked.

"It is she," Miss Hudson replied. "Were you expecting her?"

"In a manner of speaking, yes," Joanna answered. "Please be good enough to show her up."

Moments later we heard footsteps on the stairs, each producing a characteristic creak as the climber slowly ascended. Each step was followed by another, the later accompanied by the tapping sound of a walking stick.

"Would you care to approximate her weight, John?" my wife asked.

I quickly considered all the variables before stating, "I think any such assessment would prove inaccurate, for the use of her walking stick would lighten the load being applied to the wooden stairs."

"That would be so on a level surface," Joanna elucidated. "But on ascending a flight of stairs, the individual moves the good leg first, and follows with the affected leg and walking stick simultaneously. So you must ignore the creak associated with the step and stick, and concentrate on the initial step sans the noise of a walking stick. Taking this under consideration, our visitor weighs in at Miss Hudson's weight, which measures one hundred and thirty pounds."

"But from our observation, the visitor is much shorter than Miss Hudson."

"And far more rotund, which explains why their weights are the same despite a difference in height."

After a brief knock on the door, our visitor entered our drawing room. The woman was not what we expected, but rather the complete opposite of commonplace. She was rather attractive, with high-set cheekbones and dark blond hair pulled back severely into a tight bun. Her complexion was smooth with heavy makeup, but her true age was betrayed by obvious crow's-feet and deep lines in her forehead. Yet it was her pale blue eyes that drew one's attention, for they looked directly at you, without a blink, and told that she would not be easily intimidated.

"I am Mrs. Emma Adams, the owner of a pub in Whitechapel," she introduced. "And I am here to see the daughter of Sherlock Holmes."

"I have that honor," Joanna replied.

"I have come for advice."

"That is easily got."

"And your help."

"That is not so easily gotten." Joanna's eyes studied every aspect of the visitor, head to toe, before coming to rest on the woman's left arm, which appeared normal to me in every regard. "Prior to my hearing your story, pray tell why a middle-aged pub owner in Whitechapel spends hours every morning at her writing desk."

"I am a playwright," Mrs. Adams explained.

My wife rubbed her hands together gleefully, as if she had picked up the scent of an intriguing mystery. She motioned to an overstuffed chair by the fire and said, "Please take a seat and inform us how two such clearly different occupations have come to be tied together."

We gathered around the fireplace to listen to the woman's now interesting tale. Mrs. Adams proved to be quite articulate and gave a concise summary, as would be expected of a playwright who was accustomed to communicating with an economy of words. She stared into the fire while gathering her memories and telling us her story.

In her mid-twenties, Emma Adams married a young lance corporal in the British Army who shortly thereafter was sent off to fight in the Second Boer War. On his return, a handsome inheritance awaited him which he smartly used to buy a busy pub in Whitechapel. She worked as a barmaid but was free in the morning to practice her dream of becoming a playwright. With her husband's encouragement, she established a playhouse by renting a deserted warehouse at a scaled-down fee and transforming it into a theater, with a stage, dressing rooms, lighting, and makeshift seating.

"That must have been quite expensive," my father interjected.

"So one might think, but the cost was modest by all accounts," she continued on. "In the neighborhood itself were skilled carpenters, plumbers, electricians, and such, all willing to do the required work free of charge. They even rummaged about and found used materials which kept the cost to a minimum. Then there were even local directors and producers who volunteered their services, as did playwrights such as myself. Word of our endeavor spread and this attracted actors from neighboring districts to come and apply for auditions. We had far more applicants than roles to be filled, which allowed us to pick the most talented. And this is how the Whitechapel Playhouse came into existence. Initially we performed once a week, then progressed to every other night, with an entrance fee of only two shillings; and at the present there is nary an empty seat to be found. Thus, the playhouse became firmly established and to this day flourishes, all of which attests to the fact that the love of theater thrives in even the poorest neighborhoods."

There was a look of approval upon Joanna's face, as well as that of my father, for we all realized that this was not a woman to be trifled with. If ever an individual personified sheer determination, it was she.

"I take it there is an ongoing play?" Joanna inquired.

"There is," Mrs. Adams answered. "We are currently performing an updated version of *Romeo and Juliet,* which I take some pleasure in saying I wrote. The leading female role is played by a lovely teenager, and that is the reason for my visit here today."

"How so?"

"Our young Juliet has gone missing."

Joanna sighed with disappointment. "This is not the sort of case I find myself attracted to, for the meandering of a teenage girl almost always involves love and similar emotions of the heart."

"But we are not dealing with teenage love, but with a talented, self-sufficient young woman who believed that danger lurked in the darkness."

Joanna abruptly leaned forward, as if waiting for more words, which did not come. "What sort of danger? Was it obvious or presumed?"

"Listen to my story and then you can decide for yourself."

"Begin at the very beginning then, leaving out no detail, regardless of how trivial you may deem it to be," Joanna instructed. She rose to reach for a Turkish cigarette and, after lighting it, began to pace the floor of our parlor. "I shall walk about while you speak. Do not allow it to distract."

Mrs. Emma Adams took a long, deep breath as her mind seemed to be back in time. "It was the third day of auditions for *Romeo and Juliet* when I first encountered Penny Martin. Our search for the perfect Juliet was falling far short and we feared we would be forced to choose an actress of lesser talent for the role. That is when Penny appeared onstage and stole our hearts and minds. Here was this slender, beautiful young woman whose face of seductive innocence mesmerized the judges. Then she spoke with such a soft, alluring voice that all male listeners became her Romeo. To say she was talented would be an understatement. She was given the role of Juliet on the spot, and she performed in a dazzling fashion at each and every rehearsal. I gave little thought to her life off the stage until late one evening I returned to the playhouse to retrieve some books I had unintentionally left behind. There was a light on in one of the dressing rooms, and I entered to find Penny spreading an old blanket on the floor as she prepared for sleep. She was quite destitute, you see, and had no choice but to steal into the closed playhouse, where she would spend the night. The few shillings she earned sweeping the floor at a nearby jewelry shop were needed for food and other necessities."

Our visitor sighed deeply as a look of sadness crossed her face. "It was a heartbreaking scene beyond words. This wonderfully talented girl was living the life of a street urchin so she could perform on the stage, which provided no income. I immediately offered her lodging in my pub, for I live in comfortable rooms on the second floor of the establishment. There was plenty of space in that my dear husband had died of consumption ten years ago and I have the entire floor to myself. Penny initially refused, for she wanted no part of charity. But I insisted and allowed her to work in the early afternoon as a barmaid to earn her keep. And that is how I came to know and become attached to Pretty Penny."

Joanna stopped in her tracks and glanced over to our visitor. "Pretty Penny, you say?"

"That is the name she was given by her fellow players and by which she is known by everyone who saw her onstage. Mention the name Pretty Penny on any street in Whitechapel and the people will beam with pleasure, for she is both admired and loved by all." Mrs. Adams reached into her purse for a neatly folded poster which she opened for us to see. "Here is her picture, which will say more than any of my words."

The photograph revealed a stunning beauty whose soft features immediately caught and held one's attention. Her doe-like eyes and short, ruffled hair projected an aura of adolescent innocence, while her lips were parted into a most beguiling smile that seemed directed at the viewer. It required no imagination to see how mesmerizing and appealing this actress could be, both on and off the stage.

My wife crushed out her cigarette and moved in closer to study the photograph with a magnifying glass. "I note that her hair appears to glisten. Is that natural?"

"It is not a wig, if that is your question," Mrs. Adams replied. "Her hair is truly dark blond, but only glistens because pomade has been applied."

"It looks to be professionally done."

"So it is by Mrs. Marley, a widow here in Whitechapel who dresses and styles hair in her parlor on Back Church Lane. Because we have sent her so many clients, she credits us with a discount."

Joanna tapped a finger against her chin before asking, "How often does Pretty Penny avail herself of Mrs. Marley's talents?"

"Every Tuesday promptly at four," Mrs. Adams answered. "She failed to show for her appointment yesterday, which was most unusual. But when she was absent for last evening's performance, we all became greatly worried. And my worry was made even greater when she did not come home later, and this morning her bed remains unslept in."

"Were any of her personal items missing, such as clothing or jewelry?"

"All were in place, including her cosmetics and a few pieces of inexpensive jewelry which were particularly dear to her. Even the last of her asthma medications were in the bathroom cabinet, and she would never leave those behind."

"She has asthma, you say?" my father joined in.

"Indeed, sir, and how she managed to survive on the cold, polluted streets of Whitechapel is beyond me."

"Perhaps it was of the milder sort."

Emma Adams shook her head at once. "It was quite severe and almost took her life. She hid her condition from us, for fear it would disqualify her from the role of Juliet. After all, we could not have the lovely Juliet coughing and wheezing during her love scene with Romeo. But this worry became less of a concern when she moved into her warm, comfortable room and away from the dreadful night air. The frequency of the attacks diminished and they virtually disappeared when she began taking the asthma medications."

"Where and how did she obtain these drugs?" asked my father. "They can be rather costly."

"She received them from St. Bart's," Mrs. Adams replied. "They were a godsend and absolutely necessary, for once she foolishly went several days without them and that omission brought on an attack so severe I feared for her life. What I am attempting to convey to you is she would never depart without taking her asthma medications with her."

"An important observation," Joanna noted, and gazed over at me and my father, as if instructing us to docket the information. After a moment's thought, she came back to the visitor. "I take it an understudy replaced her onstage?"

Our visitor nodded gravely. "Much to the disappointment of those in attendance."

"And this has never occurred in the past?"

"Never."

Joanna lighted another cigarette and returned to her pacing. "Earlier you spoke of danger lurking about Pretty Penny. Describe when and where, and if there were witnesses."

"There are more than a few dangerous neighborhoods in Whitechapel, madam, where violence occurs all too often. Nevertheless, those associated with the theater, particularly the players, are known and well liked, and are considered untouchable and safe from harm by even the criminal element. I was therefore much surprised when Pretty Penny told me of an encounter with a stalker who remained in the shadows, but let his presence be known. It was as if he meant to frighten her."

"So there was never a face-to-face confrontation."

"Never, but at times he was close enough so she could hear a menacing laugh or highly suggestive groan. At first she thought it might be some of the local lads playing a prank, but then came the thrown bottle with the note in it." Once again Mrs. Adams reached into her purse, and now extracted a wrinkled sheet of paper. "It was most frightening—the way it was written."

She placed the note on the arm of her chair and smoothed it out so that its words printed in block letters became legible:

DO NOT ATTEMPT TO GANE
A HIGHER STASHUN
IT WOULD ONLY HASTEN
YOUR FINAL ACT
R

"The note was obviously written by an illiterate, but it is chilling nevertheless," said Emma Adams.

Joanna studied the wrinkled sheet at length before holding it up to the light and examining it further with her magnifying glass. "It is a rather clumsy effort."

"To what end?" I asked.

"To give the impression that the writer is an illiterate and from an impoverished background."

"But the misspelling of *gain* and *station* surely backs up that contention."

"So it was meant to appear," Joanna elucidated. "Allow me to draw your attention to the spelling of the word *attempt,* which is quite difficult for the uneducated because of its silent *p*. Yet the writer does so correctly. Also, recall that the word *station* is clearly seen by all as they pass or enter the underground, so even the unschooled would know its spelling. Thus, the writer intentionally wrote the words *gain* and *station* phonetically to make us believe he is illiterate. And finally, the paper has the watermark of A Pirie and Sons, a stationer of some distinction, who cater primarily to the upper class."

"But why would someone of that status send such a chilling note?" asked Mrs. Adams.

"There is a criminal element at every level of society," Joanna remarked. "A noble statesman can be just as deadly as a carpenter."

"Whoever he is, why bother to sign the note with an initial *R* which is written in script rather than a block letter?" I wondered aloud.

"It gives it a personal touch, I would suspect," my wife replied.

"Yet surely it does not stand for *Romeo,* for it does not fit the play, in which Romeo and Juliet are deeply in love," I said.

"Unless it is the delusional love of a madman," my father suggested.

Joanna flicked her cigarette into the fireplace and began pacing again. "With the danger obvious, did Pretty Penny not take precautions?"

"She was unworried because she felt she would be protected by her Romeo," Mrs. Adams answered.

"From the play?"

"Perhaps that is so, but I cannot be certain, for she refused to identify him."

"Was there any undue touching and embracing between the two on the stage or in the wings?"

Our visitor shook her head firmly. "It was all very professional, although I must say the pair did make a fine couple."

My wife came over to an overstuffed chair and sat directly across from the visitor. Their eyes locked as my wife's tone of voice became far more serious. "We have now reached the point where you must be completely open and honest, for not to do so will render it impossible to find your Pretty Penny."

"I have done so."

"No, Mrs. Adams, you have not," Joanna rebuked mildly. "There is information on this secret Romeo you are withholding, for women living under the same roof will discuss their romantic encounters in detail, and I must have those details."

Emma Adams hesitated before responding with a reluctant nod. "I did not go into this aspect of her story because I believed it unimportant."

"Permit me to decide what is important and what is not," said Joanna. "Now, if you consider their affair to be too delicate, I can ask the Watsons to retire to another room, although I assure you I will later repeat to them exactly what you reveal to me."

"Very well, then," the visitor agreed, yet I sensed a hint of reluctance in her voice. "There was nothing reproachable or reckless in her behavior. She first met him at the playhouse, and there was an immediate and mutual attraction between the two. They arranged their dates outside of Whitechapel and usually in the better districts of London. There were dinners and walks and kisses and embraces, and their love grew even more intense. But deep down she worried it was not to last, for he came from the upper class, whose members did not marry actresses, particularly those from a playhouse in Whitechapel. He assured her they would work their differences out, but she was still concerned that they would be forced apart, much like what happened in the star-crossed romance between Shakespeare's Romeo and Juliet."

Joanna considered the new information carefully before speaking. "Did Pretty Penny see her secret lover every night?"

"They met only on the evenings she was performing," Mrs. Adams replied.

"After the performance, I take it," said Joanna.

The visitor nodded. "Which always ends at nine sharp."

"And what form of transport took her to their undisclosed rendezvous?"

"Motor taxi."

"The same taxi each time?"

"I did not ask."

Joanna rose from her chair and, with a firm nod, said, "We shall look into the disappearance of Pretty Penny."

"I am ever so grateful," Mrs. Adams replied, reaching to take Joanna's hand in both of hers. "I shall somehow arrange to pay for your services, regardless of the cost."

"My fee is three tickets to the next performance of *Romeo and Juliet.*"

"And the best seats in the house you shall have." Emma Adams stood to depart, but at the door she turned and asked a final question. "How could you possibly have known I write every morning?"

"From the clues you present," my wife replied. "You have leather patches on the elbows of your jacket which prevent wear as you lean upon your writing desk. Furthermore, the left sleeve from the elbow down is obviously worn, which attests to your frequent writing. You also have a writer's callus on the third left finger from gripping your pencil too tightly, and there is a smear of graphite on the outer edge of your left palm which occurs in left-handed writers, for in those the hand follows the pencil across the paper."

"But how did you know I only write in the early morning?"

"Because that is the only time available to a busy woman who must open her pub by ten."

For the first time Mrs. Adams smiled. "You are as clever as they say."

"I take that as a compliment."

"That is how it was meant. But pray tell, is there any hope?"

"Just a glimmer."

Once the visitor departed, closing the door behind her, Joanna reached for her coat and spoke in a most urgent tone. "We must hurry, for we are dealing with the essence of evil."

"Because of the vile stalker?" I asked.

"Because he intends to kill her, if he has not already done so," Joanna said darkly. "That is the final act he writes of."

Chapter 2

The Hairdresser

The Widow Marley had rooms in a quiet, working-class neighborhood located at the southern edge of Back Church Lane. Her parlor was tiny by all accounts, but she made space for her salon by placing a wooden stool in a far corner, upon which she stood while performing her trade. Seated beneath her was a remarkably obese woman, with stringy blond hair that defied the curling iron held in the widow's deft hands. The chatter between them was incessant and only paused to allow the customer to insert a piece of chocolate candy into her brightly colored mouth. Joanna and my father sat on a cushionless bench and waited patiently, while I remained standing next to a hound of some mixture whose eyes stayed fixed on the blond customer's package of candy.

At last, the obese woman rose and paid with a few coins before departure, with the hound following her out into the street.

Mrs. Marley placed down her curling iron and studied us carefully prior to speaking. "And what can I do for you fine people this morning?"

"We require some of your time," Joanna replied.

"That will be two shillings."

"Agreed."

"And for what purpose is my time needed?"

"Our search for Pretty Penny."

The wiry widow's stern face softened noticeably at the girl's mention. "And who might you be?"

"The daughter of Sherlock Holmes."

Mrs. Marley raised her brow for a moment, obviously impressed. "So the matter is as serious as I believed."

"Quite so."

"I truly pray you can find her, for she is in many ways special. Behind that pretty face is a kind soul and a keen mind. But I must admit that I thought she was stepping out of her depth."

"In what regard?"

"She was going from one class level to another, which all too often leads to heartbreak."

"I need the details of their affair."

Mrs. Marley's face closed abruptly. "I don't know that much of her private life."

"Oh, but you do," Joanna insisted. "And every second you prevaricate places Pretty Penny in even greater danger."

"I did not pry, but only listened to what she chose to tell me."

"That is precisely what I wish to hear."

Mrs. Marley sat wearily on her wooden stool and stared down at the bare floor as she spoke. "She was not the talkative type, but she visited here twice a week, which gave us time to share stories—"

"Mrs. Adams told us she paid for only a single visit," Joanna interrupted.

"So she did, but Pretty Penny often came in a second time for the application of more pomade, which caused her hair to glisten so," Mrs. Marley clarified. "Since it required little effort on my part, I did not charge for the service, although I was rewarded with a piece of apple spice candy, which the darling girl purchased from Mr. Hardy's Sweet Shop."

"I take it that the goods at this sweet shop are somewhat inexpensive," Joanna said.

"No, no," the widow replied at once. "Some of the candy, such as the apple spice covered with chocolate, runs a shilling apiece."

"Perhaps I will stop in for a sample."

"It is only three blocks south on Prescot Street, where you will find a grand display to select from."

"I look forward to it."

"It will not disappoint," the widow assured. "Even for a lady of your standing."

"I trust not," Joanna said, with a thin smile, before flicking her wrist as if to change the subject. "But I remain interested in your pomade and why Pretty Penny considered it so important."

"For the obvious reason," Mrs. Marley answered. "It caused her hair to shine and truly brought out her natural beauty. She also adored its fragrance, which many of my customers do. I can attest to its popularity, for I myself mix up the formula, which I bottle and sell for a very modest half crown. Perhaps, madam, you would care to sample it."

"I would indeed," my wife said to my surprise.

The Widow Marley hurried over to a weathered cabinet and came back with a round green jar that had a white ribbon tied around it. She removed its top with a bit of a flourish before presenting it to the prospective buyer.

Joanna gave the jar careful attention and, after two whiffs, pronounced, "It has lard at its base and carries the heavy scent of lavender. Altogether, it is quite pleasant."

"Would you care to purchase a jar, then?"

"Very much so." Joanna held out a hand to me for a half crown, which she passed on to the widow. "Now, let us return to Pretty Penny and her secret lover."

"Which no doubt Emma Adams spoke of," the Widow Marley said, somewhat derisively. "She talks too much."

Joanna waved away the comment. "I am interested in your description, not hers."

"So it shall be," said the widow. "She never revealed his name, but only spoke of him as 'my dearest.' According to Penny, he was quite dashing, with a quick smile and a gentle voice. It was clear he came from the upper class, as attested to by his dress and manners, but he always made her feel comfortable whatever their surroundings. This lover was obviously a man of means who was accustomed to the best life had to offer."

"Which surroundings are you referring to?"

"The posh areas, such as walks along Battersea Square and expensive restaurants in Knightsbridge and Piccadilly, where they had dinner and ten-pound bottles of French wine were served."

"Did Pretty Penny ever mention the names of these delightful restaurants she visited?"

Mrs. Marley gave the matter considerable thought before responding, "Not that I recall. But there was a rather fancy restaurant in Piccadilly which Penny was quite fond of. It was high class indeed."

"Did she describe it so?"

The Widow Marley shook her head at the question. "I gathered that from the matchbook cover she brought me, for I collect such things as a hobby. It had very nice colors to it and showed a gentleman wearing a top hat."

"May I see it?" Joanna requested.

"Of course." The widow returned to the weathered cabinet and rummaged through its uppermost drawer until she found the item she was seeking. She obviously valued it, for it was carefully wrapped in tissue paper. After removing the wrapper, she held up the matchbook by its edges, so as not to soil its front with fingerprints. Proudly, she presented it for us to see. "Here it is," she announced. "And I must ask you not to touch its surface."

The matchbook cover was pale blue in color, with bright red trimming. At its center was a handsome gentleman tipping his top hat. Beneath the picture was the name of the establishment written in deep blue script.

ALEXANDER'S

ST. MARTIN'S LANE

"It is in the theater district, which she would naturally gravitate to," my father commented.

"As might her companion," Joanna added. "May I inquire as to when you received this rather striking matchbook? If possible I need a specific date."

"Tomorrow, a week ago, which was the last time I saw Pretty Penny," Mrs. Marley responded at once.

"Was this her first visit to Alexander's?"

"Oh, no. She had been there on a number of occasions, during one of which she actually spotted a royal."

"A number, you say?"

"More than a few."

"Mrs. Adams told us that Pretty Penny always traveled to their rendezvous by motor taxi and only on the nights she was performing."

"That is what I was told as well."

"Did Penny ever mention the name of the taxi or its driver?"

"Never, and there was no conversation between the two, for the taxi driver had already been given instructions as to her destination."

"Did she ever speak of the danger she was in?"

"Only when the bottle was thrown at her by some idiot," Mrs. Marley recounted, her face turning into a scowl. "I can assure you it was not done by the local lads, for everyone in Whitechapel knows that the players from the theater are not to be harmed and anyone who does so would be severely punished."

"Are you speaking of a beating?"

"I am speaking of a permanent limp and an arm which will never be used again."

With the reminder that Whitechapel could be a very violent neighborhood, particularly for those who crossed a certain line, Joanna rose and said, "We owe you two shillings for your time."

The Widow Marley waved away the fee. "You bring Pretty Penny home safe, and that will more than cover any charge."

We walked out into smoky, sulfurous air which was being polluted by the coal-burning fireplaces inside the crowded dwellings of Whitechapel. The sky itself was stained with a black mist that irritated both the lungs and the eyes. The irritants were such that we had to place handkerchiefs over our faces to filter out some of the foul contaminants. Watching our step, we walked down a slippery cobblestone street, for there was rotting garbage piled up along the footpath. The decaying refuse did not seem to bother the poorly clothed children who played within it.

"Appalling," my father commented. "Surely they must have garbage collectors serving the area."

"The backstreets are often neglected," Joanna said. "And unfortunately, that is where the need is the greatest."

"When we return to Baker Street I shall file a complaint."

"Register the complaint in the form of a letter so that the three of us can sign it."

"Do you think it will bring positive results?"

"No, but it will make us feel better."

"Revolting," my father grumbled as he stepped around a mound of spoiled food. "I daresay we will have difficulty finding a taxi or carriage along Back Church Lane."

"That can wait, for first we must visit Mr. Hardy's Sweet Shop," Joanna directed. "It is a mere three-block walk away."

As we waited for traffic to pass before crossing onto Prescot Street, I asked, "What is the importance of the sweet shop?"

"Wherever Pretty Penny stopped, we shall stop," Joanna answered. "For that is the road map the girl followed before her disappearance."

"Do you believe it represents a trail left behind by her?"

"That is what we are about to find out."

"You do realize that the girl may not be in any danger at all," my father proposed, watching a police wagon speed by. "Teenage girls can disappear for a number of reasons."

"Three come to mind," said Joanna. "First would be elopement. Here we have a young woman who is deeply in love with a gentleman of higher class whose family would be strongly against marriage. But love prevails and the couple run away and marry."

"My thought precisely," my father agreed.

"But unlikely," Joanna retorted. "You see, we are dealing

with a talented, determined individual who would not act irresponsibly, for no matter how much she loves this fellow, she has now found a perfect niche in life. She has a roof over her head, she practices her art, and she has the love of the entire community. Thus, she is strongly attached to Whitechapel and its theater, and would never abandon them."

"Yet love in young women exerts a most powerful pull," my father argued.

"True, but you are not considering her strong attachment to Mrs. Emma Adams, who provided her a comfortable home and the theater where she performs. Their relationship seemed much akin to that of a mother-daughter or at least one of close sisters. Pretty Penny, if I measure her correctly, would never suddenly desert her guardian angel and the entire stage crew at the theater who love her so dearly. Nor would she ever leave without giving some notice to Emma Adams. And remember, she shared her deepest secrets with her mother figure. No, elopement is far down the list of possibilities."

"I am still not convinced," my father persisted.

"That is because you are not taking into account the fact that she left her clothing, cosmetics, and jewelry behind," Joanna countered. "No woman would ever do that, even if overwhelmed with the excitement of an elopement."

"You raise a most important point," my father conceded.

"The second reason for her sudden disappearance would be suicide," she went on. "Like in the play *Romeo and Juliet,* a lovestruck teenager, who believes there is no resolution to the barrier separating her from her lover, sees no way out other than suicide. But we have no sign of that. She is neither distraught nor depressed, and her outward appearance would indicate she anticipates a happy ending. Furthermore, individuals who commit suicide leave notes behind and want their bodies discovered, not hidden away never to be found. No, suicide here is out of the question. Thus, we are left with the third reason and by far the most chilling one. I am afraid she is in the process of meeting her death or has already done so."

"But you cannot totally exclude elopement or suicide," I argued.

"I am dealing with probabilities at the moment," Joanna said candidly. "With that in mind, we must seek out the clues that back up my conclusion, for those same clues will lead us to Pretty Penny."

Leaving Back Church Lane behind, we strode down Prescot Street where the quality of the neighborhood changed for the better. Now there were small shops that reflected the international flavor of London itself and Whitechapel in particular. We passed a Polish food store that displayed appetizing spicy sausages hanging in its window, and just beyond was a French bakery that emitted the sweet aroma of fresh baguettes and brioches. The people strolling about were quite varied as well. There were shoppers and merchants and workmen and loiterers, most in common attire and speaking with a distinctive cockney accent.

Across the street we saw the sign for Mr. Hardy's Sweet Shop, which was written in fancy script above the door. The closer we came the stronger the aroma of sweet chocolate. Inside the shop a short, plump man, with a most cordial face, waited behind the counter to serve us. A sleepy-eyed cat looked up at us briefly before going back to sleep.

Joanna introduced us to the shopkeeper and told him of our investigation, not mentioning our earlier visit to the Widow Marley. Mr. Hardy's face showed immediate concern.

"Such a lovely girl, who meant so very much to us," he opined.

"You speak of her in the past tense," Joanna noted. "Is there a reason behind that?"

Mr. Hardy sighed sadly. "In this neighborhood, madam, when a person disappears they are for the most part never seen again."

"But we were told that the individuals associated with the playhouse were considered untouchable and free from danger."

"They were until this incident," Hardy said. "I knew something was amiss when she did not show up to purchase her favorite candy. She was quite a creature of habit, you see, and always arrived promptly at four twice a week without fail."

"Did she buy the same candy on every visit?"

The shopkeeper nodded. "Again, she was a creature of habit and always bought four pieces of chocolate-covered apple spice, but I added an extra which I know she shared with the Widow Marley, who has come on hard times since the loss of her husband." The shopkeeper sighed once more to himself. "Such a kind, sweet girl she was."

"Was she the only person in the neighborhood who fancied chocolate-covered apple spice?"

"The answer is yes, if you are referring to buying on a consistent basis. It is more expensive than the others and most cannot afford it. Nevertheless, Pretty Penny's purchases were so regular that I had to lay in a goodly supply of several dozen every month. With the girl's disappearance, I was concerned the new order would remain on the shelf indefinitely, but a new customer came in late yesterday and bought nearly an entire trayful. I shall now of course put in a much smaller supply, with Penny's absence."

Joanna's brow went up. "How many pieces of chocolate-covered apple spice were purchased by this new customer?"

"Twenty, exactly twenty."

"Was that the number you had on hand?"

"No, madam. I had twenty-five, but he insisted on me counting out twenty pieces under his careful eye," he replied.

"And most surprisingly, he paid with a five-pound note. I don't see many of those in my shop, I can tell you for sure."

"He demanded an accurate count, did he?"

"Made me count the pieces twice."

"What was the final charge?"

"One pound two shillings," Hardy answered. "And there was another odd thing. He did not bother to count the change, but simply shoved it into his pocket. In this neighborhood, I can assure you we all count our change most carefully."

"Can you give a description of this man?"

"He was an older chap, with long gray hair that was partially covered with a fisherman's hat," the shopkeeper recalled. "But he didn't have the complexion of a seagoing man."

"Do you remember his outer garments?"

"Only that he was wearing a dark sweater which had seen better days."

"Not the type of individual you would expect to pay with a five-pound note."

"Hardly."

"Did he have any facial scars or disfigurement?"

"Not that I noticed."

Joanna considered the matter further. "Did the customer speak with a cockney accent?"

Hardy shook his head. "He sounded more like an educated man."

"Had you ever seen him before?"

"Neither before nor since."

We thanked the shopkeeper for his time and bade him good-bye. Once well away from the sweet shop, Joanna rubbed her hands together gleefully and asked, "What do you make of that?"

"Of what?" I asked.

"Mr. Hardy's new customer who comes in poorly dressed

to buy precisely twenty pieces of an expensive candy with a five-pound note and pays little attention to the change he receives. A man who labors greatly for five pounds does not buy an excessive amount of expensive candy and, if by chance he did, he would most certainly count the change."

"You believe he is not poor, for he deals with a five-pound note as if it is not of great consequence," deduced my father.

"Spot-on, Watson," said Joanna. "But then, we have an individual who dresses poorly, yet speaks with an educated tongue. A strange mixture, eh?"

"Much like the individual who wrote the note and pretended to be illiterate when he obviously wasn't," my father recollected.

"So it would seem the stalker and the candy buyer are one and the same," Joanna reasoned. "I put it to you that he is from the upper class and attempting to hide it."

"But why wear a disguise to buy apple spice candy?" I asked.

"So he will not be recognized."

"By whom?"

"By Mr. Hardy, the shopkeeper," she asserted. "You see, this individual wishes to conceal his identity, for he knows the police will soon be on his trail to follow his tracks."

"For what purpose?"

"For Pretty Penny, for he is the man responsible for her disappearance."

"Based on what, pray tell?"

"The twenty pieces of apple spice candy he purchased," Joanna replied. "Is it not a rather odd number which he demanded? Not one more or one less, mind you."

"I fail to see the connection between the number twenty and Pretty Penny's disappearance."

My wife smiled thinly. "Do you not think it odder yet

that a disguised man pretending to be poor walks into a sweet shop and purchases a large amount of expensive candy which is rarely bought by anyone except Pretty Penny, who went missing a day ago?"

"He was buying the candy for her," I breathed in astonishment. "But why the number twenty?"

"It is a straightforward calculation which will give us the answer," Joanna replied. "Do you recall how many pieces of apple spice candy Pretty Penny purchased on each visit to the sweet shop?"

"Four."

"Divide that number into twenty."

"Five."

"And that is the number of days he plans to hold Pretty Penny in captivity, during which time he will feed her four pieces of apple spice candy each evening."

"And then?"

"He will bring down the curtain on the final act."

Chapter 3

The Whitechapel Playhouse

As promised by Emma Adams, we were provided with the very best seats at the Whitechapel Playhouse, where we enjoyed an updated version of Shakespeare's *Romeo and Juliet*. The performance was surprisingly good, but even more surprising was the fact that I was personally acquainted with three of the main actors, all of whom were on staff at St. Bartholomew's Hospital. The printed program listed Peter

Willoughby and Thaddeus Rudd as the heads of the feuding Capulets and Montague families, neither of whom would ever allow their children, Juliet and Romeo, to marry. Willoughby was director of pathology where I served as an assistant professor, whereas Rudd was a sharp-tongued surgeon whose skills far outweighed his manners. The third member from St. Bart's was Maxwell Anderson, who was a perfect fit for Romeo. Handsome and charming, he was the newest addition to the pathology department and all believed his brilliance was such that he was destined for an outstanding future in medicine. Despite my close professional association with the three, I had no idea how they happened to appear onstage at the Whitechapel Playhouse. But my father knew the answer and explained all at intermission, during which time the audience filed out for refreshments.

"They are members of the St. Bart's Players, an amateur actors club which was formed many years ago. I myself joined the group, for I had some acting experience during my university days in London. However, it became clear that the talents of others far exceeded mine, and I gracefully withdrew," my father recounted. "They rehearse on a regular schedule and audition for various roles on the stages of amateur playhouses throughout the greater London area."

"I take it you were a member of the group long before Willoughby, Rudd, and Maxwell," I surmised.

"By more years than I care to count," said he.

"Would it not be unusual for three actors from the St. Bart's group to be given roles in the very same play?" Joanna asked.

"One might think so, but the three onstage tonight are said to be the most talented, and I was told they often appear at the same playhouse."

"Have you ever seen them perform?"

"Not until this evening."

Joanna gave the matter more thought before inquiring, "Tell me more about the pathologist who plays Romeo."

"I am afraid I know virtually nothing of the man, for I retired prior to his arrival at St. Bart's," my father replied. "Perhaps John can assist you with that information."

"First, I must confess that I know little of this actors group, so I can only inform you of his professional status within the department of pathology," I began.

"That is where my interest lies."

I waited for a working-class couple, with sleeping children in their arms, to pass by, then continued in a low voice. "Maxwell Anderson came to us two years ago after distinguishing himself at Oxford University Hospital. He is a rather bright fellow who specializes in histopathology, a subspecialty in which diseased tissues are sectioned, placed on slides, and stained for study under the microscope. He is quite handsome and single, and thus the nurses and technicians constantly try to catch his eye, but with little success, or so the rumor goes. I am of the opinion his stay at St. Bart's will not be long, for his skills are such that he will be offered even more desirable positions at other hospitals as his reputation grows."

"He does appear to be extraordinarily handsome onstage," Joanna commented.

"As he is offstage, to the extent he turns heads and causes women to stare."

"Yet unmarried."

"To the best of my knowledge."

"He is by far the most talented of the group," Joanna noted. "And with his striking good looks, he represents the ideal Romeo."

"Just as Willoughby fits so well his role as the curmudgeon head of the Capulet family," I added. "He easily comes by acting in such a disagreeable manner, for that is his natural behavior. No one in the department of pathology, including myself, is spared the sting of his mean-spirited tongue. His one saving grace is that he is a renowned neuropathologist whose excellence is such that specimens are sent to him from all over Europe for final review and diagnosis."

"He was not always held in high esteem," my father informed us. "He was once in fact a figure of ridicule."

"I was unaware," said I, taken aback by the revelation. "This must have occurred long ago."

"Indeed so, for the incident has faded with the years." My father reached for his cherrywood pipe, which was already packed with tobacco, and slowly lighted it. "It goes back to the time I was first entering the practice of medicine and had been granted admitting privileges at St. Bartholomew's. Willoughby was a young assistant professor who, like many starting academicians, yearned for instant recognition. In contrast to the prevailing belief, he was convinced that criminal behavior was caused by a lesion in the cerebral cortex, and set out to prove it by examining the brains of recently hanged murderers. One of the initial corpses belonged to a rather handsome woman who poisoned her husband so she could gain his insurance money and enjoy life with a string of secret lovers, of which there were said to be many. Much to Willoughby's delight, she was found to have an abnormality in the frontal lobe of her cerebral cortex. Not long after, a second corpse was discovered to have a similar lesion. The latter brain was dissected from a woman of low morals who stabbed a brothel owner to death over a money issue. Willoughby claimed that in both cases the cortical lesions accounted for their criminal behavior."

"So he was about to make quite a name for himself," I supposed.

"For both he and his coworker on the study, Thaddeus Rudd."

"But Rudd was a surgeon," I noted. "How could he have been involved?"

"Back then, he was a surgeon in training and was obliged to undertake a rotation through the pathology section, where he met and soon began to work alongside Peter Willoughby. It was during that time that their startling discoveries were made."

"Startling to say the least, if they were confirmed," said I.

"But they weren't," my father went on. "Willoughby and Rudd submitted the research to the *Lancet* detailing their findings, which the medical journal refused to publish because the brain lesions were clearly the result of repeated trauma and not some long-standing structural defect. Undeterred, Willoughby decided to present his research to the Royal Society, where he was literally jeered off the podium."

"Which must have been most embarrassing," I interjected.

"For him and St. Bart's," said my father. "Willoughby, as the senior member of the project, was issued a letter of reprimand which included a requirement that all of his research be reviewed by an internal committee prior to being submitted for publication. This of course forced him to give up his unfounded theory and turn his attention to neuropathology, which he did with great vigor. Thus, with the passage of time, he was able to restore his reputation and become a leading figure in that particular field."

"What a tale," said I, wondering if Willoughby's unpleasant temperament was the result of the severe rebuke he faced in his formative academic years.

"So all is not what it seems," Joanna remarked. "But then, it never is."

"Which holds true for the prominent surgeon Thaddeus Rudd, for I am afraid he has a dark side as well," said I.

"At surgery?" Joanna asked at once.

"In a manner of speaking," I replied. "Rudd is known to be quite ill-tempered, particularly when procedures do not go smoothly. During one most difficult surgery, the nurse at his side handed Rudd the incorrect instrument on two occasions. The second mistake sent him into a tantrum, which included striking her with a metal retractor that broke her nose and caused considerable bleeding. He then chased her out of the operating room, with a string of profanities. When the nurse's husband learned of the incident, he confronted the surgeon and challenged him to step outside. Rudd responded by picking up a scalpel and slashing the husband's arm. Rudd was charged with assault, but the charges were soon dismissed, with the surgeon claiming self-defense. Obviously influence had been applied to the court from those in high places."

"Was there no punishment?" asked Joanna.

"Only that he was forced to write a letter of apology and pay a considerable sum to the husband and wife for their injuries."

Joanna shook her head at the minimal price Rudd had paid for his criminal assault. "Was it not Robert Louis Stevenson who said that the physician is the flower of our civilization?"

"I believe so," my father replied.

"Well, it is clear that he never had the pleasure of meeting this beauty."

The bell ending the intermission sounded. The audience gradually returned to their seats and quieted as the curtains were parted for the final act of *Romeo and Juliet.* The curtains consisted of stitched-together blankets which were pulled into the wings by stagehands who quickly folded them into neat stacks. Glancing around, it was clear that the entire theater was likewise makeshift, with oversized lights that dangled down on bare wires. The seats came in a number of odd varieties, including folding chairs, rockers and wooden benches, and even a nicely upholstered sofa upon which the three of us sat. What was equally remarkable was that all the seats were lined up in a fashion which gave everyone an unobstructed view of the stage. If ever there was a clear-cut demonstration of where there is a will there is a way, it was on display at the Whitechapel Playhouse.

The final act was performed without a single miscue, with the audience now completely enthralled by the poignant scene of the lovely Juliet lying stone cold in her tomb, with all evidence of life gone. Even my dear wife, Joanna, who could hide her emotions with ease, was so touched she rested her head on my shoulder as tears welled in her eyes. Then the scene abruptly changed. Romeo finds Juliet's supposedly dead body and, rather than face life without her, reaches for a vial of poison. The audience was so taken by the drama that a few stood and shouted, "Don't do it, lad! Don't do it!" And when Romeo ingested the poison, it was met with a chorus of groans and sobs, for only a moment later Juliet awakens and returns to life. The last, sad lines of the play were spoken—

"For never was a story of more woe
Than this of Juliet and her Romeo."

The words brought the audience to its feet, with thunderous applause. There were three curtain calls.

"What say you, Joanna?" I asked quietly.

"I say I would love to see the enticing Pretty Penny as Juliet," said she, and for a moment the three of us envisioned the innocent beauty of the missing girl who would have fit the role so perfectly.

We made our way through the crowded theater to a back office where Lionel Lurie, the director of the play, awaited us. Joanna felt he would know a great deal about Pretty Penny from his almost day-to-day interactions with the young actress. Yet for reasons that were unclear, Lurie was not keen on meeting with us and only did so at Emma Adams's insistence.

Our rap on the office door elicited a rather unpleasant welcome: "Well, get in!"

We found Lurie sitting behind a makeshift desk which consisted of a wide, sanded-down shutter that sat atop two barrels. The remainder of the office was equally bare, with no amenities or decorations. He did not bother to stand and only motioned to a cluster of wooden stools.

"We prefer to stand," Joanna said.

"Suit yourself, then." Lurie lighted a small cigar and leaned back in his chair. "Now, what can I do for you?"

"We require additional information which I believe you can provide," Joanna replied. "But first, I would like to know why you were so reluctant to speak with us."

"I don't care for the authorities, never have," he said with a deep cockney accent.

"Even when it comes to finding Pretty Penny?"

Lurie's face softened a bit. "Terrible business, just terrible."

"Do you fear the worst?"

"Don't you?" Lurie responded, puffing gently on his cigar. "Look, madam, this is Whitechapel, where the folks are tough as nails and the streets tougher yet. You see the audience swooning over *Romeo and Juliet* and it gives you the wrong impression. For once they leave the playhouse, they return to their cold, harsh surroundings in which violence and other unpleasantries are the order of the day."

"I must say that you do not seem overly upset over the missing girl."

"Oh, but I am," said Lurie in a calm, emotionless voice. "She was unbelievably talented, the likes of which come along once in a lifetime. But she was not long for Whitechapel, for she would have shortly moved on to a better world."

"Are you referring to her secret lover?"

"Bah," Lurie answered, and waved away the notion through

the smoke from his cigar. "That was all starry-eyed talk of women, who always look for a fairy-tale ending. In my opinion, she might well have stayed with him, but she would have never given up the stage for such a permanent union. You see, she had a natural gift that was given by God himself, and anyone with any sense realized it. Word was spreading of her remarkable talent throughout London, as evidenced by the managers and agents who came to watch her perform. No, madam, I say again that Pretty Penny was not long for Whitechapel."

"And this was her way out."

"Indeed it was."

"Yet, with her remarkable acting skills, I remain somewhat surprised that you are not more distraught over losing her."

Lurie shrugged. "In Whitechapel we do not become too attached to things or people, for in our world they tend to vanish."

"Without reason?" Joanna asked.

"Some with, some without," replied Lurie. "But gone is still gone and I am afraid that holds true for Pretty Penny."

I could not help but notice the cold, indifferent tone in the director's voice and wondered whether it was an act or he was truly that heartless.

Joanna also seemed to be measuring the man, perhaps thinking the same thought as I. His untoward demeanor at the loss of Pretty Penny was so unlike the response we had seen in others associated with the fine actress. "Did Penny ever speak of leaving?" she asked finally.

"Not to me," Lurie replied without hesitation.

"Were you aware of Pretty Penny's activities away from the playhouse?" Joanna queried.

"Only at Emma Adams's pub where the girl served as a barmaid," Lurie responded. "Even in that role she had a grace of movement and a voice that immediately grabbed and held one's attention. Those very same qualities revealed themselves when she showed up to audition for the part of Juliet. Sweet Jesus Above! She bloody well knocked us off our feet. It was like a present from heaven. In my over thirty years in show business, I was never so taken by such an individual talent, man or woman."

"You've been a director for thirty years?" Joanna inquired.

"No, madam, not as a director." Lurie ambled over to a trash bin to deposit cigar ashes. He was a tall man, in his middle years, with curly red hair and a freckled face. "First off, I was an actor, with only modest talent, I must confess. But I was addicted to the stage, so I tried my hand at playwriting, then as an assistant director at outlying playhouses. Unfortunately, the income was poor and I had a family to support at the time, so I ended up as a dockworker. Yet the stage remained in my blood and over the years I continued as a part-time director at smaller, amateur playhouses. A few years back I met Emma Adams at a dismal performance of *Macbeth* and we hit it off well enough to pool our talents and establish this playhouse. My work at the docks is intermittent, so I add to my income tending bar at Emma's pub."

"May I inquire how close you and Emma Adams are?" Joanna asked directly.

"Close enough," Lurie replied as his eyes darted briefly. "But if you are wondering if we share the same bed, the answer is no."

Joanna nodded, but I could tell from her motion that she didn't entirely believe him. "Do you have more than a passing acquaintance with the major actors in the play?"

"Only with E. T. Willoughby, who I met more years ago than I care to count."

"Who is this E. T. Willoughby?" I interrupted at once. "Are you by chance referring to Peter Willoughby in the program?"

"He is one and the same, for E.T. was a stage name he assumed many years ago as an amateur actor," Lurie replied. "As I mentioned earlier, I was a player some thirty years ago, and that is where our paths crossed. Peter Willoughby was a fine young actor whose talent far exceeded mine, and he would have made a career of it, but his family objected and demanded he become a doctor, like his father before him. While in medical school, however, he continued acting and managed to keep it a secret as far as his family was concerned. To make certain they never learned of his hidden career, he altered his stage name to Edward Thomas Willoughby, and insisted he be listed in the program as E. T. Willoughby. But now, of course, he uses his true name, for the family's knowledge of his amateur acting is no longer a concern. In any event, I went on to another occupation and so did E.T. I never laid eyes on him again until a few months ago. I was truly stunned when he showed up after all these years at the audition for *Romeo and Juliet*."

"Was he pleased to see you?" I asked.

Lurie shrugged indifferently. "To say he was cordial would be stretching it, but then again he was always somewhat of a cold fish. And now that our worlds are so far apart, I never expected any camaraderie."

"Does he take your directing without complaint?" my father asked.

"He does indeed, for he is most concerned with fine-tuning his performance," said Lurie. "Which is in stark contrast to his doctor-friend, Thaddeus Rudd, who plays the role as head of the Montague family. He is difficult to work with, for he is not nearly as talented as he believes. When he misses the mark, he has a tendency to yell and threaten, much as you would expect from a bully. But he backs down when challenged."

"By you?"

"By Harry Sanders, who guards our side entrance."

"He serves as a bouncer, then?"

Lurie smiled briefly for the first time. "Harry is a man of many skills and is most helpful to the entire crew, particularly should trouble arise. He is quite protective of Maxwell Anderson, our Romeo."

"For what reason?" asked Joanna, who had been concentrating on every word Lurie spoke. "Had this bully Rudd threatened Maxwell?"

"Nah, those two get along well," Lurie answered. "Anderson endeared himself to Harry by smuggling out some sort of aspirin cream from St. Bart's, which has worked wonders on Harry's arthritic knuckles. Anderson is exceptionally well liked, for in addition to being a kind physician, he is a superb actor, easily on a par with Willoughby."

"As evidenced by his performance tonight," she noted.

"He was particularly on point," Lurie agreed. "But you should see him perform with Pretty Penny as his Juliet. They both absolutely sparkle. You could not wait for them to return in following scenes. It was as if they were made for one another."

"It sounds like there was a perfect chemistry between them," Joanna said.

"Oh, there was indeed," Lurie concurred. "Everyone in the audience could sense their mutual attraction."

"Do you believe this attraction went beyond the stage?" my wife asked pointedly.

Lurie hesitated before answering. "It's possible, but they showed no evidence of it while performing or during rehearsals. Everything was strictly professional. And then of course you have to consider the age difference between them. She was still in her teen years, while he was surely in his thirties."

"Not an insurmountable difference."

"There never is when it comes to love involving strikingly beautiful people."

Joanna nodded at the expected reply. "I have a few more questions which I hope you can answer. They deal with Pretty Penny's acting career, and the agents and managers who visited Whitechapel to watch her perform. Did they speak with you directly about furthering her career?"

"A few did, but they were most interested in bringing her under contract and becoming her agent. One chap in particular, Richard Blackstone, the brother of the famous director, was a real nuisance, promising us the world and more to sign with his agency."

"And your response?"

"I told him that Pretty Penny had already retained an agent."

Joanna raised an eyebrow. "Which was who?"

"Emma Adams," Lurie replied offhandedly.

"Was there a formal contract?"

"Signed and sealed in the presence of a barrister."

"One last question," Joanna requested, staring out into space for a moment. "Has Emma Adams ever served as an agent in the past?"

"Not to my knowledge."

"Thank you for your time," said Joanna, and as we departed I noticed that his forehead had become furrowed and I wondered what in our conversation was causing him concern.

The playhouse was now empty and eerily silent. It was as if all life was gone from the theater and the building had reverted back to being a deserted warehouse. Near the steps to the stage we saw Emma Adams waiting for us. The lights overhead had been switched off, but the filaments within the bulbs remained red hot and gave partial illumination.

"Was Lionel Lurie of help?" she asked.

"Perhaps a bit," Joanna replied evasively. "But I must say I was somewhat surprised by his lack of worry over Pretty Penny's disappearance."

"Trust me," Mrs. Adams said. "He does not sleep at night because of his unease and anxiety."

My father and I exchanged knowing glances, for she was indeed sleeping with Lionel Lurie, which made the director a liar.

"He tends to keep things bottled up inside himself, you see," she went on. "Since the loss of his son at the Battle of the Somme last year, he finds it difficult to conjure up sympathy for anyone else regardless of their situation."

Just the mention of the battle brought sadness to every English heart. The Battle of the Somme was a fierce Allied offensive that was mounted to break through the German lines near the Somme River in northeastern France. On the first day of the battle, Britain suffered its greatest single-day loss in the country's history; there were sixty thousand casualties, one-third of whom were killed. There was not a town in all England that did not grieve.

"A sad day," Joanna commented.

"Sad indeed," said Emma Adams. "But then, we have no choice but to carry on, soldiers and citizens alike."

"And so we shall," Joanna affirmed resolutely. "Now let us return to our conversation with Mr. Lurie and to a point or two he raised. He mentioned that Thaddeus Rudd was somewhat of a bully. Did you find him so?"

Emma Adams nodded without hesitation. "He is a large, broad-shouldered man, with a deep voice that was threatening to people and caused some to back off. But he did not display this behavior often, except onstage where it was required."

"Could you give me an example?"

"Recall that he played the role of head of the Montague family, which was forever feuding with the Capulets. He performed nicely when threatening and staring down Peter Willoughby, the leader of the Capulets. You would never have known they were good friends offstage, which of course is the sign of excellent acting."

"What of the romantic scenes between Maxwell Anderson and Pretty Penny?" Joanna probed gently. "Was that entirely acting on their parts?"

"I believe so, for true love is very difficult to hide," Emma Adams responded. "It is virtually impossible to resist a secret touch or conceal a blush or look that involuntarily goes on far too long. I never witnessed those signs nor sensed they were occurring in a dark corner."

"Well judged," Joanna said, but the hint of a smile that crossed her face told me she believed otherwise. "Now please be good enough to direct us to Harry Sanders."

Emma Adams gestured to a side door on the far side of the building. "You will find him just outside in the alleyway."

We strolled toward the exit and remained silent until we were well away from Emma Adams's hearing, but even then we spoke in low voices.

"Our Mr. Lurie is a liar," Joanna whispered. "He and Emma Adams are sharing the same bed and no doubt have information they are unwilling to share with us."

"Her statement that he does not sleep well at night surely tells us that theirs is more than a casual acquaintance," I agreed.

"It was not just the statement, but the manner in which Lurie's eyes darted while denying their closeness," Joanna informed. "It is a revealing sign of a liar, every bit as telling as a facial twitch. Now we must wonder what else he is being less than honest about."

"Surely he would not withhold information on Pretty Penny's disappearance," said I. "I cannot see how that might serve his interests."

"Allow me to illustrate how it might," Joanna continued

on. "We are now aware that Emma Adams is Pretty Penny's agent and Lionel Lurie her director, and the two of them thick as thieves and then some. They decide that the talented actress is their way out of Whitechapel, so they arrange for her secret abduction, but only after setting the table with a phantom stalker and written note. We have been called in as will Scotland Yard eventually, and the story of a beautiful, talented actress who has gone missing will appear in all the newspapers. It is Juliet who has disappeared. Has she eloped with her Romeo? Has she been harmed or worse? The story is captivating and brings with it more publicity than a thousand pounds could ever purchase. Then she reappears, having somehow escaped her captors, and our scheming Emma Adams and Lionel Lurie ride her coattails to fame and fortune."

"That is beyond diabolical," my father protested mildly.

"When it comes to vast sums of money, my dear Watson, the depth of greed has no limits. Keep in mind that an actress starring at a theater on St. Martin's Lane can earn fifty pounds a week, which is more than Emma Adams's pub would profit in a year."

"But Mrs. Adams as agent would only receive a fraction of the actress's fee," my father noted.

"Ten percent to be exact, which comes to five pounds a week, twenty per month, and two hundred and forty per annum," Joanna calculated. "A rather tidy sum, wouldn't you say?"

"Quite tidy indeed."

We passed through the side entrance and found Harry Sanders sitting on a stool in the alleyway. He quickly got to his feet and gave us a half bow, having been forewarned of our presence in the playhouse. Even in the dim lighting we could see that he was a short, thick man, balding and just over five feet tall, with muscular arms that seemed oversized for his body frame. As we came closer, I noticed the physical signs which told me he had once been a boxer. There was heavy scar tissue around his eyes, most notably on his brows, together with a bent nose and huge knuckles, which no doubt had become calcified from repeated trauma.

"Did you box as a featherweight?" I asked.

"A flyweight, guv'nor," Sanders responded, with a crooked smile. "I have put on a few pounds since those days, you see."

"As a professional, I take it."

"For nearly ten years."

"A most difficult way to make a living."

"But it was in my blood, and to this day I still train with the weights and punching bag."

"Which your arms clearly demonstrate."

Harry Sanders flexed his arm to produce a bulging biceps muscle, which seemed to please him. "It comes in handy in my line of work."

"Do you remember much trouble about the playhouse?"

"Very little, guv'nor. Every now and then a fellow or two will try to sneak in via this door, but they take off when they see me."

"Are any of them older chaps?" Joanna asked.

Sanders hesitated and carefully studied Joanna for several moments. "Am I talking to the daughter of Sherlock Holmes?"

"You are."

"It is an honor, madam," said he, with another half bow.

Joanna nodded at the bouncer's deference before inquiring again, "Were any of the intruders middle-aged or older?"

"Only one that I remember," Sanders recalled. "He was a tall drunk who demanded to see Pretty Penny and actually threw a punch at me."

"Was he wearing a fisherman's hat to cover his long gray hair?"

"No, madam. The bugger was hatless and bald as an apple."

"From your description, it sounds as if you promptly sent him on his way."

"With a reminder not to return."

"Very good," Joanna continued on. "Now tell us, do you remain at this station throughout the evening?"

"I am here on the nights of every performance from five in the afternoon until ten when we lock up. And only those I know are allowed to enter. These include all the players, stage-hands, and workmen who keep the building running and in good shape."

"Do they all exit through this door as well?"

Sanders shook his head. "Most leave through the front entrance, madam. The players, however, usually exit here, so they can reach their motor taxis and avoid the autograph seekers and such."

Joanna squinted an eye as if attempting to envision the scene late at night. "Are the taxis waiting at the end of the alleyway?"

"Oh, no, madam. They only come up when I signal them."

"So the players take the next available taxi in a random fashion."

Sanders nodded at the description. "The drivers do not know who their passenger will be, with the exception of Pretty Penny. Her ride is set up previously, and that particular taxi is meant for her only."

"Does she have the same driver every time?" Joanna asked at once.

"No, madam, it varies. You see, the fare to the west side is quite hefty and the gratuity received is most generous, so I believe whoever sends the taxi must rotate it to keep the drivers happy. They consider it a real plum to carry Pretty Penny."

"Who sets the schedule for Penny's taxis?"

"I would guess the taxi company."

"But you are not certain."

"No, madam."

"Is there a way to determine this?"

"You would have to talk with one of the drivers."

"Anyone in particular?"

Sanders considered the matter at length, rubbing his chin as he did. "The only driver I know for sure who drove Pretty Penny is Tommy Maguire, an Irish lad who bragged about it for a week. He is a good boy who trains at the same gym I go to."

"He's a boxer, then?" asked Joanna.

Sanders nodded again. "Who drives a taxi at night."

"So deep down he's a boxer."

"In the making."

"Can I find him at your gym?"

"You can find him across the street, for later on we will travel to Hackney to view a heavyweight bout."

"Please signal him, for we require a taxi to Baker Street."

"Done!"

Minutes later we were riding toward the West End of London, with Tommy Maguire as our driver. Like most Irishmen, he was quite talkative and seemed to enjoy conversing about his work and how the schedule to pick up Pretty Penny was determined. "Some person calls the company's headquarters and requests a taxi be sent to the Whitechapel Playhouse at a given time, where it will wait for the actress Pretty Penny. The destination is set beforehand and we are instructed only she and she alone will occupy the taxi. We will be paid once we arrive."

"By whom?" Joanna asked.

"If it is a fancy restaurant, by the doorman, or the maître d' might step outside with the fee in an envelope. You see, the charge and gratuity are both calculated ahead."

"Where was your destination?"

"Alexander's on St. Martin's Lane."

"Who paid the fee?" Joanna queried. "Was it the doorman or the maître d'?"

"Neither. It was the gentleman waiting for her."

The three of us abruptly leaned forward, ears pricked at our good fortune. An important piece of the puzzle was at hand. "Can you describe the gentleman?" my wife asked. "We require as much detail as you can recall."

"I truly did not have a good look at him," Tommy Maguire said in an honest voice. "For as soon as she exited, she was in his arms and kissing him. A brief kiss, mind you, but it blocked my view. Being low down in the driver's seat, I only caught a glimpse of his jaw and suit, which I might add was well cut and expensive. Then he gave me an envelope with the fee and the couple entered the restaurant."

"But you must have had a rear view of him."

"I did."

"Was he tall or short?"

"Not short, for he was a head taller than Pretty Penny."

"And the color of his hair?"

"Dark."

"Was there gray in it?"

"Not that I could notice."

"From the fit of his suit, would you say he was thin or stout?"

"Average."

Joanna breathed a sigh of disappointment before asking, "Did you by chance hear him speak?"

"There was very little conversation between them," Maguire replied. "All he said was, 'You performed brilliantly as always,' and then inside they went."

A thin smile crossed my wife's face. "Very good, very good indeed."

We remained silent for the remainder of our ride, although the words spoken by the secret lover obviously had special significance to Joanna. But their meaning escaped me. So she performed brilliantly, so what? That would seem to be on a par for the remarkably talented actress.

On reaching 221b Baker Street, we stood outside our door and watched the taxi disappear into the black night. More seconds ticked by as I waited patiently for Joanna to explain the importance of the secret lover's message to Pretty Penny at the entrance to the restaurant. But she continued to tap a finger against her closed lips, as if distracted by some thoughts. Finally, I could hold my curiosity no longer and asked, "Why was the secret lover's greeting to Pretty Penny so noteworthy?"

"I saw nothing of particular interest, either," my father chimed in. "The statement 'You performed brilliantly as always' seemed innocent enough."

"It was the words *as always* which should draw your attention," Joanna instructed.

"*As always*?" my father queried.

Joanna nodded. "Those words inform us that the secret lover has seen Pretty Penny perform not one or two times, but on a multitude of occasions. With this in mind, tell me who would be expected to be in attendance at the playhouse on such a frequent basis."

The answer came to my father immediately. "The cast, of course!"

"Or perhaps an agent or manager visiting repeatedly to assess Pretty Penny's talents," I added.

"Or perhaps an individual who has paid the entrance fee evening after evening to watch his beloved," she proposed. "And when he cannot see her onstage, his fixation is such he must stalk her."

"Like a man possessed," I muttered to myself.

My father turned quickly to Joanna and asked, "Are you suggesting we may be dealing with a Dr. Jekyll–Mr. Hyde personality?"

"That thought has crossed my mind," Joanna said ominously, and reached for the door as rain began to fall.

Chapter 4

The Secret Autopsy

On my arrival at St. Bartholomew's the following morning, I encountered a most unusual sight. Standing guard outside the entrances to the autopsy room were two uniformed constables, with a sign on the door behind them that read ABSOLUTELY NO ADMITTANCE. I had never before experienced a similar situation in the department of pathology and began to mentally list the reasons for an autopsy being performed in such secrecy. The most likely cause would be a personage of lofty rank who had died under bizarre circumstances. Or perhaps the corpse was believed to carry a highly contagious disease. But then again, the latter was unlikely, for the constables were unmasked and positioned too close to the entrance.

As I approached, the taller of the two constables held up a hand and said, "Sorry, sir, but no admission other than Dr. Willoughby is allowed, on orders from the commissioner."

"Very well, then," I said, and walked on, for it was obvious from the officer's tight-lipped expression that there would be no further conversation.

With the commissioner of Scotland Yard's involvement, I

thought to myself, the matter had to be criminal and no doubt sensitive. That being the case, I would have surely been the pathologist consulted by the police, for the field of forensics was my specialty. But for the past month I had been on sabbatical leave, completing a chapter in a soon-to-be-published textbook, and was thus believed to be unavailable. Of course I could have been called in with little bother, but Peter Willoughby took advantage of the situation and was undoubtedly performing the autopsy, for he craved the publicity which would eventually arise from such a case.

I entered my small office and went directly to the shelves for the monograph I had come to fetch. It dealt with factors influencing cooling of the body after death, the subject of the chapter I was currently writing. But the monograph had been published ten years ago and the topic needed updating. For example, the older version did not discuss the effect of ventilation on the corpse's temperature, which turns out to be a most important factor. It is now well known that a body cools far more rapidly in a ventilated room as opposed to one which is closed off.

I hurried from my office, monograph in hand, and could not help but notice the constables standing guard and again wondered what purpose they served. My very best guess was that their presence ensured the secrecy of a royal who had died in a most unroyal fashion. I moved aside as the head orderly pushed an empty gurney by me. He nodded in a somewhat peculiar manner. More side to side than up and down, for his cervical spine had been badly damaged in a childhood accident.

"A word, Benson, if you have a moment," I requested.

"Of course, sir," replied William Benson, a longtime valued employee who kept everything shipshape and running smoothly in the department.

I gestured subtly with my head to the constables outside the autopsy room. "Strange business, eh?"

"Very strange indeed, Doctor," Benson replied in a low voice. "I have seen a bit of cloak-and-dagger in my time, but nothing like this. The entire area had to be cleared, from the police ambulance and down the corridor right up to the autopsy room. Only the good Dr. Willoughby, the constable, and myself were allowed to be present."

"Did you actually see the body?"

"I did not, sir, for it arrived in a wooden shell, the type the coppers use to transport their corpses. Of course its lid was closed, so no one peeping about could have a look."

"Did you alone push the gurney carrying the corpse?"

"Only me."

"And did you by yourself unload the body onto the autopsy table?"

"I did."

"Now, I want you to describe every aspect of the corpse, head to toe."

"I could only see the head, for the rest of her body was wrapped in a blanket," Benson reported. "But her face definitely belonged to a young woman."

"Was it that of a teenager?" I asked at once.

Benson thought back for a moment before answering. "I could not be certain, for her face was covered with mud and blood, with some deep cuts, like those you see in a knife fight."

"I take it that the wounds had even edges."

"Straight as can be and made with a sharp knife, I would say."

"What about their depth?"

"I could not be sure, for most of them were coated with dried blood. So was her hair, for that matter."

"Was her hair long or short?"

"Quite short."

"Was it ruffled?"

Benson shrugged. "I couldn't tell."

"Did you notice its color?"

"Light brown, with a nice sheen to it."

"Very good," said I. "So we have a young woman with short light brown hair and multiple facial cuts, probably made with a sharp knife."

"Exactly right," Benson agreed.

"Now let us estimate her weight," I went on. "Did you alone lift the body from the shell?"

"All by myself."

"What would you approximate her weight to be?"

"No more than a hundred pounds."

"Did she have an unusual smell?"

"Nary a whiff. She was freshly dead, for sure."

"One last question, Benson, and please give it careful consideration," I requested. "Did she have any distinguishing features? A facial scar? Perhaps a crooked nose or disfigured ear?"

"Her ear wasn't disfigured, but held a dangling earring," the head orderly recalled.

"Were there any gems in it?"

"Oh, no, sir. It was quite cheap, as one might expect to be worn by a working-class woman."

"The earring by itself doesn't designate a working-class woman."

"But the area in which the body was found surely does."

"Which area?"

"Whitechapel, according to the ambulance driver."

Pretty Penny! Everything about the corpse now pointed to the missing actress. It had to be her.

Benson stared at my expression, which I suspect included a dropped jaw. "Are you all right, sir?"

"I am fine," I lied. "It is just a bit of a tooth pain that comes and goes. Not to worry."

"Then I shall go about my business, sir."

"Very good," said I, regaining my composure. "Carry on."

It all fit, I continued to think to myself. A young actress goes missing one day and her mutilated body is found the next, all occurring in the district of Whitechapel. Yet I had to remind myself that absolute proof was lacking. A positive identification would require certain recognition by an individual who knew her well, such as Emma Adams or Lionel Lurie. How should I go about arranging that?

But as I walked on, there were other questions about the identity of the corpse I found baffling. If the body was Pretty Penny, why was an autopsy necessary for what seemed to be a straightforward murder that occurred in a crime-ridden area? And why was it being done in secret under police protection? Those extraordinary measures would not take place unless there was something particularly noteworthy about her death or the way she died. Ahead, I saw the entrance to Maxwell Anderson's laboratory, which received all tissues removed at autopsy for microscopic study. He would certainly be notified regarding the incoming organs and what special stains might be required. And most important, he might have the name of the individual from whom the organs were taken. He would be particularly interested if the corpse belonged to his Juliet, Pretty Penny.

I quickly entered Anderson's laboratory, which was crowded with workbenches upon which rested various machines that were used to cut organs into thin slices that were transferred onto glass slides and stained for study under a microscope. At the rear of the large room, Anderson was examining a set of dissected-out lungs while he spoke into a horn-shaped device that carried his voice to a nearby recording apparatus. He must have seen me out of the corner of his eye, for he held up an index finger, informing me that he would join me in a moment.

Like onstage, his voice had a majestic quality that captured one's attention. "The lungs are dotted with black spots consistent with the polluted air of London. There is no scarring, but a hard, calcified nodule is present in the right apex, no doubt a result of healed tuberculosis. The great vessels are unremarkable."

Stripping off his rubber gloves, Anderson strolled over and asked, "To what do I owe this honor?"

"I was wondering about the identity of the corpse currently being dissected by Willoughby," I replied.

"As are we all," Anderson said. "She has been named the anonymous Jane Smith, indicating they either do not know her identity or, for reasons beyond me, they wish to keep it a secret. I favor the latter, for even stranger measures are in place to ensure nobody learns who the corpse belongs to."

"I take it you are referring to the constables standing guard outside the autopsy room."

"Oh, it goes much deeper than that," Anderson went on. "The removed organs are not to remain in the dissecting room until all are collected, as is the custom, but rather brought to me by Benson one at a time for study. We have just completed examination of the lungs and now await the intra-abdominal contents. Once all the organs have been studied, their remains will be discarded."

"But what if they require further investigation?"

"Apparently that is of no matter, for my instructions from Willoughby were quite explicit."

"That course of action would have no bearing on her identity," I thought aloud.

"So it would seem," Anderson agreed. "But my further orders are stranger yet. Under ordinary circumstances, I record my findings and have the wax cylinders taken to the stenographer who types up the report for my signature. But with the current case, I am directed to personally walk the wax cylinder to the stenographer's office and make certain it never leaves my sight. I will then wait for the typing to be completed, read it carefully, and send it on to Willoughby for signing. Before I leave the stenographer's office, the wax cylinder is to be destroyed, so that no shred of my report remains."

"What about notes you might jot down?"

"Prohibited."

"Such extreme measures," I commented.

"To the point of being bizarre," Anderson concurred.

"All to hide the woman's identity."

"It would be as if she never existed."

"But to what end?"

"I have asked myself that very same question a dozen times in the past hour," Anderson replied before giving me a lengthy look. "May I inquire as to why you are so interested in this particular case?"

"Because there is a distinct possibility that I know her identity," I said candidly.

"Pray tell how?"

"My reasoning revolves around the still-missing Pretty Penny."

Anderson nodded worriedly. "That is so unlike her, and we are all most concerned."

"What if I told you the corpse Willoughby is currently dissecting was discovered in the dark streets of Whitechapel?"

A stunned expression came to Anderson's face. "Do you believe it to be Pretty Penny?"

"That possibility has crossed my mind."

"But if it is her, why all the secrecy?"

"I have no idea."

Anderson blinked nervously as he, too, appeared to ponder the question. "Perhaps you should bring this to the attention of your friends at Scotland Yard."

"I am afraid my friendship does not extend to the office of the commissioner."

"How will you proceed, then?"

"By taking other avenues," I answered vaguely.

"If it is Pretty Penny, you must let me know immediately," Anderson said, with distress clearly written over his face.

"I shall."

I departed from the laboratory and hurried down the corridor, taking another quick glance at the constables. Standing by them was Benson, who was no doubt waiting at the door to the autopsy room for more organs which would be carried away to be studied before being entirely disposed of. Such incredible secrecy, I thought again. From the standpoint of St. Bart's, the woman's name would remain Jane Smith and it would be as if she never existed.

Just ahead was the department's photograph section, in which photos of all hospital personnel were taken and kept on file. These included doctors on staff, nurses, technicians, orderlies, and maintenance workers. But photos were also taken of all corpses on the autopsy table, with particular attention to the faces of unidentified John and Jane Smiths who might later be recognized by family or friends.

On entering the section, I was greeted by a wave from Robbie Connery, a middle-aged Scotsman who learned his trade from his father, a well-known photographer for an Edinburgh newspaper. "And what brings Dr. Watson to these dark corners?" he asked.

"A photo," I replied.

"Of yourself?"

"Of the corpse Willoughby is currently dissecting."

"No photographs allowed," Connery said, obviously not pleased with the situation. "When I was told by Benson that a Jane Smith had arrived, I immediately assumed a photo would be required, which is always the case for an anonymous corpse. So down I go to the dissecting room and am promptly turned away."

"Most unusual," I remarked.

"Most unusual indeed," Connery agreed. "I have seen only one similar case in my over twenty years here."

"Was the identity ever revealed?"

Connery nodded. "It was a royal who did himself in, with a gunshot to the head. It was very messy, I was told."

"Eventually the true identity leaks out, then."

"It always does."

I strolled out and down the corridor, uncertain about my next step in my quest to learn if the corpse was the missing Pretty Penny. Asking Willoughby was out of the question, for he would take delight in not disclosing any identifiable features. It would be a way of him demonstrating his superiority, which existed only in his imagination. He was a small man in both frame and behavior, for he seemed most content when belittling a lesser individual who had no recourse but to stand and endure it. As I approached the constables, they seemed to straighten up in a stance of attention which I considered somewhat odd. But it soon became clear that their sign of respect wasn't for me, but for the incoming Inspector Lestrade.

He tipped his derby in greeting me. "Ah, Dr. Watson, I am

surprised at your presence, for I was told you were on sabbatical leave."

I nodded. "I am taking some time away."

"A bit of a rest, then."

"To the contrary, my time is completely consumed writing a chapter for a forthcoming textbook on pathology."

"Most important work," said Lestrade, obviously impressed. "I shan't keep you from it."

"I can spare a moment or two if you'd like, for I have information that could influence your secretive investigation," I divulged.

"Such as?" Lestrade asked at once.

"I came in to fetch a reference book, but I now find myself here for a different and more important reason which may relate to the identity of the Jane Smith corpse currently being autopsied."

Lestrade was instantly on guard. "How do you come to this knowledge, might I ask?"

"My wife, father, and I are at this moment involved in a search for a missing actress." I recounted the story of Pretty Penny in detail, emphasizing the fact that she both performed and lived in Whitechapel and had recently been threatened by an unknown stalker. "Since this Jane Smith was found in Whitechapel, I could not help but wonder if she is our Pretty Penny."

"Can you give me a description of this actress?" Lestrade requested.

"Better yet, there is a poster advertising the play which contains a picture of Pretty Penny."

"Where can we obtain this poster?"

"From the manager of the Whitechapel Playhouse."

"Excellent! And most helpful."

The door to the autopsy room opened with such a loud bang that it caused the constables to jump aside. Out strode Peter Willoughby, with blood splattered over his dark apron. He gave me the sternest of looks and demanded, "What brings you here, Watson? This matter is none of your concern."

"It is about to be," I said curtly, giving the mean little man short shrift before coming back to the inspector. "The playhouse will not be open today, but the manager, Mrs. Emma Adams, owns a pub nearby which we can visit to view the poster I mentioned."

Lestrade glanced at his timepiece. "Will it be open at this early hour?"

"If not, she will be available in the rooms above the pub where she lives."

Another officer raced in and urgently beckoned Lestrade over for a private conversation. "A moment, please, Dr. Watson," the inspector said over his shoulder as he hurried away.

"Really, Watson," Willoughby snapped. "This is most irregular."

"And most important, for the corpse you were dissecting may belong to Pretty Penny."

"I am afraid any identification will be quite difficult regardless of this poster, for her face is badly mangled, with deep, disfiguring cuts all about and her lips sliced through and spread apart down to the gums."

"Can the lips be sutured back together, which will restore some semblance to the face?"

"That is not your affair, for unless the commissioner decides to involve you and your wife in this matter, you have no place here and should be on your way."

"You don't seem very upset that the corpse you dissected may well belong to Pretty Penny," I noted, now aware of the senior pathologist's change in appearance. His face seemed gaunt and fatigued, with the lines far more obvious. Perhaps the stressful years of being director were finally taking their toll.

"I am as upset as anyone, but I will not cry over a nameless corpse until it is positively identified," said Willoughby, after giving me yet another stare of disapproval. "It is most unprofessional to do so, and I would expect more from you."

Lestrade rushed over and spoke to me in a most urgent voice. "I would like for you to ride with me over to a crime scene in Whitechapel where your wife and father will join us shortly."

"Another murder?" I inquired.

"Of the worst sort," Lestrade said darkly, guiding me away and down the corridor. "You are about to witness the return of an evil monster."

Chapter 5

The Evil Monster

We drove directly to Mitre Square, a small, open area surrounded by large warehouses, empty houses, and a few shabby shops which were still closed. It was accessible by three long, dark passageways that had narrow entrances. Spectators were lined up three deep on the far side of the square to watch the ongoing investigation.

"Word travels fast when there is a murder, and always draws a crowd," Lestrade commented.

"Even in crime-ridden Whitechapel?" I asked.

Lestrade nodded. "If the killing is gruesome enough."

Our motorcar stopped in front of the middle passageway where Joanna and my father were conversing with Sir Charles Bradberry, the commissioner of Scotland Yard. A tall, broad-shouldered man, with neatly trimmed hair and a thick mustache, he was widely respected by his officers and the public as well. He was known to be a strict disciplinarian, who would not abide by any wrongdoing at the Yard, and those found guilty were either discharged or summarily punished.

As I approached, Sir Charles greeted me with a firm handshake and said, "Thank you for joining our investigation, Dr. Watson."

"I only hope that I can be of some assistance," I replied.

"As do I," Sir Charles said, and waited for a pair of croaking ravens to pass overhead. "I was about to explain the need for absolute secrecy in the earlier murder, which I know you must be keenly interested in."

"Like everyone at St. Bart's," I added.

"So I would imagine," he went on, but not before taking a deep breath. "When I was a young officer at Scotland Yard some twenty-eight years ago, we faced the most grotesque murders one could ever envision. The victims were young prostitutes who had been sliced open in ways so gruesome I hesitate to describe them. Their faces were cut down to bone, their abdomens carved so deeply they could be disemboweled. It was all the work of a maniacal killer called Jack the Ripper. These horrific murders continued on for some months, then suddenly stopped and never recurred. It was believed that Jack the Ripper had died or gone brain-dead, and that we were rid of him once and for all. We took some comfort in that thought until two evenings ago when a young woman was so brutally murdered it brought back memories of The Ripper. Now, there were two considerations at that point." He turned to Joanna and asked, "With all this in mind, what possibilities would you deem most likely?"

"Either The Ripper has returned or you have a copycat killer in your midst," she answered.

"Precisely," the commissioner agreed. "It could very well be The Ripper, for we believed he did his earlier work while in his twenties, which would now make him in his late forties or fifties, and certainly capable of returning to his maniacal ways. Thus, we feared the worst."

"So you kept all aspects of the murder in absolute secrecy in order to avoid frightening the public and causing undue panic. You were hoping all the while it was the work of a copycat killer."

"I was indeed."

"But deep down you knew otherwise. From my reading of The Ripper, his method of killing and dissecting was rather exact, and repeated in victim after victim. I am afraid you were aware from your past experience, Sir Charles, that this murder was the doing of Jack the Ripper."

"Might not a copycat killer read of The Ripper's past exploits and accurately replicate his kills?" my father suggested.

"Possible, Watson, but unlikely," Joanna rebutted mildly. "Reading about a method and repeating it in a convincing fashion are two different matters. Furthermore, I suspect there were other indications that told Sir Charles this was yet another performance by The Ripper."

"There were," the commissioner told us. "In particular, the dissection was so neat and clean, as if done by an individual skilled in anatomy. More important, this very morning I received a letter from The Ripper which was virtually identical to the letters written by him nearly thirty years ago. And the letter could not have been copied by another, for all The Ripper's letters to Scotland Yard are now stored away in the Public Record Office on Chancery Lane. There is limited public access to them and any search is subject to inquiry about the purpose and extent of the research. Some random copycat killer could have never gained entrance. For all these reasons, I am now convinced we are dealing with Jack the Ripper."

"May we see the letter?" Joanna requested.

"Of course," said Sir Charles, reaching into his coat pocket for an envelope. "For your information, the envelope and letter have been examined for fingerprints, of which there are none. You will also note that the letter begins with the cordial salutation 'Dear Boss,' which was the very same greeting The Ripper used in his earlier messages to the commissioner."

Joanna carefully opened the envelope and held the letter up for all to see. It was written in block letters, except for the initial *R* at the end, which was done in script. It read:

> *DEAR BOSS,*
> *YOU MIGHT BE OBLIGED TO ME FOR KILLING SUCH A PIECE OF VERMIN. WHAT A PRETTY NECKLACE I GAVE HER. DO NOT FRET, FOR THERE WILL BE MORE TO COME.*
> *R*

"What is this necklace he speaks of?" I asked.

"You will see it when we view the body," Sir Charles said grimly.

Joanna slowly reread the letter aloud before saying, "It is unlike the initial letter he sent."

"What letter?" Sir Charles asked at once.

"We believe there is another, unaccounted-for victim of The Ripper," she replied.

The commissioner's brow went up. "Tell me about this supposed victim."

Joanna recounted the story of Pretty Penny, with particular emphasis on the stalker and the threatening note that appeared to be written by an individual pretending to be illiterate.

"The most current note shows no evidence of illiteracy," Sir Charles interrupted. "If anything, it is the product of a well-educated person."

"I suspect he is playing games with us."

Sir Charles nodded at her assessment. "I should add that a few of the original letters were similarly constructed, with some words spelled phonetically to leave the impression of an uneducated sender."

"Old habits are hard to break," Joanna noted.

"But this new feature of taking a victim captive would be so unlike The Ripper of old," the commissioner argued, then paused to reflect for a long moment before speaking again. "Unless former commissioner Abernathy was correct in his opinion that The Ripper had not truly gone into hibernation."

"Was there evidence to back up this assertion?" Joanna asked at once.

"It was circumstantial, but nevertheless compelling."

Sir Charles recounted a chilling story which was unbeknownst to all except those deep within the confines of Scotland Yard. It appeared that Jack the Ripper had ceased his terrifying activity, with no further mutilation-murders occurring, yet there continued to be instances of Unfortunates—a term by which prostitutes were commonly called—disappearing without reason. It was known of course that Unfortunates frequently moved on to other districts or died of illness in a hidden alleyway, but some of the missing were of a better class and stayed in rented places with roommates or boyfriends who reported their sudden absence. A few of them actually worked part-time as charwomen, which were valued positions from which they were unlikely to leave without explanation. Abernathy was convinced that The Ripper had decided to do his killing in private where there was little chance of being apprehended.

"I take it no bodies were found?"

"That is partially true, for on occasion arms and legs were put on display, which more than a few of us considered the work of The Ripper." The commissioner gazed out at the crowd gathering across the square before adding in a grave voice, "You might be interested to learn that the body parts appeared within a day or two of the reported disappearances. Thus, madam, you may not have the five days you predicted to find the missing actress. I am afraid the clock is ticking faster than you anticipated."

"If your assumption is correct," said Joanna. "Another equally plausible scenario is that the reemerging Ripper has invented a new game so he could amuse himself at length."

"Entirely possible."

"But not if the body in the passageway belongs to Pretty Penny."

"It does not," said the commissioner. "We have tentatively identified her as one Carrie Nichols, a well-known local prostitute."

"Tentative, you say?"

"Nearly certain, but we are awaiting further confirmation because her face has been so badly disfigured," he clarified. "It is the same with the corpse that is currently being autopsied at St. Bartholomew's. The latter is believed to be another prostitute named Evie Dawson, but she, too, awaits positive identification. This then is another characteristic of The Ripper in that he tends to prey on young prostitutes."

"Which are the most vulnerable."

"Indeed."

"I should now like to see his latest piece of work before the rain starts again."

"This way, then."

Sir Charles led us down the passageway at a brisk pace, but Joanna followed slowly, with her eyes fixed on the mud-covered pavement. I stepped aside to avoid walking into an upright badly weathered broom whose thick straw fibers were worn down to the stick. Beneath it was a small pile of trash.

"We see the event as happening in this manner," Sir Charles was saying. "Prostitutes usually stand at the entrance to the passageway where they offer their services to prospective customers walking by. If the customer agrees, he is taken into the dark passageway so that their business will be conducted out of view. She then positions herself with her back to him, for that is how the service is usually rendered. It is at this point we believe The Ripper slashed her throat and went about mutilating her. Whether or not she is alive at the time of mutilation is open to question."

"That may be the most likely chain of events, but the evidence shows that it occurred in a totally different fashion," said Joanna, motioning to drag marks on the muddy pavement. "Allow me to draw your attention to the deep impressions left in the mud by the victim's heels as she was dragged away. The marks begin at the entrance to the passageway where the woman was first accosted."

"How can you determine those lines were made by heels?" the commissioner asked.

"Because the two are straight without variation and less than a foot apart, which is consistent with a body being dragged," she elucidated. "There is no other explanation."

"But wouldn't she put up a struggle, which would cause the lines to become disarrayed?"

"Not if she was unconscious, which she undoubtedly was."

"But we have no proof in this regard."

"I believe examination of the corpse will prove my hypothesis," said Joanna, and gestured to the upright battered broom. "Moreover, notice how close the drag marks are to the broom. Were the victim conscious and fighting for her life, she would have certainly seen and reached for it to use as a weapon, which she obviously did not."

Ahead lay the corpse beneath a woolen blanket, with a constable standing guard nearby. The body itself was completely covered except for the victim's feet. Joanna leaned down to carefully examine them by gross inspection, before restudying them with her magnifying glass.

"You will note, Commissioner, that the heels of the woman's shoes are somewhat worn down, but are clean except for their rears, which are coated with caked mud. Since individuals do not walk on their heels, it is entirely logical to believe the mud was placed there when she was dragged away. In addition, the size of the drag marks is a quite good match for the woman's heels. Putting all these signs together, I think it is fair to say the victim was dragged into the passageway while unconscious. Now let us determine how she was rendered so. Please have the corpse uncovered."

Sir Charles signaled to the constable, who pulled the blanket away. Even for those of us accustomed to gruesome sights, the disfigured face of the prostitute was difficult to view. There were deep cuts under both eyes which were caked with dried blood and gave the appearance of artistic accents. Her lips were sliced through and through and spread apart to expose the underlying gums. But it was the woman's neck which was indeed revolting. It was so deeply slashed that she was nearly decapitated.

"It is beyond depravity," I uttered under my breath.

If Joanna was moved by the sight, she showed no evidence of it. "Why did he bother so with her neck?"

Pushing my revulsion aside, I knelt down on an unsoiled area of the blanket and inspected the work of a maniac. It was in every way diabolical, for the slashes were all delivered with deliberate intent. I could only hope that the victim was not awake as the horrific wounds were inflicted. Clearing my mind, I began to voice my findings. "I can discern two cuts to the anterior aspect of the neck, one shallow and the other wide and deep. I take it the initial stab was a failed attempt to enter the tissue below, while the second slice was far more violent and penetrated the trachea before severing the carotid arteries, which accounts for all the blood pooled and splattered about. The blade actually separated part of the cervical spine and nearly decapitated the victim. She was certainly alive during the moments she was being carved up and may have been conscious."

"What do you base the latter observation on?" my father asked.

"The initial, superficial cut to the neck, which I believe was an unsuccessful attempt to decapitate, is somewhat irregular and varies in depth," I answered. "This would occur as she was struggling and trying to pull away from the terrible pain."

"Would she not have cried out loudly?" Sir Charles inquired.

"I am afraid she did not have time, for the second cut was immediately applied and sliced through the windpipe," I explained. "Without the passage of air, the only sound she could have uttered was that of blood gurgling in her throat."

"Can you determine which direction the blade took?" Joanna queried.

"It traveled right to left, which indicates the killer was left-handed."

"Which was a characteristic of The Ripper from yesteryear," the commissioner informed. "As was the sentence in the note stating that he gave her a pretty necklace. In both letters it was referring to the wide slice that opened the victim's neck."

Sir Charles stepped in a small puddle of blood unintentionally and wiped off his shoe on a clean area. "I have put out a notice asking for knowledge of anyone who appeared with blood splattered on his garments or face."

"You won't find him," Joanna said.

"Why not?" asked he. "Certainly with all the blood spurting about, the perpetrator could not have completely avoided it."

"He is too clever for that," Joanna apprised. "An experienced killer does his work while standing behind the victim, so as to be clear of the blood spurting out of a severed carotid artery, which can travel as far as twelve inches, according to a monograph I read." She pointed to the blood splatter on the brick wall near the corpse. "The Ripper had her facing the wall for that very purpose."

"Well explained," said the commissioner.

Joanna paid little attention to the compliment as she leaned forward to examine the victim's jawline. "The deep bruise mark at the bend of the mandible is most informative."

"I was about to comment on that," said I. "Its position is consistent with a blow from the left-handed assailant. It also tells us how she was rendered semiconscious before being dragged into the passageway and sliced up."

"And nobody saw or heard even the slightest disturbance," Sir Charles remarked unhappily.

"The Ripper is very good at what he does, which explains why he has never been caught," said Joanna, and joined me to inspect the torso of the corpse.

The woman's clothing was pulled up above her waist and in total disarray. There was a huge slash that went from her pubis up to the rib cage, with its edges spread apart to allow curls of intestines to dangle out.

"Are there any organs missing?" Joanna asked.

"That determination will have to await the autopsy table," I replied.

My wife turned to the commissioner after giving the body a final look. "I trust, Sir Charles, that your cloak of secrecy will now be removed, for the corpse of this poor woman will have to be studied, not only by my husband, but by a number of experts at St. Bartholomew's. The word will certainly leak out despite your best efforts."

"I am afraid it already has," the commissioner said. "The crowd you witnessed across the square had gathered long before we arrived, and this assemblage attracted the news reporters, a few of whom are old enough to recall the horror of Jack the Ripper. I can assure you the gruesome details will appear in the evening newspapers."

"Let us hope they use some discretion," my father wished.

"They won't," Sir Charles went on. "The body was discovered by some of the locals, who invited others to view the ghastly scene, who invited yet others. We fortunately arrived before the newspaper photographers did."

"I shall do my best to prevent it from becoming a spectacle at St. Bart's," I promised.

"That would be most appreciated," the commissioner said sincerely. "I take it you will be performing the autopsy."

"Correct."

"Should Dr. Willoughby then continue to lead the hospital's investigation?"

"As director of pathology, he should of course remain in that position."

Sir Charles gave me a long, discerning look. "From your tone of voice, it would seem you think otherwise."

"I did not mean to convey that impression," I said neutrally. "But I do believe it best I alone perform the autopsy so that my concentration is not interrupted."

"Then I will suggest to Dr. Willoughby that he—"

"I would not suggest, Commissioner, but strongly recommend," Joanna advised. "It is my husband who is the forensic expert, not Dr. Willoughby. If this case is to be solved, it will require the finest of our talents."

Sir Charles hesitated briefly before acquiescing. "I shall see to it, then. Are there other matters you deem important?"

"Not at the moment," Joanna replied. "But I should like the last-known address of Carrie Nichols."

"We are in the process of having it searched."

"Excellent, but I shall require the address."

"Do you not trust Scotland Yard?"

"Not as much as I trust myself," Joanna said, with a thin smile. "And now we shall be on our way and leave you to your investigation, which at this point seems quite formidable."

"But one I mean to bring to an end," the commissioner vowed.

We left Sir Charles and Lestrade with their mutilated corpse and strolled across Mitre Square to a waiting taxi. The crowd of observers had grown even larger and some appeared to be enjoying themselves, with frolics and laughter. A young lad was moving amongst the gathering and trying to sell small bags of chips. The people quieted as we approached, for Joanna's face and skills were recognized by most of London.

In a loud voice, someone called out, "Look! There is the daughter of Sherlock Holmes."

A second voice belonging to a female shouted, "You'd better be careful, dearie, before Jack the Ripper comes after your pretty arse as well!"

The crowd chuckled at the crude remark, but I suspect they would not have found it so amusing had they known what was truly in store for Joanna.

Chapter 6

The Copper Earrings

The order that I alone perform the autopsy had been passed down from Scotland Yard and Peter Willoughby was obviously upset over it. He blamed Joanna, my father, and me for the apparent demotion, and the look in his eyes told me he would not soon forget it. To make us feel uncomfortable, he remained in the dissecting room at the beginning of the autopsy and immediately broke his word to stay silent.

"This is entirely unacceptable, Watson," said he.

"I cannot argue with the commissioner," I replied, disliking the man even more than usual. After careful deliberation, I had decided to tender my resignation at year's end, for I could no longer tolerate Willoughby's demeanor and pettiness. There were other hospitals where my services would be most welcome, although it would be painful for me to leave St. Bart's, which was considered an academic center of international repute. But so be it. Pushing that thought aside, I slipped on rubber gloves and did my best not to return Willoughby's unpleasant glare.

"Well, let us get on with the autopsy," he snapped.

"First, the victim's garments, which may hold important clues, should be examined," said I. "I trust you will allow my wife to perform this part of the autopsy, for she would be most knowledgeable about female clothing."

Willoughby took my request as a signal that he remained in charge, which of course wasn't the case. "I will permit it."

"Good. Then let us proceed."

Joanna placed on rubber gloves as well, for prostitutes were known to carry a number of diseases, some of which were communicable and easily transmitted through a scratch or abrasion in the skin. The victim's clothing had been removed and laid out on a long table for display. Joanna began with the outermost garment, which was a tattered woolen jacket that had empty pockets. Next, she patted down a man's white vest, with buttons down the front and two side pockets, one of which contained a half crown and two shillings. The latter may have been the woman's fee for services rendered. In the second pocket was a totally unexpected finding. Joanna held up a doctor's prescription from St. Bart's for my father to read.

"It is written for iodinated gauze, and signed by Thaddeus Rudd," he stated.

"There must be some mistake," Willoughby disputed at once. "A distinguished surgeon, such as Rudd, would have nothing to do with this sort of individual."

"Unless she was a patient in the charity clinic where the poor are cared for free of charge," my father explained. "I myself attended in that clinic periodically prior to my retirement. I suspect that is how she came to be seen by Rudd."

"And the purpose of the iodinated gauze?" Joanna inquired.

My father again studied the prescription. "It is an antiseptic to be inserted twice daily."

"But into where?"

"Into an infected cavity, I would surmise."

"Let us move along and stop wasting time on minor matters," Willoughby demanded.

"I work on my time, not yours," Joanna responded sharply. "If you have a complaint regarding my methods, I suggest you take it up with the commissioner."

Willoughby gave my wife a harsh stare but was wise enough to remain silent. He came from a world in which women were subservient and forever yielding to masculine dictates. Poor Willoughby simply could not accept the fact that he was outmatched in every way by Joanna.

"We should look for iodine stains on her inner garments," my father advised.

"And so we shall, Watson," said Joanna, now searching and holding up a chintz shirt that was decorated with flowers. It showed no stains. With care, she next examined the victim's blue skirt and found a single pound note sewn into its hem. "A life's savings," she presumed.

The remainder of the prostitute's clothing, including petticoat, stockings, lace-up boots, and black straw hat, revealed no additional clues.

There was a brief rap on the door and Robbie Connery, the hospital photographer, entered, carrying his equipment. He went about his business in a most professional manner, taking multiple photographs at various angles, but even he, despite his long experience, had to suppress a nauseous gag while viewing the victim's disfigured face.

"If you'd like, I can take additional photographs with her

hat on," Connery proposed. "At times a hat, if frequently worn, can bring back a remembrance."

"I do not believe it will matter much, with her marked facial disfigurement," said I.

"I am afraid you are correct," Connery agreed, and, gathering up his equipment, departed the autopsy room.

Adjusting the overhead light, I again noted how neat the facial cuts were. They were straight and obviously made with a very sharp knife, which allowed the laceration to go deep down to bone without resistance. Her lips were sliced apart, so as to give her a mocking grin. And beneath them was a badly lacerated tongue, which told a story in itself.

"I am of the opinion the victim was awake while she was being mutilated," I remarked. "In her agony she virtually chewed through her tongue. She could not scream because of her severed windpipe, and thus her only response was to bite down on her tongue in an effort to replace one pain with another."

"Perhaps she fought nonetheless and there will be defensive wounds on her hands and forearms," Willoughby suggested, trying to be helpful and lend advice.

"You raise a good point, but I see no such wounds," said I.

"There still could be blood and skin from the assailant under her fingernails," Willoughby added.

"Another good point," I said, examining the victim's nails but discovering only dirt and no evidence of chips or cracks which would indicate she had put up a struggle. "All negative."

As if the examination of Carrie Nichols's face weren't gruesome enough, the study of her neck proved to be even more so. The ghastly wound was so viciously struck that it completely severed the windpipe, as well as the surrounding thick muscles and both carotid arteries. Pooled blood was everywhere, most of it gelled, some of it still dripping. Wiping away the clots, I could see the bones of the cervical spine where the assailant had dug deep into the intervertebral cartilage in an attempt to totally decapitate the victim. As I removed yet another clot, I noticed a sliver of silver metal protruding from the interspace between the last two cervical vertebrae. I tried to remove it, but it was firmly secured in place. "He seems to have left part of his knife behind," I reported.

Joanna hurried over with her magnifying glass in hand. She gave the sliver careful study before announcing, "It would appear to be the tip of the blade, which broke off under extreme pressure."

"It requires tremendous force to completely separate well-formed vertebrae," I stated. "Although the interspace between the vertebrae consists mainly of cartilage rather than bone, it is held in place by thick, sturdy fibrous bands. A single blade would have difficulty slicing through these tissues."

"I take it that the piece of metal is fixed in its current position," said Joanna.

"It is immovable."

"Then I suggest you use pliers to remove the sliver as gently as possible, so as not to disturb any clues it may hold."

"What do you have in mind?"

"Nothing in particular," Joanna replied. "But it represents the only item of evidence left behind by Jack the Ripper and thus merits careful study."

"But it is only the tip of the blade," Willoughby noted.

"Perhaps, perhaps not," said she. "There may be more of the blade buried into the cartilage and bone."

Using surgical pliers, I proved Joanna to be correct, for I extracted an inch-long piece of blade from the vertebral interspace. It was covered with dried blood, which I did not remove for fear of disturbing any underlying evidence. After placing the metal sliver in an envelope, I continued with the autopsy and was able to determine the cause of death. Carrie's heart was normal, but her lungs were so completely filled with blood they had a deep maroon color. Carrie Nichols had aspirated huge amounts of blood and had died of suffocation.

I moved on to the abdomen and made no attempt to reinsert the intestines, which dangled out from a wide gash that extended from her rib cage to her pubis. Once inside the abdominal cavity, it became clear that The Ripper had wreaked even more havoc in a most destructive fashion.

"Unbelievable," I spoke under my breath.

"How so?" Joanna asked.

"The spleen and liver are untouched, but he has gone to the bother of removing both ovaries and her uterus."

"Surely some of those tissues must remain," Joanna wondered aloud.

I shook my head. "They were all neatly removed in a surgical fashion, with their arteries and veins expertly dissected away."

"He carried them off as mementos," my father recollected. "The Ripper of the past did the same."

"I assume these organs were not found at the crime scene?" Willoughby queried. "Correct?"

"None were present," I answered.

"Mementos beyond any doubt, for he performed the same dissection on the Jane Smith case," Willoughby noted. "But why the uterus and ovaries?"

"He must be attracted to them in a most perverted way," my father surmised.

"Or so distracted by female organs he wished to destroy them," Joanna proposed.

"It all seems to have a sexual connotation," I agreed.

"In more ways than one," said my father. "In the mutilated corpses of yesteryear, some believed The Ripper was collecting these organs in an effort to extract an elixir of youth, which would enhance his sexual powers, all of which of course was complete nonsense."

"But not to a psychotic," Joanna reminded before turning to Willoughby. "You mentioned that the uterus and ovaries were dissected out in Jane Smith, much like in Carrie Nichols. Please be good enough and recall if there were any differences."

Willoughby considered the matter at length, then began to nod. "There were several differences which were of minor consequence. Most notably, both kidneys were also neatly removed and taken away. Their dissections were carefully done, unlike the multiple stab wounds on the victim's chest that appeared to be inflicted during a frenzy. Her neck was sliced open, but only one carotid artery was severed."

"Which would have been sufficient for her to bleed to death," I added.

"More than enough," Willoughby agreed.

"Did you examine her clothing?" Joanna asked.

"As much as possible, for it was blood soaked and filthy as one might expect from a tart," Willoughby described. "Everything was cheap, including her earrings, which were made of copper."

My wife quickly pointed to the copper earrings belonging to Carrie Nichols. "Similar to these?"

"Identical, I would say," Willoughby replied. "But they are common enough and would be quite difficult to trace."

Joanna hurried over to the corpse and examined its earrings with her magnifying glass. Up and down she moved the glass to enhance the magnification. "I see a smudged fingerprint."

"Most likely hers," Willoughby inferred.

"We shall see," said she, keeping her magnifying glass in hand. "Does the corpse of Jane Smith remain at St. Bart's?"

"To the best of my knowledge."

"I should like to view it," Joanna requested. "With of course your permission."

Willoughby reached for a button on the wall to signal the orderly Benson and led the way down the corridor. He rudely brushed past technicians and junior pathologists, causing them to quickly step aside. His strident gait indicated that he believed he was again in command of the proceedings. But he wasn't. Joanna's seemingly subservient request was meant to make Willoughby more compliant and thus more useful to our investigation.

We entered the cold, dark morgue, which had a bare cement floor and walls made from plaster of Paris. Benson followed us in and switched on the overhead lights that provided sufficient illumination. Uncovered corpses on stretchers were lined up two aside against the walls, which left a more than adequate viewing area in the center of the large room. Willoughby gestured to the body of Jane Smith that lay on a nearby gurney. She was as white as the sheet beneath her.

I took it upon myself to verify Willoughby's findings and make certain he did not overlook any abnormal features. All was as the senior pathologist had described. The neck was sliced wide open, with a single carotid artery severed. There was no evidence that The Ripper had attempted to decapitate Jane Smith. The slashes across the corpse's chest appeared to be done in a frenzy, some crisscrossing, others simply stab wounds. Stepping back, I viewed the corpse in its entirety. She was quite short, no more than five feet in height, and somewhat plump, with rolls of fat about her waist and thighs. She clearly was not Pretty Penny.

Joanna moved in by my side and inquired, "Are the ovaries and uterus dissected out?"

A quick, thorough examination revealed this was the case.

"All were neatly removed by an individual who knew his way around the abdominal cavity."

"Maniacal, but skilled," Joanna noted, as her eyes drifted to the inner, upper surface of the corpse's left thigh. I followed her gaze and saw a circular, inflamed area, perhaps two inches in diameter, just where the thigh met the pubic area. In its center was a small, slit-like opening, from which protruded a strip of iodinated gauze.

"It is a carbuncle which has been incised for drainage and treated by insertion of an iodinated strip," she diagnosed correctly. "Did you notice a similar lesion on Carrie Nichols, John?"

"I did not, but my initial examination was limited to the corpse's anterior thigh," I replied. "It may be hidden, but certainly not healed, since the prescription was written on such a recent date."

"Its presence would be a most important finding," Joanna stated, now moving to the corpse's head to examine its shiny copper earrings. Like those on Carrie Nichols, the earrings consisted of copper discs which dangled and were held in place by a thin strand of wire.

"Are there fingerprints present?" I asked, watching her grasp the copper disc by its edges as she carefully studied both sides with a magnifying glass. She repeated the search twice before announcing, "Three fingerprints are evident, two smudged and superimposed, one partial and reasonably clear."

"Is the latter distinct enough for identification?" I asked.

"Only Scotland Yard can determine that."

"I see your inference here," my father joined in the discussion. "But why would The Ripper bother to touch her earrings?"

"Perhaps he did so unintentionally," I surmised.

"Or perhaps he was somewhat aroused by them," Joanna suggested. "The earrings, you see, might be considered part of the female anatomy by the killer."

"Were there any concealed similarities between these earrings and the ones you examined on Carrie Nichols?" Willoughby asked. "If so, it could indicate they came from the same source."

Joanna shook her head. "My magnifying glass is not nearly sharp enough to make that determination." She removed the earrings and wrapped them carefully in tissue paper, then handed them to my father to place in an envelope. "Now let us collect the earrings from Carrie Nichols and present them to Inspector Lestrade, who I am certain will give them his closest attention."

We hurried back to the autopsy room, with Joanna reminding Willoughby that the bodies must remain untouched and on-site at St. Bartholomew's until Scotland Yard obtained a complete set of fingerprints from the corpses. Moreover, no entrance should be allowed into the morgue until further notice. Willoughby so instructed Benson, who rushed away to carry out the orders.

Once we were back in the autopsy room, the copper earrings were removed from Carrie Nichols and, like those from Jane Smith, were carefully wrapped and secured in a sealed envelope. Only then did I reexamine the corpse, paying particular attention to her intact skin. It appeared to be remarkably clear of scars and blemishes until I reached the buttocks. Lifting the body onto its side revealed a draining incised carbuncle located in the fold between the lower buttock and upper thigh. In its center was a deeply inserted strip of iodinated gauze. All in attendance moved in for a closer view.

"An important common denominator," said Joanna.

"I am afraid you make too much of these carbuncles," Willoughby challenged. "May I remind you that personal hygiene is a low priority in Whitechapel and that various infections of the skin are quite common in their population."

"You raise an excellent point," she conceded.

Willoughby nodded, obviously pleased with his assessment. "Nevertheless, I will include this minor finding in my report, as should you, Watson."

"I shall."

"Then I will be on my way, for I have other matters to attend to," said Willoughby, stripping off his still-clean rubber gloves and hurriedly departing.

As the door closed, Joanna smiled thinly and shook her head. "It is remarkable how Willoughby can provide a reasonable comment one moment, and appear so oblivious the next."

"He doesn't seem to place as much significance on the carbuncles as you do," my father observed.

"That is because he fails to consider the most important link between the two."

"Which is?"

"Both of the similarly infected women were killed by Jack the Ripper," Joanna noted, and left it at that.

Chapter 7

The Doss-House

Carrie Nichols's last-known address was a doss-house on a street called Buck's Row that bordered the Jewish cemetery in Whitechapel. This being the case, it indicated that Scotland Yard's investigation of the premises was cursory at best, for the term *doss* was slang for *bed*. These hellish dwellings consisted of large, communal rooms that were filled with small, iron bedsteads, all of which were covered with filthy gray blankets. Sheets, when provided, were supposedly washed once a week but rarely were. The poor, the penniless, drunks, criminals, and prostitutes paid fivepence to spend a night in these dreadful places.

We entered the doss-house, accompanied by a constable furnished by Lestrade, and were met with a most disagreeable odor. The housekeeper or warden presented himself immediately, with his worried eyes darting back and forth between Joanna and the uniformed policeman.

"How—how can I be of service?" he stammered.

The constable introduced us as associates of Scotland Yard and instructed the warden to assist us in every way into the investigation of Carrie Nichols's death. The warden, whose name was Luther, was told that withholding information or evidence would be considered a crime in itself.

"I know little about Carrie Nichols, for she came and went like so many others," Luther claimed. "She was not a troublemaker, other than screaming and yelling when evicted."

"And the cause of her eviction?" Joanna asked.

"When she could not produce the fivepence required for another night's stay," Luther replied unsympathetically. "If you cannot pay by ten, you are promptly sent on your way. There is no law against that," he added, and looked at the constable for affirmation, which was not forthcoming.

"When did you last see Carrie Nichols?" Joanna asked.

"The morning before her death," Luther replied without hesitation. "She begged me to hold a bed for her and promised to return shortly with the required fee, which she did not."

"Was the bed she had occupied soon reoccupied by someone else?"

"It was," Luther answered. "By a drunk who threw up over the mattress and was evicted because of it. The mattress was scrubbed down so it would be suitable for another customer."

My father and I exchanged knowing glances, for whatever

clues that mattress might have held were long gone. "Since Carrie Nichols vowed to return soon with the fee, did she leave any of her belongings behind?" I asked.

"Ha!" Luther forced a laugh. "Any items left behind would have been stolen in the blink of an eye. Besides, these people carry everything they own in their pockets."

"Has anyone inquired about Carrie since her departure?" Joanna queried.

"Only her friend Annie Yates," Luther said. "She must have asked me a dozen times about Carrie."

"Were they close?"

"Thick as thieves they were, always huddling together to share their stories."

"Did they occupy beds next to each other?"

"Usually."

"By chance is Annie Yates still in residence here?"

"She is."

"We should like to talk with her."

Luther turned very quickly. "I will go fetch her."

"No need," Joanna said at once. "We prefer to speak with Annie in a quiet room, assuming one is available."

Luther's expression changed to one of concern. Something about my wife's request bothered the little man who had a humped back and a constant scowl on his face. "She is currently residing in a small cubicle."

"I did not realize that cubicles were available in a dosshouse," Joanna remarked.

"It belongs to me," Luther said unabashedly.

"Lead the way," Joanna directed.

We walked through a large, malodorous room filled with iron bedsteads which were packed in so closely there was barely enough room to squeeze in between them. The beds were empty, their mattresses soiled and devoid of blankets and pillows. Turning a corner, we approached a small kitchen area where a few men were gathered to cook scraps of food they had managed to find or steal earlier. An old man threw out a bone, and raggedly clothed children appeared out of nowhere to grapple over it. It was the sort of behavior one might see in wild animals, yet the man in the kitchen seemed to be amused by it.

We stepped into a tiny room, with just enough space for a bed and chair. Sitting on the bed was a most frail woman, with long, neatly parted blond hair and deep blue eyes that peered out at us over hollow cheeks. She attempted to push herself up out of respect but quickly dropped back down onto the mattress. With effort, she produced a raucous cough that caused phlegm to rattle in her throat.

"This here is Annie Yates, one of the Unfortunates," Luther introduced.

"She is obviously quite ill," my father said concernedly. "Is this the reason she was provided with a separate room?"

"I was given this bed for services I rendered," Annie said candidly. "And I shall perform this service again if Mr. Luther allows me another night's stay."

Joanna gave Luther a stern look, but he seemed unaffected by it. Rather than sit as she usually did when questioning, my wife remained standing and kept her distance because of the Unfortunate's harsh, raspy cough which came yet again.

"You of course know about the dreadful death of your friend Carrie Nichols," Joanna began.

"I do, ma'am," Annie replied in a soft voice.

"Do you have any idea who might have done this terrible act to your friend?"

"No, ma'am."

"When was the very last time you saw Carrie?"

"The night she was murdered."

"Were you both on the street at that time?"

"No, ma'am. We decided to meet at the Black Lamb, where we can pick up customers now and then."

"Were you approached?"

"No, ma'am, for the people present were from the local neighborhood. There were no gentleman drifters to be seen."

Joanna's brow went up in obvious interest, for Annie Yates had just uttered a most important clue. Gentleman drifters were known to be respectable men who seek excitement prowling the lowlife pubs of East London in search of cheap, anonymous sex. Some were said to actually be addicted to this form of secret entertainment. Clearing her throat, Joanna asked, "Had you or Carrie ever encountered such gentleman drifters at the Black Lamb?"

"On several occasions," Annie answered. "They would chat us up and arrange to meet us on the street at a later time."

"In the Mitre Square area?"

"That was a favorite place because of the dark passageways and deserted buildings."

"Did any of these gentleman drifters seem to favor you or Carrie?"

"One gentleman in particular preferred Carrie, in that she was from a neighborhood in Bristol where he claimed he was born and raised."

"Claimed, you say?"

Annie managed a weak smile. "People from Bristol have a distinct accent which he did not have. He had upper-class London written all over him."

"Can you describe this man?"

Annie shrugged. "There was nothing unusual about him.

He was of average height and frame, with long gray hair that curled at the bottom."

"Did he wear a hat?"

Annie thought before nodding. "On one occasion he wore a black hat, like the ones you see on fishermen sometimes."

The man who visited the sweet shop, I thought immediately, but that type of hat was quite common in the poorer sections of London. "Did he ever offer you or Carrie candy?" I asked.

"Never," she said promptly. "He wouldn't even buy us a pint."

"Cheap, then."

"Quite. He tried to come off as one of us, but his educated speech said otherwise, as did his finely manicured nails. You will never see those on a Whitechapel man."

"Well noted," Joanna complimented. "Now tell me, was he ever rough or threatening to you or Carrie?"

"Only when his performance failed," Annie said frankly.

"How often would this happen?"

"Always," said Annie. "He would try and try, but seemed incapable of being aroused."

"So you never truly did your business with him?"

"Nor did Carrie, despite his best efforts."

"I take it this was the moment he became threatening?"

Annie nodded as another paroxysm of violent coughing came and went. "He would scream and grow quite angry, and blame us for his failure to perform."

"Did he ever strike you or Carrie?"

"He once gave Carrie a black eye, but immediately apologized and attributed his violence and inadequacy to alcohol."

"Did she believe his excuse?"

"No, ma'am, for drunks can still perform, but not as well as those who are sober."

"After this altercation, I would think Carrie stayed clear of this gentleman drifter."

"At first she did, but he continued to apologize and gave her a gift, so she gave in and returned to him."

"What sort of gift did he give her?"

"Lovely copper earrings, like these," Annie replied, and swept back her hair to reveal earrings that were identical to those found on the two victims currently residing in the morgue at St. Bart's. "He seemed to fancy copper ones, for he presented them to me and Carrie and to yet another Unfortunate named Evie."

"Do you have any idea where he purchased them?"

Annie shrugged. "At a jewelry shop, I would guess."

"Are there many jewelry stores in Whitechapel?"

"Only a few, but none that sell expensive items."

Joanna decided to rephrase the question, for here lay an important clue. "If you wish to purchase copper earrings, which shop would you visit?"

"Froman's, for I once saw a nice display of copper jewelry in his window."

"And where would Froman's be located?"

"Half block north of here, across from the Jewish cemetery."

"Very good," Joanna said, docketing the information. "Now let us return to the Black Lamb where these gentleman drifters tend to congregate. On a usual night, how many were present?"

"Three or four, and they would always gather as a group."

"I would think that you and the other Unfortunates would keep a close eye on them."

"Oh, we would indeed, for they were most generous and willing to pay the higher fee."

"Was your business ever conducted within the pub itself?"

"Never," Annie answered, coughing loudly again and now wiping perspiration from her forehead, which no doubt arose from her fever. "It was usually done in a dark alleyway that was situated behind the pub."

"Would the gentleman drifters then depart or go back into the pub?" Joanna asked.

Annie thought for a moment before answering. "For the most part, they hurried to their waiting hansoms and carriages."

"Was this the behavior of the gentleman who favored you and Carrie?"

Annie shook her head. "He would never do business behind the Black Lamb, but insisted we follow him to Mitre Square."

"Did he give a reason for that?"

"No, ma'am."

"You stated that you followed him to the square," Joanna noted. "That implies he knew the way."

"He did indeed, for the distance from the pub to the square was seven or more blocks on the major streets, but he was aware of all the alleys and shortcuts which shortened our travel time. He was very familiar with the backstreets, I can say with certainty."

A thin smile crossed my wife's face. "Did you return to the Black Lamb after your business was done?"

"Yes, ma'am, for there may have been yet more customers to be had there."

"Did your gentleman drifter accompany you back to the pub?"

"No, ma'am. He disappeared down one of the dark passageways into the square."

"Would there be transportation awaiting him nearby?"

"Most unlikely, ma'am, for that is a very rough area where

a waiting carriage would be too tempting a target for thieves and other criminals."

"You have been most helpful," Joanna commended.

"I can only hope it leads you to the evil monster who did this terrible deed to Carrie," Annie said sadly. "Who could be so vicious?"

"As you just noted, it had to be an evil monster," Joanna replied, and turned to my father. "Do you have any questions, Watson?"

"Only a few," my father said, giving the Unfortunate a gentle, reassuring smile. "I know you are not well, so I shall endeavor to take up as little time as possible."

"Thank you, sir," said Annie, swallowing back a cough.

"Were you aware of the carbuncle on Carrie's leg?"

"Yes, sir. It had given her considerable trouble and pain to the point she could not put any pressure on it."

"So she sought care at St. Bartholomew's?"

"And excellent care it was. She was seen by a most kind doctor who drained the carbuncle twice."

"Twice, you say?"

Annie nodded. "On the first visit, the sore was opened and she was told to apply warm, salty soaks to aid in the drainage, which of course she didn't."

"Why not?"

"Where was someone living on the street going to find warm, salty soaks?"

"Your point is well taken," said my father. "So she had to return for yet another incision?"

"Which was done by the good Dr. Rudd, who was so kind that he placed some type of medicine on the skin to remove any pain from the procedure."

"And gave her a prescription for iodinated gauze to insert into the carbuncle to assist the drainage."

"Exactly right, sir."

"Did she have the funds to purchase the iodinated gauze?"

Annie nodded again. "She told me she had a little money hidden away, but did not tell me where."

"How did you come to know that she was being treated by Dr. Rudd?" I interrupted. "Did she mention his name?"

"She did, but I know the doctor as well, for he was attending me for a female problem."

"May I inquire what the problem was?"

"Something called endometriosis."

"I see," said I, recalling that endometriosis was a painful condition in which tissue that usually lines the uterus grows outside the uterus. "Was he able to give you any relief?"

"A little, with some herbal mixture the hospital provided."

My father rejoined the inquiry by asking, "I am told that the list of patients who wish to enroll in the charity clinic is very long indeed. You and Carrie were most fortunate to be allowed in. Do you know how that was arranged?"

Annie shrugged. "I wondered about that myself, for we both had such difficulty filling out the forms. It was a bit of luck for sure."

Joanna and I exchanged glances, silently telling each other that more than luck was involved here. What were the chances that three Unfortunates from Whitechapel would somehow find their way into a most selective clinic at St. Bart's?

Annie had another paroxysmal bout of coughing which provided blood-tinged phlegm. She seemed to lose her breath and struggled to regain it.

"Take slow, gentle breaths in and out," my father advised, and waited for her respirations to normalize. "You must return to the clinic as soon as possible."

"That will not be possible, sir, for my next appointment is not due for three months."

"I was once on staff at St. Bartholomew's and will make phone calls to see if I can arrange an earlier appointment."

"You are most kind, sir."

My father reached into his pocket for a half crown and handed the coin to the Unfortunate. "You are to take this money, which will pay for your continued stay here until the clinic arrangement can be made."

"I am so grateful to you, sir."

"And she is to remain in your cubicle," Joanna demanded of Luther. "If I hear otherwise, things will not go well for you."

Luther nodded his acquiescence as the scowl on his face seemed to grow.

My father gently patted Annie's shoulder and inquired, "Please forgive me, but you are both observant and well-spoken, and I cannot help but wonder how you came to be in this dreadful situation."

Annie sighed to herself as a sad memory returned. "I was once a lady's maid at an estate in Bristol where I was genuinely liked and paid a comfortable salary. My life was simple, but good, and got even better when I married a carriage driver from the estate. But then I came down with this terrible lung infection and was dismissed. Shortly thereafter my husband was killed in a road accident and everything went sour." She took another sad sigh, deeper this time, and ended by saying, "And here I am now at the lowest possible level in life."

My father patted her shoulder gently once again and instructed her in a kind voice, "You are to remain at rest until you hear from us."

"I shall, sir."

We left the doss-house and stepped out into a chilly afternoon which was made even colder by a brisk wind that sent garbage on the street flying into the air. I could barely imagine how the poor and penniless managed to survive on the mean, frigid streets of Whitechapel, where I suspected many died at a far too early age. Joanna waved good-bye to the constable and signaled our carriage to follow us as we walked along.

"What diagnosis do you give her, Watson?" she asked.

"With her obvious emaciation and bloody cough, I would put tuberculosis at the very top of the list."

"Is there any hope?"

"I am afraid not," my father said grimly. "Everything about the poor woman tells us her life on earth can now be measured in months."

"A shame in many regards."

"Indeed," my father agreed. "But I am curious how you seem to have known that someone in the doss-house would provide such a trove of information. Was there a clue I overlooked?"

"Oh, you saw it, Watson, but failed to bring it to its logical conclusion," Joanna elucidated. "Recall the struggle which Carrie Nichols engaged in at the entrance to the dark passageway off Mitre Square. The evidence showed she resisted the advances of the customer to such an extent that he was required to render her unconscious in order to make her submit. Now, why would she fight so fiercely when she was eager to accommodate virtually any customer?"

My father gave the matter long thought before nodding to himself. "She was terrified of him."

"Precisely," Joanna went on. "Some act he had done to either her or a friend previously had frightened her badly. She wanted no part of him. Now, please keep in mind that most women, unlike men, have a close friend, with whom they share all their stories, even their most intimate ones."

"And that close friend was Annie Yates," my father concluded.

"Thus, it follows that the struggle in the entrance to the passageway told us to find that close friend," Joanna said. "And even in her wretched condition, she provided us most important information which leads directly to Jack the Ripper."

"Such as?"

"We now know that The Ripper lives in Whitechapel."

"Based on what, pray tell?"

"A number of features point to that conclusion, my dear Watson," she replied, and counted off the reasons on her fingers. "First and foremost, he was keenly aware of its alleys and backstreets, even in darkness. Secondly, he was seen in various locations such as the pub, Mitre Square, the sweet shop, and now a jewelry shop, all separated by sizable distances. These are characteristics of an individual who was very familiar with the district and thus most likely has a dwelling here."

"But he is educated and obviously well-to-do," I argued. "That is not the type who would own a house in Whitechapel."

"He might if he wished to have a secret dwelling," Joanna countered. "But what is of equal interest is that both Carrie Nichols and Annie Yates were patients in the charity ward at St. Bart's."

"As was the initial victim who was autopsied by Willoughby," I added. "You will recall she, too, had a draining carbuncle that was skillfully treated."

"So we have three Unfortunates, all being looked after at a highly selective clinic at St. Bartholomew's," Joanna concluded. "That cannot simply be happenstance."

"Particularly if all three were under the care of Thaddeus Rudd," I noted.

"A most important observation, John," said my wife, with an affirmative nod. "And one which merits further investigation."

"Hold on!" my father protested at once. "It is quite a stretch to implicate a fine, distinguished surgeon in these vicious murders, only because he happened to treat them in a free clinic where he so generously donated his time."

"You may be correct, Watson, but it is a habit of mine to believe all suspects guilty until proven otherwise."

"That is so contradictory to our system of justice."

"But it works well for me."

My father stepped around a dead cat as he considered the matter further. "I would never assign this diabolical behavior to such a fine physician."

"Even one known to have a terrible temper?" Joanna inquired pointedly.

"You seem convinced we are dealing with a Dr. Jekyll–Mr. Hyde personality."

"That is because our murderer fits the profile so well."

We came to Froman's Jewelry Shop, which had only a narrow window to display its inexpensive goods. There were rows of silver rings with colorful stones, which were mixed in with earrings and bracelets made of copper. On entering we were greeted by a short, heavyset man, balding, with ruddy cheeks and a kind face. Above him, a caged parrot squawked at our presence.

"May I help you, madam?" asked he, from behind a glass counter. A framed certificate on the wall noted that Joseph Froman was a member of a jewelers association.

"We are interested in your copper earrings and bracelets," Joanna replied. "I have been invited to a costume party and would like to buy some appropriate jewelry."

"Of course." Froman reached into the showcase and extracted shiny copper items which he placed on the counter for inspection. "The copper earrings are said to come from Africa, but I am not certain that is true."

My wife examined the earrings and asked, "Will the thin wire which attaches to the ear hold up?"

Froman shrugged. "I have had no complaints."

"Do you sell a fair number of them?"

"Not very many," he said honestly. "There was no demand for them until last week."

"Oh, a lot of customers requested them, did they?"

"Only one," Froman recalled. "This strange chap came in and bought five sets of copper earrings. I usually do not sell that number in a month."

"Five, you say!" Joanna said, apparently interested. "They must have been gifts."

Froman shrugged again. "Whatever their purpose, he demanded five sets, which nearly exhausted my supply. I counted them out, after which he did the same, as if to make certain about their number."

"Strange business," Joanna probed gently. "Did he look or behave in a strange manner?"

"Not really," the jeweler said, thinking back. "He was wearing ordinary clothes, with long gray hair tucked under a fisherman's hat. What was odd was that the total charge was fifteen shillings which he paid with a ten-pound note. We do not see many of those in Whitechapel, I can tell you that."

"Did he carefully count the change?"

Froman shook his head firmly. "He simply stuffed the earrings and nine pounds five in his pocket and rushed out."

"Rushed out, eh?"

"Like the shop was on fire."

Joanna and the jeweler were now speaking like old friends, and she was collecting information which might not otherwise be revealed. Individuals in the lower class tended to clam up around the affluent as well as around the authorities, particularly the police, for fear of somehow becoming involved. Joanna had a remarkable talent for finding common ground with them by chatting primarily about their trade, yet gathering important details all the while.

My wife was now saying, "Well, as long as he was a reliable customer and his money was good, his unusual behavior is of little concern."

"Exactly right, madam," Froman agreed, before returning to the business at hand. "Do the copper earrings interest you?"

"They do indeed," Joanna responded. "I shall like a set, together with a matching bracelet."

"An excellent choice." The jeweler retrieved the items and went about shining them with a felt cloth. "This brings out their luster."

"Does it require polish?"

"No, ma'am. Like I told the chap who purchased five pairs, such polish can actually dull the shine."

"Thank you for the advice," Joanna said, as she was handed the items. "And your charge?"

"Five shillings, please."

The bill being paid, we walked out into a sunless noon, with the sky even darker than before. People hurried by, bundled up against the cold, yet still managing to steal an envious glimpse at our fashionable attire. Loud thunder suddenly roared overhead, telling us that rain would soon fall.

"Shall I signal our carriage?" I asked.

"Not yet, for we have a most important task to perform," said Joanna.

"Which is?"

"To warn Annie Yates, for her life is now in imminent danger."

"What brings you to that conclusion?"

"The five sets of earrings which Jack the Ripper bought,"

she replied, and hurried down Buck's Row back to the doss-house. My father and I had to quickstep to keep up.

"What is the significance of the five pairs of earrings?" I asked.

"Think of the *twenty* pieces of apple spice candy The Ripper bought, with four being given to each victim per day."

My answer came to me. "Divide four into twenty and that gives you the number of days Pretty Penny would remain alive, which is five."

"And of the five sets of earrings purchased, how many have been given out?"

"Three."

"To whom?"

"The three Unfortunates."

"And how many of those remain alive?"

"Only Annie Yates."

"Which designates her as the next victim."

I nodded slowly at my wife's keen conclusion. "So they are death gifts, with each set of copper earrings given to the five prospective victims. But who will be number four?"

"That is to be determined," Joanna replied. "But I know with certainty who will be number five."

"Pretty Penny," I stated the obvious.

"Who I will wager has already been given her copper earrings."

We dashed into the doss-house and entered the large communal room that was filled with crowded iron bedsteads which remained empty. Luther, who was carrying a stack of soiled blankets on his shoulder, spotted us immediately and followed us past the kitchen area into the cubicle where we had last seen Annie Yates. The bed was made up, the room itself empty.

"What is she?" Joanna demanded.

"She departed a few minutes after you did," Luther replied.

"As sick as she was?" My father raised his voice sternly.

"I guess the half crown gave her renewed energy," Luther said with an unconcerned shrug.

"Where would she have gone?" Joanna asked.

"To a pub where the drinks will be the cheapest," he answered. "I would guess to the Black Lamb, which is a favorite of the Unfortunates."

"Will she come back here this evening?"

"Only if she has fivepence remaining, which I doubt will be the case," Luther told us. "Given the chance, they quickly return to their old ways."

"But her life is now at great risk," my father blurted out. "Her days are truly numbered."

"They always are on the mean streets of Whitechapel," Luther said matter-of-factly, and turned for the communal room.

"If she returns, you must notify us at once," my father insisted, and handed the doss-house warden a personal card.

"Don't hold your breath, guv'nor," the warden said, and went back to work, placing filthy blankets on soiled mattresses.

CHAPTER 8

The Duke of York's Theatre

With the commissioner's office having made the arrangements, we found ourselves seated in the Duke of York's Theatre watching a late-morning rehearsal of Gilbert and Sullivan's musical *The Mikado*. The actual size of the renowned theater on St. Martin's Lane seemed to be exaggerated by the fact that the entire audience was comprised of Joanna, my father, and myself. During a brief intermission whilst the stage was being transformed for the final act, I took the opportunity to again glance up at the auditorium's Victorian décor, with its numerous cherubs and dragons painted in glorious colors. The extravagant embellishment was no doubt meant to impress visitors and it did so instantly in a memorable fashion. Yet it was far too bold for my tastes. As music arose from the orchestra's pit, my attention returned to the players who reappeared in their Oriental costumes and began to once more totally enchant the viewers. In particular, one of the leading actresses had a mesmerizing role which we all agreed would have been perfect for Pretty Penny. It was impossible not to keep your eyes on her beauty and incredibly graceful moves. She did not appear to take steps but rather to float through the various scenes. As the play came to an end, we could not help but applaud the players for their captivating performances, which caused them to stop onstage and give us warm smiles and appreciative bows.

The director, Roger Blackstone, hurried over to us, obviously pleased with the rehearsal. He was a short, plump man, with silver-gray hair and a bounce to his gait. His attire, which consisted of a linen suit, striped shirt, and bright red tie, was that of a showman. "Well, what is your opinion?" asked he, with an expression that told us he already knew the answer.

"Marvelous," Joanna replied. "But then, Gilbert and Sullivan's plays usually are; yet this was a notch above."

"And what of the individual performances?"

"They were magnificent," I answered. "Particularly the slender actress who seemed to float across the stage and sang her way into our hearts."

My father nodded at my assessment. "We all felt it was a role that would have been a superb fit for Pretty Penny, from what we have heard of her."

"You have a good eye, sir," Blackstone concurred. "That part requires a certain magic which few actresses possess."

"I take it you have seen Pretty Penny perform," Joanna broached the subject of our visit.

"Only once, but that was quite enough," the director said, and sighed to himself as the joy left his face. "What has happened to that poor girl is beyond heartbreaking." He paused to wave to the last of the exiting players and only spoke again when they were out of view. "Now tell me, how can I assist you in your investigation?"

"We need to hear of all your contacts with Emma Adams and Lionel Lurie," Joanna said directly.

Blackstone's brow went up. "Are they suspects?"

"Everyone connected to Pretty Penny is a suspect," she replied in a neutral tone. "Please be good enough to detail your meetings with the principals at the Whitechapel Playhouse."

"There was only one and that was to sign the contract which gave us partial control of Pretty Penny," he answered.

Joanna blinked at the unexpected revelation. "Partial control, you say?"

"Oh, yes, all signed and sealed in my barrister's office."

"Pray tell how this association came about."

"It was not my idea, but my brother's, who is a theatrical agent of some note. It is with him that the story begins."

Blackstone then proceeded to give us a most complete summary which contained some surprising information. Pretty Penny's talent was first observed by the director's twin, Richard, who brought it to the attention of his brother. Roger Blackstone promptly traveled to Whitechapel and, on seeing the young woman perform, urged the agent to take the actress under his wing, which he attempted to do, only to learn she was already obliged by contract to Emma Adams. Lionel

Lurie learned of the meeting and became infuriated, accusing the high-powered agent of attempting to steal away the talented Pretty Penny. Which in fact was true. But Lurie was of little matter, for it was Emma Adams alone who held the contract. Unfortunately, she was not interested in parting with it, despite a most generous offer.

"A stalemate, then," said Joanna.

"But not for long, for my brother did not become a celebrated agent by giving in easily," Blackstone continued on. "He surveyed the landscape—so to speak—at Whitechapel and soon discovered that the play's Romeo, Maxwell Anderson, was a superb actor as well and seemed to make Pretty Penny dazzle even more. Together they had a remarkable stage presence. My brother spoke with Anderson in private and signed on as his agent."

"Maxwell Anderson would never leave medicine for the stage; of that I can assure you," I interjected.

"One never knows, for the stage can have a captivating effect on an individual, much like a moth is drawn to the flame," he responded. "And where Pretty Penny goes, the young pathologist might well follow. They are quite a magnetic pair, you see."

"Are you suggesting they are lovers?" Joanna asked.

The director flicked his wrist at the notion. "Love is of little consequence in this instance. What matters most is that they sparkle as a pair and both know it. It is their undeniable talents which bind them together."

"It would seem you are implying that Pretty Penny would hesitate to leave for the higher position without Anderson at her side."

Blackstone smiled mischievously. "Ah, dear lady, now you are thinking like a bona fide agent."

"Did Emma Adams hear of this signing?"

"We made certain she did."

"And her response?"

"She was quite upset, for Mrs. Adams is a clever woman and knows how to read between the lines. Yet she collected herself in a businesslike fashion while Lionel Lurie became downright combative as he envisioned his chance to be a St. Martin's Lane director slipping away. He even went so far as to mention his ties to the Whitechapel underworld in an attempt to frighten us."

"Did it?"

"Hardly, for Lurie's bark is far greater than his bite."

"But there was always the distinct possibility that Pretty Penny would leave Whitechapel without Maxwell Anderson," I pointed out. "The allure would simply be too great to resist."

"Perhaps, but her success on the big stage would in no way be guaranteed, particularly with a novice agent and an unknown director. By contrast, with my brother as manager, Pretty Penny would have a direct and immediate path to both me and St. Martin's Lane. In addition, she would have been afforded the very best medical care."

"A bit fragile, was she?" Joanna asked, feigning ignorance.

"Not so much fragile as asthmatic," Blackstone replied. "During one of her performances, with my brother in the audience, he detected her intermittent difficulty breathing. To the inexperienced it might have gone unnoticed, but both he and I are very much aware of asthma, for our older brother is afflicted with this unpleasant disorder. In any case, after the performance my brother visited with Pretty Penny and could hear her soft wheezes. Now this of course could present a problem for any stage actress."

"Did this give you pause in signing her?"

"Not at all, for my dear older brother functions very well as a barrister with little problem at all. Of course he is looked after by the finest Harley Street specialists, and we assured Penny that we would make sure she was cared for equally as well. Thus, you might say we used her illness to our advantage, and I suspect it was a factor in her signing with my brother's agency. Even Mrs. Adams saw this as a distinct advantage."

"So a compromise was reached and a deal struck," Joanna concluded.

"Exactly, madam. My brother was allowed to purchase fifty percent of Pretty Penny's contract for a fee of one hundred pounds. He was also obliged to sign over half of Maxwell Anderson's contract to Mrs. Adams. So now everything was neatly tied together for all the concerned parties. My brother would send Pretty Penny to my plays, which would assure her receiving the best of leading roles and no doubt stardom. Anderson could come along if he so wished, and Mrs. Adams would prosper greatly."

"And Lionel Lurie would become an assistant director," Joanna added.

Blackstone half-shrugged his shoulders. "Unwanted, but necessary baggage."

"I am surprised he settled for that position."

"He had no choice, for Emma Adams rules that roost."

"So, in the end all benefited."

"Some far more than others, obviously."

We thanked the director for his time and strolled out of the theater into bright sunshine which promised a surprisingly warm day. The footpath on St. Martin's Lane was crowded with theatergoers hurrying to purchase tickets for the early-afternoon matinees and carrying on spirited conversations as they passed us. We waited until we reached the relative quiet at the rear of the National Gallery before speaking.

"I continue to dwell on Blackstone's last comment that

some of the participants will benefit far more than the others," my father noted. "He was surely referring to the lesser role of Lionel Lurie."

"Beyond a doubt," Joanna agreed. "He will be given the title of assistant director and little more. And should he cause any problems, he will quickly be shown the door."

"Will Emma Adams not come to his defense?"

"She will expedite his way out, for here is a strong, determined woman who will not allow anyone or anything to obstruct her path to theatrical success."

"Lurie must certainly be aware of his tenuous situation," I wondered aloud. "He might become so embittered with the position that he finds himself placed in that he resorts to the unthinkable, such as a temporary kidnapping which would bring him widespread notice."

My father quickly asked, "Are you suggesting that, with his underworld connections, he might stir up some sort of mischief which would cause both him and Pretty Penny to appear to be linked in the public's eye?"

"That thought crossed my mind, for both their names are currently mentioned on the front pages of the *Times* and *Guardian,*" I replied. "The publicity he might well continue to receive would be priceless, and he would become known prior to his arrival at St. Martin's Lane. Thus, his name on the program would become an asset, and he would not be so easy to discard. For an insecure partner, that might be motive enough."

My father stifled a laugh. "You are beginning to think like Joanna."

"I had pondered that same scenario, but for a number of reasons it doesn't ring true," said she. "To begin, it is far too risky to indulge in such a kidnapping, with the possibility of little gain. There is no guarantee Lurie's name will remain in the news, for it is Pretty Penny and not him who attracts the public's attention. Moreover, no criminal with the smallest of brains would even consider doing the deed, for to be apprehended by the police would result in a long prison sentence, and to be discovered by the locals would bring about a beating he would be unlikely to survive. And finally, we have to look at the other side of the coin and recall that Lurie has experience directing Pretty Penny and has done so admirably thus far. He might then turn out to be an asset after all was said and done."

"So you believe Emma Adams and Lionel Lurie are now completely absolved," I stated the obvious.

"Quite so, for we now see that both had far more to gain from the status quo," said Joanna. "As a matter of fact, they were always at the bottom of the suspect list, but nonetheless had to be excluded."

"With Jack the Ripper at the very top."

"Which all the evidence thus far would indicate."

"But, unlike his established modus operandi, we have no mutilated body to back up that assertion," my father argued.

"I am afraid, Watson, that one will turn up shortly," Joanna said, and, waving her parasol, signaled a passing carriage.

Chapter 9

Thaddeus Rudd

On returning to our rooms at 221b Baker Street, we received a most welcome call from Maxwell Anderson. After carefully washing the blood from the metal sliver which was embedded in Carrie Nichols's cervical spine, he discovered a definite fingerprint. Inspector Lestrade, together with a fingerprint expert at Scotland Yard, were now on their way to St. Bartholomew's and expected shortly. We hurried out and down the stairs, and past a most exasperated Miss Hudson who was on her way up, carrying a nicely laid-out tray for afternoon tea.

Outside, traffic was slow and dense in the rain, and we were fortunate to hail an empty four-wheeler. As we rode through a fashionable block of Marylebone, I could not help but compare it to the destitute neighborhood we had experienced a day earlier. The elegant shops and sparkling clean streets we were passing stood in stark contrast to the filth and poverty of Whitechapel.

"I continue to envision the horrid condition of the doss-house, with its noxious smell, that housed the poor Unfortunate," I recalled.

My father nodded at my description as his mind went back to the dreadful living quarters. "It is a breeding ground for disease."

"As demonstrated by the Unfortunate we visited," said I. "There could not be a more striking example of hopelessness."

"Indeed," my father agreed. "But I must say I was most disappointed by Annie Yates, who I believed was a decent sort underneath it all. You must admit she told a very convincing story regarding her past history."

"Which may have been true," I opined.

"We shall never know, for she is now a creature of the dark streets, who depends on lies and deceit to survive," Joanna chimed in. "And it is on those streets she will shortly die unless we intervene."

"Do you have a plan?" I asked.

"Several come to mind, but none are very appealing," she replied vaguely.

"Perhaps she will return to the doss-house, at which time Luther will notify us," my father hoped.

"That is wishful thinking, Father," I said.

"Her return or Luther informing us?" my father asked.

"Both," I answered candidly.

"Oh, Luther will notify us if she returns," Joanna predicted. "For he would expect your next half crown to end up in his pocket, which would ensure that Annie Yates will continue to sleep in his bed for a month or more, with no fee required or collected by the establishment. Thus, he would be richer by a half crown, which he would find irresistible."

"What a dreadful man," I noted.

"He is a product of his environment, nothing more and nothing less." Joanna reached into her purse and extracted a set of copper earrings which she examined at length, both with and without a magnifying glass. "Let us put Annie Yates aside for now and concentrate on fingerprints which could help identify Jack the Ripper."

"Do you believe Anderson has uncovered a complete, clear print on the metal sliver?" my father asked.

"In all likelihood, that is not the case," she replied. "If The Ripper attempted to remove the metal sliver, and I suspect he did, he would have taken hold of it between his thumb and index finger in a pincer grasp, thus leaving behind partial prints. He would have no doubt gripped it firmly and avoided the sharp edge, for not to do so could have resulted in a laceration. So I would predict we have partial prints which could prove useful, assuming Anderson did not muck them up while removing the blood."

"Holmes did not place much value on partial fingerprints," my father recalled.

"The science has improved greatly since the days of my father," Joanna informed. "I refer you to a monograph written by Sir Francis Galton, in which he describes the arches, loops, and whorls that give fingerprints their distinctive patterns. An expert does not look for an exact match but rather a specified number of characteristics in a given print and determines if they are identical to another. According to Sir Francis, you must find at least twelve identical points to consider it a match. The French demand fifteen."

"No easy task when dealing with a partial fingerprint," I presumed.

"Nevertheless, worth a try," said she.

"Perhaps the copper earrings will be more revealing," I ventured.

"That is unlikely," Joanna went on, holding up an earring for inspection. "Notice how I grasp the earring by its edges, as any woman would in order to prevent leaving smudges behind. Also, please recall the instructions given to us and The Ripper by the jeweler. The earrings were to be shined with a dry cloth to bring out their luster. I am certain our killer followed these instructions to make them even more attractive as gifts. And of course he would hold the copper earrings by their edges to avoid leaving any smudges on their surfaces."

"You make him sound so careful and deliberate at the moment," my father opined. "But it seems to me that a keen killer like The Ripper is leaving entirely too many clues behind. I am referring to the copper earrings which are a telltale sign of what he has done and will do. And then there were the daylight visits to the sweet shop and jewelry store where he was seen in public and noticed, even in his disguise. Certainly you have noted these inconsistencies."

"I have indeed, Watson," said Joanna. "And I believe he does so purposefully."

"But to what end?"

"To taunt us and show us how clever he is."

Our carriage pulled up at a side entrance to St. Bartholomew's and we hurried up and down a long corridor to Maxwell

Anderson's laboratory. But Benson was standing outside the door and held up a warning hand.

"You may not wish to enter at the moment, Dr. Watson, for Dr. Rudd is in the midst of one of his terrible tantrums," said he.

"What has set him off this time?" I asked.

"Something was lost, from the sound of it."

"Step aside," I directed, and entered, with Joanna and my father close behind.

Thaddeus Rudd was furiously pacing around the laboratory, ranting and raving at the top of his voice. For such a large man, he moved quite nimbly, and his footsteps made little noise. Rudd paused briefly to give us a mean look, then went back to shouting.

"You had better find that specimen and find it now, if you value your position here!" he roared at Anderson, who was standing off to the side in front of two frightened technicians.

"I am certain it will be found," Anderson said in a calm voice.

"You spoke those exact same words an hour ago," the surgeon replied angrily. "And have yet to produce that specimen. What am I to tell the patient and her family? That the specimen has gone missing, so we cannot determine if it was cancerous or not? Or perhaps I should suggest we operate once more and look for additional tissue to study. But then again, you would lose that specimen as well."

Rudd paused, waiting for a reply, and when none was forthcoming he gave Anderson a hostile stare and demanded an answer. "Well?"

"Well, what?" Anderson asked.

"Well, where is the missing specimen?"

"We are searching."

"Then search harder," Rudd insisted, and kicked at a tin bin, sending it flying across the room. "And I mean now."

"It is impossible to do so in the midst of your outburst," Anderson said tonelessly. "I suggest you leave and allow us to carefully comb through all of our specimens once again."

"I stay until it is found," the surgeon said before glaring over at us. "Whatever your business here, it will have to wait."

"I think not," Joanna said firmly. "And Scotland Yard will be here shortly to explain why."

"They, too, can wait."

"Tell that to Inspector Lestrade."

"Better yet, I will contact my dear friend Sir Charles Bradberry and have the commissioner intercede," Rudd coerced.

Joanna pointed to a telephone on the nearby desk. "Call him."

Rudd's face reddened as he moved toward Joanna in a most threatening manner. "You had better take leave of your own volition while you still can."

"Please keep your distance," she requested.

"I will do as I wish," he snarled, and took yet another step forward.

I was prepared to intervene and put an end to his threat, but my wife held up a hand for me to remain in place.

Rudd suddenly lunged.

In the blink of an eye, Joanna effortlessly incapacitated the surgeon with a stunning move of jujitsu, a Japanese martial art at which she was most proficient. Joanna held his arm in a joint-locking technique that totally immobilized the extended elbow and caused agonizing pain to an opponent who tried to resist. Rudd struggled to break free, which brought on even more pain, as evidenced by his loud groans.

"When I release you, you are to back away," Joanna

instructed. "Another threatening move by you could result in permanent injury." She released her hold and kept a close eye on Rudd as he rubbed at his elbow.

I hoped the surgeon would not do anything stupid, for I once accompanied my wife to her jujitsu class where she was awarded a brown belt, which is the second-highest level of proficiency in the art, superseded only by the black belt. The beauty of jujitsu was that it used an attacker's energy against him, rather than directly opposing it. A persistence in resistance could result in permanent damage, particularly in a joint as vulnerable as the elbow.

The door to the laboratory opened and Lestrade entered, followed by a tall, slender man with close-cropped gray hair. The inspector glanced at the obvious standoff between my wife and Rudd before asking, "Is there a problem?"

"It has been resolved," Joanna replied.

"You haven't heard the last of this," Rudd warned.

"For your sake, I hope I have."

Rudd gave Joanna a final glare, then spun around and brushed by Lestrade on his way out.

"A rather unpleasant fellow," Lestrade commented. "Was there a dispute?"

"A misunderstanding which has now been put to rest."

"Let us get to work, then," Lestrade said, and introduced us to Henry Overstreet, who was Scotland Yard's foremost fingerprint expert. "Where is this item to be examined?"

Maxwell Anderson led us to a laboratory bench upon which rested a metal tray. In the center of the tray was an inch-long sliver of metal that was clear of all blood. As we moved in front of the two female technicians, I could not help but notice the adoring smiles they bestowed on Joanna for the magnificent manner in which she dealt with the disgusting bully

Thaddeus Rudd. Word of her heroic deed would no doubt spread throughout the hospital, much to the displeasure of the ill-tempered surgeon.

The now-gloved Overstreet picked up the metal sliver with tweezers and carefully examined both sides with a magnifying glass under a bright overhead light. He made a tut-tut sound before reexamining the end of the blade Jack the Ripper had used on Carrie Nichols.

"Anything worthwhile?" Lestrade asked.

"One side has only a smudged print of no value," Overstreet reported. "But the other has a definable partial print."

"Is there enough to determine a match?"

"Unlikely, but we shall see."

Overstreet reached into a small kit for a tin container and sprinkled fine powder onto a brush to dust the fingerprint, explaining that the powder clung to the oil in the print and thus made it more readable. Examining the sliver once more with a magnifying glass, he proclaimed, "Ah! Much better, and if I were to hazard a guess, I would say we are looking at part of a thumbprint."

"Will there be enough points to match with another fingerprint?" Joanna asked.

"Possibly," he hedged. "But we shall know more when the print is magnified and photographed."

Anderson produced an envelope and handed it to Overstreet. "Perhaps we will have better luck with the copper earrings the two victims were wearing."

The Scotland Yard expert examined both sets, both with and without dusting powder. "They are spotless other than a scratch or two."

Lestrade sighed disappointedly. "So we are left with a partial fingerprint which may have little value."

"I am afraid so," Overstreet agreed.

"Then we shall be on our way," Lestrade said, and, tipping his derby, departed with Overstreet at his side.

"It is unfortunate we could not be more helpful," Anderson said before turning to the technicians with further instructions. "Put all of your efforts into finding the missing surgical specimen. I want you to examine every organ and tissue we have received in the past two days. Check their origin and physician, paying particular attention to the name Harriman, the patient who until yesterday possessed the abdominal mass we are searching for. No one leaves this laboratory until the specimen is found and Dr. Rudd notified."

The door suddenly opened with a bang and Peter Willoughby stormed in. He gave us at best a hasty nod before approaching Anderson. "Dr. Rudd has lodged an official complaint against you and plans to take it to St. Bart's board of trustees."

"Will it not have to go through your office first?" Anderson asked.

"It will, but I shall have no recourse other than to send the complaint to the hospital director," Willoughby said unyieldingly.

"I would very much appreciate you keeping the complaint on your desk until tomorrow morning, by which time I hope to have discovered the missing specimen."

"You hope?" the director of pathology snapped. "Do you have any idea of the consequences arising from your sloppiness? The patient we are speaking of is Martha Harriman, the wife of the chancellor of the exchequer."

"I shall find it," Anderson vowed.

"You had better, for your position here may very well be at stake," Willoughby threatened, and angrily stomped out.

Once the door closed, I approached Anderson and suggested, "If I were you, I would have the technicians open every jar and container and make certain the specimen was not inadvertently mixed in with another specimen. This happened to me some years ago."

"A capital idea, John!" he said appreciatively.

"Good hunting, then," said I, and departed, holding the door for Joanna and my father.

We walked at a brisk pace down the corridor and out the front entrance, where chances of hailing a taxi or carriage were greater. The traffic outside the hospital was heavily congested, but we were still able to observe Thaddeus Rudd riding by in his chauffeured limousine. He, too, saw us and rudely turned his head away.

"I must say, Joanna," my father remarked. "That was a bloody good move you put on Rudd."

Joanna smiled thinly. "Jujitsu does come in handy now and then."

"It was a pleasure to see Rudd put in his place, although this does not bring us any closer to resolution."

"Perhaps it does, for although I believe beyond a reasonable doubt that these horrific murders were committed by Jack the Ripper and not some clever copycat, a skeptic might wish to point out we have no definitive proof in that regard and that mutilated bodies by themselves are not enough."

My father looked at Joanna oddly. "But one would have to catch The Ripper in the act for such undeniable proof."

"Unless he left a marker behind, like a fingerprint."

"But all we have is a partial thumbprint and no prior print to match it against."

"Are you speaking of an earlier fingerprint that was known to come from the original Ripper?"

"Yes, but one does not exist."

"Oh, but I think one does," Joanna said mysteriously, and hailed a passing carriage.

Chapter 10

Alexander's

It had been a long, tiring day, but we carried on, for the lives of Annie Yates and Pretty Penny hung in the balance. Thus, we obtained dinner reservations at Alexander's on St. Martin's Lane and arrived at nine sharp, which was shortly before the scheduled time that Pretty Penny and her secret lover would have been expected to make their entrance. A doorman helped Joanna from our taxi and greeted us with a warm welcome.

"Good evening, madam and gentlemen," said he.

"And to you," Joanna replied, and glanced over at the long line of taxis waiting in line outside the restaurant. "Are the same taxis here each and every night?"

"No, ma'am," the doorman answered. "They come and go in a random manner. After dropping off passengers, they continue on their way in search of other fares. Those you see are here for our patrons who are preparing to depart. The exceptions are the few waiting limousines."

"Very good."

Joanna took my arm as well as my father's and we entered a most splendid restaurant. It was relatively small, with no more than twenty tables, all nicely placed so that nearby conversations would not be overheard. The chairs were high backed and upholstered in fine, full-grain cordovan leather which gave added comfort. High above, a sparkling glass chandelier provided soft lighting except for the corner tables where shadows allowed for more privacy.

"Good evening," a tall, handsome maître d', with a thin mustache, welcomed us. "The name under which your reservation was made, please."

"Dr. John Watson," I replied.

"Your table awaits you, sir," the maître d' said before giving Joanna a rather long, curious look. "Excuse me, madam, but your face seems familiar."

"That's because it belongs to the daughter of Sherlock Holmes."

The maître d' was taken aback momentarily but quickly regained his composure. "Is your visit official?"

"If you wish it to be."

"I would prefer not."

"Then we shall keep it unofficial, but I do have one request before we are seated," said Joanna. "I would like to see your reservation books for the past month, excluding this week's."

The maître d' hesitated as the last trace of cordiality vanished from his face. "Should that not require a search warrant?"

"I do not have one at present," Joanna responded. "But I can return tomorrow evening with such a warrant, and with Scotland Yard at my side to assist in the investigation."

"That will not be necessary, madam," the maître d' said at once, and led us past a well-stocked bar that was made of mahogany. The barkeep as well as some of the fashionably attired patrons recognized Joanna from her photograph in the newspapers, where it had appeared on a number of occasions during the past year. A few of those seated nearby commented to each other in hushed tones as we walked by.

My father whispered, "I am afraid Joanna's recognition may work to our disadvantage."

"Only if we allow it to," she whispered back.

We followed the maître d' into a small, cramped office that had no windows and a slow-moving overhead fan for ventilation.

A cluttered desk, with a battered swivel chair, rested in the center of the room. On a side shelf were thick ledgers with black covers that were stamped with the restaurant's engraved seal.

While handing over the reservation books to Joanna, the maître d' asked, "If the patrons inquire as to the purpose of your visit, what shall I tell them?"

"The truth," she replied.

"But I do not know the purpose."

"That is the truth," said Joanna, opening the initial ledger. "Please see to it that we are not disturbed."

Once the maître d' departed, my father reached in his coat pocket for a folded sheet of paper. "Here is the list you requested, which contains the dates of all performances at the Whitechapel Playhouse during the past month. I obtained the dates from Lionel Lurie, but checked them with Mrs. Adams to make certain there were no inaccuracies."

"Excellent, Watson." With effort, Joanna extracted two thick multifolded sheets of paper from her purse and carefully unfolded each. She spread them out separately on the desk, holding down their edges with books and binders and a nonfunctioning clock. Written on the sheets were long columns, with individual letters of the alphabet atop each. "I counted eighteen tables in the restaurant, which means that for each date there will be eighteen reservations between the hours of nine and ten. Since we now know there were fifteen performance dates at the playhouse during the past month, we must multiply fifteen times eighteen, which will tell us the total number of patrons present during the supposed times that Pretty Penny and her lover could have dined here. We shall go through the three ledgers and list alphabetically the visit of each patron. We are seeking an individual who has visited Alexander's more than once in the past month, for we know that Pretty Penny and her companion frequented this establishment from her conversations with the Widow Marley. Thus, the names of those who made multiple reservations may well include the name of Penny's secret lover."

My father did the arithmetic and announced, "Eighteen times fifteen equals two hundred and seventy reservations, which is a most arduous number to sift through. It may well take hours."

"But it could turn out to be most productive," said Joanna. "Now, as I call out the name of each reservation, please note it under the correct alphabet column."

"Will you be giving first and last name?" I asked.

"Just the last for now," she replied, and began to list the patrons in the first black ledger. "Bacon . . . Whitaker . . . Everest . . . Albright . . . Lewis . . . Ellington . . . Marcus . . . Covington . . . Marshall . . . Lord Bremmer . . . Dalton. . . ."

I was responsible for getting down the names that started with the letters *A* to *K,* while my father noted those that went from *L* to *Z*. After a half hour and listing seventy patrons, there was only one match. Mr. Marcus had visited twice, but the entry had two different first names—Charles and Lawrence.

"I fear we shall not be successful," my father predicted. "For the odds are against us. After all, the couple may have only visited the restaurant once."

"I suspect it was far more than once, Watson, and there are several reasons to back up this assertion," Joanna said. "First, Pretty Penny treasured her matchbook cover from Alexander's, which indicated their visit was most memorable, and such memories often result in frequent revisits. Secondly, this restaurant is located on St. Martin's Lane, which is the main theater district of London. It represents the dreamworld of the actress Pretty Penny, for it is the world she aspires to become part of. I can assure you she would beg to return time and time again."

"There is the possibility the secret lover used aliases to make the reservations and thus keep his true identity unknown," I suggested.

"If that were the case, he would use the same alias over and over, for he would be familiar to the maître d' and staff because of his many visits." Joanna reached for the second black ledger and handed it to me. "If you will, John, please call out the names as your father and I list them alphabetically."

"We shall begin with the tenth of the month," said I, and began naming the patrons. "Merriman . . . Graham . . . Grover . . . Jackson . . . Clement . . . Albertson . . . Mendel . . . Boyle . . . Poole . . . Rood—"

"Rudd!" Joanna interrupted abruptly. "Rudd, you say."

"It is spelled *R-o-o-d*," I corrected. "With the first name Samuel. He is not our surgeon."

"Underline it nonetheless, for it could be a clever, phonetically similar alias," she instructed.

"Done."

"Pray continue," Joanna requested, as the excitement of discovery faded from her face.

"Devlin . . . Courtney . . . Broadstreet . . . Duke . . . Isaacs . . . York . . . Colleton . . . Baron Rothman . . . Oliver . . . Dunleavy . . . Bayswater . . . Dubose . . . Dunbar . . . Anderson. . . ."

"I have a match!" Joanna cried out.

I blinked several times in disbelief and reread the name to make certain my eyes were not deceiving me. "The first name is Maxwell."

"Aha!" said she triumphantly. "And so we have our secret Romeo."

"But why go to such lengths to hide the romance?" asked my father. "After all, she is a quite beautiful, talented young actress."

"It is a matter of class distinction, I would guess," Joanna surmised. "But let us be absolutely certain that Maxwell Anderson is our secret Romeo. We should continue to review this ledger and the next to determine how many times Anderson's name appears. There is no need to call out the other patrons as we search for additional visits by the couple."

We hurried through the remaining ledgers that held the reservations for over a hundred and fifty patrons. Maxwell Anderson's name came up five times between the hours of nine and ten in the evening. On several of the latter visits, a small asterisk appeared next to the reservation.

"What do you believe the asterisk notes?" I asked.

"That this particular patron requires special attention," Joanna replied. "The maître d' will give us the specifics."

On that note we closed the ledgers and reentered the restaurant. As we reappeared, heads turned and the loud hum of multiple conversations quieted for a moment, then quickly resumed. The maître d' rushed over to us to inquire, "May I ask if all was in order?"

"Quite so," Joanna assured. "You should have no concern about Scotland Yard paying a visit."

"Excellent," the maître d' said, relieved.

"But I do have a question," she requested. "I noticed an asterisk by the name Maxwell Anderson. What significance does that carry?"

"Dr. Anderson wished to be seated at one of the corner tables for more privacy," he replied, and gestured to the farthest corner of the restaurant.

"Where there would be less noise and distraction," Joanna added.

"It is a preferred table for those very reasons," the maître d' agreed, and waited for more questions. When none were forthcoming, he assumed his professional demeanor and asked, "May I show you to your table?"

"Please."

We were seated only briefly before a waiter appeared and inquired, "Would you care for cocktails?"

"We shall do with just wine," Joanna responded. "When he has a moment, have the sommelier come over."

"Very good, madam," the waiter said, with a half bow, and disappeared amongst the tables.

My father whispered under his breath, "I take it you believe Anderson ordered a most expensive bottle of wine."

"What better way to impress a young beauty from Whitechapel?" Joanna said.

"Would Pretty Penny truly know the difference between an expensive and inexpensive wine?" my father asked candidly.

"It is not the wine alone which would impress her, but the large, shiny medallion that the sommelier wears around his neck."

"Does it have a function or is it simply meant for ornamentation?" asked I.

"I favor the latter," said my father.

"As do I," I ventured. "What say you, Joanna?"

"You are half-right." My wife winked at me playfully. "For, as a matter of fact, it serves two purposes."

"How so?"

"It is not actually a medallion, but a shallow silver cup used for wine tasting," Joanna described. "It is called a tastevin, which is the French term for 'taste wine.' But its gleaming silver not only catches the eye, it accentuates the color of the wines, particularly the reds, which makes them even more appetizing."

I found myself smiling at my dear Joanna, whose wits easily matched her beauty. "How in the world did you come by this information?"

"My guess would be that it was mentioned in a monograph on expensive wines which she acquired for our visit here," my father surmised.

Joanna shook her head. "I learned of it from a French murder case, in which the sommelier was strangled using the ribbon around his neck that held the tastevin."

For the hundredth time I had to remind myself that my wife seemed to have boundless knowledge on so many subjects, but only when it could be applied to a criminal activity. I would be willing to wager that not one detective in a thousand would know what a tastevin was.

The sommelier approached our table, wearing a large silver medallion that hung from a red ribbon around his neck. He was an obese man, with a protuberant abdomen upon which rested the tastevin. "How may I be of service, madam?"

"We have learned from a friend of ours, Dr. Maxwell Anderson, that you serve a most excellent Chardonnay."

The sommelier smiled, seemingly pleased with the selection. "Oh, yes. It was a fine Louis Latour."

"And the year?"

"A 1915. The best in recent memory."

"Did he always request a 1915?"

"Always, madam, for it is obviously a favorite of his."

"Did his companion enjoy it as well?"

"So it would seem, for they tasted more than a few glasses together."

Joanna nodded and lowered her voice. "I am delighted to hear that, for as you may know, Dr. Anderson is a confirmed bachelor and his family is concerned he will remain so. I would be more than happy to inform the family that the couple appeared quite affectionate and fond of one another."

The sommelier hesitated, clearly not willing to go into the

particular behavior of a highly valued patron. "That I cannot comment upon."

"Oh, but you can," Joanna said forthrightly.

"It is simply not possible, madam."

"Do you know who I am?" Joanna asked in a neutral, non-threatening tone.

"Yes, madam, but you are asking me to compromise my position."

"My questions are of no small matter and you must answer them honestly and completely, for not to do so may well make you become part of an official investigation."

The sommelier's face reddened. "I most certainly do not wish that."

"Then answer my questions to the best of your ability, with the assurances that every word you speak will be held in the highest confidence and not go beyond this table."

"Very well, madam," the sommelier spoke in a barely audible voice. "For I suspect you will learn of their quarrel from others."

"I take it all was not loving between the couple," Joanna assumed.

"There was a bit of a tiff on their last visit," the sommelier confided.

"Oh?"

The sommelier glanced around nervously, with his eyes coming to rest on the maître d', who seemed most interested in their conversation. The wine steward pasted a smile on his face and nodded at nothing. "Our talk is taking too long and I am drawing too much attention. Allow me to fetch the Louis Latour, and when I return I will slowly remove the cork and you shall slowly taste the Chardonnay. That will give me the time necessary to tell the details of the quarrel."

Once the sommelier departed, Joanna commented in a quiet voice, "It seems that all is not well in Camelot."

"Particularly when the stir occurs in public," I thought aloud. "Maxwell Anderson is usually a very calm, collected individual. It is difficult for me to envision him misbehaving in such a fashion."

"Perhaps the behavior was on Pretty Penny's part, and not his," suggested my father.

"I wonder what set off the lovers' quarrel," I pondered.

"More important, was it verbal or physical?" Joanna asked. "For if it was the latter on his part, we have a man who can be aroused to violence."

We abruptly stopped our quiet conversation as the sommelier returned to our table, carrying a bottle of wine with a bright yellow wrapping around its cork.

"A 1915 Louis Latour," he announced proudly, for the benefit of the tables closest to us. As he pierced the wrapping, he began his tale in a voice just above a whisper. "It was more of a shouting match than anything else. Their words were loud, but only became angry later on."

"Do you recall what was actually said?" Joanna whispered back.

"Not their complete sentences, madam, but phrases such as she demanding, 'You must tell them,' and he responding, 'The time is not appropriate.' I did not hear the subject of their conversation, but the word *family* kept recurring."

"Did they eventually quiet?" asked Joanna.

"No, madam. If anything, their voices grew louder, to the distraction of our other patrons," the sommelier answered. "I believe Simon, the maître d', was about to politely intervene when, in the heat of the argument, Dr. Anderson's hand tipped over a glass, with the wine spilling out and onto the lady's dress."

"Intentionally?" my wife asked at once.

"I could not tell."

"She must have been furious."

"Quite so," the sommelier went on, now slowly removing the cork from the wine bottle and carefully examining it. "She abruptly arose from the table and, rather than retire to the ladies' room, she stormed out of the restaurant, informing Dr. Maxwell to 'never bloody call me again, until you stand like a man.'"

"Did Dr. Maxwell follow her?" Joanna queried.

"He did, but only after apologizing profusely to the other patrons," the sommelier replied. "By the time he reached the street, the lady had departed in a taxi."

"Did he attempt to follow the taxi?"

"She had too much of a head start, according to the doorman." The sommelier filled our glasses, then stepped back and watched us sip and enjoy the most delicious Chardonnay. "That is the story to the best of my recollection."

"Thank you for your assistance," Joanna said, and waited for the sommelier to move away. When he was well out of earshot, she turned to us with a mischievous smile. "Well, my dear Watsons, what do you make of that?"

"A lovers' quarrel," I assumed.

"What of her demand that he must tell them?"

"She must be referring to his family and their relationship," said I.

"You would think they would eventually come to accept her," my father joined in. "After all, she is a very pretty and talented young woman who carries the trait of being instantly likable."

"You are dreaming, Watson," Joanna rebutted mildly. "Recall the disaster of the Winchester family from not long ago."

Our collective minds went back to the sad saga of the

Winchesters, a distinguished family whose lineage could be measured in centuries. Their eldest daughter fell in love with a Belgian musician of great promise. The family threatened to disown her unless she ended the relationship, which she did not. A very mysterious accident took the life of the young violinist, which gave the family some comfort. Unfortunately, it drove the daughter into a deep depression and she took her life in a well-publicized suicide.

"Make no mistake," Joanna interrupted our thoughts, "those people will do anything and everything to protect their precious family names."

My father's brow went up. "Are you suggesting that Maxwell's family knew of the relationship and arranged for Pretty Penny's disappearance?"

"Or perhaps Maxwell Anderson himself was responsible because of her threat to go to his family and disclose their affair," Joanna proposed.

"But why would she do such a thing?" my father countered. "It would only bring pressure on Maxwell to end the relationship."

"Perhaps she believed she could charm them, much like she charms everyone she meets."

The waiter approached and took our order of dover sole prepared with lemon, butter, and parsley, accompanied by side dishes of rice pilaf and sweet peppers. We waited for the sommelier to refill our glasses and depart before continuing our conversation on the motives behind the disappearance of Pretty Penny.

"Surely you are not serious about Maxwell Anderson being somehow involved," said I.

"I have not excluded him," Joanna responded.

"But it seems too farfetched."

"Not when you consider what is at stake," Joanna explained.

"Please remember that St. Bartholomew's is a distinguished medical center, with a sterling reputation. They will allow no one nor any event to place even the slightest blemish on its name."

"True enough," I agreed.

"Now, tell me what transpires when it becomes public knowledge that Maxwell Anderson is romantically involved with a common, amateur actress, who was once homeless in Whitechapel. With their marriage a distinct possibility, the family is enraged and threatens to disinherit him. The story is a scandal in the making, the type the newspapers love. The public would of course side with Pretty Penny, while the powerful aristocracy sees her as an adventuress seeking status and fortune. With all this in mind, tell me how well it would sit with those who control St. Bartholomew's."

"He would in all likelihood be dismissed," I concluded.

"So Maxwell Anderson has plenty at stake, and disclosure of the affair could harm his professional status irreparably."

"But the affair might not become public knowledge and thus no scandal would exist," I argued.

"Ha!" Joanna forced a laugh. "Word would surely leak out, if it hasn't already, for the aristocracy enjoys a good gossipy love story as much as anyone, if not more. In addition, Anderson was escorting Pretty Penny to the finest restaurants, where he was bound to be seen and recognized by others in his class."

"Particularly if one was present the night of the quarrel in the restaurant," my father interjected.

"Amen," Joanna said with a firm nod.

"Then Maxwell would have been wise to end the affair as soon as possible, assuming he had all this in mind," I opined.

"That is easy to say, but difficult to do when one is in love," said she.

"Nevertheless, I could never envision Maxwell Anderson

arranging the disappearance of Pretty Penny," I contended. "For to do so, he would have to be Jack the Ripper."

"Yes, he would," Joanna affirmed.

"That is absurd," I said too loudly.

"Perhaps not so absurd."

"I can give you more than a few reasons why it is so."

"Please do, and be good enough to list them one by one."

"First, he cannot be the stalker."

"Why not? Have you seen the stalker? Or has anyone for that matter?"

"But we do have a partial description of the individual who appeared at the sweet shop and in the jewelry store."

"In obvious disguise," Joanna countered. "Recall that Anderson is a fine actor whose talents depend on his ability to convert himself into a totally different person, with a change in voice, appearance, and behavior."

"But how do you account for the age difference between the original outings of Jack the Ripper and those now taking place? His initial killings took place twenty-eight years ago when Anderson was a mere toddler."

"He reads all the stories and events and autopsy reports which deal with The Ripper, much as I have," Joanna replied. "He is also a pathologist and that makes him an anatomist who is expert at dissection. Furthermore, he is a bachelor and does not have to account for his whereabouts late in the evening."

My father gave Joanna a lengthy, studied look before saying, "You do realize that you are once again giving us a perfect example of a Dr. Jekyll–Mr. Hyde personality."

"I am afraid, my dear Watson, that is precisely what we are up against."

"You of course are assuming that the fictional Dr. Jekyll–Mr. Hyde exists in the real world," said I.

"To some extent it exists in all of us," Joanna stated. "Which of the two arises depends on the circumstances. Think of the peace-loving farmer who goes off to war and kills or the adoring mother who one day decides to poison her children for the insurance money."

"So Maxwell Anderson could be a modern-day Ripper," I agreed reluctantly.

"I, too, must admit that is a possibility," my father concurred.

Joanna gave the two of us an affirming nod before saying, "Then we are on the same page, for we are following one of my father's most important dictums. Namely, that when you have excluded the impossible, whatever remains behind, no matter how improbable, must be the truth."

Moments later we were served and enjoyed a deliciously prepared dover sole, which we washed down with a superb Chardonnay, but all the while I kept glancing at the secluded corner where Maxwell Anderson and Pretty Penny had sat, and wondering what role he might have played in her disappearance.

Chapter 11

The Gentleman Drifters

My father and I were firmly opposed to Joanna's plan, but she prevailed by convincing us it represented our very best chance to bring this monstrous case to resolution. The plan itself was simple enough, but not without danger. Joanna and I would be in deep disguise when entering the Black Lamb, while my father was stationed in a carriage a half a block away, with his

Webley No. 2 revolver in hand. Our intent was to find and save Annie Yates, whom we would later use as bait to catch Jack the Ripper before he could kill again.

Looking into the mirror of our dressing room at 221b Baker Street, I was struck by the remarkable transformation we had undergone. Joanna was disguised as an Unfortunate, with tattered, soiled clothing and unshined walking boots. Her dark blond hair was now covered by an unkempt brown wig that showed patches of gray. She had used red lipstick to give her face a stern, yet appealing, expression. I, on the other hand, was dressed in a tweed suit and a finely woven wool cap which gave me a professional look. That was the impression I wished to show, for I was to be introduced, if necessary, as a lecturer in anatomy at a nearby college. My wig was heavily grayed, as were my thick mustache and pointed goatee. My father wore a constable's uniform, complete with hat, for even in Whitechapel the sight of an approaching policeman elicited instant fear and immediate withdrawal.

On our way out we tested the keen eye of Miss Hudson, who was taken aback by our unrecognized appearance. When told our disguises were for a hospital costume party, she smiled and shook her head good-naturedly and wished us a most happy time. It was of course the exact opposite of what we expected to encounter.

A rented four-wheeler awaited us, for we felt it would fit best in the neighborhood surrounding the Black Lamb. It would also be the most likely mode of transportation used by the gentleman drifters who wished to visit the various downscale drinking establishments. There was a definite pecking order amongst the pubs, even in Whitechapel, where Emma Adams's Prince Albert would be at the higher end, while the Black Lamb was at the lowest. It was in the latter that the guests would speak with the heaviest cockney accent.

"Now, my dear John," Joanna was instructing, "do not attempt to blend in with their dialect, for the working class will quickly see you as being an outsider, pretending to be one of them. Simply speak as a lecturer of anatomy would and they will accept you as such."

"I hope I do not have to utter a single word," I said candidly.

"That may be the case," Joanna said, intentionally smearing her lipstick at the edges. "But if they learn you teach anatomy, someone might inquire about the position of a body part or the like. It is a mistake to believe that a lack of education denotes a lack of curiosity."

After giving those instructions, Joanna returned to rehearsing a cockney accent, which she did to near perfection. She adeptly dropped the letter *h* from the beginning of words with ease. *Horse* became *'orse* and *have* sounded like *'ave*. Next, she practiced removing the letters *t* and *k* from the middle of words. *Scottish* translated to *Sco'ish* and *blackboard* became *blac'board*. I was confident we would fit in nicely, but my father still had reservations.

"The working-class pubs can be quite mean," he warned. "Ruffians heavy into drink can actually seek out fights with those they consider outsiders. I have witnessed Joanna's skill at jujitsu and I know of John's experience as a boxer at Oxford, but an all-out brawl is totally different than a one-on-one match. Thus, I would suggest you position yourself near the exit, for a quick departure is at times the best defense."

Our carriage drew up a half a block down and on the opposite side of the street from the Black Lamb. The light on the overhead lamppost was dim, which was perfect concealment for the passengers within our four-wheeler. Although my father would be the only occupant, the very last thing we wanted was for a passerby to glance in and see an individual dressed in a constable's uniform. As I opened the door for us to exit, Joanna made certain the police whistle around her neck was well hidden, while my father checked the rounds in his Webley revolver.

Joanna and I crossed the street arm in arm and entered the Black Lamb. The noisy pub was larger than I anticipated, with a long wooden bar and a row of occupied stools pushed up against it. Behind the bar were impressive mirrors that contained advertisements, the foremost of which was for Guinness. Most of the crowd was standing about in the center area, drinks in hand and conversing loudly. The room was clouded with tobacco smoke which hung in the air and gave off a stale aroma. On the far side, a rough-appearing man was throwing darts at a board and cursing his bad luck.

We found two seats at the end of the bar where we received quick glances but little else. A bearded barkeep hurried over attracted by my affluent attire and wiped his massive hands on a dirty bar towel. He was heavyset and broad shouldered, with scarred brows from countless fights.

"What'll you have?" he asked.

"'Arf-and-'arf," Joanna said, her cockney accent spot-on as she requested a half-and-half, which was a mixture of two beers, one of which was of lesser density than the other.

"If you want the Guinness, it will be pricier."

"Bring it, dearie."

While waiting for our drinks, we surveyed the people crowded into the bar, with even more coming in through the entrance. Most were from the working class, but under a bulb-like light we spotted a few gentleman drifters who were surrounded by Unfortunates offering their services. The gentlemen made no effort to hide their identities. A shoving match broke out near the dartboard but was quickly resolved by a barmaid who pushed them apart with a warning.

The barkeep deposited our half-and-halfs on the bar and said, "That'll be tenpence."

As I was paying, a rather attractive Unfortunate, with long dark hair, approached and, after giving me a careful eye, asked, "Are you taken, ducky?"

"Move on," Joanna threatened, "before I shove your arse along."

"Just inquiring," the Unfortunate said with a shrug. "Pickings are quite slim tonight."

Joanna gestured to the gentleman drifters. "What about those?"

"They are in the midst of bargaining," the Unfortunate said in a disapproving tone. "Here they are, gentlemen of some stature, trying to obtain the lowest price."

"I think the blighters take some pleasure in that," my wife remarked.

The Unfortunate nodded in agreement. "They ride up in their fancy carriages to pee down on the poor and have a jolly good time before returning to their respectable homes."

"Maybe one will take a coppery rash back to Mayfair," Joanna jested.

The prostitute smiled and revealed a nearly toothless mouth. "Now wouldn't that be a delightful present to bring home?"

I chuckled humorlessly at the term *coppery rash,* which described the dermatitis that often accompanied the dreaded disease syphilis. There was no cure for the contagious disorder and its end result was often horrific and lethal.

The door opened and a boisterous group of older men entered and immediately shouted their order to the barmaid who relayed the drink requests to the barkeep. Scratching at her armpit, the Unfortunate studied the newcomers briefly before declaring, "They are locals who wouldn't buy you a round unless their life depended on it."

"Not worth rubbing against," Joanna noted.

"It is going to be a slow night," the Unfortunate predicted unhappily.

"Well, according to my friend Annie Yates, activity picks up during the later hours," Joanna said, and sipped her beer.

"You know Annie, do you?" the Unfortunate asked.

"We are friends, but I haven't seen much of her since her illness worsened."

"It is a terrible cough she has and it never seems to stop. I don't know how she continues to work."

"She looked quite ill when I saw her last at a doss-house across from the Jewish cemetery," Joanna mentioned. "She appeared to be wasting away to skin and bones."

"Annie wasn't always that way, you know," the Unfortunate said. "Back in Bristol she was the picture of health while working as a lady's maid at a grand estate. But then she came down with a terrible cough which brought about her dismissal and forced her onto the streets without a roof over her head. That is when we both moved to Whitechapel, hoping for a better life."

"Did you, too, work at the estate?"

The Unfortunate nodded. "As a poorly paid seamstress. I had no future there, and not much of one here, either."

"Perhaps a drink will lift your spirits," Joanna said, wanting to ply as much information as possible from the prostitute.

"I would dearly love three halfpenny worth of rum, if you're offering."

The barkeep was waved over and served up the rum drink which the Unfortunate swallowed in a single gulp. She then stared at the empty glass and licked her lips hungrily, which prompted me to buy yet another round of rum, for she was our best and only clue to the whereabouts of Annie Yates.

"I am concerned about Annie and her illness," Joanna probed gently. "I have heard of a free clinic at St. Bartholomew's, which looks after the poor. Perhaps Annie might enroll there."

"It is one thing to enroll and quite another to actually be admitted," the Unfortunate informed us. "I know some girls who have been on the list for a year or more."

"But certainly someone as ill as Annie would merit more consideration."

"That is wishful thinking, dearie." The prostitute licked at her empty glass and gave Joanna a most suspicious look. "You seem overly interested in Annie. Is it only because of her illness?"

Joanna shook her head. "She had done me a favor and I wanted to return it."

"What kind of favor do you have for her?"

"I have learned of a new pub where the pickings are quite good."

"Where?"

"I will tell Annie, and if she wishes to share the information with you that will be her business."

"I will tell Annie you are looking for her."

The door to the Black Lamb opened and two more gentleman drifters entered, as evidenced by their top hats and frock coats, which could only be seen in profile. Upon noticing them, the Unfortunate licked her lips and hurried over to the prospective customers. They tipped their hats to her in a most cordial manner and beckoned the barkeep.

Joanna turned away in haste and brought her half-and-half up to her face to cover it. "Look away from the door, John," she urged, "and sip your beer while studying the mirror behind the bar."

I did as instructed and saw my reflection just below the red advertisement for Guinness. Studying it carefully, I saw nothing of undue interest. "Is there something I am overlooking?"

"Did you observe the two gentleman drifters who just arrived?"

"I saw their top hats which were being tipped."

"Now glance over to them as you sip your beer and tell me what you see."

My eyes must have widened at the unbelievable sight I was viewing. Standing in the midst of a flock of Unfortunates were Peter Willoughby and Thaddeus Rudd, attired in top hats and frock coats and obviously delighted to be showing their affluence. "Never in a million years" were the only words I could utter.

"We must leave," Joanna said in a whisper. "Although we are in disguise, their sharp eyes might recognize our telling features. I will depart first; you follow shortly after."

I watched Joanna keep her head down and mingle into the crowd, seeming to disappear. While waiting and despite my best efforts, I could not help but stare at the two physicians, for whom I had lost all respect. I immediately began to connect the two scoundrels to the two prostitutes who had been allowed entrance to the free clinic at St. Bartholomew's. A few moments later I, too, keeping my head down, walked out of the Black Lamb to join Joanna on the deserted street. We remained silent as we hurried to the four-wheeler where my father awaited us.

"Thank goodness you are safe," he said, putting his Webley revolver to rest. "Was your visit productive?"

"We are about to tell you a story which your ears will refuse to believe," Joanna replied, as our carriage rode away.

"I am afraid that I have been around too long to be surprised," my father said frankly. "It happens to the elderly."

"Well then, prepare yourself for a sudden awakening," Joanna went on. "You are no doubt aware of the term *gentleman drifters*."

"I am."

"Your son and I just saw two."

"That is not a rarity in this area."

"It is when their names are Peter Willoughby and Thaddeus Rudd."

My father's jaw dropped in astonishment. "Are—are you certain?" he stammered.

"Beyond question."

My father quickly regained his composure and wrinkled his brow in thought. "So they, too, are now part of the mix."

Joanna nodded at the obvious conclusion. "Recall last evening at Alexander's when I listed the reasons why Maxwell Anderson could not be excluded as Jack the Ripper. These two are also quite good actors who, like a chameleon, can transform themselves into a totally different individual, with a change of appearance, voice, and behavior. Moreover, they are skilled anatomists—Willoughby being a renowned pathologist and Rudd a skilled surgeon—which makes them experts at dissection. Finally, and unlike Anderson, their ages are such they could be the original Jack the Ripper."

"They fit so perfectly the Dr. Jekyll so aptly described by Robert Louis Stevenson," I remarked.

"And so the plot thickens," my father noted.

"As does the list of bona fide suspects," Joanna said, and stared out at the dense fog descending onto the dark streets of Whitechapel.

Chapter 12

Annie Yates

As a rule, early-morning phone messages bring dreadful news, and this day was no exception. Inspector Lestrade called to inform us that the body of Annie Yates had been discovered in a dark passageway just off Mitre Square. He advised us to omit breakfast before reaching the crime scene, for it was a view one did not wish to experience on a full stomach. So, after dressing and sipping only a hot cup of tea, we hailed a four-wheeler and hurried to the dour streets of Whitechapel.

We could not help but feel a pang of sadness for the pleasant girl whose once happy life had taken such a terrible, downward spiral. Bad luck and even worse circumstances had brought her to the crime-infested area surrounding Mitre Square where she now lay dead, no doubt gutted like a fish. And what remained of her would be buried in an unmarked grave in a potter's field, with no one present to mourn for her. It was the worst of all endings.

On our arrival we noted that a small crowd had already formed across the square and was being kept at a distance by a uniformed constable. Lestrade greeted us with a tip of his derby and moved aside to reveal a corpse covered with a gray blanket. There was a faint, somewhat unpleasant aroma in the air which seemed familiar, but I could not place it.

"We have another savage murder," Lestrade reported. "But on this occasion, we have an eyewitness."

He gestured to a thin, hollow-cheeked woman, of undetermined age, who was bundled up in an oversized coat and shivering against the chilly morning air. She hesitantly stepped forward, but Lestrade held up a hand. "In a moment," he instructed before giving us the details of Annie Yates's encounter with Jack the Ripper, which began innocently enough.

Annie Yates and her friend Sally Hawkins were walking the streets in a pair for safety's sake at just after ten last evening. A man called out from across the square, saying, "I want you again, Annie!" He obviously knew her from a prior encounter, but did not mention his name. The prospective customer came out of the dark, walking with a terrible limp, but was not using crutches or cane. The light was poor, so it was difficult to make out his face.

"Are we to conclude that the eyewitness saw none of the man's facial features?" Joanna interrupted.

"She was quite clear on this point," Lestrade replied. "But if you wish, I have no objection to you questioning her."

"Have her come forward," Joanna requested.

Lestrade motioned to the still-shivering Unfortunate who haltingly came over, with her head down in a position of submission. "This lady is the daughter of Sherlock Holmes," he introduced. "She is an associate of Scotland Yard and you will answer her questions as if I were the one asking."

"Yes, sir," Sally Hawkins said meekly.

"I want you to think back to when the man first stepped out of the shadows," Joanna began. "What was your initial impression?"

"That he was old," Sally answered at once.

"Why was that?"

"Because he had such trouble walking."

"Did that cause Annie concern?"

"No, ma'am. I asked Annie if he was a cripple and she said no, because there was no limp when she met him before."

"When they walked away together, did he continue to limp?"

Sally thought back for a moment. "I did not notice it, but then he had his hand around her waist."

I nodded to myself, for a genuine limp would have persisted despite the support. A limp that comes and goes in a matter of minutes was a fake one that was put on for show. The killer was not disabled in the least.

"Surely you must have glanced at his face," Joanna went on.

"I did, ma'am, but the light was not good and he was wearing a fisherman's hat pulled down over his forehead."

"Did you see his lips?"

"I am not sure, for things happened so quickly."

"Think back," Joanna urged. "I am interested in his lips and whether you could see teeth behind them."

Sally shook her head. "I cannot remember it. But there was something about one of his cheeks that struck me as odd. When he turned to escort Annie down the passageway, what little light there was seemed to reflect off his cheek."

"Are you saying it glowed?" Joanna queried.

"No, ma'am. It only seemed so smooth."

"Were there lines or wrinkles?"

The Unfortunate shook her head again. "Smooth as stone."

"As they entered the passageway, did the man use any force?" Joanna asked.

"No, ma'am. She was quite comfortable with him, almost like they were friends. You see, he had given her a gift in their last meeting, which Annie had mentioned."

"Are you referring to the copper earrings?"

"Yes, ma'am."

"So you could see nothing amiss?"

"Nothing at all. Once they entered the passageway, there were no calls for help or shouts of distress." Sally hesitated as she thought back. "I did hear the sound of glass breaking in the darkness, but did not make much of it. Perhaps he had dropped a bottle of spirits, for some customers need a nip or two before transacting their business. In any event, I continued on my way unconcerned."

"Very good," Joanna said, and signaled to Lestrade that her questioning was done.

After Sally Hawkins departed, Lestrade said, "Not much to go on, is there?"

"Not much," Joanna agreed.

"But the smoothness of the killer's face is somewhat confusing," the inspector remarked. "It denotes a young man, which does not fit well with our contention that we are dealing with the return of an older Jack the Ripper."

"Unless he is wearing a mask which would be quite smooth."

"A disguise!" Lestrade said too loudly, which drew the attention of a constable standing by the covered corpse. "That would explain it."

"It would, but it brings us no closer to resolution."

"Unhappily so."

Joanna pointed to the concealed body and said, "Now I think it would be appropriate for us to view the remains of Annie Yates."

"Prepare yourself," Lestrade warned.

But no amount of preparation could ward off the revulsion we experienced when the blanket was lifted from the corpse. Annie's face had been defleshed. Vertical incisions penetrated deeply into her forehead and cheeks, with the skin and muscles peeled back to reveal white facial bones. Even her lips had been sliced and spread apart down to the gums. The only recognizable feature of Annie Yates was her neatly parted blond hair. Her abdomen was split wide open, her greenish-tan intestines dangling out. The monster had even cut off her breasts.

"My God," my father murmured. "This is beyond barbaric."

"Let us hope she wasn't awake for any of this," I said softly.

Joanna pointed to the corpse's neck, which was lacerated down to the cervical spine. Both carotid arteries were completely severed, with their spurts of blood covering a nearby wall. "If she was alert, it was only for a very short time. Such massive exsanguination can bring death in under a minute."

Joanna appeared to be unmoved by the grotesque sight as she went about the business of examining the corpse and crime scene. Nevertheless, I noticed my wife wince on occasion and stepped in closer to her in the event she faltered, for the scene was that gruesome and unsettling. Even I, as an experienced pathologist, found it difficult to view such despicable mutilation. Perhaps our feelings were influenced by the fact that we had known this pitiful, yet likable, Unfortunate.

My wife was now carefully examining the corpse's head, for some feature there had drawn her attention. "She is missing an earring."

Lestrade leaned down for a closer look, then said with a shrug, "Perhaps she was wearing only one."

"No, Inspector," Joanna refuted the notion. "Not the hardest-pressed woman, regardless of her station in life, would ever wear a single earring in public, for it would show a lack of taste and true poverty, which no female would wish to exhibit."

"But then, why would she have on only a single earring?"

"Two explanations come to mind," Joanna replied. "Either it became loose and she lost it, or someone took it."

Lestrade considered the possibilities before saying, "But why take one rather than both as any worthwhile thief would do?"

"You raise a good point," Joanna said, with a thin smile.

"Then, it is most likely she lost it."

"Perhaps, but I think it a good idea to have your constables search the area for the missing earring."

"Is it that important?"

"It very well could be."

A puzzled look crossed the inspector's face, but his expression suddenly brightened as the answer came. "Ah, yes! The killer may have ripped it off and later discarded it, leaving us his fingerprints."

"Excellent, Lestrade," Joanna commended, and turned to me. "When the body is prepared for autopsy, please have all of her clothing sent to Maxwell Anderson's laboratory for a most careful examination, for the earring may have slipped off or be in one of her pockets. Also search her abdominal cavity in the event it somehow found its way in through the wide incision."

"Are you certain you wish the examination to be done in the histopathology laboratory by Maxwell Anderson?" I asked, recalling that Anderson was now considered a prime suspect.

"I am quite certain, for the lighting there is of the best quality," she said, with a subtle wink. "Of course we shall accompany the garments to his laboratory."

And of course we shall observe Anderson's reaction should a major clue be found, I thought, and returned my wife's subtle wink.

Using her foot, Joanna was now moving the shattered glass next to the corpse over a wider area. Most of the pieces were smashed with sliver-like splinters, but a few were goodly sized and could be measured in inches. It was the largest piece which she picked up with small tweezers and examined under the magnifying glass. "I see fingerprints."

"Are they complete prints?" I asked at once.

"It is difficult to tell until they are dusted and reexamined."

"Do you believe he tried to fetch the broken pieces?" my father queried.

"That is unlikely, Watson, for they would serve no purpose," Joanna responded. "Moreover, he would have difficulty seeing them in the darkness. I suspect these fingerprints were placed on the bottle while it was still intact."

"But you must also consider the possibility that the bottle did not belong to the killer," Lestrade proposed. "Perhaps he kicked over an old bottle in the dim light."

"You raise an excellent point, Inspector, except for one factor," Joanna said, and held a piece of broken glass under my nose. "What do you detect, John?"

"The smell of formaldehyde," I realized quickly. "He brought along a bottle of formaldehyde to preserve the organs he removed."

My wife nodded as she wrapped the larger pieces of glass in tissue without touching them. "This bottle belonged to Jack the Ripper and so do these fingerprints."

"How can you be so certain the prints were made by Jack the Ripper?" Lestrade questioned. "Perhaps a passerby picked it up and, noticing its odor, discarded it."

"The pattern of broken glass on the ground says otherwise," Joanna elucidated. "When a glass bottle is accidentally dropped from a height of three feet or so, it breaks into relatively large pieces. That was not the case here. The vast majority of the shattered pieces were small slivers, many of which were ground into the passageway. It is quite obvious that here is the work of a man intent on destroying evidence. In the dimness, The Ripper must have overlooked the large piece which held his fingerprint."

"Outstanding," Lestrade approved. "We shall have Henry Overstreet give them a most careful look."

"Would it be possible for you and Overstreet to come to Anderson's laboratory?" Joanna requested. "That would be doubly important if we discover the missing earring in the corpse's garments."

"I see no problem with the initial examination being done there, but I must insist that the specimens be further studied and housed at Scotland Yard."

"Then we are agreed," Joanna said, and deposited the wrapped pieces of glass into her purse.

Lestrade glanced down at the scattered glass next to the corpse and remarked, "It seems our Ripper is becoming a bit careless and may have left an identifiable fingerprint behind."

"So it would appear," Joanna said, following his gaze. "Please have Overstreet study the piece of glass at his earliest convenience, for it may contain the best clue we have thus far."

"So I shall," said the inspector, and looked at his timepiece. "Well then, I will detain you no further and hope to rejoin you at St. Bartholomew's before noon."

As our four-wheeler rode away, I noticed the crowd gathered on the opposite side of the square had increased greatly in size, now lined up three deep, with newspaper reporters at the front and calling out to us. Accounts of Jack the Ripper were currently in the headlines of all London's newspapers, with the public eagerly awaiting his next horrific outing to occur. A photograph of a mutilated corpse would fetch a hundred pounds or more, which reminded me to alert Benson to be on the lookout for any trespassers to the pathology section at St. Bart's.

I brought my mind back to the investigation and commented to Joanna, "The inspector seems to be following the correct avenue in this case, do you not agree?"

Joanna nodded as she searched for a Turkish cigarette and carefully lighted it. "At times Lestrade can be quite a good detective, but then he spoils that impression by overlooking important clues which were obvious and placed directly in front of his eyes."

"Pray tell what did he fail to notice?" I asked, leaning forward for the answer, as did my father.

"Three clues, which give us important information on Jack the Ripper," Joanna replied, and held up three fingers to count them off. "First, what did you make of the broken glass bottle? In particular, please estimate its size."

I shrugged. "It was not small."

"A quart, perhaps?"

"I would think so."

"So we have a quart bottle filled with formaldehyde," she went on. "With this in mind, tell me what excised organs would fit into such a bottle?"

"A uterus, ovaries, and two Fallopian tubes, and not much more."

"Then why cut off her breasts?"

"In a maniacal frenzy, I would guess."

"Or deliberately so, simply to disfigure her," my father advanced.

"Excellent, Watson, for I believe it is the latter," said Joanna. "The uterus and ovaries were to be mementos, while the breasts were sending us a message. He is telling us and Scotland Yard that he is doing whatever he wishes and whenever he wishes, and that the mastectomies were just a bit of added pleasure."

"What makes you so certain that this is not all maniacal in nature?" I asked.

"Because he makes it his business to methodically remove each and every clue," said she. "This is a man who crosses his *t*'s and dots his *i*'s."

"Are you saying he can turn his maniacal behavior off and on?" I queried.

"That is the second part of his message to us. He is telling us he will never be caught, for he is far too clever."

"Another taunt," my father commented.

Joanna took a final puff on her cigarette and flicked it out the window. "He is very good at that."

"What was the second clue Lestrade and the Watsons overlooked?" I asked.

"The missing copper earring," she replied. "The Ripper may have intentionally taken it to give to another victim."

"But even an Unfortunate would look with disdain at a gift consisting of a single earring," I argued.

"Not if it is given after she is dead and mutilated beyond recognition," Joanna countered.

"Evil personified," I muttered.

"To the nth degree," my father agreed before turning to Joanna. "And the third clue we missed?"

"The prostitute's description of The Ripper's cheek," said she. "The woman recalled that it was smooth, without lines or wrinkles."

"But the possibility that he was wearing a mask has already been raised," my father noted.

"But what if it wasn't a mask?" Joanna asked.

"Then what else could it be?"

"Allow me to draw your attention to the fact that our three main suspects are talented actors," she prompted.

My father's brow went up. "You can produce a smooth face with makeup."

Joanna nodded. "Actors use it all the time, for it not only

smooths the skin but gives it a bit of a glow under bright stage lights."

"Greasepaint," my father recollected the name of the theatrical makeup.

"Which stage actors would have easy access to," I added.

A mischievous smile crossed my wife's face as our carriage approached St. Bartholomew's. "Everything seems to point to the Whitechapel Playhouse, doesn't it?"

"But which of the three suspects is Jack the Ripper?" I asked.

"The cleverest of the bunch," Joanna said, and left it at that.

Chapter 13

The Main Suspects

The bright lights in the autopsy room only exaggerated the gruesome mutilation of Annie Yates. Even on gross inspection I could determine that the attack on the Unfortunate had been more vicious than originally believed. There was, in addition to the previously described wounds, a huge abdominal incision that extended down to her genital area which had been neatly dissected out. It, too, could fit in a quart-sized bottle of formaldehyde, but I saw no need to comment on that hideous feature, for it would serve no purpose.

As per my usual protocol, I began the autopsy at the corpse's head and neck, which were covered with dried blood. After a thorough washing, I could better view the damage done to the victim's cervical spine.

"Like in the others, he attempted to decapitate her," I

noted. "There are gouges in the intervertebral cartilage that indicate he tried to do so."

"Why the emphasis on decapitation?" my father asked.

"I would surmise that he wished to dehumanize the victim," I replied. "A headless corpse has no face and thus no identity to who he or she was. It is a cruel act done with a most cruel purpose.

"Both carotid arteries were severed, so she no doubt bled to death," I went on. "It required a minute or two for her to exsanguinate, during which time she was aware of what was transpiring."

"The perverted killer probably took great pleasure in watching her blood spurt onto the nearby wall," my father envisioned.

"To him it would be an opening act, like the curtain going up." I continued with the autopsy, which showed that her heart was normal, while her lungs were not. They exhibited chronic inflammation and pulmonary lymphadenopathy, all characteristic of extensive tuberculosis. But it was her abdominal cavity which provided the most surprising finding. Both excised breasts were stuffed in between the liver and stomach. I held them up for the others to see.

"His perversion deepens," my father stated. "But why excise the breasts only to return them to the body?"

"I suspect because it is the most drastic female disfiguration one can imagine," Joanna answered. "To savagely remove a woman's breasts is one matter, but to jam them into a distant cavity is quite another. He was obviously intent on destroying every feminine feature Annie Yates possessed."

I pointed to the genital area which had been carefully denuded. "He is remarkably good at it."

"And exceedingly practiced," she added, then requested, "Please reexamine the thoracic and abdominal cavities to determine if The Ripper deposited the copper earring there as well."

A careful search was unproductive and only revealed that Annie Yates's tuberculosis had spread far beyond her lungs, with massive involvement of the liver, spleen, and pericardium, which was obvious to the others as well. "Death was truly at the doorstep of this poor Unfortunate."

On that note I completed the autopsy, having discovered no further clues or abnormal findings. Leaving my rubber gloves on, I retrieved the stack of the Unfortunate's garments from a nearby table and led the way out. At the door to Anderson's laboratory I encountered Benson, whom I instructed to immediately remove Annie Yates's remains to the morgue, where they would be secure from intruders.

On entering the laboratory, we were surprised to find the three main suspects who were discussing the missing surgical specimen which had now been located.

"I covered for you yesterday," Rudd was saying to Anderson, "by telling the family that the specimen required further study and review by experts to determine if a cancer was present."

"That was most kind of you," Anderson said gratefully.

"Do not allow it to happen again," Rudd warned in a gruff voice.

"Extra precautions have been put into place to ensure it doesn't," said Willoughby, and turned to us, with a sour expression on his face. "You will have to wait, for we are in the midst of a most important study."

"So are we," Joanna responded, "as the soon arrival of Scotland Yard will indicate. I am afraid that Jack the Ripper has struck again."

The three physicians gave appropriate reactions to the dreadful news. Rudd growled in displeasure, while Anderson and Willoughby shook their heads soulfully. Their suitable expressions were not unexpected, even if guilty, for each of the three was a talented actor who could conceal his true feelings.

"This madness has to be brought to an end," Willoughby demanded.

I was struck by the director's appearance, for he was wearing a white laboratory coat which seemed far too large for his frame. But then I realized the coat belonged to him, for it had his name embroidered above a chest pocket. Willoughby had obviously lost weight and this was becoming more and more noticeable. He was known to be suffering with severe peptic ulcer disease and had recently been hospitalized because of it.

"Let us hope it was not Pretty Penny," Anderson broke the silence on a hopeful note.

"It was not," Joanna assured. "The victim was another Unfortunate named Annie Yates."

There was no detectable reaction from the three.

"Who was brutally mutilated," my wife went on. "Her face was defleshed to such an extent she was unrecognizable."

"How then was she identified?" asked Anderson.

"There was an eyewitness," Joanna reported.

Almost in unison the three physicians raised their eyebrows, but it was Rudd who spoke. "Was she able to give an accurate description?"

"Only a partial one, but Scotland Yard believes it could be helpful." Joanna glanced over to me with a thin smile, which I returned, for Thaddeus Rudd had just made a revealing mistake. My wife had not mentioned the gender of the eyewitness, but Rudd correctly called her *she*. How could he have known that without being present? Of course it was common knowledge that prostitutes often walked the streets in pairs for safety, but still . . .

"A partial description is better than none at all," Willoughby commented. "Although such descriptions rarely hold up at official inquiries."

"There are other clues in this regard," Joanna lied easily. "And we expect to learn more when we examine the victim's garments."

"May we participate in the latter?" Willoughby requested.

"Your participation would be welcome, for I suspect you have considerable experience in the examination of clothing from murder victims."

"I do, indeed," said Willoughby, obviously pleased with the acknowledgment. "Allow us a moment to complete our study on Dr. Rudd's surgical specimen."

"Of course."

As the two pathologists returned to their Zeiss microscope, Joanna sorted through Annie Yates's garments, paying particular attention to the victim's shoes. Using a damp cloth, Joanna dusted off the dirt and dried blood from the boots, which unexpectedly had silver buckles on their tops. With care she placed the feminine boots on a workbench and covered them with other garments.

"I say no cancer," Willoughby announced, rising up from the microscope.

"I agree," Anderson concurred. "The findings are consistent with a walled-off abscess that shows intense inflammation."

"Excellent," said Rudd, obviously pleased that the lesion was benign. "The family will be delighted with the report."

"Let us then proceed to the victim's garments," Willoughby directed, and walked over to us, with Anderson and Rudd at his side. "Should we not wait for Scotland Yard?"

"There is no need, for I have been authorized to conduct the search by Inspector Lestrade," said Joanna. "I am in favor of the following plan, which I believe will work to everyone's satisfaction. On holding up the garment for inspection, I will comment on my findings before passing it on to you and Dr. Anderson for your assessment. No notes or recordings are to be made unless instructed to do so by Scotland Yard."

I kept my expression even, although I was amazed at Joanna's decision to include Willoughby and Anderson in the examination of Annie Yates's garments, for my wife's ability to detect and decipher even the smallest clue was a hundredfold superior to that of the two pathologists combined. But I had learned long ago that there was a purpose to even the oddest of Joanna's plans.

"Let us begin with her gloves," she was saying as she held up a pair to the light. "They are old and ragged, but intact, which is unfortunate, for they would have prevented the victim from digging her fingernails into her attacker's face and arms. This would have left some of the attacker's skin and blood under her nails, which would show up as defensive wounds on The Ripper."

Joanna passed the gloves to Willoughby and Anderson, who gave them a cursory look before nodding their agreement with her assessment.

"Next, we come to the scarf, heavy coat, sweater, and petticoat that are soaked through and through with dried blood," she continued on, carefully examining each garment. "The amount of blood loss is consistent with both carotid arteries being severed, which no doubt resulted in exsanguination."

The pathologists again nodded at Joanna's description, but did not reach out for the items she offered to them.

Annie Yates's dress was likewise drenched with old blood, but Joanna still bothered to examine it at length, top to bottom. She abruptly stopped at the hem as she palpated a small object that was sewn securely within and hidden from sight. "A blade, please," she requested, and was handed a scalpel which she used to remove the stitching from the hem. Deep inside was a male wedding band. With her magnifying glass, Joanna read the inscription, "'Love, AY.'"

"No doubt from her marriage to the estate carriage driver," my father recalled.

"Which ended so tragically," I added.

Anderson asked quizzically, "How did you come by this information?"

"The eyewitness informed us," I replied.

"Did the witness say when this supposed marriage ended?" Anderson queried, raising the possibility that the ring was stolen.

"Some years ago," I answered.

"Yet she still holds on to it so dearly," Anderson wondered. "Is it not strange she continues to do so?"

"Sometimes it is difficult to let go." A look of melancholy came and went from Joanna's face as she no doubt thought back to her former husband who died young of cholera. Shaking her head at the memory, she exhibited the prostitute's stockings for the group to examine. She sniffed at them briefly and said, "They have an aroma which I believe will be familiar to you."

Willoughby whiffed at the stockings, holding them at arm's length before commenting, "They carry the smell of formaldehyde."

Anderson nodded on detecting the same aroma. "That is how The Ripper preserves the organs he carries away."

"Absolute madness," Rudd blurted out. "This terror has to be put to a stop."

"I can assure you Scotland Yard is doing all in their power to apprehend this barbarian," Joanna said. "You might be interested to know they are simultaneously working day and night to find the missing Pretty Penny, for they believe the two are connected."

Anderson's jaw dropped. "Then they must think her dead."

"Or being held captive," Joanna suggested.

"To what end?" Anderson asked anxiously.

"To kill her when it best suits him," she replied.

"A murderous maniac who remains on the loose and does as he pleases," Rudd growled. "He is making Scotland Yard look like a bunch of idiots."

"Much as he did twenty-eight years ago," Joanna reminded. "He was very clever then, as he is now. But eventually he will make a mistake."

"I don't think that gives the public any comfort," Willoughby noted. "That is particularly so when the gruesome details appear daily in the newspapers. It makes all involved seem so helpless."

"Sadly so," said Joanna, and reached for the Unfortunate's boots, which she grasped by their heels. "These shoes are of great interest, for they are far too good and costly to be found on the feet of a prostitute. They are constructed from fine leather which has held up well, and their silver buckles speak of high quality."

"Where would a common prostitute obtain such shoes?" Willoughby asked the obvious question.

"Perhaps they were a gift," Anderson advanced.

Willoughby waved away the idea. "An Unfortunate who plies her trade for a mere shilling or two would never be given such an expensive gift."

Joanna and I exchanged quick glances, thinking that of course the distinguished pathologist would be aware of the price a prostitute charged for her services. He was a known gentleman drifter.

"Perhaps they are fake," Willoughby said at length. "They may only be cheaply made replicas."

"A worthwhile thought," Joanna lauded, and attempted to

examine the insides of the tall boots with her magnifying glass. "I cannot obtain a clear view and unfortunately I have left my reading glasses at home. Perhaps you can see the inside label better than I." She handed one boot to Willoughby and the other to Anderson before prompting, "I believe the manufacturer's name begins with a *T*."

The two pathologists carefully examined the inner sides and soles of the boots, while I was left wondering why Joanna was lying about her vision. She had excellent sight and never wore glasses for reading.

Rudd yawned rudely without covering his mouth, obviously bored by the discussion of the Unfortunate's boots. It was then that I noticed one of his incisors was missing. How clever Joanna was! She had no doubt observed this dental finding during her earlier encounter with Thaddeus Rudd, and it was for this reason she wondered whether Sally Hawkins had seen Jack the Ripper's lips and teeth. Unfortunately, she had not, for had she it would have revealed a telltale sign.

"Travistock," Willoughby and Anderson announced the brand name on the innersoles simultaneously.

"Ah, yes," Joanna noted. "They make the finest boots."

"So they are not fakes," my father said.

"They are most likely genuine, which is also evidenced by the high quality of their leather," my wife remarked. "This will all be mentioned to Scotland Yard, who can perhaps trace the origin of the boots, which might prove helpful."

"How could that possibly help?" Willoughby asked.

"I am not certain," Joanna said. "But these boots are out of place for an Unfortunate's attire and, when an item is out of place, it hangs like a loose thread and must be tied off, for that is how most crimes are solved."

"Please keep us informed of any developments, particularly those which relate to Pretty Penny," Willoughby requested.

"Of course," she assured, and gathered up all of Annie Yates's belongings before bidding the gathered group good day.

Once we were in the corridor and well away from Anderson's laboratory, I asked in a quiet voice, "Why is the origin of the boots so important?"

"Oh, it is not the origin of the boots which is so significant, but what is now on their surface."

"Which is?"

"The fingerprints of two main suspects."

Chapter 14

The Omen

It was well into the evening before Joanna and I rested on the comfortable sofa in front of a cheery fire which nicely warmed our parlor against the outside chill. My father had retired early, but only after applying heat and aspirin cream to his painful arthritic knee in hopes the joint would improve and allow him to travel to Brighton in the morning. For it was there that his beloved Northumberland Fusiliers would be holding their reunion, an event he so looked forward to, despite the sad memories it carried from the Second Afghan War. But a train trip, no matter how short, would surely cause his knee to stiffen and only worsen his discomfort. I found myself wondering if I should accompany him on his journey.

"The answer is no," said Joanna. "For he will not wish to appear old and infirm in front of his comrades-in-arms."

I could not help but stare at my wife in astonishment. "How in the world did you come by that? And please do not tell me it was simple observation, for there was nothing to observe."

"But there was," she replied. "You continued to glance over to your father's packed suitcase by the door, then up at the rack which holds your hat and topcoat. The heavy tweed coat was of particular interest, for it is the one you favor while traveling. Thus, it was obvious you were dwelling on your father's journey and whether you should be by his side."

"I must learn how to perform that magic," said I, as the crackling fire drew my attention. "Nevertheless, you were spot-on and I may have no choice other than to accompany him."

"He will not permit it," Joanna stated. "For in the end, the final decision will be made by him, not you."

I nodded at my wife's assessment. "Perhaps his treatment will bring about improvement in short order."

"That is wishful thinking, if past experience is any indication."

"Let us then hope for a miraculous recovery."

Joanna chuckled softly to herself. "It is unfortunate that my son Johnny is not here to offer Watson some new and revolutionary treatment."

We shared a warm smile as the memory of the remarkable conversation between my father and Johnny came to mind. It occurred last year during the lad's spring holiday from Eton, at a time my father's knee was again flaring up and resisting all therapy.

The ever-inquisitive Johnny had asked, "Why do you limp so, Dr. Watson?"

"I am afraid I have arthritis in my knee," he had replied.

"What is the cause of that, may I inquire?"

"The cartilage degenerates and becomes uneven."

"Only in one knee?"

"Only in one."

"Why not add a lubricant to the affected knee?"

"It already has excessive lubricant called joint fluid, but it does not seem to help."

"Perhaps it is of inferior quality."

"Perhaps."

"Then why not take fluid from the good knee, which seems to function well, and inject it into the painful one?"

My father had grinned at the suggestion. "Do you truly believe it would be beneficial?"

"It seems to be protecting your good knee."

I looked over to my wife, saying, "Do you know my father actually proposed Johnny's treatment to an orthopedic surgeon?"

"What was the surgeon's response?"

"He shrugged, calling it nonsense."

"Did Watson pursue it further?"

"Indeed he did. My father brought the idea to the attention of a pediatrician at the Hospital for Sick Children who cares for the young with arthritis."

"And the result?"

"He promised to look into it."

"Good show! Was my son so informed?"

"He will be, if and when such a study is undertaken."

"Johnny will be pleased to learn of it, for to him it is an experiment that should give a definitive answer. It is the type of inquiry he enjoys the most."

"Like his mother."

"And his grandfather before him."

"So much so," I noted. "My father says that young Johnny is an exact replica of Sherlock Holmes."

"But far more thoughtful in that he never forgets my birthday," Joanna said, and nudged me playfully with her elbow. "Unlike some men I know."

I cringed briefly for effect. "I almost forgot that important day."

"Almost?"

"Almost." I reached into my vest pocket for a small velvet jewelry box. "Fortunately, I was passing by a shop on Regency Street a few days ago and saw this little item in the window."

Joanna quickly opened the case to reveal a cameo broach which had a white figurehead against a sky-blue background. It was framed in a delicate gold lace. "It is so lovely," she whispered, softly kissing my cheek. "Thank you, my dearest."

"You are welcome, dear heart."

"And now my birthday is in fact complete."

"I suspect it would be even more complete if young Johnny was here with us."

"Indeed so, but I take some comfort in knowing he is safely tucked away in Eton and far away from the dreadful crimes now pervading London."

At that moment, as Joanna nestled her head upon my shoulder, a log in the fireplace split in two and sent up a great shower of sparks. In retrospect, I wondered if that noisy interruption was an omen of how unsafe Johnny's future truly was.

Chapter 15

The Baker Street Irregulars

The mood was somber in our rooms at 221b Baker Street as we awaited the results of the fingerprint comparisons. We had learned earlier there were problems with the items that had been submitted to Scotland Yard for investigation. In particular, the fingerprints on the broken-off blade and piece of glass were partial prints that only captured the tips of the fingers. Thus, any match would be most difficult to obtain since at least twelve identical points had to be compared and confirmed. Nevertheless, there was another avenue which might match the new fingerprints on Annie Yates's shoes to those of Jack the Ripper. It would also prove beyond a doubt that the past and present Jack the Ripper were one and the same.

"How did you come to know there was a definite fingerprint of The Ripper's that dated back to 1889?" my father inquired, with his leg resting on an ottoman. His knee was much improved, but some swelling and stiffness persisted, so he wisely decided to forgo his journey to Brighton.

Joanna was standing by the window, watching the comings and goings on Baker Street below. "By reading all the old, available documents which recorded his murderous activities. There was one letter he wrote in red ink, which also included a fingerprint that was clearly stamped on the paper in red ink as well. He obviously did so intentionally, as a taunt to Scotland Yard."

"Have you actually seen this letter?" I asked.

"I have not, for it along with dozens of other such documents are under seal at the Public Record Office," Joanna replied. "Lestrade is now applying to the commissioner to have the seal broken."

"Let us hope that print can be matched to those on the blade and broken glass," my father remarked. "And those then matched to one of the fingerprints on Annie Yates's shoes."

"That would be a perfect world which rarely exists, Watson," Joanna said. "You must keep in mind that a match on the broken glass, which is highly improbable, would still not convict, for any barrister worth his salt would state that the bottle was stolen from St. Bart's by an intruder. After all, Willoughby and Anderson frequently touch bottles of formaldehyde, which are in great use in their department. Rudd might also come in contact with such bottles, into which he would place his surgical specimens. Thus, it is the print on the blade which connects the owner to Jack the Ripper, and thereupon rests the weakest print of all."

"So we must depend on matching a fingerprint on the shoe to the one on the letter The Ripper wrote," my father concluded.

"But here again there may be a problem," she continued on, walking over to the Persian slipper which held her Turkish cigarettes. She carefully lighted one before returning to her position at the large window overlooking Baker Street. "You see, it is believed that the majority of letters written by Jack the Ripper to Scotland Yard and the newspapers were in fact hoaxes. Some idiot actually included a piece of kidney in his letter for added effect."

"But if the fingerprint on the shoe matches that on the letter, we have our killer," I stated.

"Ah, if it were only so simple," Joanna countered. "Again, any worthwhile barrister would claim the letter was written as a hoax by the defendant while in medical school. And of course the suspect would swear under oath that he did so. You would have to prove otherwise, for under Anglo-Saxon law an individual is innocent unless you can prove him guilty."

"But such a match would certainly point the finger of guilt at its owner," I contended.

"Unfortunately, there is a huge difference between pointing a finger and establishing guilt," said she.

My father sighed dispiritedly. "I am afraid the letter stamped with his fingerprint is indeed a hoax. Only a simpleton would send such an identifying feature."

"Perhaps," Joanna agreed mildly. "But then the study of fingerprints was not used in criminal cases back in 1889 when the letter was written, and The Ripper, being such a clever fellow, would have known this and have no hesitation in sending the taunt."

"So he remains a step ahead of us," I noted.

"At the least," Joanna said, and suddenly craned her neck for a better view of the street. "But I intend to close that gap a bit."

"How so?" I asked.

"By recruiting some assistants," she replied, and, after extinguishing her cigarette in an ashtray, pointed out the window.

My father and I hurried over to view three figures, darting between traffic as they approached our doorstep. I instantly recognized the Baker Street Irregulars, as did my father, for the sight brought a smile to his face and no doubt recalled his exciting days with the long-dead Sherlock Holmes. There was a most interesting history behind the Irregulars which few were aware of. The Great Detective had somehow gathered up a gang of street urchins whom he employed to aid his causes. They consisted originally of a dozen or so members, all streetwise, who could go everywhere, see everything, and overhear everyone without being noticed. When put to the task, they had a remarkable success record. For their efforts each was paid a shilling a day, with a guinea to whoever found the most prized clue. Since Holmes's death, more than a few of the original guttersnipes had either drifted away or become ill, but their leader, Wiggins, remained and took in new recruits to replace those who had departed. He had last employed them in the case of *The Disappearance of Alistair Ainsworth,* in which they played an important role in uncovering the plot behind the cryptographer's disappearance.

Joanna knew Miss Hudson would recognize the group and allow them immediate entrance, for it was our landlady who sent for the messenger to carry the message to the Irregulars. On hearing their footsteps on the stairs, Joanna quickly turned to us. "The Irregulars are to be given the barest facts and nothing more. Then we shall set them loose."

"To what end?" asked my father.

"Why, to track our gentleman drifters of course."

After a brief rap on the door, Wiggins entered, followed by two children, in their teens, whom I knew well. On closer examination it was clear the trio had not changed much over the past two years. In his late twenties, Wiggins was tall and quite thin, with hollow cheeks and dark eyes that seemed to dance around, as if searching for something that might be hidden in the background. To his right was Little Alfie, who was fifteen but appeared younger, with his unkempt brown hair and the look of innocence about him. On the other side of Wiggins was Sarah The Gypsy, a dark-complected girl who had grown a head in height since last seen. The young lass possessed an extraordinary sixth sense that told her when she was being watched or if there was a constable nearby.

"Got your message, I did, and came at my quickest," Wiggins

said in a deep cockney accent. "That will be a shilling twopence for our ride over, if you please, ma'am."

Joanna handed over some coins and spoke directly to the point. "I take it you know Whitechapel well."

"It is my home turf, ma'am," Wiggins said proudly.

"Are you familiar with the Black Lamb?"

"It is a pub at the lower end."

"Have you visited there?"

Wiggins shook his head. "Rarely, for they overcharge and underpour."

"On your few visits there have you noticed gentleman drifters?"

"They come and go, but never stay long."

"There are three I am most interested in." Joanna went to her small writing desk for a large manila envelope. She opened it and gave the photographs of Peter Willoughby, Maxwell Anderson, and Thaddeus Rudd to Wiggins, who studied them at length. "Do you recognize any of the three as being gentleman drifters?"

I glanced over at the head shots which were made by the photography department at St. Bartholomew's for identification badges. The three physicians appeared so proper and distinguished, which belied the savage cruelty one of them possessed.

Wiggins carefully looked at the photographs once again before saying, "I can't be certain, ma'am, for the gentlemen are usually dressed in top hats and I have only seen them at a distance."

"And you may wish to keep your distance, for one of this lot is a cold-blooded murderer."

If Joanna's depiction affected the Irregulars, they did not show it. Wiggins gave each of the photographs another cursory glance and asked, "Do their killings in Whitechapel, do they?"

"So it is believed."

He nodded knowingly. "Like old Jack the Ripper, eh?"

"Like Jack the Ripper," Joanna agreed. "But it would be best that you not mention this to anyone, for word would spread and reach his ears, which would surely put him on guard."

"Not a word, then," Wiggins vowed, making the motion of sealing his lips shut. "Are you interested in their activities inside the pub, then?"

"I am interested in their activities when they *leave* the Black Lamb," Joanna instructed. "Once you recognize any of the three, I would like you to signal Little Alfie and Sarah The Gypsy that he is to be followed noiselessly. I need to know where he goes and with whom."

The leader of the Irregulars hesitated as he appeared to be searching for the correct words. "You do realize that the gentlemen often depart with one of the Unfortunates?"

"I do."

"It would be very difficult to witness their acts, for they are usually performed in dark alleyways, with only scant light from an outer lamppost," Wiggins said frankly.

"That will not be necessary, for I suspect this particular gentleman will depart alone and travel to a place where he will change his appearance and attire, such that he is no longer recognizable."

Wiggins quickly formulated a plan which would meet Joanna's requirements. "I can spot the gentleman as he departs and signal Little Alfie and Sarah by stepping outside and lighting a cigarette. I can assure you they will neither be seen nor heard, but that will be the easiest part. It is when he travels that the difficulty sets in. If he goes by carriage or taxi, he will be impossible to track unless I hire a similar mode of transportation, which will add greatly to your expense." He paused to consider the matter further. "It will take some doing, and will require an extra pound or two, for it has to be done without being noticed."

"So be it," Joanna agreed, and went to her purse. "Here is a pound up front in case the need arises, and a shilling each for your work tonight."

"I shall return when there is news," said he, and led the other Irregulars to the door.

She hurriedly called after him, "There is one more precaution you must take. If the gentleman drifter changes into a totally different character and begins to bargain with an Unfortunate, you are to somehow sound the alarm, for he means to do her great harm!"

"Which we will do with police whistles," Wiggins decided at once. "And of course there will be an additional charge for the whistles."

"Done."

Once the door closed, Joanna began pacing the floor, head down, hands clasped behind her, as she no doubt reviewed the plans and possible pitfalls of the instructions given to the Irregulars. She rarely second-guessed herself, but with so much at stake even the smallest detail could be consequential.

"I believe your plans are quite good, with a high benefit-to-risk ratio," I opined.

Joanna stopped pacing and smiled at me. "You are becoming very adept at reading my mind, dear John, but my primary thought was not with the plan itself. I was wondering if it would be worthwhile to alert Lestrade that there will be observers on the streets of Whitechapel who can sound an alarm with whistles if The Ripper makes an appearance."

"A rather worthwhile idea, I would think," said my father.

She shook her head at the notion. "At first glance perhaps, but then I worry that Lestrade would place even more constables on the streets, which would alert The Ripper and postpone his next attack."

"But a postponement works to the benefit of prospective victims," my father noted.

"It might also make The Ripper disappear, which is not to our advantage," said Joanna. "No, I think it best we leave things as they are for now."

"As do I," I agreed. "Nevertheless, I have real doubts that the Irregulars will be capable of performing the task you have given them, for it will be particularly difficult to follow the suspect through the dark streets of Whitechapel if he departs in a taxi or carriage. I think it unreasonable to believe that Wiggins will have such transports waiting for hours outside the Black Lamb."

"That may not be a recurring problem, for you must bear in mind that The Ripper requires a place to change his appearance and it is unlikely he will travel home or to the playhouse, where he might well be seen in his new identity."

"He could change clothes in the back of a four-wheeler or limousine," my father suggested.

"Again that is unlikely, for the strange transformation would be noticed by the driver, and his suspicion would grow if the suspect departed at Mitre Square," Joanna pointed out. "Furthermore, he would need a place to apply greasepaint, which requires good lighting which a carriage or taxi will not provide."

"Where will he change and transform himself, then?" my father asked.

"I have a strong suspicion that he has a dwelling within walking distance of the pubs, which he uses for the singular purpose of disguising himself and later removing said disguise."

"Assuming he does have such a dwelling, he has used it for

twenty-eight years, which covers the time of the original Jack the Ripper," my father calculated.

"Precisely," Joanna concurred. "And on that optimistic note I will brew a fresh pot of Earl Grey while we await Lestrade's phone call."

"During which time I will endeavor to finish reading this morning's *Guardian,*" said my father, reaching for the folded newspaper.

I watched Joanna clear her workbench and light a Bunsen burner in order to prepare the Earl Grey black tea, which she made far darker than that brewed by Miss Hudson. My wife firmly believed that strong tea and equally strong nicotine from a Turkish cigarette provided a most excellent stimulus to the brain. She was obviously still searching for answers to the perplexing case we now were facing. As Sherlock Holmes would have said, this was quite a three-pipe problem. My attention went over to my father, who was deeply immersed in the morning newspaper. Its front page was filled with reports and speculations regarding the latest victim of Jack the Ripper. I was certain my father had read every line, for he believed one could gather more information about criminal activities from a single newspaper than from a dozen magazines and periodicals. Something had caught my father's interest, for he brought the newspaper in closer to his eyes.

"Joanna, you did not tell us that young Johnny would soon honor us with the pleasure of his company!" my father called out.

"I wished my son's visit to be a surprise," she explained.

"It will be a most delightful one, for his presence always lights up our rooms."

"How did you learn of it?"

"It was noted in the *Guardian*'s society column that Lord

Blalock will be hosting a splendid birthday party for the lad later this week."

"I am afraid his dear grandfather does tend to overdo it for Johnny," Joanna noted. "I predict the party will be somewhat extravagant."

"To which I was not invited," my father grumbled good-naturedly.

"Oh, I was hoping you would accompany John and me to the festivities."

"I shall look forward to it," said he, and returned to the opened newspaper. But before he could turn the page, the nearby phone rang. He quickly reached for it and answered, "Yes?"

My father pushed the newspaper aside and quietly apprised us, "It is Lestrade."

He listened intently and intermittently asked, "When? . . . Where? . . . Was there any resistance? . . . Escaped? . . . Conclusive evidence, you say?"

The conversation continued at length, but my father saw no need to take notes. However, he did move his lips silently, which was a habit of his while memorizing. He nodded a few times as he brought the call to an end, saying, "We shall join you immediately."

My father gave us a most serious look before telling us the nature of the phone call. "Inspector Lestrade has apprehended Jack the Ripper."

"Is he one of the physicians from St. Bart's?" Joanna asked at once.

My father shook his head. "He is an escaped inmate from the Hanwell lunatic asylum."

"And the proof?" asked she.

"Conclusive, for it definitely places the suspect at the scene of Annie Yates's murder," he informed.

"Did Lestrade give you the particulars on this evidence?"

"He did not, telling me only that it is beyond dispute."

"We must see this evidence before it can in any way be distorted or placed under a court's seal."

"It sounds as if you have your doubts."

"I doubt everything Scotland Yard does, particularly when a solution is given to them on a silver platter."

"But conclusive evidence is still conclusive evidence."

"Did Lestrade invite us to see the evidence and interrogate the suspect?"

"He did."

"Then he, too, has some underlying doubts."

"Based on what?"

"That Jack the Ripper is far too clever to be an out-and-out madman."

Chapter 16

The Hanwell Asylum

Approaching Hanwell, our carriage was waved through the gated entrance without inspection. A delivery lorry leaving the mental institution was likewise allowed to pass without stopping. I also noted there was only a single guard at the gate and that the metal fence which surrounded the facility was at the most three feet high, all of which would make for an easy, unnoticed escape. The medical facility itself was unprotected and far more expansive than I had anticipated. It consisted of a cluster of imposing stone buildings that encircled a very large garden where men were busily at work.

Drawing up to the most impressive of the structures, we were greeted on the steps by Inspector Lestrade, who introduced us to the superintendent at Hanwell, Dr. Charles Marshall Ellis, an elderly physician with snow-white hair and a kind, welcoming face. As we walked down a long, quiet corridor, we encountered expressionless inmates, with dazed, faraway looks in their eyes, which was characteristic of the mentally ill. They, however, nodded to us and seemed pleased that we were visiting. Some even spoke a few cordial words, which we returned.

"We encourage them to walk about and interact with others," said Ellis. "It seems to make them feel they are part of the outside world."

"Are drugs used as well?" my father asked.

"Not as much as before," Ellis replied. "We employ bromides which help soothe the most agitated and paraldehyde to quiet those at bedtime."

We passed by a very large room that was filled with row after row of empty bedsteads which were no more than three feet apart. But unlike the beds at the doss-house, these were covered with clean sheets and pillows, all neatly arranged.

"May I ask where the inmates are?" I inquired.

"We refer to them as patients, for it gives them a bit more dignity," Ellis corrected gently. "In answer to your question, we have a very tight schedule for those housed here, which for the most part keeps them occupied. They are awakened at six, at which time they are washed, their hair combed, and their skin inspected. At nine they are served breakfast, after which they begin their day's work. Men work and farm the garden for the food we consume, while women are employed in the laundry and needle room. By eight in the evening, all are in bed."

"It is not what I anticipated," my father admitted. "Back in my days in medicine, the mentally unstable were not treated nearly as well, with filth, violence, and restraints being the order of the day."

"Fortunately, we have changed and progressed, Dr. Watson," Ellis said, as we approached a clearly agitated patient in a straitjacket being accompanied by an attendant. "But on some occasions, we have no recourse other than to keep the violent ones restrained."

The patient glared at us as we passed, and snarled menacingly while making a sudden, aggressive move toward our group. His attendant held him back with a gentle tug on his straitjacket, much like he would do with a mean dog on a leash.

"Walter is one of the unfortunate exceptions," Ellis said unhappily.

"What of the man who claims to be Jack the Ripper?" Joanna asked.

"He, too, is one of the exceptions."

We came to the end of the corridor where a burly attendant and a constable stood guard in front of a padded door. Within, there were no sounds to be heard. A slow-moving overhead fan provided scant ventilation, for the air held a musty odor.

Reaching for the doorknob, Ellis cautioned, "I should warn you that psychotic patients can quickly transform from absolute compliance to excess motor activity and excitement, which may end in acts of violence."

"So those around them must be protected," Joanna noted.

"They must also be protected from themselves," Ellis added.

"I take it they may also have false beliefs and delusions, which can intensify this violence," said she.

"Sometimes to extremes," the superintendent agreed, and opened the door.

We entered a narrow, rectangular room whose floor and walls were covered with canvas pouches, which we were told had been filled with horsehair to prevent patients from harming themselves. In the center of the padded room was a heavyset middle-aged man, with gray, unruly hair and dark brown eyes that stared at you without even a hint of a blink. He didn't seem bothered by his straitjacket as he conversed with an imaginary figure.

"I tell you there is no excuse for it, Thomas," he said. "Such behavior will cause you to be expelled from Hanwell."

The delusional man nodded at the silent response.

"Good, then," he went on. "Play it on the straight and you will do just fine."

"Artie, there are people here who wish to speak with you," Ellis said in a comforting voice.

"Can't you see I am involved in a most serious conversation?" Artie shouted, suddenly agitated.

"Forgive me, but I would very much like you to hold that conversation in abeyance while you speak with the police. I know you are most interested in telling them of your recent activities in Whitechapel."

"As long as it doesn't take too long," Artie conceded.

"Thank you," Ellis said, and stepped aside.

Joanna studied the patient carefully, paying particular attention to the straitjacket covering his torso. For a moment, he seemed to be attempting to wiggle his way out of it. "That restraint must be very uncomfortable," she said.

"It is," Artie answered.

"Would you like it removed?"

"I would."

"With the understanding that should you misbehave, it will immediately be placed back on you."

"That is a lot to ask."

"Yes or no?" Joanna pressed.

"I will behave," Artie promised reluctantly.

Ellis quickly interceded. "That would be most dangerous, for he can turn violent in an instant."

"If the removal were not important, I would not have requested it," Joanna said, unconcerned. "Besides, should Artie become violent, your burly attendant and the constable, along with the inspector, will have no difficulty subduing him."

"Still, you do so at your risk," the superintendent warned.

"So be it," she replied. "Please call in your attendant."

Artie was surprisingly compliant when the attendant freed him from the straitjacket. He moved his arms about in a circular motion to relax the muscles and increase the circulation. Finally, he stretched his back and uttered a sigh of relief. "I hope this doesn't take up much time."

"That depends on your answers," Joanna said, and asked that he hold his arms out in front of him, so she could examine his bloodied hands. He did so without hesitation but had difficulty maintaining the outstretched position with his left arm. "Your left arm seems a bit weak," she noticed.

"It was the result of an accident," Artie explained.

"Did this accident occur while you were Jack the Ripper?"

"Oh, no. It occurred some years ago."

"I would like to hear the details of the accident."

"It is not important."

"It is to me."

Artie hesitated and for unknown reasons sniffed at the air. He did so again, moving a little closer to the group of visitors. "I smell tobacco smoke."

"I smoke," Joanna said.

"Cigarettes?"

"The Turkish variety."

"I would dearly love one."

Joanna looked over to Ellis, who nodded his approval. She

extracted a cigarette from her purse and, after handing it to Artie, lighted it with a strike-anywhere match. The patient inhaled deeply to soak up every trace of nicotine and did so yet again.

"There is nothing quite as delightful as a strong smoke," he said happily.

"Which Turkish tobacco always delivers," Joanna added.

"They must be expensive."

"Not so when you consider one smoke from them is worth two or more from an ordinary cigarette."

"I shall have to remember that," Artie said, and took another deep inhalation.

I was struck how Joanna and Artie were now chatting like old friends. He appeared completely at ease and sane as he told her of the brands of common cigarettes he once so enjoyed. She of course knew of not only these brands but also the type of ash they left behind, which Artie found most interesting. Even the good Dr. Ellis seemed surprised by the ease of conversation between the two, for he was unaware of Joanna's ability to sound nonintrusive while being the exact opposite.

"How do you come to know so much about tobacco?" Artie asked.

"My father instructed me," Joanna said truthfully, then waved her hand to end that portion of the conversation. "Now, please tell me about your unfortunate accident, which must have been horrific."

"It was indeed, madam," he commenced, now walking around the padded room with a noticeable limp. "I was a butcher's assistant in Whitechapel and pushed a large cart to deliver beef and poultry to various addresses. Everything was going quite well that day when a horse suddenly bolted from the backfire of a lorry. The bloody animal ran over both me and my cart, knocking both of us to the cobblestones. The accident crushed my left leg, which left me with a hobble that I have to this day."

"I see your shoulder was injured as well," Joanna observed. "It must have been very painful."

"Oh, the pain eventually passed, but the complete use of my left arm never returned." Artie lifted his left arm up to shoulder height, but it quickly dropped down to his side. "The weakness cost me my position at the butcher shop, and from that moment on things went badly for me."

"A terrible handicap," she commiserated. "Can you perform any functions with your left arm?"

"Very few, madam, for it tires so easily."

"Are you able to hold up a pint of bitters?"

"Not for long, but that is of little matter, for I am naturally right-handed."

Lestrade decided to intervene, now seeing where the conversation was headed. "But his right arm is quite powerful, for he uses it for all things and thus its strength even grows. I will wager you can hold your own in a fight, eh, Artie?"

"That I can, guv'nor, as more than a few men will testify to," Artie replied, now looking longingly at the very last of his cigarette. He attempted to draw a final puff, but the burning end was too close to his lips. "I wonder, madam, if I might have one more of your Turkish cigarettes."

Joanna gave him another cigarette, which he lighted from the one he was smoking before stamping out the latter on the canvas-covered floor. "Please be good enough to tell me of your attacks on the Unfortunates," she probed in a neutral tone.

"It was easy, for they were weak."

"Surely they resisted."

"But to no avail, for my strength was overwhelming."

"Did they scream?"

Artie chuckled inappropriately. "It is most difficult to scream through a slit throat."

"Did you leave them there to die?" Joanna queried.

"I enjoyed watching them bleed to death," Artie replied. "It reminded me of my days at the butcher shop, where we would slaughter the animals and watch their blood flow into the street. It was similar to a flowing red stream, you see."

"Did you take anything from the Unfortunate's body?"

"Her organs?"

"Which?"

"Any I wished."

"And what did you do with them?"

"I offered them up to God to show him that I was accomplishing my mission on earth."

"What was the mission God assigned to you?"

"To rid the streets of Whitechapel of dirty prostitutes who cause decent men to sin."

"Does God give you a name?"

"He calls me his Angel of Death."

"How many Unfortunates have you killed?"

"A great number."

"And this pleases your God?"

"Quite so, for he encourages me to kill more and more until we have cleansed all of Whitechapel."

"Perhaps he will tell you to stop."

Artie suddenly turned angry and began to move his arms in a threatening manner. "He would never! I am his special servant."

"But suppose he does?"

"You are planning to talk with him, aren't you?" Artie's voice was now a menacing shriek. "I will not allow you to speak with him, and I will harm you if you attempt to do so."

Joanna responded with only a silent stare.

Artie suddenly lunged for her throat with outstretched arms, which caught the constable and attendant by total surprise. In an instant Joanna effortlessly swept Artie's arms aside and, using her foot, kicked his legs from under him. Artie hit the canvas floor headfirst, with a loud thud which rendered him dazed and powerless. The attendant had no difficulty reapplying the straitjacket.

"I say!" Lestrade said, astonished by Joanna's martial art skill. "What type of fighting is that called?"

"Jujitsu," Joanna replied. "It comes in handy for self-defense."

"So I noticed," Lestrade said, stepping around the still-stunned inmate.

Out in the corridor, Joanna firmly pronounced, "He is not Jack the Ripper."

"But you have not seen the evidence which clearly states he is," Lestrade argued.

"I have seen enough," said she. "To begin with, we know from the pattern of the victim's wounds that The Ripper is left-handed. Artie is right-handed, and his left is so weak it can barely support a pint of bitters. He, for all intents and purposes, is a one-armed man. It is beyond the realm of reality for him to subdue an alert Unfortunate and slit her throat simultaneously."

"Perhaps he first rendered them unconscious," Lestrade proposed.

"That is not The Ripper's modus operandi, for he wishes to see their final fear and agony," Joanna countered. "Even Artie was aware of this, for he took some delight in telling us that his supposed victim could not scream through a severed windpipe. Moreover, Artie has a permanent limp whereas The Ripper, as described by Sally Hawkins, appeared to be feigning such a disability. It is also rather odd that neither Annie Yates nor Sally Hawkins mentioned that The Ripper had a palsied arm, which both would have noticed. And finally, Artie could not name the female organs that were dissected out of the victims, which Jack the Ripper would have had no difficulty describing. Thus, I believe you have the wrong man, Lestrade."

"Your points are well taken, but I am convinced that your opinion will change once you see the all too convincing evidence," the inspector insisted.

"We shall see," said Joanna.

Following Lestrade and Ellis down the corridor, I whispered to Joanna, "That was a clever move to have the suspect's straitjacket removed, for it certainly put him at ease."

"That was not the purpose of the removal," she whispered back. "I noticed that his right shoulder was overly developed and his left withered. To make certain this apparent finding was not a distortion caused by the straitjacket, I had it taken off. This allowed me to clearly demonstrate that he was right-handed for the most part and had a palsied left."

"I missed that," I said regretfully.

"You must learn to observe more carefully, John," Joanna said, with a playful smile.

Ellis led the way into a musty room which was used to store cleaning equipment. On a large, centrally located table Lestrade had spread out all the evidence taken from the suspect. I could detect the stale blood and the even stronger aroma of formaldehyde which emanated from the garments removed from Artie upon his readmission to Hanwell. The evidence included shoes and socks, trousers, shirt, coat, pieces of blood-stained glass, and the feathered leg torn off a bird, most likely a chicken.

"Allow me to tell you how the suspect was apprehended earlier today," said Lestrade. "He was seen by more than a few to be walking around Mitre Square, wearing bloody clothing and crying out, 'I am Jack the Ripper and you will never catch me.' When approached by police officers, he drew a large, bloodied knife and dared them to come closer, so they might join the company of the dead Unfortunates. A prolonged struggle ensued before he was shackled and returned to Hanwell for examination."

"How was it determined he was an inmate at Hanwell?" Joanna asked.

"He told the officers and produced a card stating this was the case," the inspector replied.

"How convenient," she commented, and carefully eyed the items of evidence on the table. "Where is this large knife you just spoke of?"

"I am afraid it has been lost," Lestrade said unhappily.

"I would do my very best to find that knife, for it may carry more evidence than all the other items put together."

"Such as?"

"Its purpose, other than to be used as a weapon," Joanna replied. "You may wish to determine its origin and in particular whether it came from the butcher shop where he once worked."

"What relevance would that hold?"

"Would you not like to learn whether that very same knife was used to dissect out organs from slaughtered animals?"

"Excellent point," Lestrade admitted, and appeared to be making a mental note.

Joanna reached for the suspect's trousers, with their pockets turned inside out, and carefully sniffed at them from belt to bottom. She did so yet again before performing the same act on Artie's shoes. "Formaldehyde," she said finally.

"Which no doubt splashed on him when the bottle slipped from his pocket and broke open on the cobblestones," Lestrade construed.

"Well considered," Joanna said, "except for the fact that the formaldehyde is concentrated on the knees of his trousers and nowhere else."

He gave the matter thought before saying, "I fail to see the significance to that finding."

"If the bottle of formaldehyde had broken open near the suspect's feet, it would have splashed up onto his shoes and the entire lower portion of his trousers, which it did not. The aroma of formaldehyde was for the most part limited to the knees of his trousers."

"How did it get there and nowhere else, then?"

"There is only one explanation," Joanna informed. "The suspect knelt down in a puddle of formaldehyde which was made earlier by the genuine Jack the Ripper."

"But you found the same aroma on his shoes," the inspector challenged.

"Only on the soles when he stepped into the already-formed puddle," she responded, and turned her attention to the torn-off feathered chicken leg. "What are we to make of this?"

"I suspect Artie was starving and scavenging for anything edible," Lestrade answered.

"Why would he leave the feathers on, then?"

Lestrade shrugged. "I would guess he planned to defeather it once he found a place to cook it."

"But starving men do not wait for an ideal location to cook their food," Joanna countered.

Lestrade moved his head from side to side as he further considered the matter. "Perhaps he was in no rush, for he had dined earlier on the other parts of the bird."

"I believe you are correct in that assumption," said Joanna, but the humming sound that followed told me there was more to this puzzle than she was revealing. Next, she closely inspected the suspect's heavy coat and tattered shirt, which was soiled but free of blood. The lining of the coat had been torn out long ago and what remained held no hiding places. A search of the shoes and socks was likewise unproductive.

"I see you are avoiding the most important item of evidence," Lestrade broke the silence.

"Are you referring to the large, bloodstained piece of glass?" she asked.

"I am."

"And pray tell what renders it so important?"

Lestrade gave my wife a rather perplexed look. "Because he no doubt used it to slit the last victim's throat."

"So our suspect did not do the deed with his knife after all."

"If we find the knife, all well and good, but for now the bloodstained piece of glass will do nicely."

"Perhaps not so nicely," Joanna said as she furrowed her brow in thought. Again she hummed to herself at length until she found the fact she was searching for. Turning to me, she asked, "Tell me, John, is it not true that avian blood differs from that of humans?"

"It does indeed, but it requires microscopic examination to distinguish between the two," I replied.

"Excellent, for much depends on that distinction."

"We have a microscope in our small laboratory, if you wish to use it," Ellis offered.

"Do you employ a technician?" I inquired.

"Part-time, for she performs only the simplest of tests," Ellis answered.

"Such as peripheral blood smears?" asked I.

"Oh, yes, she is very good with Wright's stain."

"Is she present today?"

"She is until noon."

Joanna picked up the large piece of bloodstained glass and

held it up to the light. "This will do quite well for our purposes. Now, Dr. Ellis, if you will, please show us the way to the institution's laboratory."

We hurried a short distance down the corridor and entered a very small laboratory whose only major instrument was an ancient microscope. A middle-aged technician, with gray-streaked hair held back in a bun, quickly got to her feet.

"Alice, would you be good enough to do a Wright's stain on a piece of broken glass for us?" Ellis requested in a soft voice.

"Of course, sir, but for the best results we would need a flat surface," she complied.

"I believe this will do," said Joanna, and gave Alice the blood-soaked piece of glass.

After holding it up to a bright light, she cleansed the undersurface with saline, then added purple Wright's stain to its top. Within minutes, the stained piece of glass was under the microscope and ready for viewing.

I quickly studied the glass and pronounced, "It is bird blood, as demonstrated by the nucleated red blood cells. Human erythrocytes are devoid of such a nucleus."

"Well done, John, for everything now fits together," Joanna said, and, after thanking the technician, departed the laboratory, with the rest of us close behind.

In the corridor, she asserted, "I am now even more certain that Artie is not our Jack the Ripper. He no doubt used the sharp piece of broken glass to open the bird and remove its edible parts. He consumed all except for the chicken leg, which remained protected by its feathers and which he planned to later dine on. Before this event occurred, however, I believe that Artie, while roaming the dark streets of Whitechapel, happened onto the corpse of Annie Yates and took advantage of the find."

"Why didn't Artie use the knife he was flashing to section

the chicken?" Lestrade argued. "It would have served the purpose far better than broken glass."

"Here I would be guessing, but I believe it to be a guess of high probability," Joanna replied. "I believe The Ripper slipped the knife into Artie's pocket unnoticed."

"Why not simply hand it to him?"

"It would be most reckless to give a madman a large knife in a dark alley."

Lestrade nodded and held up an envelope which he emptied onto a nearby gurney. We gathered around to view a single copper earring that also had blood on its surface. "In all likelihood this, too, was slipped into Artie's pocket," the inspector deduced.

Joanna stared at the bloodied earring as a thin smile crossed her face. "How clever he is."

"Based on the earring?" Lestrade asked quizzically.

"Precisely so," she replied. "Allow me to draw your attention to the attachment which permits the earring to be fastened to a woman's ear."

"It appears to be perfectly intact," Lestrade noted, with a shrug.

"Which it should not be," Joanna said, turning back in the direction of the padded room. "We must question Artie once more."

"I am afraid he will be most uncooperative now," Ellis informed. "He will remember his last painful encounter with you."

"I can persuade him to behave," she responded, unconcerned.

"But the straitjacket must remain on."

"That will present no problem."

As we rushed down the corridor, I continued to dwell on the bloodied earring and why its intact attachment was such an important clue. The common type of attachment, which this one possessed, made it simple to fasten and remove. Certainly even a madman would have little difficulty detaching the earring. Why then all the attention on an intact attachment?

We entered the padded room, with the burly attendant and constable by our sides. Artie remained restrained in a straitjacket and was angrily pacing the canvased floor, all the while muttering nonsense to himself. He paused briefly to give us a menacing glare as he seemed to struggle against his restraint, which made him even angrier.

"Get out!" he shouted at the top of his voice.

"I have more questions for you," Joanna said calmly.

"Go bugger yourself!"

"Perhaps we can reach an agreement which would make my interview more appealing."

Artie stopped pacing abruptly, now giving thought to such a proposition. His anger appeared to subside while he contemplated and searched for an advantage. Then a smile came to his face. "Remove the straitjacket and we can talk," he negotiated cleverly.

"That is not an option," Joanna refused.

"Then leave, for I soon have a meeting with another Angel of Death which cannot wait."

"He will wait."

"Blasphemy!"

"He will understand as we discuss matters over a Turkish cigarette."

Artie considered the offer and continued to bargain despite his madness. "Only one?"

"Three, for that is the number which remain in my pack."

"How do I know you will hold up to our agreement?"

"I will give the pack, with its three cigarettes, to Dr. Ellis, who will pass them on to you once the straitjacket is removed."

"I want to see you hand him the pack now."

Joanna did so, but with a warning. "If you do not answer my questions truthfully, I will take the pack back and our conversation will come to an end. Understood?"

Artie nodded, his eyes still riveted on the pack of cigarettes. "Understood."

"Describe the man who gave you the copper earring," Joanna requested.

"He was an ordinary bloke."

"Did he speak cockney?"

"No, ma'am. He spoke more like a gentleman."

"Could you see his face?"

"Not much of it, for he was wearing one of those fisherman caps pulled over his forehead."

"I would guess he gave you the chicken as well."

Artie nodded unhappily. "A scrawny bird, if ever there was one."

"Did he supply you with a knife to carve it up?"

"No, madam. I had the good fortune to find it later in my pocket."

"Do you have any idea how it got there?"

"I suspect God put it there," Artie replied. "To do his work, you see."

"He is good at those sorts of things."

"He is indeed."

"Let us turn to the copper earring," Joanna redirected the conversation. "Did the man you described give you only a single earring?"

"I asked for the other, but he refused. So then, I asked him what good one earring was, and he told me to go to Froman's Jewelry Shop where the owner would purchase it from me, for people are always seeking a replacement for one that was lost. He assured me it would bring a shilling."

"Why did you not take it to Froman's?" asked Joanna.

"I was on my way there when I was nabbed by the coppers; otherwise I would have—" Artie stopped in midsentence and stared up at the bare ceiling. "Here comes the other Angel of Death. You must leave or the meeting will be canceled."

"So we shall."

"Leave! Leave! Before it is too late."

In the corridor and away from the padded room, I could not help but ask Joanna, "What was the significance of the intact attachment on the earring?"

"It was dark in that passageway where Annie Yates lay, and I think it fair to say that Artie could have hardly seen a copper earring under her long blond hair. And had he somehow noticed it, with such little light and being a man unfamiliar with such jewelry, he would have surely ripped it off her ear, which would have left the flimsy attachment behind."

"And Annie's ears showed no signs of traumatic injury," I recalled from the autopsy.

"Very good, John," Joanna went on. "So why then was Artie given only a single earring?"

"I have no idea," I admitted.

"As a clue, which would inform the police that Artie was present at the crime scene and, in all likelihood, was the person who murdered Annie Yates," said she. "It was a nice touch to give him a single earring, for that is how a totally crazed individual might be expected to behave."

"But why the chicken as a gift?"

"It wasn't a gift, but a nicely contrived bribe," Joanna elucidated. "You see, our Jack the Ripper, being a physician, knew he was dealing with a psychotic who he could manipulate. He no doubt had shadowed Artie earlier, and when he saw Artie coming down the passageway, he indulged him with conversation and bribes. He might have actually known Artie from the poor soul's days at the butcher shop."

"Of course, of course," my father interjected. "Being a longtime resident of Whitechapel, The Ripper knew all about Artie, including his psychosis and traumatic injuries."

"Which made Artie the perfect pigeon to carry all the clues that would at first make him appear to be Jack the Ripper," Joanna concluded. "But The Ripper knew that we would uncover the charade after a careful investigation."

"Why do such a charade?" Lestrade asked.

"He is playing a game with us, Inspector, which leads us off in different directions," she replied. "He is taunting us and telling us how clever he is. In a silent way, he is saying, 'I am much smarter than you and you will never catch me.'"

"He is a most clever madman," my father noted. "And the worst of all opponents."

"Or the best, depending on one's point of view," said Joanna, obviously pleased with the competition. "Here is a man who I am happy to do business with."

Chapter 17

The Copper Cuff Links

Joanna spent the entire night pacing back and forth across our parlor, lighting one cigarette after another, which left the air polluted with dense tobacco smoke. My father and I did not interrupt, for we were aware that a break in her concentration would be most unwelcomed. We had seen this type of behavior before and knew it represented a puzzle that refused resolution.

But the interruption in her thoughts occurred nevertheless when Miss Hudson entered after a brief rap on the door. "I was wondering when it would be convenient for breakfast to be served."

"Later," Joanna replied absently, still pacing.

Miss Hudson waved away the thick smoke and hurried to the window which she opened to allow in a crisp, fresh draft. "I do not understand how you can tolerate such foul air."

"It suits my brain," Joanna replied, and rushed to close the window.

"A nicely prepared breakfast could suit it better," Miss Hudson retorted.

"Give us a bit more time, if you will," Joanna requested, and reached for another cigarette.

"Really, Dr. Watson," Miss Hudson addressed my father, "you must discourage her from such an evil and unhealthy habit."

"I shall do my best," my father promised. "And rest assured our appetites will soon demand one of your most sumptuous breakfasts, which we always look forward to."

"Very good, sir," Miss Hudson said, pacified by my father's gentle words, and departed as quietly as she had entered.

Once the door closed, Joanna remarked, "On occasion, she interrupts my thoughts at the most inopportune moment."

"She means well," my father said.

"I am aware of that," Joanna agreed. "But her entrance occurred just as my brain was formulating a solution to a most troubling problem which demands an answer."

"What so troubles you, may I ask?" I queried.

"The copper earring that Jack the Ripper gave to Artie," Joanna answered. "There is a purpose to that move which escapes me."

"It was his marker," said I.

Joanna shook her head at my notion. "He had already left an earring behind on the corpse of Annie Yates."

"But then he gave the other one to Artie to further convince us that the psychotic was Jack the Ripper."

"He was far too clever for that," Joanna countered. "There was more than enough evidence on Annie Yates to show it was the work of The Ripper. Moreover, all the clues planted on Artie were superficial and would be seen through by a worthwhile observer. The single copper earring on the corpse of Annie Yates and the one given to Artie are beyond a doubt interconnected, but not in the manner we think. There is another purpose to the madness; of that I am convinced."

"You may be stretching it a bit, Joanna," my father said.

"Not if my suspicions are correct."

"Which are?"

"My initial impression, like Lestrade's, was that The Ripper may have decided to split the pair and leave a single earring on the corpse as a marker. He then gave the other to Artie to indicate the inmate was at the crime scene and was most likely the murderer."

"But why give one to Artie when it is The Ripper's custom to bestow a complete set on each of his victims?" my father asked. "After all, as you just mentioned, there was abundant evidence to show that it was the work of The Ripper and not Artie."

"Well thought out, Watson, for it makes my initial suspicion untenable," Joanna replied. "The true reason continues to escape me, but we must keep in mind that our killer is most clever and enjoys playing games, particularly when he holds the advantage."

"Are you saying he is intentionally leading us on?" my father queried.

"That thought has crossed and stayed in my mind, for I am of the opinion that the single earring on the corpse and the one on Artie were presented to us as clues he wishes us to follow."

"To what end?"

"One that we will no doubt find surprising."

"Yet it must surely be to his benefit."

"Oh, it already is and continues to be, for I believe he derives great pleasure in knowing that he is controlling us again and again, while he goes on his merry, killing ways."

"Leaving only bits and pieces behind," my father grumbled.

"Bits and pieces indeed," Joanna agreed. "As you pointed out a moment ago, it was The Ripper's custom to bestow a *pair* of earrings on each victim, but in the case of Annie Yates he leaves only one."

My father shrugged. "So that he could give the other to Artie, as an obvious lead disguised as a gift which had no value by itself."

"No value by itself!" Joanna exclaimed as a sudden epiphany came to her. "The Ripper was leading us to Froman's Jewelry Shop, not to Artie. He purposefully removed an earring from Annie Yates and gave it to Artie, with instructions to take it to Froman's where it would be purchased, which was absolute nonsense."

"But not to a psychotic," I interjected.

"Precisely, John. All Artie could envision was a shilling in his pocket, which was a tidy sum to a man starving on the streets of Whitechapel. The Ripper was directing Artie to Froman's, knowing we would follow."

"But why specifically there?"

"Because that is where the next clue will be," Joanna said,

obviously pleased with her reasoning as she reached for the bell to summon Miss Hudson. "And now for a hearty breakfast, for we have a long day ahead of us."

The commercial section of Whitechapel was quite busy, with all of the stores now open and the footpaths filled with shoppers and merchants and tradesmen, as well as the ever-present loiterers and vagrants. I was again impressed with the international flavor of the neighborhood we were riding through. There was a French bakery, Polish restaurant, Jewish clothier, and Irish pub on a single block. A recent article in the *Guardian* stated that over twenty-five languages and dialects were spoken in the district. But behind the façade of legitimate businesses were the slums, gangs, and brothels that brought violence and crime along with them. The same article in the *Guardian* noted there were twelve hundred prostitutes and sixty-two brothels that were known to exist in Whitechapel. Our carriage passed by the doss-house which once housed Annie Yates, the poor girl from Bristol who now lay in the cold earth of a potter's field. It reminded me of how fragile one's existence could be. Had she not come down with tuberculosis, she might still be employed as a lady's maid on a grand estate. I quickly cleared my mind as we approached the block which contained the jewelry shop. Joanna was now telling us her plans for the investigation.

"There will be no pretense on this visit," she informed. "We will not be casual shoppers, but rather the daughter of Sherlock Holmes, and the Watsons."

"Are you certain you wish to go that route?" I asked. "As you know better than I, people in this neighborhood are somewhat reluctant to speak with the higher class."

"I do not believe that will be a problem, for the good people of Whitechapel are more than eager to see an end to the escapades of Jack the Ripper."

"It reflects poorly on them," my father opined.

"And more important, it is bad for business," Joanna added. "Because of this evil violence, shops close and people vacate the streets at the first signs of darkness."

"You would think that the local gangs would happily dispatch Jack the Ripper," said my father.

"They would do so if they knew his identity, but to them, like to us, he is little more than a moving shadow."

"And how do you propose we catch a moving shadow?" my father asked.

"We don't," Joanna replied, as our carriage drew up to the curb outside Froman's Jewelry Shop. "We must allow him to trap himself."

"How do you propose we do that?"

"By enticing him into a trap."

"With what?"

"An irresistible bait," she said, and left it at that.

We entered the jewelry shop and found its owner, Joseph Froman, cleaning the top of a glass counter. He immediately recognized us from our previous visit and greeted us warmly.

"It is a pleasure to see you once again," he welcomed.

"I am afraid we are not here as shoppers, but rather on official business," Joanna said frankly. "Allow me to introduce myself."

"There is no need, madam, for your face is familiar to all London," Froman replied. "I knew who I was dealing with on your first call to my shop."

"Were you not concerned about my visit?"

"I am an honest man and thus have no such fears."

"Excellent," Joanna approved. "Let us get down to the

matter at hand. Do you recall the man who purchased five sets of copper earrings from you last week?"

"It is impossible to forget such a customer, for they are rare indeed."

"Has he returned, as I suspected?"

Froman's brow went up in surprise. "How could you possibly be aware of that?"

"It is my business to know things others do not," Joanna answered simply. "Now I need to be told everything about his visit in detail, beginning with when he last entered your shop."

"It was in the late afternoon two days ago, and he came in with a most unusual request," the jeweler described, as he thought back. "I offered to show him my newly arrived supply of copper earrings, but he was uninterested and seemed in a bit of a hurry. What a strange fellow he was."

"How so?" she asked.

"He wished for me to make him a set of cuff links from farthing coins," Froman said, shaking his head at the idea. "What respectable gentleman would publicly display such cheap jewelry?"

"Gentleman, you say?"

"That would be my guess, for although he attempted to sound like one of the local residents, a phrase or two gave him away."

"Could you recall an example of that?"

Froman considered the request briefly before saying, "He waited in the store to see if the final product was satisfactory. His exact words were, 'I shall await here to be certain the cuff links meet my expectations.' There was not a hint of cockney in his voice, and I can assure you the people of Whitechapel never speak the phrase *meet my expectations*."

"What exactly were these expectations?"

"He wished the cuff links to be constructed of new, copper

farthings only," the jeweler detailed. "I suggested that silver coins might be more appropriate, but he insisted on copper in a most demanding tone."

"Could they also be used as earrings?" Joanna asked pointedly.

"I think not, for their attachments were far too large to pass through pierced ears."

"Even if forced into place?"

"I am afraid that would cause too much discomfort."

"I take it he was satisfied with your workmanship?"

"Quite so, and paid my charge of two shillings without hesitation."

"Did you have any further conversation with him?"

Froman tapped a finger against his chin as he searched his memory. "He seemed to be keen on copper jewelry, so I tried to tempt him to buy a bracelet and other items made of that particular metal. He refused my bargain prices, yet his interest picked up considerably when I mentioned the famous daughter of Sherlock Holmes had visited my shop earlier and had purchased a similar item. He wanted to know the details of your purchase, and I saw no reason to withhold that information."

Joanna smiled thinly, obviously pleased that all of her predictions had been accurate. "That is most helpful."

The jeweler gave Joanna a lengthy look, moving his lips before forming words. "Would it be inappropriate for me to ask why you are so interested in this fellow? He seemed harmless enough."

I had to strain to keep my expression even at the jeweler's description. What an actor Jack the Ripper must be! One moment he appeared to be a harmless customer, and the next he could transform himself into the most vicious killer London had ever known.

"I can only tell you that he is involved with a group of

thieves," Joanna lied easily. "He disguises himself as a workman to gain entrance into the houses of the well-to-do."

Froman nodded to himself. "And the farthing cuff links fit well with his disguises as a workman."

"Precisely so," she agreed. "Now, if you will, permit me to see the attachment placed on the cuff link."

Froman reached into a drawer behind the counter and produced a tiny bar, the top of which could be pushed into a horizontal position to secure it into a cuff.

"You are correct," Joanna assessed. "This attachment could never pass through a pierced ear."

"Not without great difficulty," the jeweler said, and, after loudly clearing his throat, asked, "Exactly how, madam, should I behave if he returns?"

"Simply be yourself, and be good enough to tell the thief that the daughter of Sherlock Holmes was inquiring about him."

As we were departing, Joanna suddenly turned back to the jeweler and said, "Oh, yes, there was one final question I wish to ask. Did Pretty Penny ever visit your shop and show an interest in copper earrings?"

"She was never a customer, but rather a cleaning girl," Froman replied. "Before she took to the stage and was given a room by Mrs. Adams, she worked here to sweep and mop the floor and shine the counters twice a week for a fee of one shilling. On more than a few occasions she admired the copper earrings which she thought would be an excellent match for her copper necklace. Of course, the lass could ill afford the earrings."

"That is most interesting," Joanna said, as another piece of the puzzle fell into place. We immediately wondered if Pretty Penny's desire for the copper earrings was somehow brought to Jack the Ripper's attention and gave him the idea to use them as gifts to his prospective victims.

Outside, the day was turning cold and misty, with a light drizzle beginning to fall. I was about to hail a carriage when my wife intervened. "Do not bother, John, for we have other, nearby visits to make."

As we waited for traffic to pass, I asked, "How in the world did you know of Pretty Penny's visit to the jeweler's?"

"The copper earrings," she replied. "I will explain all later."

Walking along briskly, we focused our attention on the copper cuff links which Jack the Ripper had purchased. They seemed so out of character for the murderer and went against the profile he had carefully constructed for himself.

"Why the farthing cuff links?" I queried. "They are part of masculine attire, and The Ripper has never shown an interest in men. His prey are always prostitutes of the lowest possible class."

"Perhaps they are not meant to be used as cuff links," my father suggested. "The links could be sewn into the sleeves of a woman's coat, such as buttons are placed for style on a man's garment."

"Or they could serve as top buttons on a blouse or sweater which would brighten their outfit," I proposed.

My father nodded at the idea. "Any Unfortunate would welcome such a gift, for their clothes are typically worn and threadbare."

"You are overlooking an important fact," Joanna interjected. "He already has in his possession another set of copper earrings which he purchased earlier and could use as a gift. And if he wished to have yet another pair, he would have simply bought them from the jeweler. But he did not and demanded copper cuff links and only copper cuff links."

"But to what end?" I asked.

"He is leaving us an obvious clue to decipher," Joanna replied.

"He appears to be toying with us yet again," my father said unhappily.

"And doing a splendid job of it," Joanna added.

"Perhaps we are making too much of it," I wondered aloud. "I propose he is simply following his usual custom of giving copper jewelry to a prospective victim he has already selected."

"But why switch from earrings to cuff links?" Joanna asked, and waited for a response, but her question was met with silence.

We crossed the street and ducked into Mr. Hardy's Sweet Shop just as the rain began to pour down. Mr. Hardy, like the jeweler Froman, recognized us from our previous visit and welcomed us with a warm smile.

"How nice to see you again," he greeted.

"And we, you," Joanna returned the greeting. "We were passing by and could not help but think of your apple spice chocolate."

"And I have a goodly supply on hand."

"Ten pieces, wrapped, should do nicely."

"A tidy dessert, then."

"Our intent exactly," said she, watching the shopkeeper prepare our order. "You mentioned a goodly supply, so I take it there has not been a great demand for the apple spice chocolate."

"It is a bit pricey for most."

"But not for the fellow who bought twenty pieces earlier," Joanna prompted. "I would wager you'd love for him to give your shop a return visit."

"Oh, but he did return, madam, a few days ago."

A thin smile came and left Joanna's face. "Did he purchase more apple spice chocolate?"

"He did not, much to my disappointment," Hardy replied.

"He wished only a few pieces of the regular fudge which is a favorite for many."

"I am surprised he was not tempted by the delicious aroma of the apple spice."

"He appeared uninterested, even though I offered it at a reduced price, for I now have an oversupply since Pretty Penny's disappearance. But the customer was most good-natured and told me not to worry, for others would soon come in for the apple spice chocolate. Are you by chance those individuals?"

"We are indeed," Joanna said tonelessly, despite the obvious, yet surprising, clue.

As I paid for the candy, the door to the sweet shop opened and the Widow Marley rushed in, leaving her drenched umbrella at the entrance.

We exchanged pleasantries, but the conversation soon turned to Pretty Penny, and all of our faces went serious and solemn. I saw tears welling up in the eyes of the Widow Marley.

"Is there any news of Pretty Penny?" she asked.

"I am afraid not," Joanna replied.

"We are all worried sick, and with each passing day our worries grow," the widow remarked sadly. "I fear the very worst has happened."

"As do I," Hardy agreed. "I would give anything for her to bounce in for her normal purchase of apple spice chocolate."

"Which is the reason for my visit," the widow said. "I can no longer resist the lure of that wonderful candy."

"How many pieces, then?" asked Mr. Hardy.

"Two please."

"Two it is," the shopkeeper announced the order. "And I shall add an extra piece, free of charge, in hopes it will change our luck."

"Business is down, is it?" asked Mrs. Marley.

"Most notably since Pretty Penny's disappearance," Hardy responded. "Attendance is down at the playhouse as you no doubt know, and more than a few of the audience usually stop in for candy prior to the performance."

"And my sales of hair pomade have decreased as well," the widow commiserated. "I have sold only a single jar in the past few days and that to a man who accidentally dropped a recently purchased one that fell to the floor and shattered."

Joanna's eyes suddenly narrowed. "Is this the same man who bought a jar shortly after Pretty Penny's disappearance?"

"The very same, for he is my only male customer."

"Well, let us hope for better days," Joanna said, and picked up the wrapped order of apple spice candy.

"Which cannot come fast enough," the Widow Marley wished.

"Before we depart, I wonder if you could supply me with one more bit of information on Pretty Penny."

"Of course," the widow replied, while Mr. Hardy leaned over the counter so he would not miss a word.

"As a rule, do women remove earrings and necklaces when you dress their hair?"

"For the most part the answer is no, but a few take off their necklaces to avoid them being touched by the hair pomade."

"Did Pretty Penny ever remove her copper necklace?"

"Always," Mrs. Marley said at once. "You see, it was a family keepsake which she greatly treasured. She often told me that the day would come when she could purchase matching copper earrings from Mr. Froman." The widow shook her head dolefully. "Such a sweet girl."

"Indeed."

After bidding all a good-bye, I led the way outside and hailed a carriage from Mr. Hardy's doorstep. We hurried into the coach, protected from the downpour by the driver's umbrella.

"How illuminating," Joanna said over the sound of rain pounding on the roof. "It is clear that Jack the Ripper is leading us down a deliberate path he wants us to follow. He purposefully made those copper cuff links to tell us there is another victim in store. But who and where and when? Then he visited the sweet shop, but purchased only chocolate fudge and not the apple spice variety which Pretty Penny favors. Therein lies another message."

"Which is?" I asked.

"That Pretty Penny remains his fifth and final victim," Joanna replied. "Her execution date is fixed and on schedule, and thus he requires no additional apple spice chocolate. And lastly, the purchase of yet another jar of hair pomade carries yet another message."

"But it accidentally fell to the floor and shattered," my father contended.

"Nonsense, Watson," she rebutted. "That jar is made of thick glass and would have to be forcefully thrown to a wooden floor to cause even a crack. He bought more pomade to prepare Pretty Penny for her final act and for no other reason. He will add more and more pomade until her hair glistens brightly in the light, just as it does onstage, and then he will slit her throat."

"He is truly an evil monster," my father commented yet again.

"And one who is clever enough to stay one step ahead of us."

I shook my head in confusion. "But how could he know so much about Pretty Penny's itinerary that he could predict where she would visit? After all, there was no way he could shadow and follow her in broad daylight."

"He didn't have to," Joanna explained. "Remember, he is a part-time resident of Whitechapel and has a secret dwelling there. Thus, while in disguise, he could periodically mingle with the local inhabitants and hear all the gossip relating to Pretty Penny. It was common knowledge that Penny visited the Widow Marley for her hairstyling and most importantly for the pomade that made her hair glisten. Everyone knew she regularly stopped into Mr. Hardy's Sweet Shop for apple spice chocolate which she shared with Mrs. Marley, who no doubt told of the girl's kindness to all of her customers. And both the widow and the jeweler Froman were aware of Pretty Penny's copper necklace and her desire to one day purchase matching earrings. They chatted about it to us as they did to others earlier. So it is clear that Jack the Ripper had no difficulty learning of Pretty Penny's routine itinerary through Whitechapel."

"And he left clues behind to tell us exactly that," I noted.

"He laid them out rather nicely," said Joanna.

"But how did you know of Pretty Penny's visit to the jeweler's, which was not common knowledge?"

"The copper earrings, for they are the established link between Penny's disappearance and Jack the Ripper. He learned of her desire for those earrings and she must have mentioned where they could be purchased."

"So clever," I conceded. "I suspect he will continue to leave us clues."

"All except for one."

"Which is?"

"The one which tells us where he is holding Pretty Penny hostage."

Chapter 18

The Aroused Gentleman Drifter

After a brief rap on our door, Miss Hudson entered with a look of urgency on her face. "I know it is late, but the street urchins are downstairs and demanding to be seen."

My father placed aside a copy of the *Lancet* and glanced at his timepiece, but there was no need, for Big Ben was chiming the ten o'clock hour in the distance. "Please show them up, Miss Hudson."

"Such an inconvenient hour," she noted. "I trust their visit will prove to be worthwhile."

"As do I," said Joanna, but her eyes brightened with anticipation.

Once the door closed, my father asked, "What do you make of this?"

"Prepare yourself for a surprise," Joanna replied. "You must keep in mind that the Baker Street Irregulars have seen, heard, or witnessed virtually every misdeed you can name or imagine. They are streetwise and hardened because of it, so it requires a most unusual event to set them off."

"I can't remember them ever reporting back at such a late hour, even during my days with Sherlock Holmes," said my father.

"Which denotes the gravity of their call."

We heard the chatter and footsteps of the Irregulars coming up the stairs and repositioned our chairs, so that each of us would be facing the visitors. I added a log to the fire, for the night had turned most chilly, as evidenced by the ice crystals forming on our windows.

The door opened without a preceding knock, and the three Irregulars rushed in and over to the fireplace to warm their ungloved hands. They were dressed in work clothes which consisted of heavy, well-worn outer coats and faded multicolored scarves around their necks. Only Wiggins wore a woolen cap that was pulled down over his ears.

"I take it you bring important news that could not wait until morning," said Joanna.

"Indeed, madam, for I am certain you will wish to hear it now," Wiggins informed.

"Why so?"

"Because it concerns Pretty Penny."

The lad now had our immediate and undivided attention and knew it. "I believe that portion of our report will merit a guinea, madam."

"We shall see," Joanna said, and hid any signs of impatience. She reached for a Turkish cigarette and slowly lighted it. "You must begin at the very beginning and leave out no detail."

"At the start, then." Wiggins took a deep breath and cleared his throat, like an individual about to give a formal presentation. "Little Alfie and Sara The Gypsy had placed themselves in the shadows across the street from the Black Lamb to await my signal. A half a block down, my good friend Lewis was parked in his taxi, motor off of course."

"Does he work for a taxi company?" Joanna asked.

"In a way he does."

Joanna's face hardened. "It was a bad idea to bring in an outsider, for he might tell of his adventure, which would not be to our advantage."

"He will not talk, madam," Wiggins assured. "You see,

he is a mechanic in a garage which services taxis. We—shall I say—borrowed one for a few hours, which could cost him his position if discovered. To cover matters, I gave him a pound and promised the same to the night guard at the garage. I told them we were following a man who was believed to be cheating on his wife."

"Well done," said she. "Please proceed."

"I entered the Black Lamb, which was quite crowded, and had a beer or two while I waited. The usual locals were there, laborers, tradesmen, and more than a few Unfortunates. Just after eight, the gentleman drifters made their entrance and were warmly greeted by the Unfortunates. I must say that at first I did not recognize them, for they were wearing top hats and frock coats. Apparently one of the crowd took offense at the presence of the gentleman drifters and tried to provoke a fight. He shouted out, 'Here to look down on us, are you? Go back to Mayfair where you belong!' Of course the pub went silent on that note and expected violence on the drinker's part. But the biggest bloke of the three gentlemen, the one with the broad shoulders and heavy chest, stepped forward and threatened to smash the troublemaker's face in."

That description fit Thaddeus Rudd, who had a bad temper and the strength and size to back it up.

"Did a brawl occur?" Joanna asked as she crushed out her cigarette.

"No, madam. The barkeep quickly intervened and threw the agitator out, for the gentleman drifters would spend ten times more in a night than the troublemaker would in a week. Yet tension remained high in the pub and it would not take much for an argy-bargy to ensue."

"Is *argy-bargy* cockney for a full-blown fight?" my father asked.

"It is, sir."

"Please continue."

"For this reason, I suspect, the three gentlemen departed, much to the unhappiness of the Unfortunates. I stayed put for a few ticks on the clock, then followed them out. They hurried along their way and I feared their evening out had ended. I signaled Little Alfie and Sarah The Gypsy to track two of the gentlemen as best they could, while I trailed the big bloke I just mentioned, for I thought he was the one you would be most interested in."

"Were they not going to their carriages?" asked my father. "That being the case, Little Alfie and Sarah The Gypsy could not hope to keep up."

"But luck was with us, for the gentlemen walked only a few blocks to the next nearest pub, called the Randy Tar. I followed them in and could immediately tell they were well-known, for they were warmly greeted by the barmaid and entire lot of Unfortunates. It was clear that the gentlemen had experience with these Unfortunates, for they called them by their first names."

"Do you recall any of the first names?" Joanna interrupted.

"Alice and Mary or Marie come to mind," Wiggins answered.

"Any last names?"

"No, madam."

"Proceed."

"Well then, the gentlemen stayed for a while and had a jolly good time, with plenty of drinks and a round or two of darts. They were always surrounded by eager Unfortunates who were looking for work. Eventually two of the gentlemen paired off with their selections and went outside."

"Which of the trio remained in the pub?"

"The youngest and best-looking one."

"Did he not pair up?" Joanna asked at once.

"Oh, yes, and with the prettiest of the Unfortunates," Wiggins replied. "Yet they seemed to be in serious talk, without laughter or touching."

"What transpired next?"

"I stepped out to signal Little Alfie and Sarah The Gypsy, who were well hidden in the shadows. He was instructed to follow the big, tough bloke, while she was to watch the older gentleman. I then returned to my place at the bar to keep a close eye on the handsome one, who was still chatting up the same Unfortunate. Now things turned interesting, as Sarah and Little Alfie will testify to."

Sarah The Gypsy took a step forward and spoke in an emotionless voice. "The older gentleman and his selection went into a dark passageway to conduct their business. I stayed back a good distance, so as not to be discovered, but I could still clearly hear their grunts and groans. He was encouraging her with words like, 'Go, my beauty, go!' It was then I heard a woman's scream and the sound of Little Alfie's whistle. The pair I was watching came running out of the darkness and reentered the pub moments before a constable arrived. I remained hidden in the passageway, so only Little Alfie can describe what happened next."

Joanna quickly interrupted and said to Little Alfie, "Begin with the big gentleman leaving the Randy Tar with his selection."

"There was nothing untoward at first," Little Alfie recalled. "They walked out of the pub hand in hand, with him offering an additional fee for a special service. They seemed to agree on a price without bargaining. Into the darkness they went and disappeared from sight, for I remained crouched down and hidden behind a bloody big garbage bin. Things became rough, with her telling him to stop, which he did not do, for she cried out even louder for him to stop. That was when she let out a bloody shriek that chilled to the bone. I thought it best to blow my whistle and prevent further harm to her."

"How much time passed before a patrolling constable arrived on the scene?" Joanna asked.

"A few minutes at most."

"Did the Unfortunate come running out of the passageway?"

"At first I heard her footsteps approaching my position, but then she stopped abruptly. Not on her own accord, mind you, for she yelled at him to release her."

"Did he?"

"Only after she bargained for another fee."

"I want to hear that portion of their conversation word for word," Joanna requested. "The more you can remember the closer you come to placing a guinea in your pocket."

Little Alfie hesitated, as he thought back in time, and tried to retrieve every sentence that was uttered. A guinea, which equaled one pound one shilling, was a most tempting offer to a street urchin who had rarely ever seen a pound note. His lips moved silently as more and more of the conversation returned from his memory bank. Finally, he announced, "I will repeat it in a he said–she said fashion, if that is good with you."

"It is."

"I heard his footsteps come up to her, and that is when he must have grabbed her."

"And the first words he spoke?" Joanna prompted.

"He said, 'I meant you no harm.'"

"She then said, 'You intended to hurt me.'"

"He then said, 'I became overly aroused.'"

"She then said, 'By squeezing my throat?'"

"He then said, 'It was unintentional.'"

"She then said, 'Tell that to the police.'"

"Were those their exact words?" Joanna asked, and watched for the street urchin's reaction.

"Pretty much so, madam," Little Alfie replied.

Wiggins interjected, "I should tell you, madam, that Little Alfie has the best memory of all of us. He can still remember lines from books he read while in school."

"Which book did you enjoy the most?" Joanna asked Little Alfie.

"*The Jungle Book* by Rudyard Kipling."

"Can you recall its most famous line?"

Little Alfie nodded and recited, "The Law of the Jungle—which is by far the oldest law in the world."

I looked on in astonishment, for although we knew Little Alfie had some education and was the smartest of the lot, his memory from a story read long ago was quite remarkable.

"Excellent," Joanna praised, "for I, too, am familiar with the book."

"I once had a copy, but someone swiped it," Little Alfie said unhappily.

"I shall see you get another."

"Thank you, madam."

"Now, do go on with the conversation between the two before the police arrived."

"She threatened to tell the constable and he pleaded with her not to," Little Alfie continued on. "He offered her a pound to make up a story that her scream was one of joy and pleasure. She refused and demanded more for her lie. They settled on two guineas. That is when the constable arrived and listened to her story. I suspect he recognized the big bloke as being from the upper class and let the matter go, with a warning to the Unfortunate."

"Did she reenter the Randy Tar?" Joanna asked.

"She went on her way, while the two gentleman drifters hurried to their carriages, which raced away," Sarah replied.

Joanna turned back to Wiggins. "What of the handsome gentleman you were watching at the pub?"

"When I entered, he was still chatting up the Unfortunate, all the while checking his timepiece," Wiggins replied. "Then he bought her a drink and dashed out to his carriage all by himself. I strolled down to my waiting taxi, which allowed me to follow the gentleman's coach at a distance. My driver, Lewis, was very good at not being seen or detected. He would suddenly park and turn off the vehicle's lights, for he knew the carriage would have to stop at the next major intersection. When the carriage continued on, Lewis turned the motor on and stayed on the chase. After a somewhat roundabout route, the carriage came to a stop at Mitre Square. There it waited."

"For what purpose?" I asked impatiently.

"For an Unfortunate who came out of the shadows," Wiggins replied. "She climbed into the carriage, but it did not drive away."

"Could you determine if they were conducting business?" my father asked.

"If you are inquiring if the carriage was bouncing up and down, the answer is no," Wiggins reported. "But I knew you would inquire as to what transpired inside the coach, so in the darkness I crept closer and closer until I reached a side alleyway at the rear of the carriage. And that is when I heard them discussing Pretty Penny. I could clearly hear her name over and over."

"On both of their parts?" Joanna asked promptly.

"Yes, ma'am."

"Did you hear complete sentences?"

"That was most difficult, for other carriages and motor vehicles were producing noise as they passed by, and the bloody horse kept whinnying. But I heard them mentioning who and when along with Pretty Penny's name. I suspect they reached some sort of agreement because she finally said, 'That is how it will occur.' And with that, she bounded out of the carriage and disappeared into the darkness."

"Well done," Joanna approved, and gave Wiggins a five-pound note. "One pound for the Irregulars uncovering a most important clue, a second is for the night guard at the taxi repair garage, and the next two are for Lewis and the garage guard for your upcoming outing to track the gentleman drifters."

"And the final pound of the five-pound note?"

"Find the Unfortunate who was in the carriage and offer her a pound for the conversation she had with the handsome gentleman."

"I am afraid, madam, that I did not obtain a good look at her face, and only saw her in profile," Higgins said honestly. "Moreover, she may not wish to discuss that secret conversation."

"Ask around and learn her identity," Joanna coaxed. "There will be a fiver in it if you can discover her name and address."

Wiggins licked his lips at the irresistible offer. Five pounds was the equivalent of a hundred shillings, which was a hundred times greater than the daily fee paid for the services of an Irregular. They would scour the streets and work day and night to find that woman's name and whereabouts. "What are your instructions when we return as lookouts at the Randy Tar?"

"I would think it unfeasible to have three taxis waiting near the pub."

"Totally, madam. There is no possible way to snatch three taxis from the garage without being noticed. And to have three taxis outside the Randy Tar late at night would surely draw attention and suspicion."

"Then make do with one."

"Which of the three gentleman drifters should I follow?"

"The one who departs without a carriage."

"Done."

The Baker Street Irregulars hurried out, no doubt anxious to begin their search for the Unfortunate who met and carried on a secret conversation with Maxwell Anderson. It seemed like a hopeless task, but I had learned from past experience not to underestimate the cleverness of the Irregulars.

"What do you make of all this, Joanna?" my father asked.

"I make that it takes us one step closer to Pretty Penny," said she.

"I agree, particularly with the information we have on Maxwell Anderson," my father concurred. "Should we now not confront him and learn of his conversation with the Unfortunate?"

"Not yet," Joanna advised.

"But he could surely advance our case."

"He could also invent a dozen stories to cover his meeting at Mitre Square."

"Such as?"

"He could state that the Unfortunate recognized him as an actor from the playhouse and offered him information on the whereabouts of Pretty Penny. With this tempting offer, he agreed to meet her secretly at Mitre Square where she would be given a substantial reward for her knowledge. But alas, it all turned out to be a hoax."

"Or the truth," I opined.

"Either way, we must play our cards carefully and wait for the opportune moment to confront Maxwell Anderson."

With that final statement, Joanna lighted a Turkish cigarette and began pacing across our parlor, for it was clear that all the pieces of the puzzle had not yet come together.

Chapter 19

The Threat

The letter arrived mixed in with the remainder of the morning mail to 221b Baker Street. But it was uniquely different in that the addressee was THE DAUGHTER OF SHERLOCK HOLMES spelled in block letters which had been pasted onto the envelope. We immediately recognized who had sent the letter and that was enough to cause a chill to run down our collective spines.

"It's him," Joanna whispered under her breath.

"He means to taunt us at home," I surmised.

"We shall see." After donning rubber gloves, Joanna carefully opened the envelope and inspected its interior before extracting a neatly folded letter and placing it on the dining table for all to see.

It read:

STILL PUZZLED?
ASK THE BOSS ABOUT JOHN GILL
YOURS
NEMO

"Could it be a hoax?" my father asked.

"Probably not," Joanna replied. "Note that he uses the term *BOSS,* which was how Jack the Ripper referred to the Metropolitan Police Commissioner in his letters to Scotland Yard twenty-eight years ago. It is his method of telling us this mail is genuine."

I reread the letter and wondered about its purpose. "Who is this John Gill?"

Joanna shrugged. "I have no idea, but obviously the commissioner does."

"And why did he sign it with the name Nemo?" I asked.

"That, too, is beyond me," said she. "But again, he is leaving two clues we must follow."

Joanna reached for the phone and dialed Inspector Lestrade's number, which she had long ago committed to memory. She requested he immediately set up a meeting with the commissioner on a most important matter dealing with Jack the Ripper. Although the letter was mentioned, she decided to give none of the details.

Joanna placed the phone down, saying, "He will call back shortly." She examined the letter again and held it up to the light for further study. "It carries the watermark of A Pirie and Sons, just as did the earlier message."

"I wonder if the cut-out block letters of the alphabet come from the same source?" I queried. "Perhaps they could be traced."

"This is to be determined," she replied. "But it is the content of the letter, not its composition, which merits our closest attention and that of Scotland Yard. It is the mention of John Gill and Nemo which is most worrisome, for I fear they point to yet another victim."

"Would it have not been wise to give the inspector the names in the letter?" my father suggested. "That would have surely piqued the commissioner's interest."

"He will be greatly interested as it is," Joanna responded. "I was also concerned that if Lestrade were to only inquire about the names, the commissioner might reply with short answers from a distant memory, which will not work to our advantage. I have questions to go with those names, for they have some deep purpose which must not be overlooked."

"I take it you have already made some deductions from the letter," I surmised.

"More than a few come to mind, but all require confirmation from the commissioner," said she. "Let us begin with the name John Gill, who is known to the commissioner and thus must be one of The Ripper's victims from the long-ago past."

"But I thought The Ripper only killed females who were prostitutes, and John Gill would certainly not fall into that category," I argued.

"An excellent point, John, for our Ripper has followed the same course thus far," Joanna concurred. "Which begs the question—why does he mention John Gill in his letter?"

"It must relate to the next victim," I reasoned quickly.

"Precisely, but who and why?" she went on. "There is more to this than simply a name. Then we come to the signature at the end of the letter, Nemo. In Jules Verne's novel *20,000 Leagues Under the Sea,* the captain of the *Nautilus* is named Nemo, a rather heroic figure, who obviously bears no resemblance to our Ripper. Yet he signs his letter with that name."

"There must be a hidden, nonfictitious meaning to Nemo," my father ventured.

"Such as?" Joanna asked.

"An abbreviation of his true name."

"Most unlikely, for that would be too revealing."

"Perhaps Nemo also points to the next victim," my father suggested.

"Oh, I am certain it does," Joanna said. "And I am equally certain that it is somehow connected to the aforementioned John Gill."

We sat in silence and tried in vain to put together the strange pieces of the puzzle. But one question continued to weigh heavily on our minds. Were the present-day Ripper and the monster from twenty-eight years ago one and the same?

The evidence at hand spoke in the affirmative, for our Ripper followed the identical killing pattern as his supposed predecessor and both wrote letters remarkably similar to those written at the end of the last century. Yet we had no proof to back up this assertion. And this distinction was of more than just historical interest, for if these murderers were one and the same, it would exclude thirty-two-year-old Maxwell Anderson as being the current-day Ripper. But what of his outings as a gentleman drifter and his secret meeting with the Unfortunate at Mitre Square and their whispered conversation regarding Pretty Penny, whose life was slipping away before my very eyes? These happenings would have to be explained.

The phone sounded loudly and broke into our concentration. On the second ring, Joanna quickly picked up the receiver and, after speaking briefly with Lestrade, announced that the commissioner would see us immediately.

We departed our rooms in haste and were able to promptly hail a passing taxi. But traffic was dense and slow, which only heightened our anticipation that important clues were about to be deciphered, either of which could point to The Ripper's next victim. Nonetheless, our hopes that we might be able to save a life were dimmed by the indisputable fact that this madman seemed clever enough to remain one step or more ahead of us.

Twenty minutes later we found ourselves being ushered by Lestrade into Commissioner Bradberry's office. The décor, like the man, was solid and polished, with nicely worn oak furniture and an orderly desk that was free of clutter. Except for a large photograph of King George the Fifth, the walls were bare.

The commissioner waved us to our seats and, without the usual amenities, we proceeded directly to the business at hand. Using her still-gloved hands, Joanna opened the envelope and spread the letter upon the desk, then moved back. Both Bradberry and Lestrade leaned in to read and reread the letter. The expression on the inspector's face indicated he was as puzzled as we were by the message it contained.

"Who is this John Gill?" the inspector asked.

"A victim," the commissioner replied curtly before turning to Joanna. "Was the letter examined for a watermark?"

"It was produced by A Pirie and Sons," she replied.

"He still favors them, much as he did so many years ago," Bradberry remarked. "We attempted to track down the seller of such fine stationery, but it was an impossible task then and would be now. We shall of course look for fingerprints on the envelope and letter, but he is much too clever to leave any behind. Which reminds me, we tried to match the prints on the shoes to the other items you supplied, but were only able to determine three identical points, which were far too few."

"What of the red ink fingerprint on the old letter written by The Ripper?" Joanna inquired.

"The old print was cracked and badly smudged, and thus was of little value," the commissioner reported. "In addition, that was one of the letters which was considered to be a hoax."

"Do you suspect the letter before us is likewise a hoax?" Lestrade asked.

"I think not," he answered. "The same watermark says otherwise, and the use of the names John Gill and Nemo confirms that opinion. Furthermore, he employed the same term to denote the commissioner which was a hallmark of Jack the Ripper."

"Might he have gathered that by studying The Ripper's past history?" my father asked.

"Possibly," the commissioner replied. "But then he connects my name with that of John Gill, which only someone very familiar with The Ripper's past would be aware of."

"I take it John Gill was a known victim of The Ripper's?" said Joanna.

"Most believe so, although some disagree. I was of the opinion the mutilated lad was the work of this vile murderer, and no doubt the most ghastly of the lot," he continued on, and for a moment I thought I saw a wince come and go from his face. "Please prepare yourself for this horrific story, for it is the sort which can give one nightmares." He took a deep breath as the unpleasant memory returned. "John Gill was a sweet little lad of almost eight when he disappeared without notice or reason. Two days later his body was found in a stable not far from his home in Bradford, Yorkshire. His navy-blue topcoat was wrapped and tied around him. When he was unwrapped, those present saw the most gruesome sight imaginable. Both of the lad's ears were sliced off, and his severed legs were propped up on either side of his body and secured with cord. He had been stabbed multiple times, with his abdomen slashed open and his organs placed on the ground next to him. His heart had been torn out and wedged under his chin. The police begged the mother not to view her son's body, but she insisted. It was said that her wails and sobs could be heard a quarter of a mile away."

We sat motionless in stunned silence at the most horrific murder we had heard of or witnessed. It was far beyond savagery and barbarism, and an unforgettable nightmare to all who viewed the ravaged body. And what of the lad's poor mother, who would never know a peaceful moment for the remainder of her life?

"And to top it all, the bloody bastard had sent a letter to the *Times* which read: 'I have come to Liverpool and you will soon hear from me.'" The commissioner's face hardened at the recollection. "He had the message delivered a week before the murder occurred."

"Did he kill others so young?" Joanna asked.

"There may well have been another, for during the same time period a second schoolboy named Percy Knight Searle was found murdered near Portsmouth, with vicious slashes to his throat," Bradberry responded. "The Ripper was merciless in all of his attacks, but particularly so in the case of John Gill. To add to the misery of the family, he had somehow learned about the lad's upcoming birthday and performed his terrible deed a week prior to the planned party, which should have been a most joyful time. Can you imagine a more malevolent act? Here the family was about to gather to celebrate the little boy's birthday and—"

Joanna abruptly straightened up in her chair. "Johnny! He plans to kill my Johnny!"

The commissioner stared at my wife, mystified by her reaction. "Who is this Johnny you speak of?"

"Her young son who is about to turn fifteen," my father answered for the still-stunned Joanna. "A grand birthday party at Lord Blalock's manor is scheduled for tomorrow."

Bradberry nodded slowly as he assimilated the new information and the similarities between the cases. Both the previous victim and the prospective one were named John, and both had upcoming birthdays which would mark the end of their lives. "Jack the Ripper plans to repeat the terrible deed he performed twenty-eight years ago and, as before, he is announcing it."

"Except this time he will be looking at the business end of a Webley revolver," my father said coldly.

Joanna regained her composure and lighted a Turkish cigarette as she thought through the problem. Unlike her father, she was endowed with emotions, but was able to compartmentalize her feelings from the harsh realities of a brutal case. She took several deep puffs on her cigarette before speaking.

"He will not come at Johnny while my son is under our close watch, but rather when for some reason our guard is down. And it will not be a frontal attack, but a kidnapping."

"Then we shall provide round-the-clock surveillance and protection for your son," Bradberry assured.

"How exactly are we to closet him away from all of his activities?" Joanna wondered aloud. "He is a busy student at Eton and it would be impossible to protect him twenty-four hours a day. You cannot expect—" She stopped in mid-sentence as her face lost color. "He is at Eton at this very moment and unguarded."

The commissioner quickly reached for his phone and dialed a single-digit number. "Mrs. Jeffries, I wish to speak with the headmaster at Eton on a most urgent matter." He replaced the phone and came back to Joanna. "Your son will have to withdraw from Eton for the near future."

"For the foreseeable future," she corrected worriedly, "assuming he has not yet been harmed."

"But surely the headmaster would have informed you of such a happening," said I.

Joanna shook her head. "Johnny could be missing for hours without causing concern."

"But the warning letter only arrived this morning," my father noted.

"It may not be a warning, Watson, but a notice of what has already transpired."

The phone on the commissioner's desk rang and he promptly answered it. "Headmaster, I am in my office and by my side is the daughter of Sherlock Holmes, who wishes to speak with you." He handed the receiver to Joanna with a quiet caution. "Be careful with your words, for I have a plan in mind which requires secrecy."

"As do I," Joanna replied in a soft voice. "But rest assured my son will not be used as bait."

"We may have no choice."

"There is always a choice, Commissioner," she said, and directed her attention to the phone. "Headmaster, listen most carefully to what I am about to say and do so without interruption. There is a distinct possibility that my son may be facing danger. I need to know of his whereabouts at this very moment. If you are unaware, then determine so while the phone line is open."

Joanna's eyes suddenly widened. "He departed? When? What method of transportation did he use?" she asked, and followed with a string of questions.

"Did you notice if it was a taxi company? . . .

"Exactly what time did the taxi driver arrive at the boys' hall? . . .

"Was he alone? . . .

"No, no, Headmaster, you need not do anything further. If we require more information, you will be contacted."

Joanna placed the phone down and quickly went over the contents of her conversation with the headmaster. "Johnny departed Eton at two o'clock after informing the headmaster that his early departure to London was to surprise his mother, for both of us were to attend a grand birthday party at his grandfather's manor the following day. The taxi Johnny had summoned arrived on time, but the headmaster did not know if it was a taxi from a local company, nor did he notice the driver other than when he opened the door for my son. And finally, Johnny was alone when he entered the taxi, which did not appear to have any other passengers."

After giving the matter more thought, my father said, "The route from Eton to the train station goes through heavily populated neighborhoods. Even The Ripper would not be so bold as to attack Johnny en route when they could surely be seen."

"But Johnny could be rendered unconscious and hidden in the rear compartment," Joanna rebutted. "Nevertheless, the fact that the taxi was summoned and arrived on time strongly suggests the taxi and its driver were legitimate."

"Then the lad should be safe and secure once he boards the train," I said, injecting a note of optimism.

"Not necessarily," she countered. "If memory serves me correctly, the early-afternoon train to Paddington makes a stop at Reading. The Ripper could have boarded earlier in Eton or later in Reading and done his work in the first-class cabin Johnny prefers."

"But how could The Ripper reach Reading before Johnny's train?" my father queried. "He could not have known the lad was departing Eton early."

"He could have been shadowing Johnny," Joanna responded. "And the moment he realized where my Johnny was headed, The Ripper could have raced by motor vehicle to Reading."

"I have taken the train from Windsor to Paddington on a number of occasions," Bradberry recalled. "The stop at Reading lasts at least ten minutes."

"Which is more than enough time for The Ripper to inflict horrific damage," Joanna said hurriedly, as she crushed out her cigarette. "Commissioner, please be good enough to contact the stationmaster at Reading and see if the train from Windsor has arrived. If it has or is about to, instruct him to hold it there until a local constable is on the scene. And that constable should be armed. Of course no one should be allowed to board or leave that train until a thorough search is completed."

In under thirty seconds, the commissioner was speaking with the stationmaster at Reading. "The train has already departed, you say, and is due at Paddington in fifteen minutes," he repeated for our benefit.

Joanna abruptly pushed her chair back. "It will take fifteen minutes for us to reach Paddington if traffic allows. Let us make haste, for I wish to be on the platform the moment the train arrives."

"Provide them with a car," the commissioner ordered Lestrade.

"Done, sir."

"And report back on any mishaps the lad might have experienced on the trip home."

We sped to Paddington station in a large Scotland Yard motorcar, with both Lestrade and the driver armed and prepared to fire, for we had learned from hard experience The Ripper's uncanny ability to evade capture. But our minds were all fixed on young Johnny and the horrid possibility that he had encountered the madman, with a gruesome ending. The butchery of The Ripper was so ghastly that I hesitated to write of it, but I decided it was necessary to do so in order to demonstrate the man's true and savage nature. Although the abolition of public hanging had been instituted in 1868, I wished for the law to be briefly suspended should Jack the Ripper be apprehended.

We pulled up in front of Paddington station and hastily exited, with both Lestrade and the armed driver Harrison at our side. Two constables were guarding the entrance, and I noticed yet another two standing watchfully near the platform for the train from Windsor which was just arriving. A telephone call from the commissioner brought immediate results for all to see, I thought to myself. The pair of constables straightened their posture and saluted as we approached.

Lestrade rushed over with instructions. "Fetch the other two constables immediately and stand guard at all the exits of the train from Windsor. No one is permitted to disembark until my search of every car is completed. The individual we are interested in may well be dressed as and have the manner of a gentleman, but he is quite dangerous, so be aware and take no chances."

But before the constables could reach their assigned positions, the passengers were stepping out onto the platform. We observed each closely, looking for any sign or behavior which might be telltale. First off was an elderly couple, the man bent at the waist and using a cane for support. He required a porter to help him disembark. Then came a soldier, with shining boots and a ramrod posture, and behind him a pair of chatting nuns. More couples stepped down onto the platform, followed by a group of teenagers dressed in their school uniforms. None of the students were Johnny and none were wearing the well-known Eton suit. Finally, the disembarkation ended.

"The Ripper could have seen the police activity and remained on board," Lestrade suggested. "The constables will be stationed at the exits, while the train is searched. I shall begin in the car nearest the locomotive, while Harrison, our driver, takes the opposite end. You may follow me if you wish."

The inspector loosened the revolver in his holster and climbed aboard, with the three of us only a step behind. The first car was quiet and empty, with all the first-class cabins vacated. The second car was likewise still, but the door to the end compartment was closed. Lestrade waved us back and, upon drawing his weapon, rapped on the door.

"This is Scotland Yard!" he said in a stern voice. "You are ordered to immediately open."

We heard the sound of someone stirring about before the door opened. It was Johnny, who was rubbing at his sleep-filled eyes.

"Why all the commotion?" the lad asked, watching Lestrade place his revolver back in the holster.

"We were most worried about you," Joanna said, with a

broad smile, and hurried over to give the tightest of hugs. She kissed his forehead, saying, "I take it your journey was uneventful."

Johnny gave his mother a most puzzled look. "Please tell me why a train ride from Windsor merits such great concern."

"Because we thought you might be in danger."

"From what, pray tell?"

"An evil which you shall shortly learn of."

"And this evil has me in mind?"

"So it would appear."

Johnny's face brightened. "Is he formidable?"

"Quite," Joanna said candidly.

"On the order of Moriarty?" Johnny asked, mentioning the name of a mastermind criminal whom Sherlock Holmes referred to as the Napoleon of crime.

"Every bit as evil, but far more vicious."

"Well then, we shall endeavor to catch this chap."

It was most certainly not the response we had expected, but then again here was the grandson of Sherlock Holmes who had already demonstrated to us that he carried the Great Detective's genes. Like his grandfather and mother, the young Sherlock would never dream of backing down, for deep within all three was the unquenchable desire to confront and defeat any criminal element which came their way.

After thanking Lestrade for his assistance, we departed Paddington and found a four-wheeler waiting for us at the entrance. The door to our carriage had barely closed before the ever-inquisitive Johnny began his questions.

"Pray tell who is this evil?" he asked.

"Jack the Ripper," Joanna replied, and watched for her son's reaction.

"I have read of him," Johnny said, unmoved. "So he has returned, has he?"

"With you in mind, I am afraid," Joanna cautioned.

"How so?"

Joanna hesitated, as if wondering how many of the gruesome features she should tell her son. She decided to hold back nothing and spoke in vivid detail of the letter and the significance of the name John Gill. I was somewhat surprised that she repeated, literally word for word, the commissioner's ghastly description of the little boy's butchered body. Perhaps she did it to reinforce that this was not simply a criminal investigation and merry chase but rather dealt with a conscienceless murderer whose savagery had no end. Joanna's next sentence proved my assertion was correct.

"You must place the utmost gravity on this horrid case, for lives are very much at stake, including yours."

"He is simply a killer, Mother, who is driven by some mad impulse, which will eventually lead to his downfall."

"Does it not concern you that your life is in danger?"

"Of course, for that reason I have a plan to defend myself."

"How will you accomplish this feat?"

"With a weapon."

"With a revolver?" my father asked in astonishment.

"With jujitsu, Dr. Watson," Johnny replied. "You see, I have followed in my mother's footsteps and enrolled in such a school near Windsor."

Joanna's head spun around at the unexpected revelation. "How long have you been attending this school?"

"For seven months."

"Have you earned a belt?"

"A solid gray one."

"I am afraid that is at the lower end of the spectrum."

"That is so, but I can break a man's arm so that he will never use it again," Johnny said confidently.

"The elbow lock," Joanna described.

"Which I practice daily on one of my roommates."

My father and I exchanged knowing glances, for here again was the indelible proof that physical talent can be genetically transmitted. Sherlock Holmes was a skilled boxer, Joanna a black belt in jujitsu, and now her son was climbing the ladder in that very same martial art. That trait had to run in the genes.

Joanna took a long, deep breath, which she tended to do while carefully choosing her words. "I must warn you that your experience in jujitsu is still somewhat limited and you may not be developed to the point of defending yourself against a sudden attack that comes out of nowhere. That requires a split-second, nearly involuntary, reaction to your opponent. And if he comes at you with a weapon, such as a bat or club, a simple jujitsu move will not protect you."

"I am aware of that, Mother, and for that reason I plan to stay close to the three of you."

"Well considered," Joanna said, obviously relieved.

"Wherever you go, we shall go," my father chimed in.

"Accompanied by your trusted Webley," Johnny said in an even tone, but his face was now deadly serious.

"I shall sleep with it."

Joanna nodded her approval at my father's comments, for they reinforced the danger the lad was facing and the necessity that all precautions be taken. We rode on in silence, but our collective thoughts no doubt remained centered on Jack the Ripper. My mind drifted back to the letter he had sent to Joanna, for therein lay the clues to his next victim, presumably our Johnny. The mention of John Gill indicated that the victim would be a young lad nearing his birthday, which told us who and when. But it was the important *where* that seemed to elude us. The only other clues in the letter were the nickname The Ripper assigned to the commissioner and the mysterious

Nemo at the end of the message. Was the latter a clue as to where the next murder would take place?

"We neglected to ask the commissioner about the name Nemo in the letter," I mused aloud.

"I was too concerned with Johnny's well-being to inquire," said Joanna. "But I shall do so by phone when we reach home."

A curious look came to Johnny's face. "What would Jack the Ripper have to do with *The Odyssey*?"

"Are you referring to the ancient story in Greek mythology?" she asked at once.

"I am," Johnny replied. "Nemo was the alias Odysseus used to overcome his opponent."

Joanna was taken aback by her son's knowledge of the Greek myth, as was I. "How did you come by this information?"

"Some weeks ago there was a play at Eton entitled *The Odyssey,* which was based on Homer's work and performed by a group of traveling actors from London," the lad replied. "We were encouraged by our tutors to attend."

Traveling actors from London! The words reverberated in my brain and immediately brought to mind the St. Bart's Players, who often performed in cities near London. Most important, three of the St. Bart's Players were prime suspects in the Jack the Ripper murders. I quickly glanced over to Joanna and my father, and it was clear we all had the same thought.

"How did you learn of this play?" I asked, trying to keep my voice neutral.

"There were posters placed all about," Johnny replied. "That and the fact it was the talk of the town."

"Did the posters happen to mention where these players originated from?"

"They were called the Hammersmith Players."

My spirits sank at the lad's answer. So much for connecting *The Odyssey* to our prime suspects, I thought unhappily. Although the Hammersmith district had a hospital, it was a military facility reserved for those wounded in the Great War and was in no way associated with St. Bartholomew's. "And so goes a possible link to Jack the Ripper," said I.

"Not necessarily," Joanna countered, and turned to her son. "Please tell me about these posters which advertised the play. I would like a description."

Johnny thought back briefly before answering. "There was nothing unusual about them other than they were quite colorful, with a figure of Homer taking up most of the poster."

"Was the name Nemo mentioned?"

Johnny nodded slowly, as the memory returned. "It was indeed. A giant figure of a Greek warrior was holding out both hands, with the name Odysseus, who was the hero, printed on one, and Nemo, the alias, written on the other. Those of us unfamiliar with the myth wondered what their meaning was."

"The poster caught your eye, did it?"

"It caught everyone's eye, Mother."

"Including Jack the Ripper's," Joanna said grimly.

"Pray tell how you reached that conclusion?" I queried.

"Because of the letter he sent us," she elucidated. "All of the pieces of the puzzle now fit together. John Gill was mentioned to inform us that his next victim would be a young boy nearing his birthday. That indicated to us he was planning to bring harm to our Johnny, who had the same profile. *NEMO* was signed to tell us The Ripper has visited Eton and seen the colorful posters. He may well have been shadowing Johnny and waiting for the most opportune moment to strike."

"And he was no doubt taunting us again, with a notice of what was yet to come," I added.

"That, too."

There was a sudden loud bang which caused our carriage to rock violently from side to side. We were thrown against one door, then the other, with nothing to hold on to other than each other. Joanna landed on my lap and Johnny on hers, while my father was tossed to the floor. As the carriage came to a rest, we could hear our horse make a frightful sound, followed by the noise of tires squealing on the asphalt pavement. We quickly checked ourselves for injuries and fortunately there were none, save for a nasty bruise on my father's knee.

The door to our coach slowly opened and a bloodied hand reached into the cabin. I hurriedly leaned back and prepared myself to kick at the intruder, while Joanna removed a shoe to use as a weapon. Then the remainder of the body that belonged to the bloodied hand showed itself. It was our driver, with a profusely bleeding nose. We stared at him and tried to collect ourselves as our pulses continued to race from the adrenaline flowing through our veins.

"Anyone hurt?" he asked anxiously.

"We are fine," I replied. "What caused our accident?"

"A bloody insane driver who of course sped away to avoid penalty and punishment."

"Did he come directly at us?" Joanna asked.

"So it would appear, madam," the driver responded. "My horse seemed to sense it and turned away just in time."

The horse made another frightful sound, although less intense than the previous one. Then he snorted loudly as air was forced through his nostrils.

"I had better attend to him," the driver said.

"One more question," Joanna requested quickly. "Did you actually see the driver of the vehicle?"

"I did, madam, but only briefly and in passing, as he fled the scene."

"Describe what you saw."

"It was a man, in his middle years, I would guess, who was for the most part hunched over the wheel."

"Could you make out his hair?"

"No, madam, for he was wearing a hat of some sort."

"Like a fisherman's hat?" Joanna asked promptly.

The driver hesitated before answering. "It could be, but then again he was driving away and I did not have a good look."

"Thank you," Joanna said. "You may now attend to your horse."

Once the driver had withdrawn, I hurriedly asked, "Do you truly believe it was The Ripper?"

"It might well have been," Joanna replied. "It would have been a variation of the smash-and-grab technique. With all of us dazed and perhaps seriously injured, he could have carried Johnny away."

"But would there not be witnesses and onlookers who would stop him?" Johnny asked.

"Oh, there would be, but he could have explained that you were most badly injured and he was rushing you to nearby St. Mary's Hospital."

"Is he that clever, Mother?"

"There is a long list of dead people that can attest to that very fact," Joanna said, and reached for the door to climb out of the battered carriage.

Chapter 20

Maxwell Anderson

"You do not fit the profile of a gentleman drifter," Joanna remarked.

Maxwell Anderson's brow went up a notch. "I believe you have been misinformed."

"My sources do not misinform," said she.

We were seated in the parlor of our rooms at 221b Baker Street, enjoying glasses of sherry as yet another storm blew in from the North Sea. Anderson had been invited on the premise that his knowledge of Pretty Penny might assist us in our investigation, but our prime purpose was to determine if he was in any way involved in the disappearance of the missing actress. He showed no hesitation in accepting our invitation.

"You were seen in the Black Lamb, well dressed indeed and cozying up to an Unfortunate," Joanna went on. "Yet your age and manners are not in keeping with those of a gentleman drifter."

"My intent was not to slum, but to find a trail that Penny may have left behind."

"In the Black Lamb?"

Anderson nodded his answer. "For that was one of the places where she might have crossed paths with her abductor."

Joanna, my father, and I looked at the handsome pathologist in total disbelief, with my wife asking the question on our collective minds. "Surely you are not telling us Pretty Penny worked part-time as an Unfortunate."

"No, no," Anderson said at once. "Never in a million years."

He sighed sadly, then recounted the desperate plight Pretty Penny found herself in prior to being taken in by Emma Adams. The young girl was penniless on the mean streets of Whitechapel and barely managed to subsist by taking on the most menial of positions which paid only a pittance. These included cleaning floors at local shops and washing dishes at the Black Lamb. It was the latter work she valued so highly, because the pub owner allowed her to partake of leftover food. There were times when that was her only form of nourishment.

"What a dreadful experience," my father noted.

"Dreadful indeed, sir," Anderson continued on. "Made even worse by her seemingly endless attacks of asthma."

"She confided in you, then."

"She did, Dr. Watson, but only after she began wheezing noticeably after a late-evening performance. From her history, it was clear she had never been adequately treated, so I arranged for her to be seen by a specialist at St. Bart's who was having some success with a combination therapy that included belladonna alkaloids and atropine. His stock of these agents was limited, but he was good enough to deliver a weekly supply to me, which of course I gave to Penny. The results were spectacular, with only an occasional wheeze to be heard now and then."

"Until she decided to have a go without them," Joanna interjected.

The handsome pathologist nodded again. "Like most patients with chronic disease who become asymptomatic, she assumed the drugs had cured her, which of course they had not."

"You stated that you supplied Penny with her medications on a weekly basis. Correct?"

"Correct, for as I just mentioned, the stock of these agents was in short supply and a week's worth was all the specialist could provide to me."

"Which you promptly handed to Pretty Penny."

"Every Tuesday following the performance."

"But she went missing on a Tuesday."

"Which continues to cause me even greater concern, for without her medications the severe life-threatening attacks of asthma are certain to return," Anderson said worriedly. "That is why I set out on my own to find my dear Penny before such a terrible event occurs. But alas, my ventures into the Black Lamb were in vain. None of her coworkers were able to help in even the smallest way."

"And the clock on Pretty Penny now ticks even faster," Joanna said, more to herself than to the pathologist.

"So it would appear."

My wife paused to light a Turkish cigarette which Anderson viewed with obvious disfavor. She ignored his look of disapproval and spent several moments assimilating the new information. "But a dishwasher would not come into contact with the unruly crowd that usually populated the pub, and that is where the abductor would have placed himself."

"True enough, madam, but on weekends when the pub was busiest, Penny would also help out as a barmaid. She was always kind and considerate to the Unfortunates, who adored her for it. Thus my interest in the Unfortunates, for they would have noticed any unsavory character who paid unwanted attention to Penny."

"And one Unfortunate did," Joanna reasoned. "Which is why you decided to meet her secretly in a carriage at Mitre Square."

Anderson's jaw dropped. "How could you possibly know that?"

"I have my sources," she replied. "But pray tell why in such secrecy and why at Mitre Square?"

"At the square because she lived nearby, and in secrecy away from the pub for two reasons. First, when Unfortunates spend excessive time talking to an individual rather than performing a service, people become suspicious and ask questions. Secondly, pubs have ears that listen to the patrons talk. The Unfortunate did not want word reaching the abductor that she might be a witness."

"Clever girl."

"Clever enough to keep her distance from Jack the Ripper."

Joanna abruptly moved in closer and asked, "Did she actually see The Ripper?"

"Not with any degree of certainty, but she recalled an older patron repeatedly offering to buy Penny a drink, which she of course refused."

"Could she describe the man?" Joanna inquired quickly.

"Only that he was older, with long gray hair," Anderson replied. "I informed her that should she obtain his name and address, a most generous reward awaited her."

"I take it she has not responded."

"Not as yet."

"Nor will she, for Jack the Ripper will shortly bring his reign of terror to an end, and he will then again go into seclusion."

The young pathologist gave my wife an odd look. "What allows you to be so certain this will occur?"

"Because his letters state that once he has done away with Pretty Penny, he will retire for good. She will be the last to die, you see."

Anderson sank into his chair, crestfallen. "The thought of losing her forever is more than I can bear."

"Which no doubt makes you deeply regret the fight you two had at Alexander's."

"More than you will ever know," he said ruefully. "All she wanted was a commitment to marriage which I foolishly refused to give—all because of societal pressure which means so little now."

"Was that the last evening you saw her?"

"The very last and it had been so perfect," he reminisced. "We were enjoying hors d'oeuvres when a well-known actress entered and the seated patrons received her with warm applause. Penny envisioned the day when she, too, would walk into Alexander's and be recognized with spontaneous applause. It was shortly after that pleasant moment that our fight occurred and she stormed out."

"Did you subsequently attempt to apologize?"

"On a number of occasions, but she turned a deaf ear," Anderson answered. "It had gotten to the point where I planned to propose."

"Was she aware of that?"

"Sadly, no."

Joanna crushed out her cigarette and gave our visitor a long look before saying, "Men tend to lack timing in such situations."

"As I am keenly aware at this moment," said he. "And I suspect I was trying to make up for it by performing my own amateurish investigation."

"You have not caused any harm," she assured him. "But dressed as a gentleman drifter, you are unlikely to discover any worthwhile clues. The Unfortunates will speak with you, but say little."

"Particularly since I am not nearly as glib as Willoughby and Rudd."

"They are frequent drifters, are they?" asked I.

"Quite so," Anderson replied. "They travel to such places at least once a week and, from their descriptions, the seedier the pub the better."

"I would expect better of them," my father said in a voice of disapproval.

"They show no shame and actually boast of their unsavory outings."

"But not to their families."

"I should think not."

"And not to their medical associates."

"Only to those who also take part in such adventures."

Joanna rejoined the conversation. "How many others are there?"

Anderson shrugged. "A few from other hospitals, I am told. But I was not given their names."

"Do they partake of the activities at the Black Lamb?"

"Of that I am not certain."

"While at the Black Lamb, did you speak with other Unfortunates?" she inquired.

"One other," he replied. "But she had little to offer and only wished to be served one drink after another. In addition, she continually scratched at herself, which made me wonder if she had some sort of infestation." Our visitor paused as if to ponder a problem. "Do you consider it best for me not to return to the Black Lamb and continue my pursuit?"

"I would suggest you avoid that pub, for frequent visits and offers of reward will in all likelihood elicit false information which will be of no value."

Anderson nodded in agreement. "False data is worse than no data, so I shall follow your advice and desist."

"A wise decision." Joanna rose to indicate the interview was over. "Thank you for your time and accurate information."

"I trust you will keep me informed of any further developments."

"We shall."

At the door, Anderson turned and said, "There was one more feature the Unfortunate described of the individual in the pub who seemed so intent on buying Penny a drink."

"And that was?"

"He wore a fisherman's hat pulled down far over his forehead."

As the young pathologist departed, a sleepy-eyed Johnny looked out from his bedroom. "Did I miss anything of importance, Mother?"

"Only if you consider the exclusion of a prime suspect important," she replied, and, with a warm smile, gestured him back to his bed. "We'll talk more in the morning, at which time I shall provide you with all the details."

"I will hold you to that," the lad said before retiring.

As quiet returned, I looked to my wife with both a statement and a question. "That narrows it down to Willoughby and Rudd. Which of the two do you favor?"

"Both, for now."

Chapter 21

The Birthday Party

I believe this was the very first instance in which my father joined in the festivities of a birthday party fully armed. He made no effort to hide the bulge beneath his coat which concealed the holster that held his Webley No. 2 revolver. Standing off to the side of the expansive garden at the rear of the Blalock manor, he sipped from a cup of punch but kept a sharp eye on all those present and arriving.

I found myself in conversation with Johnny's grandfather, the esteemed statesman Sir Henry Blalock, who showed his displeasure that Jack the Ripper remained on the loose and was now threatening his only grandchild.

"Why hasn't this madman been brought to justice?" he demanded.

"He is most clever, Sir Henry," I responded. "But I am certain his capture will come."

"I take it that the full force of Scotland Yard is engaged in the hunt for this so-called Ripper."

"They are, for it represents their number one priority."

"I am afraid I do not place much confidence in that lot." The elder statesman was a tall, broad-shouldered man, with sharp, aristocratic features and a voice that commanded one's attention. "You see, I recall their lack of success nearly thirty years ago when Jack the Ripper went about his work without interruption. Oh, they had their suspects, but could never bring forth enough evidence to prosecute. One of those under close scrutiny was the Duke of Clarence, who had rather unusual sexual preferences. He had, shall we say, a tendency to play both sides of the net, for which he was often blackmailed. One story, for example, found him in a compromising position from his association with two ladies of low standing who were paid off for their silence. Thus, he appeared to solve his problems with money, not murder."

He paused to flick an ash from his cigar into a large fountain which contained gently running water. A huge goldfish came up to investigate but showed no further interest and swam away. "The second suspect seemed more promising. He was an actor and gentleman drifter named Thomas Blake."

"Blake, you say?" I interrupted, my interest piqued by the fact that he was a gentleman drifter and actor, as were our three main suspects.

"A strange fellow who came from a quite good family, but seemed to find enjoyment amongst those of a lower class," Lord Blalock went on. "He had a vile temper to go along with his shady tastes and was a prime suspect. Blake died some years ago, but the suspicion that he was Jack the Ripper always hung over his head."

"Until now, of course."

"Indeed, for dead men don't kill." Sir Henry turned to greet his grandson with a warm smile. The lad was dressed in stylish attire, which included an ascot tie, and looked every bit the young gentleman. "Are you having a fine time, Johnny?"

"It is a splendid party, Grandfather," Johnny replied. "And I thank you heartily for it."

"It was my pleasure, for I want my grandson to be happy, even in these most trying times."

"Not to worry, sir, for I am well protected."

"So I see," Sir Henry said, and gestured with his head to my father. "The ever-vigilant Dr. Watson will guarantee that."

"As will the armed detective here in attendance for my safety," Johnny noted.

The elder statesman quickly glanced around the gathering. He studied the ten-foot-tall hedges surrounding the garden, then the children playing a game of charades with their parents watching, and finally his gaze went to the table holding the birthday cards brought by the guests as gifts.

"Where is this so-called detective located?" he asked.

"Observe the man by the card table, Grandfather," Johnny prompted.

Sir Henry looked over to the young man wearing a black waiter's jacket. "He is one of the hired help, I assume."

"Your assumption is incorrect, Grandfather," the lad pointed out. "Notice that he is wearing brown shoes rather than the customary black."

"Bad taste," Lord Blalock suggested.

"It is out of order, as is the bulge under the left side of his jacket where his revolver no doubt resides."

Sir Henry signaled to the head butler, who hurried over. "James, who is the help by the card table?"

James replied in a quiet voice, "He was sent by Scotland Yard, sir."

"Very good," the elder statesman said. He waited for the servant to return to his previous position, then patted his grandson affectionately on the shoulder. "You are so much like your mother, laddie."

"That is high praise indeed, Grandfather."

"It was meant to be," Sir Henry said. "And I take some comfort in the knowledge you will be safe with your mother in the confines of 221b Baker Street."

"I shall not be limited to Baker Street, sir, for there are a number of activities planned elsewhere," Johnny divulged.

"Will that not present some danger?"

"Not in the least, for I shall be accompanied by my mother and the Watsons when I visit the British Museum to pursue my studies in hieroglyphics."

"Why hieroglyphics?"

"Because it interests me," Johnny replied simply.

"I see," Sir Henry said, suppressing a grin. "What other activities are on your schedule?"

"A most important one, in which the good Dr. Watson will escort me to the firing range, where I shall endeavor to become a skilled marksman."

"Excellent!" Lord Blalock approved. "Pray tell what sort of weapon will be used?"

"Dr. Watson carries a heavy Webley No. 2 revolver, but he feels it would be too large and unwieldy for me. Thus, we shall begin our practice with a smaller .25-caliber Webley and gradually work our way up to the more powerful revolver."

"A well-thought-out plan," said Lord Blalock. "The .25-caliber is easy to handle and has the force to drop the enemy in his tracks when it finds its intended mark."

"Are you experienced with that caliber weapon, sir?"

"I am indeed, and have a .25-caliber Webley and Scott revolver residing and unemployed in my library. I would be more than delighted to give it to you as a birthday present."

"How generous of you, Grandfather!"

"Not at all, my boy."

Joanna strolled over to join us and playfully asked, "Do I sense a conspiracy in the making?"

"You do indeed," Sir Henry replied. "Johnny informs us that Dr. Watson has plans to turn the lad into a skilled marksman, which I applaud. To add to his pleasure and with your approval, I shall give my grandson a quite serviceable Webley and Scott .25-caliber revolver as a birthday present."

"A splendid gift," Joanna consented before turning to her son. "Allow me to repeat my instructions once more, Johnny. You must treat the weapon with deep respect, for it can do great good and great harm. And please remember there is no pleasure to be had by shooting an individual."

Johnny nodded solemnly. "Dr. Watson told me he has done so in both war and peace, and never felt an ounce of satisfaction."

"Well put," Joanna said. "Now I think it is time for you to join your friends in the festivities."

Johnny glanced over to a group of teenagers who were attempting to interpret gestures being made by a pretty young girl. "Oh, charades! A game which on occasion has some merit."

"Why so?" asked she, somewhat surprised, because her son rarely showed interest in such forms of amusement.

"Clues, Mother," he replied. "It is a game of clues."

Sir Henry watched his grandson move toward the play making and waited for him to be out of hearing distance. "We can only hope this extreme unpleasantness will not scar the lad."

"It is up to us to see that it doesn't," Joanna said determinedly.

"You must bring this monster to justice, Joanna," Sir Henry demanded. "You really must!"

"That is my plan."

"The quicker the better," he said, his expression now turning cold. "And if by chance one of Dr. Watson's bullets finds its mark, no one in London will grieve."

With that remark, he strode away to greet newcomers in a most cordial manner. But I noticed that he positioned himself so that his dear grandson was clearly in view.

"Your father-in-law made a most interesting comment on a prime suspect in the Jack the Ripper murders of yesterday," I whispered. "His name was Thomas Blake and he was a gentleman drifter and actor, with a violent temper."

Joanna quickly leaned in and asked, "Is he still alive?"

"Not according to Sir Henry," said I.

"Check with Lestrade, who may have to consult with the commissioner, to see if that report was accurate," she requested. "The common denominator here are gentleman drifters associating with and murdering Unfortunates."

"But for some reason our Ripper now seems to be fancying young boys."

"Only when the young boy is the son of the daughter of Sherlock Holmes, who happens to be nipping at his heels."

"Do you truly believe it bothers him that much?" I asked. "After all, the killings go on despite our presence."

"I can assure you it is of concern to him," Joanna replied. "But it will only cause him to choose his opportune moment more carefully. After all, Johnny will not be some defenseless Unfortunate standing alone, but rather a target surrounded by the three of us."

"Surely he will not confront us head on."

"Do not underestimate him, John. He is every bit as clever as Moriarty, who my father deemed the Napoleon of crime," my wife went on. "What is a certainty is that he will not do the expected."

"I may be overly optimistic, but I feel deep down that he invented this threat to Johnny in order to distract us as he goes about his business," said I.

Joanna shook her head in disagreement. "His type does not distract; they kill."

"Hope is one of my flaws, I suspect."

"Hope has its place, but not when it comes to solving crimes." Joanna gazed around the crowded garden in a leisurely fashion before suddenly craning her neck in the direction of the children playing charades. "I don't see Johnny!"

I quickly followed her line of vision and could not spot the lad. Nor did he appear to be by the fountain or tall hedges or elsewhere in the garden. I was about to signal my father when one of the young girls shrieked loudly. Our collective eyes went to the shrieker, who was now laughing as Johnny appeared from behind a tree after having apparently performed a particularly clever charade.

"He disappeared as part of the game," I remarked.

"We have to be ever vigilant," said Joanna, breathing a sigh of relief. "All that is required is one slip on our part and he is gone forever."

"But surely The Ripper would never attempt such an abduction here, with the garden so well guarded," I assured.

"You must keep in mind that he is a master of subterfuge," Joanna cautioned. "He can come and go and slip by without arousing suspicion. That is why we must never allow Johnny to be out of sight on Baker Street, at the British Museum, or even on the firing range."

"I shall reemphasize that to my father."

"There is no need, for our Watson is watching Johnny like a hawk."

"Speaking of the lad," I said, motioning with my head, "here he comes now, holding what appears to be a gift."

"Which would be most unusual, for birthday cards are customarily brought by the guests, not presents," Joanna commented.

"Look, Mother," Johnny said, as he opened a small velvet case.

Joanna's jaw dropped, for the case contained a pair of shiny copper cuff links which were made from farthing coins. She quickly regained her composure and glanced around the garden, measuring each and every guest except for the children. She paid particular attention to the hedges and the trees beside them, then to the circulating butlers. Suddenly her head jerked to the large fountain where a man dressed in work clothes appeared to be hunched over and hurrying down a pebbled path. She pointed to the individual and shouted, "Stop that man!"

In an instant my father had his revolver drawn and aimed at the apparent workman who froze in his steps. We rushed over, as did Sir Henry and the disguised detective from Scotland Yard. Joanna carefully studied the man being held at gunpoint and came to the same conclusion as I did. The thin middle-aged workman, with shaggy salt-and-pepper hair, was not one of our prime suspects.

"Does anyone know this man?" Joanna asked.

The head butler of the manor answered, "He is the repairman we sent for to unplug the fountain drain, madam."

"So you recognize him."

"I do, madam, for he is often called upon."

"Very good," Joanna said, and turned to the repairman. "You may be on your way, then."

"Yes, ma'am," he said, still shaken by the incident.

Sir Henry watched the repairman depart before asking Joanna, "What made you so suspicious of him?"

"His clothes seemed so out of place amongst your smartly attired guests," she replied, with a half-truth.

Sir Henry nodded at the explanation. "Better safe than sorry."

"Exactly," said Joanna, then suggested, "Perhaps we should now enjoy a glass of punch and rejoin the festivities."

She guided my father and me to the card table where the opened jewelry was exhibited for all to see. "Let us not upset the gathering by explaining the presence of copper cuff links."

"How did The Ripper manage to place the gift on the card table without himself being here?" I queried.

"I can think of a number of mechanisms," Joanna answered. "It could have been sent by a delivery service or mail or messenger. He might have even disguised himself and dropped it off as an invited guest who could not attend because of a prior engagement."

The head butler appeared, carrying a silver tray with three glasses of punch which he proffered to us.

"Thank you, James," Joanna said. "By chance, do you recall how the lovely jewelry box found its way to the card table?"

"It was delivered by messenger, madam."

"Did you recognize the messenger?"

"The package was taken at the door by one of the staff," James replied.

"Was a signature required?"

"No, madam."

"Do you recall the time the package arrived?"

"Only a few minutes ago, madam," James answered, and glanced at his pocket timepiece. "I would say as the clock was about to strike two thirty."

Perfect timing, I thought, for the gift was delivered at the height of the festivities when little attention would be paid to the delivery. I waited for the head butler to be out of earshot before asking Joanna, "Is there any hope to track the messenger?"

"None, for he is far too clever to leave that trail."

"And now there can be no doubt that our Johnny is his next intended victim," my father chimed in. "The meaning of the gift is crystal clear."

"He is sending us another message that is equally as clear and even more sinister."

"Which is?"

"That he can reach my son and take him captive whenever he wishes."

At that very moment, whether it was maternal instinct or happenstance, Joanna abruptly began to glance back and forth across the Blalock garden. A worried expression came to her face as she spoke. "I do not see Johnny."

"Perhaps he is still participating in the game of charades," I suggested.

We quickly walked over to the playing children and could immediately see that Johnny was not amongst them, nor was he hiding behind a tree as before. Joanna approached a pretty teenage girl and asked, "Is Johnny no longer with you?"

The lass pointed to an area between the fountain and tall hedge. "He dashed over there for a better view of the intruder, ma'am. But he promised to return shortly."

Our eyes went to the far section of the garden beyond the fountain, with its water now running smoothly. Not a soul was to be seen and from a distance there was no apparent opening in the hedge.

My father asked, "You are quite familiar with the garden, Joanna. Does it contain a rear gate?"

She responded with a shake of her head, "Only a high hedge."

We rapidly surveyed the entire garden end to end, searching behind every tree, fixture, and piece of furniture that had been placed on the lawn for the birthday party. A butler was instructed to enter the manor and determine if the lad had retired to use the bathroom. He had not.

Joanna was desperately trying to maintain her composure as her brain sought an answer to explain the disappearance. Once more she gazed around the garden, now peering between the closely gathered guests. Her son was not amongst them.

"Let us examine the place where he was last seen," she said finally, and led the way to the high hedge behind the fountain.

I saw nothing which was noteworthy, but apparently Joanna did, for she was now on her knees examining the bottom of the tall hedge. As she leaned in even closer, her attention seemed riveted on several protruding slender branches. "Broken," she announced, and, using both hands, parted the thick base of the hedge for a better view. It was at that instant my dear wife uttered a primal shriek, the likes of which I had never heard before. "Oh God! The Ripper has my Johnny!"

"What?" I asked with alarm. "How do you know this?"

Joanna gestured to a pair of drag marks through the lush grass beneath the hedge and next to them was one of Johnny's shoes. "The Ripper was secluded here, watching and waiting for his chance."

"And he used the disturbance of the repairman as a perfect distraction," I stated the obvious.

My wife waved the deduction aside. "Kick through the hedge, John! Hurry! Hurry!"

The branches were quite thick and required more than a few boots to reach the outer side of the hedge, which revealed only grass and no additional clues. There were no further drag marks and thank goodness no bloodstains. Joanna continued to study the ground, searching for the most trivial of signs, but found only indistinct footprints in the soft, wet grass.

"A single set of prints which were made by a man's shoe," she said, more to herself than to us. Her gaze next went to the surrounding area and, in particular, a narrow paved back road that was free of vehicles. Step by step, with her head down, she walked over to the road and at its curbside found Johnny's other shoe. "This is where he parked his automobile."

"Or his carriage," I ventured.

Joanna shook her head. "That would be too slow and require a driver."

Next, her gaze went to the adjoining manor which was also surrounded by a tall, thick hedge that was being trimmed by a middle-aged gardener who was perched on a wooden ladder. He turned and stared at us, obviously curious as to our presence.

"A possible witness," said she, and hurried over to the gardener, noting that he was not wearing spectacles. "And one with good vision, I would think."

As we approached, the workman descended from his ladder and respectfully removed his hat. "Yes, ma'am?"

"Did you happen to see a young lad with an older man pass through a short time ago?" Joanna asked anxiously.

"Yes, ma'am, I did. It was no more than ten minutes back, if that. And they seemed in a rush because the lad was ill."

"Ill? How so?"

"The gentleman was carrying the lad in his arms, with the boy's head hanging down. He must be sick, I thought to myself."

"Did he continue walking?"

"Until he reached the motor vehicle which was parked over there." The gardener pointed to the place where Johnny's second shoe was discovered.

"Can you describe the man?"

"No, ma'am. He was too far away."

"What was his attire?"

"He was wearing a hat and overalls, but I could not tell their brands," he answered. "I could, however, tell it was a boy he was carrying. The lad looked so ill that he was not moving at all. I began to wonder—!"

"The motor vehicle," Joanna interrupted. "Can you describe it?"

"Long and black."

"Do you know its make?"

The gardener shrugged. "I have no way of knowing."

"Was it chauffeured?"

"It did not appear so, for no one opened the rear door for the gentleman."

"Had you ever seen that car before?"

"No, ma'am."

"Thank you for your time."

As we turned and headed back to the Blalock manor, Joanna made no effort to hide the tears that gushed down her cheeks. Her voice cracked pitifully when she finally spoke. "My Johnny must be so frightened, so terribly frightened."

"I should have never taken my eyes off the lad," my father berated himself.

"That holds true for all of us," said Joanna, sniffing back her tears.

"I shall notify Sir Charles, who I am certain will place the full force of Scotland Yard behind—"

Joanna made a loud dismissive sound. She took a deep breath and regained some measure of her composure. "It will be up to us to find Johnny, not those bumblers at the Yard."

"But where do we begin?" asked I.

"By determining if either Peter Willoughby or Thaddeus Rudd has an alibi for this time period," she instructed, as her face suddenly hardened and her deductive mind took over for the moment. "John, you must hurry to St. Bartholomew's and question the two as to their whereabouts between the hours of two and four."

I looked at my wife quizzically and asked, "Why the time period between two and four?"

"Because my Johnny was taken from us at two thirty," she explained quickly. "If you consider the entire kidnapping sequence, it requires two hours to bring it to a successful completion. Do the math on your journey to St. Bart's. And while questioning the two main suspects, demand precise answers and, even if they provide alibis, double-check and verify with eyewitnesses."

"And if they are not present at the hospital?"

"Then we shall have them tracked down."

"What if they use each other as an alibi?"

"That would be most unlikely, for only one of them is guilty," said she. "Remember, verify with eyewitnesses and if needed written statements. Now go!"

Before I could move, my wife's intense anguish returned as tears again poured out and streamed down her cheeks. She flew into my arms and embraced me tightly, saying, "Leave no stone unturned, for my son's life hangs in the balance."

Chapter 22

The Alibis

There being no motor taxis outside the manor, I hired a waiting hansom and instructed the driver to make haste to St. Bart's, for an emergency awaited me at the hospital. As we rode by St. James's Park, I mentally calculated the time frame necessary for the kidnapping to be successfully carried out. The birthday party began at 2:00 PM and The Ripper had no doubt secreted himself in the thick hedge earlier, waiting for the opportunity to snatch young Johnny, which occurred at 2:30 PM. The Ripper would then have to travel to Whitechapel to deposit and secure the lad in the hidden dwelling, which would have taken an hour or so. Then he would hurry back to St. Bart's to resume his usual activities and establish an alibi. That would require another thirty minutes. Total time elapsed two hours. Next, my mind went to the two prime suspects and their alibis, which I believed I could predict. Thaddeus Rudd would claim to be either performing surgery in the main amphitheater or seeing patients in the clinic during the hours between two and four. In both places, eyewitnesses would abound. Peter Willoughby would also seemingly have a sold, verifiable alibi, for he was scheduled to attend a noon luncheon-conference on neuropathology at St. George's Hospital in Knightsbridge, which was only a stone's throw away from the Blalock manor in Belgravia. The renowned conference that I was invited to and spoke at a year earlier would conclude at 2:00 PM. Willoughby and Maxwell Anderson had in all likelihood traveled together from St. Bart's to the meeting, since both were scheduled to present their work on traumatic brain injuries. That being the case, they would then travel back to St. Bart's, reaching the hospital at 2:30 PM, which was the time of the kidnapping. If this time reference was correct, Peter Willoughby could not be The Ripper. And he had a perfect eyewitness to account for all his time away from St. Bart's.

We passed through Trafalgar Square as I again went over the predicted time sequences. They were absolutely correct, which meant that neither Rudd nor Willoughby, our prime suspects, could be Jack the Ripper, and that depressing fact would demand we begin our investigation anew. And this would consume entirely too much time, which we had precious little of. But then again, I had to remind myself, all of my calculations were based on assumptions and one of Joanna's cardinal rules was to never bank on assumptions until they can be verified by firsthand accounts.

Ten minutes later we drew up to the side entrance at St. Bartholomew's. Hurrying down the corridor in the department of pathology, I cleared my mind of all preconceived notions and decided to begin my investigation with Peter Willoughby. The door to the director's office was closed, so I rapped gently and entered to find Willoughby's meek, but ever-efficient, secretary sitting behind her desk struggling with a typewriter ribbon.

"Good afternoon, Rose," I greeted her.

"And good afternoon to you, Dr. Watson," said she, looking up from her task. "May I be of help?"

"I need to speak with the director on an important matter," I replied.

"Oh, I am afraid his schedule is rather full," the secretary informed. "Can you wait until tomorrow?"

"I'd rather not," I urged. "Has he returned from his luncheon-conference at St. George's?"

"I suspect so, for the affair was due to be over promptly at two."

"Did he stop by his office on his return?"

"Not that I noticed, but then I was away from my desk for a while dealing with a problem at the stenographer's station," said she. "Shall I notify the director of your request once he is done with his other meetings?"

"No need," I responded. "I will catch up with him later today."

"Very good, Dr. Watson."

On leaving the director's office, I spotted Benson, the head orderly, pushing a cart loaded with dissected specimens. I waved and walked across the corridor. "A moment of your time."

"Of course, sir."

I glanced down at the coils of large intestines, upon which lay a lacerated spleen. "Are these from an autopsy?"

"No, sir. They come from an ongoing surgery being performed by Dr. Rudd," he answered. "Multiple stab wounds to the abdomen, you see."

"A knife fight, I presume."

Benson shook his head. "It was a revenge stabbing, so I am told, that inflicted terrible damage. The patient was indeed fortunate to have such a fine surgeon on hand, who is at his best in these situations."

"I think I will have a look-see myself, for such cases of trauma interest me."

"I am afraid you will find the amphitheater's seats filled, as the good Dr. Rudd always draws a large audience."

"That will present no problem, for I will stand at the rear if necessary to watch a surgical genius at work," I exaggerated, and turned away but then remembered a final most important question. "Benson, have you by chance seen Dr. Willoughby this afternoon?"

"Briefly, as he was entering Dr. Anderson's laboratory."

"What time was that?"

"A little after four."

I hurried down the corridor and took the brass elevator to the third floor where the operating rooms were located. I had to squeeze my way into the main amphitheater, which was filled to the point of being overcrowded. At the base of the amphitheater, a woman with long brown hair lay on the operating table, her face covered with an anesthetic cone. Thaddeus Rudd, gowned and masked, was cursing loudly as he went about his delicate dissection.

"Hold the bloody retractor steady," he growled.

"Sorry, sir," said a gowned surgical nurse.

"Don't be sorry; be proficient," Rudd snapped. "It is impossible to tie off a bleeder if one cannot see it."

I turned to a nearby surgeon, Harry Askins, and inquired, "Horrendous case, eh?"

"The worst, with the patient going in and out of shock," he answered quietly. "Rudd has been on his feet for the better part of three hours, dealing with one complication after another."

"No rest break at all?"

"Not for a second, and I have been in the amphitheater from the very start. I tell you, Rudd has the energy of ten."

"Make that twenty," said a young surgeon who had overheard our conversation. "Rudd had to open her up the moment she was anesthetized. Blood was spurting everywhere, and had he not stopped the hemorrhaging immediately she would have not lived a minute longer. I tell you that poor woman should have died a dozen times, but Rudd refuses to let her do so."

I had seen enough. Despite being covered with cap, gown, and mask, the surgeon in the operating room was Thaddeus Rudd, who had been in place since one o'clock and would remain there for hours more. Thus, Rudd could not have been responsible for the kidnapping, which also meant he could not be Jack the Ripper.

As I dashed down the stairs to the pathology department, I decided to question Maxwell Anderson next, for he in all likelihood could verify Willoughby's alibi. And what if he did substantiate it? Then we had no suspects, I thought miserably, and no hope of rescuing Joanna's son. As I reached for the door to Anderson's laboratory, a chilling picture of a bound and gagged Johnny came into my mind, which reminded me how terrified the poor lad must be at this moment.

On entering the histopathology section, I spotted Anderson and Willoughby standing near a machine that was churning out slices of tissue and placing them onto glass slides. Both men were attired in long white laboratory coats and appeared to be chatting amiably above the noise of the machine. If there was an expression of concern on the director's face, I could not detect it.

He glanced at me for a long moment, now apparently annoyed by my intrusion. "Rose tells me you wish to speak with me."

"If you have a moment," said I, caught off guard but quickly fabricating a reason. "I was interested in borrowing your excellent neuropathology slides for a talk I have been invited to give."

Willoughby eyed me suspiciously. "Are you now an expert in neuropathology?"

"Hardly," I explained. "The symposium deals with generalized trauma and your slides will simply demonstrate its effect on the brain."

"I will allow the lending as long as they are carefully looked after and returned in the same condition they were given."

"They shall be," I promised. "By the way, did your conference at St. George's go well?"

"Quite well, until the accident occurred."

"Accident?" I inquired.

"A splash of red wine was spilled onto the director's shirt and tie," Anderson interjected.

Willoughby growled at the unpleasant memory. "Some clumsy waiter placed a glass of wine on the edge of a napkin and it tilted over."

"It must have resulted in a most untidy appearance," I said sympathetically, but saw no such spotting on his attire.

"I covered it with a fresh napkin as best as I could, and as soon as the conference ended I hurried home to change into new garments."

"Your wife must have been surprised to see you away from the hospital so early in the afternoon."

"She would have been indeed, but she was out shopping and it was the servants' day off, so I had the entire house to myself. In any event, I quickly changed into fresh attire, which I must say brightened my day." Willoughby ran a hand across his freshly laundered collar and striped red tie. "Even Rose noted the change and complimented me on it."

"Very stylish," said I.

"Hmm," the director made a low-pitched guttural sound indicating the pleasant exchange was over. "Now, in regard to the slides you wish to borrow, I am afraid I unintentionally left them on my desk at home. I had placed them there while I took the quiet opportunity to answer correspondence which had accumulated over the past week. Time slipped by and the next thing I knew it was past three thirty. I dashed from my house and neglected to take my slides with me."

"No worries," said I. "I will come by your office in the morning for them."

"Very good." He checked his timepiece with a glance and turned for the door. "I must now attend to other matters which await me."

I waited for Willoughby to be well gone before asking Anderson, "Did he put up a big brouhaha over the spilled wine?"

"And some," he replied. "It required several minutes for him to finally calm down. But then he recouped and made a bit of a jest over it during his presentation. However, his fury returned when he left the conference and walked to his automobile."

"So I take it you two had come to the meeting in separate vehicles."

Anderson shook his head. "We drove over in the director's automobile. But when he was forced to return home, I was obliged to hire a hansom and enjoy a pleasant ride back to St. Bartholomew's."

"While Willoughby hurried home, where he spent a relaxing, yet productive, afternoon."

"So it would seem, but he complained about losing two hours of laboratory time the moment he returned."

"It was around four o'clock, then."

"A little after."

Docketing that final piece of information, I departed Anderson's laboratory with a singular thought going through my mind. Both Willoughby and Rudd had seemingly solid alibis, but there was a difference. Rudd's could be verified. Willoughby's could not.

Chapter 23

Fading Hope

Red-eyed and grief-stricken, Joanna managed to push her heartache aside as she listened intently to every word I spoke without interruption. But I could tell from her expressions that there were several points of the report which did not register well. My father sat in his chair by the fireplace, hanging on to every syllable, with his Webley revolver close at hand. The weapon served no purpose at the moment, other than to remind the three of us we had let our guard down with disastrous results.

"We should begin with Rudd, for I believe he has the firmest of alibis," Joanna said finally. "However, you say there was only one confirmed eyewitness."

"Actually two and no doubt a dozen more if we wish to pursue it," I replied. "A second surgeon present in the amphitheater at the start of the surgery commented that the patient would have died on multiple occasions but for Rudd's heroics."

"I take it he was never absent from the operating room."

"Never and certainly not for the hours required to carry out a kidnapping."

"Which leaves us with Peter Willoughby, whose alibi is obviously contrived but most difficult to disprove."

"We could of course question his wife to document her absence from the house," I suggested.

Joanna flicked her wrist at the notion. "She would not in all likelihood bear witness against her husband and under the law could not be forced to do so. Moreover, he could conjure up a story of having crept into the house without her being aware. And today might well be the servants' day off. You must keep in mind that he is a very clever fellow."

"I must say the spillage of wine was a cunning ruse indeed, which allowed him to absent himself from the hospital," my father added.

"Oh, that was well orchestrated," Joanna agreed. "Even the clumsiest of waiters does not set a filled wineglass on a napkin. You will also note the manner in which Willoughby openly displayed his freshly laundered shirt and new tie for all to see. This behavior is so unlike that of a man who routinely dresses so poorly it causes others to wince."

"He seemed to go out of his way to exhibit his stylish attire to his secretary as well," said I.

My wife nodded. "This man is beyond clever and knows how to cover his tracks. Even his timing was precise, with every hour of his absence accounted for." She paused to light a Turkish cigarette and gave the matter more thought, before turning back to me and asking, "Are you absolutely certain of the time sequence?"

"Quite so," I assured. "On my return from St. Bartholomew's, I hired a taxi and clocked the time required to travel from St. George's to Belgravia, then to Whitechapel and onto Hampstead Heath, and finally back to the hospital. My estimates were spot-on."

"Well executed," Joanna grumbled under her breath.

"But I see a possible flaw," my father argued mildly. "It would still be daylight when the kidnapper reached Whitechapel. There would be a real chance the pair would be seen by his neighbors."

"Not so," she disagreed immediately. "He could conceal Johnny in a blanket or roll of canvas, which would not arouse suspicion. And stage actors can change their appearance in a matter of minutes, being the gentleman one moment and a shabbily dressed commoner the next."

"And he would have the lad bound and gagged so he could not move or cry out," I surmised. "That of course assumes The Ripper has not already done the worst."

My father sighed sadly. "I must admit that at times I am troubled by the feeling that Johnny is gone from us."

"I think not," said my wife. "The Ripper enjoys his work too much to hurry through it. He will wait until he can perform it at his leisure."

"So there is some hope he remains with us," my father tried to inject a note of optimism.

"But he will not be for long," Joanna warned. "The very last thing The Ripper wants is a sharp-eyed witness."

The phone rang. We all went silent, wondering who would be calling at this mid-evening hour. Deep down we expected the worst as my father reached for the phone.

"Yes . . . good evening, Commissioner," he greeted, pressing the receiver to his ear. "No luck there, eh? . . . Any additional witnesses? . . . Of course, that might be helpful. . . . What of the fingerprints on the lad's shoes? . . . A worthwhile thought . . . We know you will do your best."

My father placed the phone down, his face now holding a grim expression. "There is no promising news. Additional witnesses in and about the manor could not be found. The lad's shoes did contain fingerprints, but they do not belong to our main suspect. They will now be checked against known pedophiles and suspected kidnappers."

My wife shook her head firmly. "This is the work of The Ripper, with all evidence pointing directly at him."

"Sir Charles is simply covering every possibility, but, like us, he believes The Ripper is responsible and feels certain the madman will soon return to his dwelling in Whitechapel, if he has not already done so. Accordingly, the commissioner has doubled the number of constables patrolling the district and has detectives in motor vehicles circling the entire area. In addition, Scotland Yard has more than a few snitches in the community who are on alert as well, with the promise of a handsome reward should their information lead to a rescue."

"They will all be of little use, for Johnny is now well concealed in The Ripper's secret dwelling, where he will remain until his life is ended," Joanna said glumly.

"But for how long will he keep Johnny alive?" my father asked.

"It is impossible to say, but certainly for no more than a day or two," she predicted. "He will plan the awful deed so as to gain the most notoriety from it. The Ripper will wish it widely publicized that he killed the son of the daughter of Sherlock Holmes."

"The effect being that since you carry the Great Detective's genes, he has in fact bested Sherlock Holmes himself."

"Precisely."

"And all we can do is sit in our comfortable chairs and worry."

"To the contrary, Watson, I believe we can do much better than that." Joanna crushed out her cigarette and, after lighting another, began to pace the floor of our parlor, head down, with each step more determined than the last. Minutes passed before she spoke to us, without looking our way. "This criminal, like all criminals, has made a mistake and I shall find it."

Chapter 24

The Scent

I attempted to sleep that night, but slumber would not come, and the best I could do was to twist and turn and doze fitfully before I awakened to the living nightmare we were facing. Finally, shortly after daybreak, I arose and entered the parlor to find my father fully dressed and awake, but the dark circles under his eyes told me he had not slept. Joanna gave me the slightest of glances, then continued to pace through a cloud of smoke so dense it was difficult to see her completely. But as she drew closer, it was obvious her face was drawn and fatigued.

"You should rest, my dear, if only for an hour or so," I advised.

Joanna ignored my suggestion and continued to pace. "The answer will not come with my eyes closed."

"Father, please instruct my wife that the brain will not function well without at least a modicum of respite," I urged.

My father lighted his cherrywood pipe and added to the smoky air before commenting, "She will do fine, for she is like her father, Sherlock Holmes, who could go days without sleep when the answer to a difficult problem escaped him. He simply could not rest until the solution came."

"It is there, directly in front of my eyes, yet I cannot grasp it," Joanna said without inflection.

"I take it you are speaking of a clue," said my father.

"It is more than a clue," she responded. "It is the loose thread that untangles the knot."

Our conversation was interrupted by a gentle rap on the

door. It was Miss Hudson, with tear-stained cheeks, bringing in an armful of the morning newspapers.

"Oh, please tell me it is not true," she lamented. "Tell me the lad is still with us."

"I am afraid he has been kidnapped," said my father.

Miss Hudson looked directly at my wife for a long moment, with her lips moving before she spoke. "You must find him, madam, and bring the lad back to us."

"That I shall do," Joanna vowed.

Once our landlady had departed, we eagerly reached for the newspapers and hurriedly read their front pages. The *Guardian* summed up the matter best with its bold headline stating:

GRANDSON OF SHERLOCK HOLMES MISSING

It went on to describe in detail how the kidnapping had occurred, even delineating the cover of the high, thick hedge at the rear of Lord Blalock's garden. Obviously someone at the party had rushed to the newspapers with the horrific story. It was surely not one of the servants, for such a disclosure would put their position in jeopardy. In all likelihood, the source was one of the guests.

"There is no mention of The Ripper," I noted.

"That will come soon enough," Joanna predicted as she placed down the *Daily Telegraph*. "And once the publicity intensifies and grows, The Ripper will make his move."

"And no doubt leave his mark," I added dolefully.

The phone rang loudly and drew our complete attention. The three of us wondered collectively what news it might bring at just past eight. As a rule, early-morning calls were the most distressing. My father lifted the receiver on the second ring.

"Yes, and good morning to you, Commissioner," he replied.

We all breathed a sigh of relief, for *good morning* would never be used as a greeting if the call carried a devastating message.

"No match, eh?" my father was saying. "But most were the same and unidentifiable. . . . Yes, yes, the lad's fingerprints must be excluded. . . . I understand. . . . We shall have the item available when your detective arrives. . . . We will continue to hope for the best."

On placing the receiver down, my father gave us the details. "The fingerprints on the shoes do not match those of any suspect or known criminal who participates in childhood abduction. He believes they most likely belong to the lad, but this has to be confirmed. He will shortly send around a detective to pick up an item which contains Johnny's fingerprints, so a comparison can be made. There is always the possibility that the prints were placed there by the kidnapper."

"They are Johnny's," Joanna said with certainty. "The Ripper is far too clever to leave his fingerprints behind. Moreover, why would he bother to touch the shoes? What purpose would that serve? No, no. He would wish to make his getaway as quickly as possible and would not be concerned with the shoes."

"I am afraid you are correct," my father concurred. "But it is best to do the comparison and thus exclude the possibility they originated from the abductor. With that in mind, which item should we give to Scotland Yard?"

"His text on hieroglyphics," my wife answered. "He is constantly referring to it."

My father stood and stretched his back, which cracked noisily. "It appears we are facing a perfectly executed crime, with only a pair of discarded shoes left behind, which in themselves hold little value."

"In an ideal world, those shoes could magically walk their way back to their owner," I mused. "Which of course would lead to The Ripper's secret dwelling."

"But unfortunately, we live in the real world, where shoes cannot walk without feet in them." Joanna reached for a Turkish cigarette and was in the process of striking a match when her brow suddenly went up. The cigarette dropped from her lips. "The dwelling! The dwelling! I was concentrating on the wrong object. I was focusing on the person rather than the place."

"Please explain," I urged.

Joanna lighted her cigarette and began to pace back and forth with quick steps as she organized her thoughts. "Leaving the shoes behind was The Ripper's mistake, for they may well lead to his hiding place. It was so obvious I almost missed it. My father once said that there is nothing more deceptive than an obvious fact. Allow me to paraphrase by stating there is nothing more deceptive than an obvious clue."

"You have lost me," I complained. "What about the shoes renders them so important?"

"They carry Johnny's scent," she explained. "Follow the scent and we will find my son."

"Can Toby Two do it?" I asked at once, referring to a hound that possessed the keenest nose in all London and had aided us so well in several important cases.

"That is what we are about to determine," Joanna said, and rapidly turned to my father. "Watson, please call Scotland Yard and have the detective bring me one of Johnny's shoes with him."

"They will ask for a reason."

"Tell them I wish to study it and no more," she replied. "Next, hire a taxi, which we will need for an extended period of time. A vehicle with a large rear compartment would suit our purpose best. And finally, you must remain here in the event Scotland Yard requires additional information which only a member of our household can provide."

"Done," said he, and began dialing numbers he knew by rote.

"Now I must freshen up and change clothes, for my husband and I are about to embark on the most important journey of our lives."

After picking up Toby Two from her kennel in lower Lambeth, we sped to Whitechapel, hoping to arrive before yet another storm coming in from the North Sea. The newspapers predicted it would reach London by early afternoon, which gave us only a few hours to search. But dark clouds were already gathering and a light rain beginning to fall, indicating our time might be limited even further. As we approached our destination, Joanna reached for the airtight container which held her son's shoe, but did not open it until we reached the Whitechapel Playhouse. She allowed Toby Two a quick sniff of Johnny's shoe before returning it to its container.

With her head out of the taxi's rear window, the hound sampled the air joyfully as we circled one square block after another. On occasion her tail would wag and she would let out a happy bark, but these encounters were short-lived and did not arouse great interest.

"I suspect that Johnny's scent has become quite faint," I remarked.

"And fading even more with the falling rain and increasing wind," Joanna said discouragingly.

"Perhaps another piece of Johnny's clothing will serve our purpose better," I suggested.

My wife shook her head. "The shoe is best, with its tight fit which causes perspiration and elicits the stronger scent."

"It is indeed unfortunate that Johnny does not favor a men's cologne," I thought aloud as heavy drops of rain tapped against the roof of our taxi.

"Capital, John!" Joanna shouted happily. "A most excellent idea."

"But your son does not wear cologne," I agreed.

"But I will wager that Pretty Penny indulges in perfume which would render the same result, for where she resides, so resides our dear Johnny." Joanna rapped on the window in front of us. "To the Prince Albert, driver."

Five minutes later we arrived at the pub and hurried to find Emma Adams busily serving lunch to diners crowded into a half-dozen or so booths. On seeing us, she quickly signaled to Lionel Lurie to come from behind the bar and take her place, then dashed over to greet us.

"I am very sorry to hear of your terrible news," she said sadly. "I pray for your son's safe return."

"Thank you for your concern," Joanna replied. "But we find ourselves in a great rush and require your immediate assistance in search of our Johnny."

"Anything you need will be happily provided."

"I take it Pretty Penny wears perfume."

Emma Adams nodded. "Like most young women she favors a rather strong, inexpensive variety."

"Which I presume she left behind before she went missing."

"She did."

"Then I request the bottle."

"For what purpose, may I ask?"

"To find Pretty Penny and my son in the process," Joanna said simply. "Now, time is of the essence, so please fetch the perfume without further questions."

Mrs. Adams raced for the back stairs which led to the rooms above the pub. Lurie watched her every step from near the bar before turning to us. His face was most inquisitive, but Joanna's blank expression told him that he would not be included in the business at hand.

"Let us hope Emma Adams does not wear the same perfume," my wife cautioned. "For if she does, Toby Two's nose will continue to return to the pub, where the scent would be the strongest."

"Perhaps you should have requested a jar of the hair pomade Pretty Penny uses in excess."

"That would have proved useless, for countless women in Whitechapel no doubt apply the Widow Marley's special blend on a frequent basis."

Loud thunder roared close by and caused the fixtures in the pub to rattle. The men seated in the booths laughed at the sound, but I found nothing amusing about the promise of an approaching storm. Time was short enough as is and it was soon to become much shorter.

Mrs. Adams skipped down the stairs and sprinted over to us, with the small bottle of Pretty Penny's perfume in hand. "There is only a little remaining, so you need not bother to return it."

"Pray tell do you wear the same perfume?" Joanna asked.

Emma Adams shook her head. "I prefer the more expensive French variety."

"Very good," said my wife, snatching the bottle and dashing for the door, with me only a step behind.

In the taxi Joanna dampened her handkerchief with a dab of Pretty Penny's perfume, and held it well outside the window. Once we had traveled a mile away, she placed the bottle alongside the shoe in the airtight container and had the driver deposit both in the boot of the taxi. Only then did she allow Toby Two to whiff the perfume-dampened handkerchief, with instructions to "go, girl!"

The hound eagerly responded and positioned her head and

nose so far out of the taxi window that I held on to her for safety's sake. Once again the taxi slowly circled the square blocks of Whitechapel, beginning at the major thoroughfare of Prescot Street. Toby Two continued to sample the air but showed little interest, as her tail remained flaccid and still. On reaching Back Church Lane, however, the hound suddenly came to life, with her tail straightening.

"Ah!" I exclaimed. "She is picking up the scent."

"We are approaching the Widow Marley's house and salon where Pretty Penny visited to have her hair cut and styled," Joanna explained. "Let us see what occurs when we pass the house."

Toby Two's interest rapidly faded once we moved beyond the makeshift beauty salon. But a moment later her excitement returned, with her tail wagging vigorously. She let out a happy bark as we approached the Whitechapel Playhouse. Yet, as before, her interest subsided as we drove away from the playhouse where Pretty Penny had performed so often.

Suddenly lightning cracked and thunder boomed so loudly it caused our taxi to vibrate. Then the rain poured down in drenching torrents that quickly began to flood the streets. The wind also picked up and blew heavy droplets into the taxi, which necessitated us bringing Toby Two inside and closing the window.

"We can proceed no further," said Joanna dispiritedly. "The storm will remove all traces of a scent."

With heavy hearts we began our journey home, knowing full well that we had lost our best and perhaps only opportunity to rescue dear Johnny.

Chapter 25

Johnny

That evening we gathered around our fireplace in the saddest of all possible moods, with virtually all hope now gone. Unencouraging reports continued to flow in, the latest being from Scotland Yard, which despite its best efforts had not turned up even a hint regarding The Ripper's secret dwelling. And to make matters worse, the storm from the North Sea had persisted, with heavy rain and strong gales that made further investigation impossible.

A powerful blast of wind noisily rattled our window overlooking Baker Street and drew Joanna's attention. "The din of the storm also works in The Ripper's favor, for any screams and cries for help will never be heard above it."

"Perhaps the dreadful weather will force the monster to remain at home, at least for the immediate future," my father opined.

"On the other hand, it provides him with perfect cover to move about as he wishes," Joanna countered.

"It is unfortunate we could not convince Scotland Yard to place a tail on Willoughby," I complained.

"Ha!" Joanna scoffed. "On the surface it seemed like a good idea, but in this weather Lestrade would have difficulty following a bus around Piccadilly Circus."

"Come morning, the commissioner informed me, the Yard will begin a house-to-house search of the entire Whitechapel district, using every available officer," my father noted. "He promised that no door will be left unopened."

"A valiant effort no doubt, but one unlikely to bring results," said my wife. "The Ripper conducts his horrific business in a well-hidden place, and simply opening a door will not reveal it."

My father and I had to nod at the unpleasant conclusion.

A prolonged silence ensued before my father spoke again. "I am afraid we are reaching the last of our options, and so is Scotland Yard. With each tick of the clock the chances of a rescue grow dimmer and dimmer."

"Then we must redouble our efforts," Joanna said firmly. "And not sleep a wink until my son is safely home."

"But what other recourses are available to us?"

"We shall repeat what we failed to accomplish today," she replied. "In the morning, John and I shall again travel to Whitechapel, with Toby Two at our side, and allow her to track Johnny by the scent of his shoe. Perhaps the clearer air will make the scent more noticeable."

"Let us pray so."

As Big Ben struck the hour of ten, we collectively sank down in our overstuffed chairs to mull over the seemingly unsolvable dilemma facing us. Our return to Whitechapel with Toby Two was a long shot at best, I thought miserably, for Johnny was no doubt being held in an enclosed hidden space which would hide his scent as well. I kept this worrisome thought to myself, not wishing to add to my wife's torment. If the lad does perish, poor Joanna would never— We abruptly stiffened in our seats as we heard Miss Hudson cry out from downstairs. My father raced to his room for his Webley revolver, while my wife and I positioned ourselves as far as possible from the entrance to our parlor. My father returned and assumed the firing position, with his weapon pointed directly at the door. We held our breath as footsteps approached, followed by a gentle rap on the door, which slowly opened.

To our joy and amazement, standing before us was a rain-drenched Johnny who was accompanied by an equally wet constable. Joanna rushed to her son and held him in the tightest of embraces, rocking back and forth, smiling and tearing up at the same time. "Oh, my sweet Johnny!"

"I am glad to be home," he said in a neutral tone.

"Are you now?" Joanna laughed and, wiping away her tears, turned to the constable. "How did you find him?"

"It was the lad who found me, madam," he replied. "I am simply the officer who has the honor of bringing your brave son home."

"Then I must thank you from the very bottom of my heart," said she. "Won't you come in and dry off by the fire?"

"I must return to my post, madam, but again, it was my privilege to escort him back to you." And with a half salute he departed.

Joanna again embraced her son and kissed him, which caused him to wince and withdraw. "I am afraid it is a bit tender there, Mother."

Our attention went to the deep bruise on the lad's jaw that extended up to his ear. It was black-and-blue, but fortunately the skin had not been broken.

My wife's expression suddenly hardened. "Did he hurt you otherwise?"

"No, Mother, I have no further injuries." Johnny walked over to the fireplace, where I assumed he would warm himself and gather his wits. But this was not the case, for he casually removed his jacket to dry and in the bright light seemed remarkably well composed despite the terrifying ordeal he had just endured. I did notice a bit of a tremor in his hands, which might have been caused by the outside chill. In profile, the lad's resemblance to Sherlock Holmes was as always startling. "I have quite a story to tell."

My father hurried over to vigorously shake the boy's hand. "We are so delighted to have you back with us, but I would think a comfortable bed is quite in order to allow for a complete recovery."

"Thank you for your concern, Dr. Watson, but I am fine in every way."

"Then perhaps a spot of dinner," I suggested, patting the lad's shoulder and giving it a gentle squeeze. "Surely you must be famished."

"Miss Hudson made the very same comment and is currently heating her oven," said Johnny, with a smile that quickly left his face. "Now you must listen to my story, for I was close enough to Jack the Ripper to feel his breath."

We returned to our chairs and drew them in closer so as not to miss a word.

"You must start at the beginning, my dear son, with the last memory you have before being rendered unconscious," Joanna instructed.

Johnny's face remained impassive, not showing even a trace of fear or anxiety. He picked up a metal stoker to stir the fire and seemed to tell his tale to the flames. "I was near the hedge watching Dr. Watson pointing his Webley at the intruder when I heard a strange noise in the thick shrub. I looked in, wondering if an animal had become trapped, and suddenly everything went black. When I awakened, I was in a very dark room, tightly bound hand and foot to a wooden chair. As I regained consciousness, I heard a conversation between a man and a young woman. She was crying and begging to be released. He told her that she would soon be lifted up; then there was the sound of someone retching, followed by footsteps which appeared to be going upstairs. A moment later a door closed. It was then that my senses cleared and I realized I had been taken captive by Jack the Ripper."

"You must have been terrified," Joanna said in a near whisper.

"No, Mother, for what fright I had passed quickly as I concentrated on my predicament. My singular thought was to somehow free myself, for I knew what the madman had in store for me."

If there was any fear in the lad's voice, I could not detect it. It was Sherlock Holmes's brain at work. If there was a problem, solve it. Emotions were of no benefit.

"I soon realized the ropes securing me were far too thick to break and the binding so tight I could barely move my arms and legs. It took me a while to think through the conundrum. The answer was quite simple: If you can't break through the ropes, break through the structure they are attached to."

"The chair!" Joanna exclaimed gleefully.

Johnny nodded. "It was wooden and rather rackety and squeaked when I attempted to move my body. With my fingers, I could feel the arms of the chair and determined they were somewhat thin. I next proceeded to rock the chair back and forth until it tilted over and crashed to the floor. The right arm of the seat broke off, which freed my right hand, and I was thus able to untie myself. I searched for the young woman who had been crying, but could not find her in the darkness. I felt my way until I found the stairs, which I quietly mounted to reach a closed but not locked door. I listened intently with my ear pressed to the door for a full five minutes, and when no sound was forthcoming I made my exit to the alleyway." Johnny hesitated and took a deep breath, as if reliving the moment. "I then ran for my life, Mother, for how many blocks I do not know, but it was a great number. On approaching a major thoroughfare, I came upon the good constable Godwin, who called for a motor vehicle and was kind enough to accompany me home."

"Good show!" my father bellowed out.

"Good show indeed," said Joanna. "Now tell us, did you perceive any aspect of The Ripper?"

"Only his voice."

"Not even a glimpse?"

"Not even that, for it was very dark in the room and he spoke from behind me."

"Think back to the woman's voice. Was there anything noteworthy about it?"

"Only that it seemed to originate from an enclosed space."

"Did you notice the name of the street this dwelling was located on?"

"No, Mother, for it was pitch black with no lampposts until I reached an intersection a good many blocks away. There were no street signs and, if any were present, they would have been impossible to see through the drenching downpour. At that moment, I thought it best to continue running and distance myself from the dwelling."

"I would like you to think back to your initial encounter with The Ripper," Joanna probed gently. "Were there any features you happened to observe, such as a blemish on the hand that struck you?"

Johnny considered the question at length before responding. "He had a very thin neck, which I noticed just prior to the blow. It was as if it was surrounded by a collar three sizes too large."

Peter Willoughby, I thought immediately, showing the evidence of his obvious weight loss.

"And there was one other feature I failed to mention, Mother."

"Of the man?"

Johnny shook his head slowly. "Concerning the young woman in the enclosed space. She seemed to be wheezing badly, with each breath requiring considerable effort."

"Pretty Penny and her asthma," my father diagnosed quickly. "With her condition worsening by the hour in the absence of her much-needed medication."

"Is her life in danger, Dr. Watson?" asked the lad.

"Quite so, I am afraid, for she cannot last long with her deteriorating lung function."

Joanna arose from her chair and took her son's hand. "Enough questions for now. I believe a short rest would be most welcomed by you as we await one of Miss Hudson's sumptuous dinners."

"Agreed," Johnny said, and, as he turned for his bedroom, an expression of concern crossed his face. "Mother, do you think he will come after me again?"

"I do not believe so," Joanna replied, but the tone of her voice told all of us she thought otherwise.

CHAPTER 26

Ruby

I returned to St. Bartholomew's the following morning, for my brief sabbatical had ended and young Johnny was now safe and secure under the watchful eyes of Joanna and my father. In addition, Scotland Yard had placed a constable round the clock at the doorstep of 221b Baker Street. With that confident thought, I approached Peter Willoughby's office and peered in, only to see him berating his meek secretary over no doubt some minor issue. He gave me the slightest of glances before turning his back to me. I wondered if his early-morning tirade was brought on by the loss of his prized catch last night.

Perhaps I continued to stare too long, for the director hurried over to shut the door in my face.

The mutual dislike between Willoughby and myself seemed to be intensifying through no apparent fault of my own. Perhaps he had somehow learned of my plans to leave St. Bartholomew's at the end of the academic year and was showing his displeasure at my decision. Whatever the reason, he continued to assign mundane tasks to me in the department of pathology, and one of those assignments was to choose appropriate corpses in the morgue to be used as cadavers in the medical school. I was able to bypass most of the tedious paperwork that accompanied the selection process, with the assistance of the head orderly, Benson, who was helpful in completing the forms required to transfer the corpse out of the morgue. Benson was totally illiterate and incapable of filling out the various papers, but he had a remarkable memory for the details given by the police when they delivered a body. Thus, in a strange fashion, he would dictate and I would transcribe.

It was nearly noon when I freed up enough time to attend to the selection process and found myself hurrying down the busy corridor to meet with Benson. As I passed Willoughby's door, I again glanced in and briefly studied the director who no doubt was Jack the Ripper. He clearly met the profile of the Dr. Jekyll–Mr. Hyde character so ably portrayed by Robert Louis Stevenson, but it remained beyond me how a distinguished physician could be transformed into such a savage killer who had no conscience whatsoever. Of course Stevenson brought about the transformation with the use of a hallucinogenic agent. Such drugs, like opium and peyote, would be readily available to Willoughby without arousing suspicion. I docketed this possibility with the intent of mentioning it to Joanna, for she had a knack of making much from little. So many times in the past, she had demonstrated to us that the most trivial of clues can at times turn out to be the most important.

I reached the end of the corridor and entered Benson's office, which resembled a large, windowless closet. There was barely enough room for two chairs and a small bookcase that was packed with papers and folders and various writing materials. Yet everything seemed neat and in place, just like the man who rose to greet me.

"There is a long history behind this one," Benson said, handing me a stack of forms fastened to a clipboard.

"Oh?" I asked, mildly interested as I seated myself.

"Well known, she was."

"In what capacity?"

"She was an Unfortunate who was known to roam the streets of Whitechapel."

I tried my best to keep my expression even and professional. "Do we know the cause of death?"

"She was struck by a motor vehicle while crossing Prescot Street."

My mind quickly went back to the vehicle which deliberately rammed us as we were returning from Paddington station. "Was the driver apprehended?"

"No, sir. According to the police, he fled the scene," Benson reported.

"Were there witnesses?"

"There was one witness, sir. I was told that a shopkeeper cleaning his doorstep saw the Unfortunate stagger into the street a moment before the accident occurred. It was his opinion that she was the worse for drink."

"Did he see the driver?"

"No, sir."

I continued to wonder if the motorcar accidents outside Paddington and on Prescot Street were somehow related. And if so, how?

"The police insisted they were most thorough in their search for other witnesses, but were unsuccessful," Benson added.

"I am certain they gave it their best," said I, still thinking it could have been The Ripper at work in both instances. But why would he kill a wandering Unfortunate in broad daylight on a busy street where he could have been seen? But then again, the man's madness seemed to serve no purpose. I decided to determine if Willoughby had an alibi for the time of the supposed accident. "Dr. Willoughby usually shows a keen interest in accidental deaths. Was this case presented to him?"

"Oh, no, sir," Benson responded immediately. "The good doctor wants nothing to do with cadaver selection and has made that abundantly clear to me. Even the mention of the process can set him off on a tirade."

"This being a case of accidental death, I should notify him, in the event he's not aware of it," I lied easily. "Was he in his office when the corpse arrived?"

Benson shrugged. "I assume so."

Assumptions were not good enough, I thought at once. "What time did the accident occur?"

"Around ten, sir."

"Was she brought directly to St. Bart's?"

"Right away, for she was obviously dead at the scene," Benson replied. "She was a bit smashed up, but only her legs were mangled."

"Were they maimed enough to disqualify her from being a cadaver for the medical school?"

"No, sir. She will do just fine."

I quickly began filling out the forms with the information

Benson had provided, but there remained a goodly number of blank spaces. "Do we have her name?"

"She was called Ruby on the streets, but no one was aware of a last name."

"Relatives?"

"None known."

"Friends?"

"Probably a few Unfortunates, but they of course rapidly disappear when the police arrive."

I heard grumbling and heavy footsteps approaching in the corridor and sensed we were about to have a most unpleasant visitor who barked at everyone. I wondered what his current complaint might be.

Peter Willoughby stopped abruptly in front of Benson's small office and stared in. He appeared to be even thinner than before, with his white laboratory coat seeming to hang on his frame. I wondered if his severe peptic ulcer disease was taking its toll and causing him to be even more disagreeable to those around him. The head orderly hurried to his feet, while I remained seated to display my defiance to this mean-spirited man. "Ah, there you are," he said curtly to me. "Hiding away, eh?"

"We are in the process of selecting a cadaver for the medical school," I explained.

"That should not take all morning."

"It is somewhat complicated, for we are dealing with an Unfortunate who was struck by a motorcar in Whitechapel," I recounted, and waited for his reaction.

Willoughby waved his hand dismissively. "That should require only a minimum of your attention."

"That is true under ordinary circumstances, but here we have to carefully examine the body to determine if there are any clues regarding the driver and vehicle responsible for the woman's death."

"You will not find any," Willoughby predicted.

"We shall see."

Willoughby made another dismissive gesture, indicating that particular topic of conversation was over. "Do not waste a great deal of time on it, for we have a most important matter to deal with. Do you recall the surgical specimen from Rudd's patient that was lost and then found by Anderson?"

I nodded. "It was deemed benign."

"That is now being brought into question. It seems the patient has developed similar lesions about the incision site and nearby muscle which may unhappily herald the spread of an aggressive cancer."

"Were the new lesions warm and tender to the touch?"

"I did not ask."

"Does the patient have a fever?"

"What difference does that make?" Willoughby snapped, losing patience.

"Because it may be an infection which is spreading, and that would be accompanied by a fever," I replied.

"We are not here to be bedside physicians, but to be straightforward pathologists," Willoughby said, obviously not interested in the patient's well-being, but only her tissue diagnosis under the microscope. "Rudd, Anderson, and I will meet in Anderson's laboratory at two sharp to reexamine the specimen and determine if it is malignant or not. Be there."

I watched Willoughby storm away, clearly upset and justifiably so. It was one matter to give a patient an unpleasant diagnosis, but quite another to render a favorable diagnosis, only to later return with a dreadful one. It was horrible for the patient and a dark stain on the department of pathology. Hoping our initial diagnosis would stand, I turned my attention back to the cadaver forms. "I take it we have no address for the victim."

"The Unfortunates never stay in one place, sir," Benson

said. "At best they will reside in a doss-house, but only for a night or two, and then they move on."

"But there are exceptions."

"Rarely."

"If such an address were to be had, it would be present in a purse, would it not?"

"We have seen that on occasion, but unhappily no such purse accompanied the victim to St. Bart's."

"Was the scene thoroughly searched?"

"It was, but none was found. Either she did not carry one or it was snatched by a passerby."

The missing purse was of some relevance, for of all the apparel a woman wore, the purse was most likely to contain items of identification. "So we have no way of knowing her full name, address, or origin," I noted, and drew a line through the blank spaces on the form.

"Even the name Ruby may be false, for it is not uncommon for Unfortunates to use an alias out of shame."

"We shall list her as Ruby, nonetheless."

"Very good, sir."

I legibly wrote down the corpse as being one Ruby Smith from the Whitechapel district in London. And if the body was not claimed by family or friend within twenty-four hours, she would lose even that semblance of identity. For after that short period of time, the corpse would be delivered to the medical school where it would be dissected and what remained deposited in an unmarked grave in a potter's field. A sad life, I thought, with an even sadder ending.

We quickly went through the rest of the questions, many of which could not be answered. Incomplete forms were frequently seen in the selection process and proved to be no hindrance in having a given corpse transferred to the morgue. Pushing our chairs back, we left the closet-like office and walked down a silent corridor in which all the doors were closed except for the one to Maxwell Anderson's laboratory. I glanced in and saw Willoughby and Anderson peering into microscopes, while the technicians stood well back, no doubt awaiting Willoughby's next outburst. Thaddeus Rudd was not to be seen.

At the end of the corridor we entered the morgue, which had a cement floor and uninterrupted plaster of Paris walls. The room was brightly lighted, which allowed for a thorough examination of the corpse that lay on a slab table. As was my custom, I began my investigation with her garments that were neatly stacked, with her well-worn, nondescript shoes atop. Her sweater, blouse, and petticoat were unremarkable, but the lower end of her skirt was heavily stained with dried blood. Her topcoat was badly soiled and ragged, with its hem torn in places. The pockets contained two shillings, a dirty handkerchief, and a folded slip of paper which I carefully opened. It was a prescription from St. Bart's. On it was written the Unfortunate's true name, Clara Collins, without an address. The doctor's orders were to collect and strain her urine for stones, and it was signed by Thaddeus Rudd. For a moment, I could not help but have sympathy for the Unfortunate, for she had kidney stones, which could elicit one of the most excruciating pains known in medicine. I could not imagine a worse set of circumstances than being caught on the dark streets of Whitechapel with the agony of a passing stone and no place to go and seek treatment.

I handed the prescription slip to Benson, who could not read yet knew from its form what it represented. "No doubt a patient in the free clinic," said he.

"No doubt," I agreed, and turned my attention to the corpse, with her mangled right leg. Her tibia had a compound fracture that caused the sharp, splintered end to penetrate the skin and produce a huge tear that was filled with blood. Beyond question, a large artery had been severed and that accounted for the massive hemorrhaging. The left leg was in reasonable condition, with only scrapes and bruises, and thus could be used for dissection and teaching purposes. The abdomen showed extensive ecchymoses and contusions which no doubt extended down into the organs. But it was her head that revealed the fatal injury. Just behind the frontal hairline was a wide gash that went so deep as to expose brain matter.

Benson peered over my shoulder and remarked, "That is what did her in."

"Death was instantaneous," said I.

"So she felt little."

"If anything."

I swept her long blond hair away from the occipital region of her head, for that was where crush injuries often occur in victims of motorcar accidents. There were no apparent wounds and I was about to release her hair when her somewhat pointed ears came into view. Attached to them were shiny copper earrings! My expression must have changed, for Benson immediately moved in for a closer look.

"I see no injuries there, sir," said he.

"It is her copper earrings," I muttered under my breath.

"Do you believe they caused harm?"

Quickly collecting myself, I shook my head. "It was just surprising to see an Unfortunate wearing jewelry."

"Occasionally they do, sir, but it is usually of the cheap variety."

"Such as those made from copper?"

Benson shrugged. "More often glass beads or the like."

"Well, let us proceed then," I said, now examining the corpse's eyes and eyebrows, but my thoughts were elsewhere. Clara Collins represented the fourth Unfortunate Jack the

Ripper intended to butcher. But it was now clear that her death was not the work of The Ripper, for he killed to dissect the victim, which gave him the most pleasure. What would he do now when he learns that his Ruby is dead? Will he search for another Unfortunate or will he simply move on with the execution of Pretty Penny? After all, his supply of apple slice candy must be running low. The last consideration brought to mind a most gruesome thought, for the loss of a prospective victim might so anger The Ripper that he would make the butchery of Pretty Penny even more savage and prolonged to enhance his twisted pleasure.

"Sir," Benson interrupted my thoughts, "is there something about the eyes we should note?"

"Nothing of importance," I responded. "I was searching for any hidden infection that might prove contagious to the medical students."

"I have never seen such an affliction."

"It occurs," said I, and left it at that.

"So we are done here."

"All except for the copper earrings," I replied, and rapidly thought back to what The Ripper might do once he learns that his fourth victim has been denied him. But suppose he is not made aware of Clara Collins's death? It now seems most likely that her death was accidental and unrelated to The Ripper. If this was the case, I might be able to keep her demise a secret and buy us and Pretty Penny more time. "I want those earrings removed and kept in a safe place."

"May I ask why, sir?" Benson inquired. "They truly have little worth."

"Not to her," I responded. "For they well may have been the sole possession of any value she had. And we should allow her to be buried with some dignity, and with her copper earrings on."

"A fine idea, sir," Benson said, moved by my sympathy. "I shall keep them in my office."

"Very good," I approved. "Now not a word to anyone about the Unfortunate and her copper earrings, for some stickler may come along and insist that such possessions, no matter how small, become the property of the Crown."

"In addition, sir, if the earrings were to accompany the corpse to the medical school, a student might decide to take them as a trinket or memento."

"Which is the very last thing we want."

"Indeed, sir."

I tapped a finger against the slab table, thinking of how to phrase a question I needed an exact answer to. "How many people at St. Bart's would be aware of the sad plight of Ruby, the Unfortunate?"

"Only you and I, sir."

"Not even Professor Willoughby's office?"

"No, sir. I bypass him and his office on any and all matters relating to the selection process, for he becomes most upset when the subject is even mentioned."

"A wise decision, and with that in mind there is no reason to talk more of her," said I. "But if by chance someone arrives and claims the body, I should like to be informed, for another corpse will have to be selected."

"I shall see to it."

I departed the morgue and hurried down the corridor, hoping that the head orderly would keep his word, but the tale of an Unfortunate, who a professor insisted be buried wearing her copper earrings, was so juicy, it was bound to leak out and become a popular subject of gossip at St. Bartholomew's. Such talk was almost certain to reach the ear of Willoughby and could thus seal the final fate of Pretty Penny.

Chapter 27

The Resurrection

Later that afternoon I returned to our rooms at 221b Baker Street and found Joanna alone, for following Johnny's hieroglyphics lessons at the British Museum the young lad and my father retired to the firing range to begin instructions in the use of a Webley & Scott revolver. My wife glanced up at me briefly before sinking back down in her overstuffed chair and furrowing her brow in concentration.

"Has something untoward occurred?" I asked.

"It is something very much untoward which may occur," she replied.

"Concerning Johnny?"

Joanna nodded, with a most serious expression. "Do you recall Sir David Shaw?"

"I do indeed."

Sir David was a curator in charge of ancient Mesopotamian script and languages at the British Museum. He had been one of England's most celebrated code breakers during the Second Afghan War and was knighted by Queen Victoria for his wartime skill deciphering top secret, coded messages, some of which were so sensitive they would never be allowed to see the light of day. My introduction to Sir David took place when he helped Joanna break an extremely difficult code in our first case together, which I entitled *The Daughter of Sherlock Holmes.*

"I thought it a good idea to show Sir David the letter we received from Jack the Ripper and ask for his interpretation,"

Joanna went on. "I was hoping the message could offer a clue as to the whereabouts of The Ripper's dwelling. I thought the name Nemo might be of importance in this regard."

"And?"

"I could not have been more wrong," she said. "His explanation of the signature *NEMO* was interesting, but held no significance. Sir David was aware of The Ripper's earlier letters and informed me they were often signed *NEMO*. I was told that *nemo* was a Latin word which meant 'nobody.' Thus, some believed The Ripper was simply saying that the murders were being committed by an ill-defined person, which conveyed the message that you think you see him, but you truly do not see him."

"As if he is one individual, but appears to be another," I assumed.

Joanna nodded. "Much like a chameleon who can disappear from sight, yet remain present."

"So he was referring to a Dr. Jekyll–Mr. Hyde character," I reasoned.

"Precisely," Joanna agreed. "But Nemo could also represent a double entendre, in which the name also indicates that Jack the Ripper was at Eton, shadowing and following my son until the most opportune moment for capture arose."

"No promising news there," I concluded.

"Now comes the most disconcerting interpretation," she said grimly. "Sir David believes the inclusion of John Gill in the letter portends the very worst. He recalled the case of the young lad, which was widely reported at the time. In Sir David's view, The Ripper plans to not only recapture Johnny, but then he will perform the most gruesome of tasks." She paused to swallow audibly, which told me that what was to come was most unnerving. "As you noted so well at autopsy, The Ripper often wishes to decapitate his victims. In the case of Johnny, he will take off my son's head and have it mounted, as if it was some sort of trophy."

I shook my head in revulsion. "Like a hunter does with a lion he has killed, or a fisherman with a giant blue marlin."

Joanna nodded at my assessment. "They do it to remind themselves that they were more powerful and far smarter than the prey they tracked and killed. Likewise for Johnny, he will mount the head to document and confirm he had outwitted the famous daughter of Sherlock Holmes and brought upon her a lifetime of misery and grief from which she can never escape. And that by definition is the most supreme of powers."

"It is beyond insanity," I noted.

"Those were Sir David's exact words," Joanna continued on. "Furthermore, to make certain all England knows of The Ripper's extraordinary feat, he might well take a photograph of the mounted head and send it to the newspapers for publication. You see, he wishes to be known as Attila The Hun of his time."

"What he truly desires is for his name to go down in history as a byword for cruelty," I added darkly.

"And thus far he is succeeding admirably at it," said she. "With all these eventualities in mind, Sir David has strongly advised that we double the precautions we already have in place and never leave the boy unguarded."

"And so we shall," I vowed.

Joanna flicked her wrist at the notion. "We would only be fooling ourselves. There is no way we can hover over him twenty-four hours a day, seven days a week, fifty-two weeks a year. At some point in time, The Ripper will find an opening and use it."

"What then do you plan to do?" I asked.

"I plan to destroy him."

"You had better do so quickly, for the fourth Unfortunate wearing copper earrings is now dead."

Joanna's brow went up. "Has he struck again?"

"I think not, but when he learns of Ruby's death it will force his hand," I replied. "And I am afraid it will seal Pretty Penny's fate."

"Details," she insisted. "I need details of the woman's death and do not leave out a single word."

I watched my wife hurry to the Persian slipper and remove a Turkish cigarette which she lighted, then began to pace the parlor, leaving a trail of dense smoke behind. Outside, there was the sound of screeching brakes, followed by the noise of metal banging against metal, which she totally ignored. "Begin, begin," Joanna said impatiently.

I recounted the story of the Unfortunate's apparently accidental death, recalling every fact from the moment she stopped off the curb on Prescot Street in Whitechapel until the discovery of her copper earrings on the corpse in the morgue.

"There were no witnesses, you say?" Joanna asked at once.

"Only the shopkeeper who saw the inebriated Unfortunate step onto the street only moments before she was struck by a motor vehicle which sped away."

"The death was surely accidental," she concluded. "The Ripper kills, but only when he can dissect, which seems to give him the greatest pleasure. Thus, it is most unlikely that this is The Ripper's work."

"In addition, I learned that Peter Willoughby was in St. Bartholomew's at the time of Ruby's death, with a solid alibi," I noted. "This information was firsthand and obtained at an afternoon conference which was convened to certify that a surgical specimen initially said to be benign was in fact benign. Of course Willoughby could have arranged for another to do the deed."

"Why would he do so?" Joanna asked quickly.

"Perhaps she somehow became aware of his true identity and threatened to blackmail."

"That, too, is most unlikely," Joanna argued. "Had she attempted to blackmail him, he would have agreed to meet her in a dark alleyway with the money, and begged for another sexual encounter, at which time he would have slit her throat. This fellow is very clever and he knows how to tie off loose ends."

"Another macabre possibility just crossed my mind," I thought aloud.

"Let us have it," said she.

"Suppose The Ripper arranged for the killing and further arranged for himself to do the autopsy, which he could easily do as director of pathology," I envisioned. "Of course that, too, would be a form of dissection."

"Possible, but again unlikely, for The Ripper requires his victims to be alive while he dissects them. In that fashion, he can enjoy their suffering and agony."

"And listen to their gurgles as blood fills their severed trachea, making it impossible for the victim to scream," I appended.

"That, as well," Joanna said, taking a final puff on her cigarette and tossing it into the fireplace as she continued to pace. "Tell me more about the prescription slip you discovered in the corpse's coat pocket. In particular, I wish to know the date it was written."

I thought back briefly. "Nearly a month ago."

"Which fits the schedule he had set up for his intended victims. A month provides him with more than enough time to plan five executions," she calculated before asking, "You mentioned her true name was Clara Collins, with the slip dated and signed by Thaddeus Rudd. Correct?"

"Correct."

"Was an address given?"

"That section was left unanswered," I replied. "But as you know, most Unfortunates do not have a permanent address and only seek shelter in doss-houses when they can afford it."

"That does not exclude the possibility that she had some sort of permanent address."

"But none was noted on the slip."

"Doctors often leave that section blank, for they are usually in a hurry when filling out prescriptions, as evidenced by their illegible handwriting." She paused to gaze out the window at the minor motor vehicle accident and, apparently unimpressed, went back to pacing. "Clara Collins was a patient in the free clinic and thus will have a chart at St. Bart's. Please review that chart at your earliest convenience and see if it lists an address."

"And if she has one, how do you plan to make use of it?" I asked.

"She may have a roommate or friends there, who can tell us about the Unfortunate's wanderings and in particular any encounters she might have had with Thaddeus Rudd away from the free clinic. We need to know if there was a specific time and place where they met to conduct their sordid business."

"That is a very long shot."

"It is all we have at the moment," said Joanna as she lighted yet another Turkish cigarette and took several rapid puffs in succession. It was a sure sign that a solution to our problem remained far out of reach. "We require more data if we are to predict The Ripper's movements and set a trap which he is unaware of. You see, he may not have been informed of the Unfortunate's death."

"I am afraid I may have given that information away," I admitted.

"How so?" Joanna asked, abruptly stopping in her tracks.

"I asked the head orderly to remove the Unfortunate's copper earrings, for fear they might be misplaced or stolen," I replied, again second-guessing myself. "I suggested they be replaced onto the Unfortunate's ears when her remains are finally buried. I told the orderly it might give her a touch of dignity at the end of her miserable life. Of course my main reason was to hide the copper earrings from sight so that our one main suspect would not become aware of their presence. But I now worry that the tale of a professor insisting that an Unfortunate be laid to rest wearing her copper earrings might end up becoming juicy hospital gossip that could come to the attention of The Ripper."

"How many people know of this?"

"Only myself and the head orderly, Benson, who I enjoined not to say a word of my unusual request."

"Which of course only increases the temptation to do so."

"And if word of Ruby's death does leak out, I worry that The Ripper will speed up his schedule and proceed directly with the execution of Pretty Penny."

"Your point is well taken," Joanna said, concerned. "It is important that her identity remains unknown."

"Gossip is virtually impossible to stop."

"Not if it is blocked at its source," Joanna contended, and gestured to the telephone. "I would like you to contact the head orderly at once and tell him you have spoken to the police about the copper earrings. Scotland Yard insists the earrings be moved to a most secure place, for they may represent an important clue in the death of the Unfortunate. For this reason, their existence is not to be discussed with anyone."

"But what if he already has?"

"Then we have lost a pivotal advantage."

I was able to reach the head orderly by calling my office and having him summoned immediately. Speaking in an urgent voice, I relayed Joanna's instructions and added a few misstatements of my own as well. The answers were encouraging, if true. Placing the phone down, I said, "Benson informs that he has not yet removed the earrings from the corpse, for his time has been taken up with other duties. He swears, for whatever that is worth, that he has not mentioned the copper earrings to a soul."

Joanna grumbled under her breath, "Whenever someone swears to an answer, it is a certain sign they are lying."

"I am aware of that," I went on. "Which explains why I told Benson that Scotland Yard would shortly be searching about and questioning anyone who may have touched or been told of the earrings."

"What was his response?"

"He admitted that the subject was mentioned to a junior orderly only a few minutes earlier."

"As we expected."

"But there may be time to intercede, for the junior orderly was just down the corridor awaiting instructions on another matter. I can assure you that class of individuals want no contact whatsoever with Scotland Yard on any criminal investigation. Thus, we may have prevented the gossip from spreading."

"Only if we assume that Benson is telling us the whole truth."

"You have doubts?"

"Don't you?"

There was a brief rap on the door and Miss Hudson peeked in. "The street urchins are here to see you."

"Show them in, please," Joanna requested.

The Baker Street Irregulars must have been standing on the staircase directly behind our housekeeper, for they rushed in only a moment before the door closed. Wiggins, Little Alfie, and Sarah The Gypsy were attired in their working clothes, which were unpressed and obviously worn. The latter two members had smudges of dirt on their innocent faces to signify they were truly street urchins. Yet it was still difficult for me to envision them as being so savvy and experienced when it came to the most sordid of criminal activities.

"We have important news, ma'am," Wiggins announced.

"Do you have the name of the Unfortunate who was gutted by The Ripper?" Joanna asked at once.

"No, ma'am, we do not."

"How disappointing."

"To us as well," said Wiggins, no doubt thinking of the handsome reward for that information. "But in our search for her identity, we came across matters regarding the gentleman drifters which will be of interest to you."

"What was the source of this information?"

"The Unfortunates themselves."

"And why do you believe they were being truthful?" Joanna asked in a skeptical tone.

"Because I gave them two shillings, with the promise there would be more should their descriptions prove accurate," Wiggins replied. "In addition, ma'am, the Unfortunates have a true dislike for these gentleman drifters, for reasons I shall shortly tell of."

"Proceed."

"One of them was quite rough and mean to the point that some of the Unfortunates did their best to avoid them, while others demanded a much higher fee for their services," Wiggins detailed. "One of the Unfortunates actually went to the hospital for injuries to her throat and neck. It was painful enough to—"

"Describe the injuries," Joanna interrupted.

"Deep bruises and damage to the voice box which caused the poor woman to speak with a squeak."

"But how could she afford a hospital visit?" I asked. "The cost would be far beyond the means of most Unfortunates."

"It was paid for by the gentleman drifter," Wiggins answered.

"Which of the drifters?" Joanna asked quickly.

"The big, broad-shouldered one."

Joanna and I exchanged knowing glances. The abuser was Thaddeus Rudd, with his vile, hair-trigger temper.

"Did the injured woman have any further encounters with this particular gentleman drifter?" she asked.

"No, ma'am," Wiggins replied. "She was badly frightened by the experience and refused his advances, despite being offered triple her usual fee."

"What so attracted him to her?"

"I asked that very same question, and was told it was her long blond hair and attractive face which appealed to him."

I could not help but wonder if that particular Unfortunate was Clara Collins, also known as Ruby, who now lay dead in the morgue at St. Bartholomew's. "Did you by chance learn the name of the Unfortunate who refused his advances?"

"She was called Ruby."

"Did you have the opportunity to question Ruby?" I inquired.

"No, sir," Wiggins replied. "She was not to be found."

I believed this line of questioning had come to an end, but it was good fortune that Joanna did not. I could almost sense the wheels of her brain switching to yet a higher gear. Although she was not a chess player, she thought like one, always pondering several moves ahead.

Wiggins misinterpreted our silence as a sign of disbelief. "We truly did try to find her, ma'am."

"I am certain you did," Joanna said in a reassuring voice. "For the Unfortunates can disappear quite quickly when the need arises."

"Indeed they can, ma'am."

"Did you consider the woman who gave you the information on Ruby to be reliable?" Joanna asked.

Wiggins nodded his reply. "She seemed so, for she gave her answers freely and without hesitation. Liars usually require time to conjure up their stories."

"So I have noticed," Joanna said, then tapped a finger against her closed lips before continuing. "Was the large gentleman, who had been so mean to Ruby, equally harsh with the other Unfortunates?"

"I cannot say for certain, ma'am," Wiggins replied. "But the other bloke in the trio could also be quite aggressive, to say the least."

"Which are you referring to?" Joanna inquired at once.

"The oldest of the lot."

Peter Willoughby! My mind went directly to the head of pathology, who seemed to take delight bringing his nasty behavior to those who could not defend themselves.

"How did the older gentleman exhibit the aggressiveness you mentioned?" Joanna asked.

"With a black eye he gave her," Wiggins responded. "Once they were in the alleyway and about to conduct business, he struck her with some force. She threatened to tell the others, but he begged her not to and paid her a half crown for her silence."

"But she still spoke of it."

Wiggins shrugged. "A quid may have bought her silence, but not a half crown."

"Were you able to obtain the name of the Unfortunate he struck?"

"No, ma'am. She apparently was a newcomer who no one knew well."

"Disappointing."

"Yes, ma'am."

Joanna reached for yet another Turkish cigarette and, after carefully lighting it, strolled over to the large window which overlooked Baker Street. She gazed out and stood there for some time, obviously lost in thought as she moved her head in quick motions while she sorted through various ideas, most of which did not appear to merit consideration. The Irregulars shifted around nervously on their feet, no doubt wondering if their mission was over and done and, if so, wanting to be paid for their service.

Wiggins cleared his throat audibly. "Ma'am, should we continue to search for the Unfortunate's name?"

"That will not be necessary," Joanna replied.

"What of the surveillance of the gentleman drifters?" Wiggins asked hopefully.

"That, too, should be discontinued."

"Are we finished and done, then?"

"Except for one more important task," Joanna responded. "I wish you to circulate amongst the Unfortunates of Whitechapel and deliver the following message. Beginning with your informant, tell them you have found and spoken with Ruby, who has come on hard times and will shortly be leaving Whitechapel for an area which holds more promise. You must convey this information in a most convincing yet subtle manner. Are you up to it?"

"That will present no problem, ma'am."

"Give me the particulars you will say about Ruby's departure."

Wiggins gave it only a moment's thought before speaking in a deep cockney accent. "I will tell them that I met up with Ruby as she left a doss-house where she had spent her last five-pence. The poor woman is now on hard times, with business very slow, and she has no option but to depart Whitechapel for greener pastures."

"Where will she go?"

"To Notting Dale."

"A good choice."

I agreed as well silently. Notting Dale was a district where the population consisted mainly of beggars, tramps, thieves, and prostitutes. But it was also frequented by gentleman drifters from Mayfair and Kensington.

"I will say that Ruby has an unnamed friend there who will introduce her around the various pubs," Wiggins added.

"A nice touch, for it will show some preparation," said Joanna. "I would also like you to mention that she will try her luck at Mitre Square before leaving, for she has heard that business there is improving. But if this turns out not to be the case, she will promptly depart for Notting Dale."

"How long will she ply her trade in that area before deciding to leave?"

"A matter of days, no more than three."

"A believable number."

"Be on your way, then."

Joanna waited for the door to close before flicking her cigarette into the fire and giving me a most satisfied look. "And so the trap is set, using bait that Jack the Ripper will find irresistible."

"But Ruby, the Unfortunate, is dead," I asserted.

Joanna smiled at me mischievously. "She is about to be resurrected."

Chapter 28

The Trap

My father was clearly disappointed that he would play no role in setting the trap for Jack the Ripper, for the kindly gentleman had been given the task of safeguarding Johnny in our rooms at 221b Baker Street. He was aptly prepared to do so, as evidenced by the shoulder holster he was wearing that held his Webley No. 2 revolver.

"I worry that Joanna is exposing herself to great danger," said my father.

"As do I," I agreed. "But she feels the risk is well worth the opportunity to capture this evil monster."

"Does it not concern you that she will be out in the open unprotected?"

"There will be multiple eyes on her."

"But from a distance," my father cautioned. "Remember, this devil acts with such speed that the victim barely has time to scream for help."

"I am quite aware of that and I can assure you that Joanna is as well."

"Perhaps you should accompany her in the role of being her procurer," my father suggested. "Then you could depart, but remain in the shadows."

I shook my head at the notion. "Prostitutes at the lowest rung do not have procurers, for their fee is so minimal it would hardly be worth splitting with another. Besides, the presence of a male associate would surely frighten away The Ripper."

"Then have an alert constable hidden nearby."

"Whose presence would be noticed by the ever-watchful locals, particularly in the late evening, which would be a tip-off that something was amiss."

Johnny, who was seated next to my father and listening to every word of our conversation, interjected, "Perhaps my mother should carry a revolver for added protection."

"That would give me no advantage," Joanna said, stepping out of our bedroom. "The weapon would have to be hidden and my hands in the open to place The Ripper at ease. His knife would be at my throat long before I could draw a revolver."

I could not help but stare at Joanna, as did my father, for her transformation into Ruby, the Unfortunate, was absolutely remarkable. Like Ruby, she was tall and slender, with long blond hair that reached her shoulders and beyond. The lengthy strands of her hair were pulled back just enough to expose a pair of shiny copper earrings. Her garments were well-worn, particularly her topcoat, with its collar raised to cover her lower face.

"The Ripper will surely believe you are Ruby," I complimented. "There is not a trace of Joanna to be seen."

"Which was my intent," she said, and looked over admiringly at her son. "Now I heard your conversation through the door and want you to know I shall not be harmed."

Johnny rushed over to Joanna and gave her a firm hug. "Oh, Mother, do be careful."

"I promise you I shall."

"I do not know what I would do without you."

"Do not worry, for I plan to return safely to you."

"But what if your life is lost?"

"It will not be," she assured. "But I would gladly give my life to save yours."

Johnny embraced his mother even tighter, saying softly, "As I would give mine for you."

Joanna kissed the lad's forehead and smiled down at her most treasured possession. "Worry not, for your mother will return with the scalp of Jack the Ripper under her belt."

Johnny suddenly brightened. "And we shall dance around it."

"With pleasure," Joanna said, her expression turning stone cold as she headed for the door.

We ensconced ourselves in an empty warehouse facing Mitre Square, with Inspector Lestrade at our side. The street below was dark and quiet at the late hour and showed little activity other than the occasional motorcar which noisily passed by. Lestrade had a small torch in his hand which he flashed briefly and only once. A return blink of light came from an adjacent warehouse where two armed detectives were stationed as lookouts. In addition, there was a sharpshooter on a nearby roof, with a high-powered rifle that carried a telescopic sight. No constables were to be seen, nor would they be.

"How did you manage to position your detectives without them being noticed?" Joanna asked. "You well know that the people in this area are very suspicious of Scotland Yard."

"It was not so difficult," Lestrade replied. "We chose a nearby empty warehouse and had ten detectives disguised as workmen enter the building at midday. They came and went, and pretending to be working on the site, with various tools and materials. At sunset, only eight departed. The two remaining are my most experienced detectives."

"Well played," Joanna lauded. "And what mechanism did you use to place the sharpshooter on the roof?"

"He disguised himself as a vagrant seeking shelter, with a large, battered suitcase that carried his weapon," Lestrade recounted. "For added response, we have a half-dozen darkened trucks parked off the streets a block or two away. In each of those vehicles are a driver and armed detective, ready to engage at the slightest stirring."

"I take it they have been instructed to seal off the exits of the passageways that lead from Mitre Square."

"That will be their first reaction."

"And their second?"

"To pursue and shoot anyone who refuses to stop when ordered to do so."

"Then we are prepared to capture, and if necessary kill."

"Assuming he shows."

"Oh, he will," Joanna assured.

"Dangling an attractive prostitute at him may not be enough," Lestrade worried. "And even if it were, he might not choose this night to act out his sexual impulses."

"I have made this evening the perfect opportunity for him."

"How so?"

"The play *Romeo and Juliet* was scheduled to be performed at the Whitechapel Playhouse tonight," Joanna replied. "I have had it canceled in such a manner that it will not arouse suspicion. Thus, our three main suspects have what one might call a free night to be in the area. The Ripper is almost certain to take advantage of that, particularly since Ruby will only be available for another night or two."

"But would not abruptly closing down a performance at the playhouse cause The Ripper concern?" Lestrade asked.

"Under ordinary circumstances it might, but I arranged for the closure in a most convincing fashion," Joanna elucidated. "I had to bring Mrs. Emma Adams into our confidence, but told her that one loose word from her lips could ruin our plans to take down The Ripper. She understands that her Pretty Penny's life is at stake, so she shall beyond a doubt remain silent. In any event, Emma, being familiar with the stage's lighting, caused a short circuit to occur, which produced smoke and of course alarmed everyone. Tonight's performance was called off to give the electricians time to rewire the lights on the stage. Of course the players were notified, as was the public, by word of mouth."

Lestrade gave the matter further thought, obviously still concerned. "It is all too convenient," he opined. "Here we have one individual, Mrs. Adams, who was questioned thoroughly by both you and me, which connects her to the daughter of Sherlock Holmes and Scotland Yard. Everyone in Whitechapel is aware of that. And suddenly she calls off a performance because some people detected a bit of smoke from a short circuit? I am afraid it will not sit well with a clever devil like The Ripper."

"That also crossed my mind," Joanna responded. "Fortunately, there was an earlier incident in which the stage lights flickered off and on during the touching tomb scene when Romeo was about to poison himself upon believing his Juliet was dead. It was a most inopportune time for the lighting to go amiss and the audience was quite disturbed by it. With all this in mind, I believed it was plausible indeed to cancel a performance to make certain the stage lights did not go away again."

"Nicely done," Lestrade said. "But a character as clever as this one might still see through it."

"Let us hope he doesn't."

A four-wheeler passed along the cobblestones of Mitre Square and stopped briefly before disappearing into the darkness. We pricked our ears, listening for other movements in the dim light, but heard none. Still, as the silence returned, the noise of the wheels riding over cobblestones put our nerves on edge. In the distance, Big Ben began to toll the ten o'clock hour.

"It is time," Joanna said, without a hint of fear.

"Be most careful," I cautioned. "And blow your police whistle at the first sign of danger."

"I suggest you keep it in your hand and at the ready," Lestrade advised.

"That would be a dead giveaway were he to see it." Joanna adjusted her blond wig and scarf so that the copper earrings were clearly visible. "Let us finish this business once and for all."

Lestrade and I watched her depart via a rear exit that opened on to a dark alleyway just to the east of Mitre Square. The inspector flashed his small torch twice to alert the detectives in the adjacent warehouse and the sharpshooter on the roof that Joanna was now on the move.

"I worry," I said.

"As do I," Lestrade concurred.

"I wish my father was here, for he is such an excellent marksman."

"So is the sharpshooter on the roof, who can hit an apple at two hundred yards."

"In the darkness?"

Lestrade had no answer.

Joanna appeared on the square, now standing next to the lamppost, which gave off scant light. At a distance and even closer in the dimness, she could easily pass for Ruby, the Unfortunate. A motorcar crossed the far side of the square without slowing down. It was a large vehicle, similar to the one we had seen Thaddeus Rudd being chauffeured in outside St. Bartholomew's. Our senses heightened even more as the silence and stillness returned.

"He will act soon," Lestrade predicted.

"Based on what?" I asked.

"An itch I feel when mayhem is about to occur."

As if on cue, a figure wearing a heavy topcoat appeared out of the shadows and approached Joanna. He hesitated for a moment, then strode by for a good ten steps, only to quickly turn and come back to her. They gestured and exchanged brief words before disappearing down a dark passageway.

"He makes his move!" Lestrade whispered loudly.

We dashed for the stairs and hurried down, taking them two at a time, until we exited into a dim passageway. Lestrade led the way, silently creeping along with his revolver drawn. Now there was not even a hint of light in the darkness, which made the going slow and even more precarious. Then we heard Joanna's screams and the sound of a struggle, with a tin bin rattling against the cobblestones.

We raced toward her voice, almost tripping over ourselves, and found Joanna leaning against a brick wall, catching her breath but nonetheless unharmed. She pointed into the darkness and shouted, "That way!"

We sprinted for the dim light at the end of the passageway where we were joined by the two detectives from the adjacent warehouse, both with revolvers at the ready. There was no sign of Jack the Ripper. The nearby walls were windowless and free of any ladders which would allow one to climb up and escape. We could hear no sounds that night be followed.

The sharpshooter on the roof called out, "He is heading eastward!"

"How far?" Lestrade called back.

"A short block down from you, no more."

"Keep him in your sight."

"Will do."

Trucks carrying more detectives pulled up beside us and their occupants hurriedly exited, most with revolvers, a few with long rifles. The entire group of fifteen detectives gathered around Lestrade and awaited his instructions. He was about to speak when the sharpshooter shouted down from the roof, "He has turned off the street and is heading north down a narrow passageway!"

"Is he still visible?" Lestrade shouted up.

"Not now."

"Are there intersecting streets off the passageway?"

"One for certain, if you go by lampposts."

Lestrade came back to the assembled detectives and gave them the location of the last sighting of The Ripper, with the following instructions: "Divide yourselves into three groups, with each covering a segment north of the passageway. The entire area is to be blanketed, and every house, room, and roof searched thoroughly."

"What about the passageway itself, sir?" asked a young detective.

"The Watsons and I will scour every inch of it," Lestrade replied. "In addition, I would like the trucks placed in a semicircle three blocks north of the last sighting. Nothing is to be allowed through without being stopped and searched."

As per the inspector's instructions, the group divided itself into three and dashed off in different directions. Just behind them, a bevy of trucks raced their engines and sped away to their designated locations. We hurried to the passageway on the next block just as a heavy rain began to fall, which, unfortunately, would wash away any tracks left behind by The Ripper. Nonetheless, we pushed on, realizing this was our best and perhaps only chance to apprehend the maniacal killer.

We could hear doors being pounded upon and see lights suddenly turning on in otherwise dark houses as the detectives conducted their search. In a few homes, babies were crying and dogs barking, all of which served to drown out any sounds The Ripper might make.

Suddenly the shrill sound of a police whistle filled the night air. We ran full speed to the site of its origin and were soon joined by a phalanx of detectives, with their weapons drawn and ready to fire. Trucks pulled up at both ends of the street, thus blocking entrance and exit.

Lestrade approached the detective at the doorstep of a dark home, who had his revolver in one hand and a police whistle in the other. He was young, but with a face hard as steel, and if he had any fear it did not show.

"What do we have here?" Lestrade asked.

"A very dark house in which the occupant refuses to answer my knock," the detective replied.

"How do you know the house is occupied?"

"Because I heard him moving about, sir."

Lestrade checked the rounds in his revolver, saying, "Rap on the door once more and if there is no response you are to kick it open."

"Very good, sir."

Lestrade motioned to two burly detectives and, with hand signals, instructed them to rush in once the door was crashed open.

The young detective pounded on the door a half-dozen times, then stepped back and waited. When no response was forthcoming, he stepped back and prepared for a forceful kick.

"Did you try the doorknob?" Joanna asked, as all eyes went to the young detective.

"Yes, ma'am," he replied. "It is fixed."

"Proceed, then."

With a mighty kick, the door cracked but did not open. A second kick caused the thick wooden door to fly off its hinges.

The detectives raced in with their torches and weapons pointed ahead, only to find the parlor empty. But there were wet footprints leading to a narrow staircase. Again with hand signals, Lestrade directed two detectives to follow him up the stairs. Silently, he ascended with measured steps. I knew that Lestrade would attempt to take The Ripper alive and give the man his day in court, but were the cruel murderer to come down the stairs lifeless, I would not be disappointed. We could hear footsteps and doors opening and closing on the floor above, but there were no sounds of a struggle. I feared the worst, with The Ripper remaining at large and Joanna and her son continuing to be put through a never-ending nightmare. Joanna and I kept our eyes on the staircase as Lestrade descended.

"I suspect he escaped via a ladder that led to the roof, which is now vacant," he reported in a monotone, but the setback was clearly written on his face. "These are all row houses and he could have easily gone a block without being noticed."

"He may still be here," Joanna said, walking about the parlor and repeatedly stomping her foot on the floor. "I suggest searching for a hollow space beneath."

"What makes you so certain there is one?" Lestrade asked.

"Because here is where he would hide Pretty Penny," Joanna replied. "There is no other place."

The entire squad of detectives eagerly stomped every inch of the floor, hoping to find a secret compartment underneath the parlor, dining area, and kitchen, but their search proved futile.

"I am afraid he is gone," Lestrade declared dispiritedly, glancing around the bare room once again before returning to Joanna. "Were you able to make out any of his physical features in the dimness?

"None of note, for he was well disguised," she replied. "His face was for the most part covered with hat and scarf."

"What of his voice?"

"He altered that as well by giving it a hoarse quality."

"So clever," Lestrade grumbled. "It appears he has given us the slip, just as we had him within our grasp."

"Maybe, maybe not," Joanna said, stomping on the floor yet again. "There are ways to hide the hollow sound of a secret space."

"It would require a court order for us to tear up the entire floor, which might not be given since our evidence is so scant."

"We do not require a court order, but rather a keen nose."

"And where will one be found?"

"At Number Three Pinchin Lane in lower Lambeth."

"Where Toby Two resides," I recalled.

Joanna nodded and smiled confidently. "Who carries with her the keenest nose in all London."

Chapter 29

The Hiding Place

Toby Two was more than delighted to see me, for dogs have the unique ability to immediately distinguish between the scents of friend and foe, and once this difference is learned, their remarkable memory never allows them to forget. Yet, after a quick lick of my hand, the hound busied herself sniffing around the rear seat of the Scotland Yard motor vehicle, obviously attracted by an aroma I could not detect. This was not surprising in that a monograph on this subject, which Joanna gave me long ago, emphasized that the sense of smell in dogs was at least a thousand times more sensitive than that of humans. I had actually seen Toby Two in action when she followed the faint whiff of a perfume across London to Victoria station and in doing so led to the exoneration of a prime suspect. But it was beyond me what so attracted Toby Two to the cushion in the rear compartment.

"Have you carried any unusual cargo in the back of this motorcar recently?" I asked the driver.

"Not that I recall," the driver replied.

"Perhaps you transported food or an unwashed captured suspect."

"Nothing of that sort."

"Another animal?"

The driver paused to think back. "Some weeks ago I gave the commissioner a ride to pick up his sick collie."

"That explains Toby Two's interest in the rear cushion," I said, nodding to myself. In the aforementioned monograph, it was noted that a dog could not only easily detect the aroma of another hound but also determine whether it was male or female and, if female, whether it was pregnant and how close to delivery. A scent left behind a month ago was quickly picked up and identified, all of which indicated that a dog's nose was truly one of nature's most sensitive instruments. But how would Joanna employ Toby Two in the search for Jack the Ripper? Was it the smell of formaldehyde, which either Peter Willoughby or Thaddeus Rudd would carry from their visit to Maxwell Anderson's laboratory? Quite possible indeed, for although their visit occurred last week, to Toby Two it would be as if the scent were deposited an hour ago.

We arrived at the entrance to the dark passageway and, as instructed, I remained in the motor vehicle with the hound, while the driver raced on foot into the dwelling from which The Ripper had supposedly escaped. Most of the windows in the neighborhood were now lighted, with the occupants leaning out to view the ongoing police activity. A few came down to the passageway but were quickly turned away. Toby Two's tail began to wag happily, which informed me that Joanna was approaching.

"Well, well, it is good to see you again," said Joanna, reaching down to scratch the head of the most peculiar-appearing animal. The dog had many features of a long-haired spaniel, but the floppy ears, sad eyes, and snout were those of a bloodhound. Being the offspring of a second-generation Toby and an amorous bloodhound endowed her with the keenest sense of smell imaginable, which she merrily put to work. Toby Two sat on her haunches and stared up at Joanna, as if awaiting directions.

"Now we are about to play a game you so enjoy," Joanna said, and delved into her purse for the jar of hair pomade she had purchased from the Widow Marley. She placed the unopened jar under Toby Two's nose for a brief few seconds and watched the dog's tail wag at its distinctive lavender aroma. Only then did Joanna hand the jar to the driver and ask, "Which way is the wind blowing tonight?"

"East to west, ma'am," he replied.

"I would like you to drive west, with the wind, and after you have traveled several miles dispose of the jar."

"Very good, ma'am."

Joanna took hold of Toby Two's leash and led her into a brightly lighted parlor, where the dog abruptly stopped in her tracks, with her tail now pointed straight as an arrow. Lestrade and his team watched with great interest while they stepped away from the dog's intended path. Toby Two began straining on her leash, with her nose directed to the kitchen area. Another detective came out of the kitchen and, seeing the circumstances, quickly moved aside.

"Go, girl!" Joanna commanded, and released the leash.

Toby Two dashed through the kitchen door and into an

oversized storage closet next to it. She went directly to a worn rug near the wall and pawed furiously at it. Joanna hurried over and stomped on the rug, expecting a hollow sound to return, but none came. Stepping back, she reconsidered the situation before kicking the rug away. Under it and against the wall was a metal handle lying flat on the floor. Joanna reached down and pulled on it, which caused the floor to give, but no more than a centimeter. She released the handle and the floor dropped back into place.

"I need a strong hand!" she called out.

A burly detective, with the physique of a wrestler, came over and, with a mighty jerk, opened up a most unusual trapdoor. Its top had a wooden surface, while its underside was lined with thick sacks of sand which accounted for its heavy weight.

"Clever," Joanna remarked. "I suspect the entire ceiling of the cellar is covered with sandbags, which keeps the sound dull when the floor above is stomped upon. It also renders the space soundproof, which would prevent screams from his victims being heard."

Lestrade quickly stepped over and peered down at the narrow staircase that led to the darkened cellar. "He may be hiding in there."

Joanna shook her head. "He is gone."

"What makes you so confident?"

"The rug," Joanna replied. "Had he entered via the trapdoor and closed it, he could not have pulled the rug back into place."

"Still," Lestrade said, reaching for his revolver, "we will take no chances."

With two detectives close behind him, Lestrade slowly stepped down the stairs, lighting the way into the darkness with his torch. There were no sounds to be heard as we all wondered what ghastly sights awaited us in this secret chamber of horrors. Toby Two's nose had informed us that Pretty Penny was imprisoned there but could not tell us if she was alive. Finally, after a long silence, Lestrade called up, "All clear!"

Joanna and I carefully descended the stairs, with the inspector's torch lighting our way. The air was quite musty and stale from lack of ventilation. In addition, I detected the smell of body decay, which I was all too familiar with from my time in the autopsy room. One of the detectives found a light switch on the wall and turned it on, but it provided limited illumination, for there was only a single lightbulb dangling from the ceiling. But it was enough to bring into view the most macabre sights imaginable. On a wall above a workbench was nailed a collection of Jack the Ripper's trophies. There were row upon row of dried-out ovaries and uteruses, some still attached to intact vaginas, which had been dissected out en bloc. It was so disgusting that even a seasoned detective was forced to look away and swallow back his nausea.

"Only the most evil of minds could construct a museum for such mementos," Lestrade commented, directing his torch at the dissected organs. "Yet they seem so well preserved, with little evidence of rot."

"That is because they have been mummified," Joanna elucidated, and pointed to the workbench, upon which were scalpels and other dissecting instruments. Sitting next to them were airtight glass containers that held several noses and ears which were heavily dusted with white powder. "This is how one goes about the process of mummification. The various organs are placed in airtight jars and covered with baking soda, which removes every drop of moisture, causing desiccation, which in turn prevents decay."

"An absolute madman," said Lestrade, glancing around the dimly lighted cellar.

"But one with a mission," Joanna noted, and walked over to the far corner of the room, which held a metal table, six feet in length, with side drains to siphon off unwanted bodily fluids. Close by was a stand filled with a variety of surgical instruments, including knives, scalpels, saws, hemostats, retractors, and toothed forceps.

It took me a moment to make the connection. "Good Lord! He was performing autopsies down here."

"But why and on whom?" Lestrade asked at once. "The bodies of his victims were always found at the crime scene."

"Not all," Joanna informed, and reminded him of the missing Unfortunates in the past whose corpses were never found.

"So he is back to his old tricks."

"So it would seem."

A detective hurried over and said, "Inspector, there is no sign of the girl."

"Please do not tell me he has escaped with his captive," Lestrade growled unhappily.

"But that appears to be the case, sir."

"She is here," said Joanna.

"What allows you to be so certain, may I ask?"

Joanna motioned to the end of the workbench beyond the instruments and organs being preserved.

Lestrade squinted his eyes in the dimness. "I see nothing other than his gruesome workings."

"Look again."

"I see a jar," Lestrade noted as he directed his torch to the item.

"It is the jar of pomade Pretty Penny uses to make her hair glisten, and which The Ripper recently purchased from the girl's hairdresser," said Joanna. "And next to it is a final helping of apple spice candy that is meant to be served to Pretty Penny on her execution day."

"But there is no sign of her," Lestrade argued mildly.

"And there was no sign of a trapdoor leading down to the cellar, either," Joanna rebutted, and turned to the detective. "You and your men must search again, and be certain to stomp on every square foot."

"But we have done that, madam."

"Do it once more," she insisted. "But this time stomp harder and listen for even the slightest echo."

Lestrade nodded his consent and watched the detective hurry away before coming back to Joanna. "Assuming he did autopsies in this cellar, how could he dispose of the corpses? That would be no easy task even if dismembered."

"Not as difficult as one might suppose," Joanna said, and gestured to a large container of lye beneath the instrument table. "He simply buried them in the earth."

"But where? This cellar is not nearly large enough for a graveyard."

Joanna pointed to a stack of large canvas sacks in the near corner. "I suspect the bodies were placed in those sacks and covered with lye, which transforms them into a brown pulp in a matter of days."

"But those sacks are not large enough to hold a whole corpse," Lestrade argued.

"He dismembered them first and spread their limbs elsewhere around London, as the commissioner so aptly described."

The inspector rubbed at his chin, considering the matter further. "But burying these large sacks is no simple task, for he'd have to dig a bloody big pit."

"Oh, there are ways around that," Joanna explained. "All he needed was to find abandoned water wells in the countryside, some of which go a hundred feet or more deep. The Ripper could drop the sacks in, cover them with a layer of rocks or sand, and move on to the next."

"The lye no doubt offsets the noxious smell as well."

My wife nodded. "An added benefit."

A young detective called out from the workbench, "Sir, we have found a framed letter in one of the lower drawers!"

"What does it say?" asked Lestrade.

"It seems to be a notification from the *Lancet*."

"A notification of what sort?"

"One of rejection, I would say."

"Ah, yes, the final piece of the puzzle," said Joanna, as a look of satisfaction crossed her face.

"Which is?" Lestrade inquired.

"His motivation for the mutilated murders," my wife said, reaching for the framed letter which she dusted off before reading aloud, "'From the editor of the *Lancet*,' dated 1889."

"Denying publication of his research no doubt," I interjected.

Joanna nodded. "It reads as follows:

> *"Dear Sir,*
>
> *"We regret to inform you that we shall be unable to publish your study in the* Lancet. *Your contention that the criminal behavior of the two women can be attributed to lesions in the frontal cortex is not supported by the data. Our panel of experts was of the opinion that the brain lesions were the result of repeated trauma and did not show the structural lesions you proposed were present. Furthermore, your conclusion that the increased size and weight of the female sex organs accounted for the subjects' promiscuity is without merit. Should you wish to resubmit your study at a later date, we would be obliged to again review it, but only if the underlying data is far more convincing."*

"Is Willoughby's name on the letter?" I asked quickly.

"It is not to be seen, for it has been blacked out with dark ink," she replied, holding the frame closer to Lestrade's torch. "It would seem he wanted the motivation of the rebuke, but not the shame associated with it."

"So he persevered, even to the point of embarrassing himself before the Royal Society," I recalled. "Which of course was the sternest of rebukes."

"That, too, was well deserved."

"So it was all an experiment," Lestrade concluded. "He murdered those women hoping to advance science."

"It was done mainly to advance himself and gain the fame of an important medical discovery," said Joanna. "Now let us find his laboratory books, which will prove the obvious."

"What would their appearance be, ma'am?" asked the young detective.

"They are large notebooks, with thick covers."

The detective pointed to an opened drawer beneath the workbench. "Such books were beside the framed letter."

"Excellent," Joanna said, and hurried over to the drawer to extract a well-worn laboratory book, which she opened and held up to the light.

We gathered as my wife began to slowly turn its pages one by one until she came to the most revealing one.

"That is something you would expect to find in Dr. Frankenstein's laboratory," said I, making no effort to hide my revulsion, as I read over her shoulder.

Before me was a chart that listed the horrific data on the organs Willoughby had dissected from the mutilated corpses. Every detail was so carefully printed out. The only blank spaces were next to the letters *P.P.,* which no doubt stood for *Pretty Penny.*

"Please interpret for us, Dr. Watson," Lestrade requested.

Name	Ovarian Weight		Uterine Weight	Brain Lesion
T.M.	5 gm		49 gm	—
R.P.	4 gm		55 gm	—
J.G.	7 gm		60 gm	—
B.H.	14 gm		82 gm	Meningioma
A.D.	6 gm		45 gm	—
P.P.				

"He has recorded the names of his victims and the weights of their ovaries and uteruses. All are within normal limits except that of B.H., with readings of fourteen grams and eighty-two grams, which are far above normal. She also had a benign brain tumor called a meningioma."

"Which Willoughby no doubt believed would prove his hypothesis that the sex organs' large size, together with the brain lesion, would account for the woman's abnormal behavior," Joanna reasoned.

I turned to the following page, which contained a more detailed description of the brain lesion. "Except that the meningioma was located in the occipital area, where it would cause visual problems and not personality change."

"Science gone mad," said Lestrade, and again studied the rejection letter from the *Lancet*. "Perhaps our experts at the Yard can remove the black stain and reveal Dr. Willoughby's name."

"It would be interesting, but not proof that the addressee was The Ripper," Joanna rebutted. "Any good barrister would claim the letter was stolen long ago and no one could disprove it. We require an eyewitness to satisfy the court."

"Or a clear fingerprint."

"That would do nicely as well."

The lead detective returned, shaking his head. "I am afraid we have come up empty, ma'am."

"Perhaps we should bring Toby Two down," I suggested.

"Unfortunately, she will be of little help in this instance," said Joanna. "This entire cellar is contaminated with the smell of cadavers, which all dogs find irresistible. She would literally roll around on the floor next to the autopsy table, oblivious to all other scents."

"So we must conclude that Pretty Penny is gone," Lestrade said gloomily.

"She is here," Joanna asserted once again, and began to walk back and forth across the cellar, head down, stomping on the floor with each step. She continued carefully pacing over every square foot, even testing the floor under the workbench and autopsy table, but without results. Finally, she moved over to the staircase and examined the area beneath it but found nothing of interest. Her gaze went around the cellar once more and came to rest on the stack of large canvas sacks which stood in a far corner.

The detective followed her line of vision and anticipated her question. "We searched the stack as well and found nothing hidden."

"Did you look beneath them?"

"Yes, ma'am. We wheeled the trolley aside and inspected every inch under it."

Joanna's brow went up. "Wheeled, you say?"

"Yes, ma'am. Like most trolleys used for transport, this one had four wheels."

"But why?"

"Why what?"

"Why wheels, my good fellow? It has wheels because it was meant to be moved," she explained. "Well then, we must ask ourselves for what purpose? Certainly not to travel around the cellar, for if you wished a sack, you would simply walk over and take one. Which leaves us with only one explanation for its movement. It must be concealing something and needs to be periodically pushed aside."

"But there was no evidence of a pit or space beneath it."

"Did you see tracks on the floor made by the trolley?"

"Yes, ma'am."

"And how far did those tracks travel?"

"Only a yard or so."

"Which is all that would be required for The Ripper to reach his desired object," Joanna deduced. "Please move it out of the corner."

Once the area beneath the trolley was cleared, she used her foot to sweep away the thick grime that covered the floor. A deep, straight crack appeared, which was connected at right angles to yet another. Again using her foot, my wife cleared aside more grime, and the outline of a trapdoor came into view. If there was illumination below, it was not enough to pierce through the cracks in the wood. No sounds could be heard. As with the trapdoor upstairs, a metal handle was situated next to the wall itself.

The burly detective was beckoned and hurried over to pull open the trapdoor, which had sandbags attached to its underneath surface. Warm air rushed up at us and in a moment dissipated. Below was total darkness and the strong odor of stale, dried blood. We collectively held our breaths, expecting the worst.

"Hello!" Joanna called down.

There was a stretch of time before a weak, tiny voice replied, "Please let me go."

"We are Scotland Yard here to rescue you," said Joanna.

A stream of torches lighted the dark pit, which had dimensions of approximately ten by ten feet. The floor, but not the walls, was covered with planks of wood. In the center of the small dungeon was the badly frightened Pretty Penny, whose attractive face was still recognizable but whose lower body was painted with old blood and dark dirt. She was sitting on the floor, for there was no furniture to be seen.

"Are you injured?" Joanna asked.

"No, ma'am," Pretty Penny replied pitifully.

"Is the blood not yours?"

"It is his," she responded. "He threw up on me."

To a man there was not one of us who did not wish to have his hands on the throat of this maniacal monster whose cruelty knew no bounds.

"We shall come down for you and have you cleaned up properly," Joanna told her in a gentle voice.

"Thank you, ma'am," Pretty Penny said, and began to weep.

A ladder was found in a nearby corner of the cellar and brought over, which a detective used to descend into the pit and, with care, bring the young actress up to freedom. A bucket of water was retrieved from the kitchen, which Joanna used to wet her handkerchief and wash away much of the blood and grime that covered Pretty Penny's face and arms.

"Thank you," the young actress said gratefully. "Thank you for saving my life."

"I am delighted we were able to do so," Joanna responded. "But now we must find the man who did this dreadful thing to you. Do you feel like answering a few questions?"

"I am more than up to it," Pretty Penny replied, regaining a measure of strength and composure.

"Did you recognize your assailant?"

"I did not, for I was rendered unconscious when he took me hostage. When I awakened, I found myself in this hellish pit. I rarely saw his face, for he only exposed himself while opening the trapdoor briefly to throw food down to me."

"Were you able to make out any of his features?"

"Only that he always wore a fisherman's hat which was pulled down over his forehead."

"What of his voice?"

"He rarely spoke."

"I take it you were never in a conversation with your captor?"

"Never. He spoke only a few words, except when he retched his blood down on me."

"How many times did this occur?"

"Twice."

"And then he would talk to you at length?"

"Not at length, but to apologize."

Joanna paused to assimilate and digest all the new information, for in her mind something was out of place. "For him to apologize, it would appear he did not throw up blood on you intentionally."

"He could have stepped away," Pretty Penny refuted, now showing a flash of anger. "But he vomited again and again on one occasion, and remained in place."

"So you believed his apology was insincere," Joanna concluded.

Pretty Penny nodded. "Particularly when he told me that the blood I was drenched in would bind us together, whatever that meant."

"It was the talk of a madman," Joanna explained, although the implication was obvious. It was an attempt to bond an old, make-believe Romeo to his Juliet in a lasting, diabolical fashion.

Pretty Penny licked nervously at her parched lips before asking, "This madman planned to eventually kill me, did he not?"

"I am afraid so," Joanna replied candidly.

"Then what is to protect me now, with this lunatic on the loose?" Pretty Penny asked in a quivering voice. "I cannot go home and expose my dear Emma to this terrible danger."

Lestrade stepped forward and said, "You can indeed go home, for there will be a constable at your front door and an armed detective at your side until this villain is apprehended and brought to justice."

"The sooner the better, sir."

"We shall do our very best," Lestrade vowed, and motioned for the two detectives to approach. "And now you will be taken home where I am certain a warm bath and bed would be most welcome."

Pretty Penny tried to arise from her chair, but her unsteady legs would not allow it. The detectives hurried in and assisted her to a standing position. She smiled briefly and in a clear, theatrical voice said, "Thank all of you for saving my life. If I live to be a hundred, I will never forget your faces or your kindness."

Lestrade waited until the young actress was escorted out of the cellar before turning to Joanna. "It would appear we have been outfoxed again."

"Maybe not," Joanna said, undeterred. "You should have every inch of this house and cellar searched for fingerprints which might match those that you already have on file."

"He must have left some prints behind," Lestrade hoped.

"I would not be overly optimistic in that regard," Joanna downplayed the possibility, and pointed to the rubber gloves on The Ripper's workbench. "He knows how to cover his tracks."

"Clever devil," Lestrade said sourly. "But surely he had to leave some hidden clues for us."

"Oh, indeed he did, and they are directly in front of your eyes."

"Pray tell where?"

Joanna gestured to the wall which contained The Ripper's hideous mementos. "How many do you count?"

"Several dozen," Lestrade approximated.

"And their age?"

"Some new, some old."

"How many are relatively new?"

Lestrade counted quickly. "Perhaps a dozen or so."

"Which tells us that the other dozens came from The Ripper's activities which took place twenty-eight years ago," Joanna calculated.

"So?" asked Lestrade, who like the rest of us did not see its relevance.

"Which further tells us that The Ripper has occupied and in all likelihood owned this home for nearly thirty years."

"So?"

"Someone had to pay property taxes on this dwelling," Joanna concluded. "Show me the taxpayer and I will show you Jack the Ripper."

Chapter 30

Jack the Ripper

The Tax Office opened promptly at 8:00 AM, but the property records were not made available to us, for they were under seal and held in confidence. Even Scotland Yard would not be allowed access to the files without a court order. One was obtained, facilitated by a phone call from the commissioner, and the tax record for the Whitechapel dwelling unsealed at 10:55 AM. The house was registered to Peter Willoughby.

We drove to St. Bartholomew's in a Scotland Yard motor vehicle driven by a detective, with Lestrade in the front seat next to him and Joanna and me in the rear compartment. Despite our lack of conversation, we were all well aware that the interrogation of Willoughby had to be done in a most careful manner, for there was no solid evidence to show that he was Jack the Ripper. Incredibly, after a painstakingly diligent search, not a single fingerprint was found in the subterranean chamber of horrors. Not one! The Ripper had no doubt worn rubber gloves while performing his work and may have even washed down the area with bleach, for several empty bottles of the liquid were found in the pit Pretty Penny occupied.

"That is the crucial clue," Joanna broke the silence. "We have to place Willoughby in that cellar with his captive."

"But there are numerous, clearly defined fingerprints on the first floor," Lestrade argued. "Surely some of those will belong to him."

"What if they do?" she asked with a shrug. "A clever barrister would claim they were made by his client while showing the house to a prospective buyer or lessee."

"Would he not have to show that such an act had taken place?"

Joanna flicked her wrist dismissively. "They would say that no transaction occurred and thus no paperwork was required. They would also suggest that someone else must have surreptitiously occupied the premises on an intermittent basis."

Lestrade nodded dolefully at the assessment. "And the nearby neighbors swear they rarely saw anyone coming or going. That dwelling could have been vacant most of the time."

"I suspect it was until Willoughby decided to reoccupy the house and resume his role as Jack the Ripper," said Joanna. "But proving it is quite another matter, for there is nothing to show that he was ever in that horrific cellar, and Pretty Penny, the only one of his victims still alive, cannot identify him as her captor. In essence then, the evidence we have on hand would never stand up in a court of law."

"It would seem our interrogation of Willoughby will not be very productive," I predicted. "There appears to be no opening to pursue."

"Let us first determine if he has an alibi for his whereabouts between the hours of ten and eleven last night," Joanna advised.

"He might simply tell us he was taking a long walk alone," I envisioned. "And of course challenge us to prove otherwise."

"And how would he explain the bite mark on his arm?" she asked.

"What bite mark?" Lestrade and I inquired simultaneously.

"During the attack last night, he pushed me against a wall and grabbed at my neck," Joanna described. "As I attempted to place his elbow in an armlock, he raised his other arm and tightened it under my chin. It was a sudden, unexpected move which caught me by surprise. He then brought his forearm up to my mouth to silence me, which allowed me to bite down through his sleeve and into his skin. He promptly released his hold, which gave me the opportunity to call for help."

"Did you draw blood?" I asked at once.

"I can't be certain, but my teeth went deep enough to elicit a loud cry of pain," she replied. "A moment later I was able to lash out at his shin and land a solid blow. We should look for a bruise mark there as well."

"Perhaps Willoughby will claim he was attacked on his evening walk," Lestrade countered.

"Did his so-called attacker leave a distinctive bite mark behind?" Joanna queried.

"Are such bite marks truly distinctive?" Lestrade asked.

"We are about to find out."

Moments later we pulled up to a side entrance to St. Bartholomew's and quickly exited, then hurried down a long flight of stairs and into a busy corridor. Lestrade and the other detective from Scotland Yard led the way, with Joanna and me only a few feet behind. There was something about the inspector's expression and stride which caused people to move aside and stop their conversations. Even the wheelchairs and gurneys came to a sudden halt. I could not help but wonder what Peter Willoughby's response to the interrogation might be, for here was a man accustomed to being in command and in control of all that transpired in the department of pathology. He would shortly be exposed to a much different and unexpected situation.

As we approached the door to the director's office, Lestrade asked, "Should I begin?"

Joanna nodded and replied quietly, "I shall intervene when we reach the issue of his alibi."

We entered Willoughby's office and went directly to his secretary's desk. The meek little lady looked up to study the group but paid particular attention to my presence before asking, "May I help you, gentlemen?"

"You may indeed, madam," Lestrade replied. "I am Inspector Lestrade of Scotland Yard, who, along with my associates, wish to speak with Dr. Willoughby immediately."

"He has left instructions that he is not to be disturbed, sir," the secretary responded. "He is in the midst of a most important study."

"He must be interrupted now, for we are here on official business," Lestrade said in an authoritative tone. "There will be no delay."

Pushing her chair back, the secretary quickly walked to a large door and rapped against a frosted glass pane, upon which was printed Willoughby's name and title. "Sir, there are detectives from Scotland Yard here who wish to see you."

There was no answer, so she waited a moment and rapped once more, a bit louder this time. Again there was no reply.

"Please stand aside," Lestrade requested, and tried the door, which was locked. "Do you have the key, madam?"

"No, sir," the secretary replied. "The only other key is in the possession of the head orderly."

"Call him immediately."

While the secretary busied herself on the phone, Lestrade moved us aside and asked me in a low voice, "Are there windows in the office?"

"None whatsoever, for the pathology department is in a subterranean location," I answered.

"So the only way out is via the stairs?" queried Lestrade. "Is that correct?"

"Correct," I replied.

"Does Willoughby have a closet in his office?"

"Not that I recall."

"Is there any place for a hidden staircase?"

"None."

The secretary called over, "Inspector, the head orderly will be here shortly!"

"Did you request that he bring his keys?"

"He carries them with him, sir."

"Very good," Lestrade said, and came back to us. "Is there an escape hatch in the ceiling?"

"If there is, it is well hidden," I replied.

"Is there a door to an adjoining office?"

"Not that I am aware of."

"Do you recall seeing any structures or forms of art that cover a wall?"

"Such as?"

"A giant screen or tall bookcase."

"There are floor-to-ceiling bookcases," I recounted.

"We must look behind them." Lestrade again peered over at the frosted glass pane in the door to Willoughby's office, as if trying to see through it. "Assuming he has made good his escape, it surely points the finger of guilt at him."

We waited impatiently for the orderly with his keys, all of us wondering what lay behind the closed, locked door. Had Willoughby truly managed to escape? Was there a secret way out that only he was aware of? Being the all-powerful director, he could have had a hidden exit installed without the rest of us knowing. And then a final, most disconcerting thought came into my mind. With Peter Willoughby in fact being Jack the Ripper, it would cast a terrible stain on St. Bartholomew's that would be indelible and forever lasting.

"Something is amiss here," Joanna said, more to herself than to us. "A clever man, even if guilty, would never run, for he would soon be apprehended. The smart move would be to claim innocence, say little, and call your barrister."

Lestrade gave Joanna a puzzled look. "Are you saying he is still in his office?"

"I am saying it makes no sense to run."

Benson, the head orderly, hurried in and waited for instructions, although he quickly glanced around the room, looking for any signs that might tell him what was transpiring.

"You are to unlock the office door, then be on your way," Lestrade directed before turning to the secretary. "And you, madam, may wish to excuse yourself."

The lock gave way on the initial try, and the door cracked open to absolute silence. On Lestrade's hand signals, the accompanying detective escorted the secretary and orderly out, then closed the door behind them. Waving us back, the inspector pushed the office door wide open and peered in. He was the first to see the ghastly sight.

Sitting behind his desk was a very dead Peter Willoughby. His entire body was twisted and contorted, with his arms and legs convulsed into severe contractions. But it was his face that was most startling. Its color was deep blue, with lips drawn back in a mocking grin that seemed to be directed at us.

"Strychnine poisoning," Joanna pronounced.

"A classic case," I agreed, and walked over to examine the corpse. There was no pulse and the skin felt cool, indicating that death had taken place several hours earlier. On the desk in front of him was an open container of the toxic agent. "He obviously committed suicide."

Lestrade stepped in for a closer look, not in the least moved by the grisly sight. "I take it his appearance is entirely the result of strychnine."

"Every feature points to that diagnosis," I elucidated. "The drug causes excessive, powerful muscular contractions, which accounts for the markedly twisted extremities and arched back. The respiratory muscles do the same and can no longer function, which brings about death by suffocation, with the lack of oxygen giving the skin its bluish, cyanotic appearance."

"And what elicits the disgusting smile?" Lestrade inquired.

"The muscles of the jaw contract violently and pull the lips back into a demonic grin."

Joanna glanced down at a nearby trash bin that was splattered inside and out with dried blood. "He threw up blood here as well. He must have had a very sick stomach."

"Willoughby had lost some weight recently, but no one

made much of it, for he was known to have unrelenting peptic ulcer disease," I recalled.

Joanna's gaze went to a letter on the desk which she held up for all to read. It was penned in Willoughby's handwriting. "Ah, a suicide note from the dearly departed."

It read as follows:

Dr. Virchow has paid me a visit and I am now obliged to make my final exit.
PW

"Does anyone know this Dr. Virchow?" Lestrade asked.

"He was a famous German pathologist who died some years ago," I replied, thinking how clever Willoughby was in leaving us his terminal diagnosis. "Virchow was the first to describe a large, palpable lymph node above the clavicle which indicated a metastasis from an advanced gastric carcinoma. That was the cause of Willoughby repeatedly throwing up blood."

"So he must have had a Virchow's node," Joanna diagnosed.

I pulled back the corpse's tie and collar and exposed a sizable group of matted lymph nodes in the left supraclavicular fossa. "Indeed he did."

"Yet I suspect that his terminal illness was not the sole reason for his suicide," she commented, after studying the cancerous mass.

"As do I," I concurred. "For I believe, like you, that he realized that the forces of the law were closing in on him and it was only a matter of time before he was discovered to be Jack the Ripper."

Joanna next unbuttoned the corpse's right shirtsleeve and rolled it up to uncover a bare forearm. On the area just below the elbow was a deep bite mark that had not drawn blood. "Jack the Ripper," she pronounced.

"Who has escaped the hangman and his noose," Lestrade said unhappily. "And sadly, we shall never have the evidence to prove he was in fact The Ripper."

"But strychnine causes a most unpleasant death which I think we all believe he richly deserved," I said, now rereading the suicide note and determining yet another underlying meaning. "Even in death, the conceited monster had to be onstage, as shown by his phrase 'I am now obliged to make my final exit.' I suspect he envisioned himself to be some tragic Shakespearean figure."

Joanna smiled humorously at my remark. "It brings to mind Shakespeare's immortal words that 'all the world's a stage, and all the men and women merely players; they have their exits and their entrances; and one man in his time plays many parts.'"

"Those words certainly apply here, for Peter Willoughby, like the original Dr. Jekyll and Mr. Hyde, played a number of parts," said I, feeling no sympathy whatsoever for the man for his dreadful ending. "I think we can all say that his exit was long overdue."

"And will be welcomed by all of London," Lestrade added.

But this was not to be.

Closure

Peter Willoughby was given a grand funeral, with many notables, including the Duke of Cumberland, who represented the Crown, in attendance. Scholars from medical academia eulogized the man with high praise for his many contributions to the field of pathology. Mention was made that he had edited a number of textbooks and monographs which were considered to be gold standards in his specialty. Although the cause of his death was not spoken of, one eulogizer hinted at Willoughby's courage in taking his life to spare his family watching him linger in such terrible agony. There were of course tears from the family, but none from Joanna or myself. I was present only because I had been named interim director of pathology at St. Bartholomew's and it would have been unseemly for me not to attend. Joanna was good enough to accompany me in this most unpleasant task.

But there were developments of note which the reader should be made aware of. At Joanna's insistence, the cellar of horrors was again searched for fingerprints, with particular attention paid to The Ripper's mementos that hung on the wall, for they would have been placed up nearly thirty years ago when there was no fingerprint section at Scotland Yard and thus criminals never bothered to wear gloves. A single fingerprint belonging to Peter Willoughby was found on the outer surface of a mummified ovary, proving beyond a doubt that he was Jack the Ripper. In addition, Joanna performed an experiment in which she compared her bite mark, which was made into a waxlike material, to the one present on Willoughby's forearm. The marks were identical, even including a slight notch on Joanna's most anterior incisor. But none of these findings would ever be disclosed, for sadly there was never to be a trial. By Anglo-Saxon law, a dead man cannot be tried for any crime, no matter how vicious, for he would be denied the opportunity to defend himself. However, there are exceptions in cases of homicide, but only if the court is presented with evidence to exonerate the guilty or the defendant has submitted a declaration of guilt prior to his demise. Neither of these applied to Jack the Ripper. Accordingly, the records and files related to the mass murderer were to be permanently sealed and hidden from public eye. As Lestrade regrettably stated, it appeared that Peter Willoughby had escaped the hangman's noose he so richly deserved. Nonetheless, we took some comfort in knowing that Jack the Ripper now lies beneath six feet of good English earth and that his reign of terror is forever ended.

And on a final, happier note, Maxwell Anderson has arranged for Pretty Penny to be under the care of a physician at St. Bartholomew's who specializes in the treatment of patients who have been subjected to severe emotional trauma. It is said that Maxwell visits her often and that by all accounts she is convalescing well.

Acknowledgments

Special thanks to Peter Wolverton, for being an editor par excellence, and to Scott Mendel, for being such an extraordinary agent. And a tip of the hat to Danielle Prielipp and Hector DeJean, my superb publicists, and to David Baldeosingh Rotstein, for his wonderful cover designs.